Acclaim for 'A Quirk of Destiny'

'.. great romp of a novel, populated by a host of well-drawn characters, and with a gradually emerging, sinister plot twist.' **Brian Page, Editor Mensa Magazine**

'I was hooked by the dramatic first chapter. This book illustrates present dangers we may already face. It has certainly made me think about what I eat. The ending is a bit of a cliff-hanger to set the scene for the sequel. I hope it comes soon.' **Amazon reader**

'A readable, engaging thriller with a message that makes you think! A compelling storyline, once you pick up this book you can't put it down.' **Amazon reader**

'This book is rather scary at times as to the scenario it presents and even more so when one considers the author's background. The reader may be left wondering, and possibly rightly so, I should say, as to whether this might not be whistle blowing disguised as fiction. A definite must-read book.' **Michael Smith, Editor Green Living**

'The manipulation of genes places huge powers in the hands of the few and that is why books such as the 'Quirk of Destiny' can be so valuable in sounding the alarm bells in time for people to regain control.' **Peter Riley, GM Freeze Campaign Director**

'The threat of Genetically Modified (GM) Plants and its impact on our health may be a greater risk than we realise.' **Phil Exon, Mensa Science Fiction SIG Editor**

'This is a compelling novel in the style of John Wyndham. It shows how a single event can cause our complex society to break down very quickly.' **Amazon reader**

'**The Best of the Year 2013**. **Best books (joint number 1)** On the same level we have then "A Quirk of Destiny" – another must read book – though different, as it is about GMO and more a thriller and a novel rather than a memoir.' **Michael Smith, Green (Living) Review.**

'This is definitely NOT a run of the mill post-apocalyptic tale! It's very intelligently written with some decent plot twists. I also like how the author gave the "genies," or the genetically mutated people special attributes you wouldn't expect them to have. It definitely made them creepier. An exciting and enjoyable read that makes me want to eat more organic foods.' **Amazon reader**

Acclaim for 'Return to Gallanvaig'

'Return to Gallanvaig is a work of fiction but it's message comes through loud and clear: we disrespect nature at our peril. The second in a post-apocalyptic trilogy, this novel pits a group of vegan environmentalists against horribly deformed "Genies" and a shadowy group intent on restoring the old-world order. Twists and turns abound. From GM crops and the powerful pesticides they are so liberally sprayed with, to nuclear weapons and the banking crisis, current, real-world problems are taken to extreme conclusions that should make readers think and take stock.'

Liz O'Neill - Director of GM Freeze.

'In her first novel, A Quirk of Destiny, Catherine Greenall gave us a terrifying look at a world where genetically modified food has caused a deadly epidemic to sweep the globe causing death and destruction. The subject matter is close to the author's heart. Mensa member Catherine wrote what was the first in what is to be a trilogy with a career as a government scientist behind her – and a remaining passion for veganism and environmentalism. Now she continues the story with Return to Gallanvaig. It's two years on since the first outbreak of the epidemic and mutants, the evil 'Genies', are plotting to increase the reach of their diseased race – while another, secretive, group emerges with plans of its own to take control of what's left of the Earth's population. And the GM-free survivors are caught in the middle... Will they lead a fightback? Can humankind survive? You'll gather from the plotlines that while Catherine is obviously using her background – and her beliefs – to provide us with a message it is done not in a leaden-fisted manner but by way of an exciting and multi-layered tale which takes us on an exciting, page-turning, spine-chilling journey. A combination, then, of taut story-telling and thoughtful science.'

Brian Page Mensa Magazine

Catherine Greenall
Destiny of Light
Final Book in Quirk of Destiny Trilogy

To Elspeth

my Rock Rebel

Friend!

love

Catherine

The Third Book in the 'Quirk of Destiny' Trilogy

Also by Catherine Greenall

Short Stories

Non-Fiction

About the Author

After a long career as a government scientist, Catherine Greenall wrote the first novel in a trilogy, 'A Quirk of Destiny,' an apocalyptic tale, which was awarded joint best book of 2013 by Green Living. 'Return to Gallanvaig' continued the story and the final book in the series is 'Destiny of Light.'

Her work includes ghost, horror, science fiction and vegan cookery, as well as scientific works. She is a long-term vegan and environmentalist. Her published works also include a cookbook 'Vegans Can't Eat Anything!' The short stories include 'Burnview' and the collection 'Echoes and Reverberations.'

Her scientific works include 'The Mersey Measure.'

'Destiny of Light' is a work of fiction based on a huge body of scientific facts. Many events occur in real places. Any mistakes or alterations to places and facts are the author's own mistakes or creative inventions. All characters in this publication are fictitious and any resemblance to real persons, living or dead, is purely coincidental.

A CIP catalogue record for this title is available in the British Library.

ISBN-13:   9781079474855

First Published 2019
Freebo Amazing Jumpfrog Publishing
Adams & Co.
Office A05
Towngate Works
Dark Lane
Mawdesley, Lancashire L40 2QU

Dedication

This book is dedicated to the Soil Association, Greenpeace, Friends of the Earth, GM Freeze, GM-Free Cymru, GM-Free Scotland, GM-Free Ireland, David Icke and all those who fight untiringly for the truth to be heard.

Despite a growing mountain of scientific evidence, governments and multinational corporations are not admitting the truth about the disastrous effects that genetically-modified substances are having on human and animal health, as well as on the planet Earth.

Acknowledgements

Thanks go to the organizations, individuals and academics below, who have published a vast amount of scientific research and information on the subject material in the 'Quirk of Destiny' trilogy, which have been an invaluable source of information to the author.

GM Freeze, GM Free Cymru, GM Free Scotland, GM Free Ireland, Friends of the Earth UK, Greenpeace UK, The Soil Association, Institute for Responsible Technology, Ban GM Food, Center for Food Safety, Gene Watch, Food Standards Agency UK, The Vegan Society, Martin Teitel, PhD and Kimberly A.Wilson, Tom Philpott, Don Lotter, Joël Spiroux de Vendômois, François Roullier, Dominique Cellier and Gilles-Eric Séralini, the Guardian newspaper UK, BBC News, Thomas J.H. Chen, Kenneth Blum, Daniel Mathews, Larry Fisher, Nancy Schnautz, Eric R. Braverman, John Schoolfield, Bernard W. Downs, David E. Comings, *Dr. Barry Starr,* Global Psychics Inc., Mary Desaulniers, Spin Profiles, Natalie Geen, Chris Firth, European Commission, Sail North Scotland, Scottish Tourist Board, Martin Desvaux, Johan van der Heyden, Royal Air Force, Rahni Anomalies Unlimited, David Icke for his far-sighted wisdom about the history of Earth and what is really going on. Also, thanks go to Google Maps for showing me where and to Wikipedia for always knowing the answer to everything.

Thank you to my editor Alan, my publisher Freebo Amazing Jumpfrog Publishing and my cover designer George Stephenson.

"Power tends to corrupt, and absolute power corrupts absolutely." **Lord John Acton**

"All that is necessary for the triumph of evil is that good men do nothing." **Edmund Burke**

"Give me control over a nation's currency, and I care not who makes its laws."
Mayer Amschel Rothschild

"A great star fell from Heaven, blazing like a torch and it fell on a third of the rivers and on the fountains of water. The name of the star is Wormwood. A third of the waters became wormwood and many men died of the water because it was made bitter."
Revelation 8, 10-11

"And there were flashes of lightning, loud noises, peals of thunder and a great earthquake such as had never been since men were on the earth, so great was that earthquake."
Revelation 16, 17-18

"Today, the stranglehold of the controlling negative forces upon Earth is extremely advanced and is choking the very life from our planet. The effects of this are evident everywhere in the form of fear, separation, war, disease and multifarious kinds of disharmony on all levels." **David Icke**

Contents

1. The Master's Victory

The Master looked around his elite and he was very satisfied. They had done well. He was particularly happy with his new disciples, the long-time inhabitants of this land now called America.

Inola and Keezheekoni had proved to be excellent at pyrokinesis, bringing fire to their distant enemies.

Megedagik and Nashoba were ruthless killers, who could project their lethal venom over a great distance.

Shappa could bring thunder and earthquakes at will.

Yes, Balthazar was pleased with them. He clapped each of them on the back.

"You have shown yourselves to be obedient and able disciples," he said. "The Master is very pleased with you."

They teleported in a swirl of black cloud and were instantly back at home, beneath the ground.

They had cut down the Master's enemies and it was good.

2. Confusion

Calum searched desperately around the faces of the villagers sheltering in the old smugglers' caves high above the swirling seas.

Where on earth was Jessie? She should have been here ages before him. He had been forced to take shelter with his friends in the old coastguard's tower when the sea had suddenly risen. Huge waves had crashed down over the harbour road.

David, Chloe and Rob came in after him, Rob calling out for Hannah. Spotting James, Shaun, Rachel and Joanna huddled in a corner with Millie, Calum went over to them.

"Have you seen Jessie or Hannah?" he asked.

"Not since the storm," said James. "We thought they were with you."

"Is Jessie okay?" asked Joanna looking worried.

"I hope so, sweetheart," said Calum, with a weak smile. "We just need to find her."

"Where *are* they?" asked Rob. "They were just in front of us when Lauren fell down the rift in the road. How could they have got lost between the village and here? They were calling at your house Millie to collect you and the kids."

"Well, we didn't see them. We left in a hurry when we heard the tremors. We just followed everyone up here."

Calum looked around desperately.

He said nothing. He was very worried now but didn't want to let the kids know.

But, he knew that the last time he had seen Jessie was just before the huge tidal wave had breached the harbour wall.

What if she and Hannah hadn't made it to the caves before then?

He felt a wave of horror sweep over him as the full, tragic possibility struck him.

Had he lost his beloved Jessie for good?

3. The Devastated Elite

Sir Michael Goldman was angry. It wasn't very often that he got to take a holiday with his family. He had just arrived at Heathrow airport for his flight to the Caribbean to rendezvous with his luxury yacht, which the crew had waiting for him at St Lucia.

His butler had been given strict instructions that he was to contact his master only in a dire emergency. And yet, he had only been gone from his mansion for a couple of hours and he was being disturbed. His mobile phone continued to ring insistently.

Impatiently, Sir Michael pressed the button to take the call.

"Yes?" he barked.

Then, after listening to the caller for a few minutes, he shouted "What? The whole mansion? How could it catch fire *again*? What the hell happened?"

He shot questions at his anxious butler, who had the unenviable job of breaking the bad news.

"Look, I will be leaving it to Justin to do damage limitation, I will contact him now. We don't want the local security forces sniffing around again. If they turn up, you are to refer them to Justin. And by the way, I am now out of contact for the next three weeks, as far as you're concerned. If I do need to be involved, Justin will contact me."

He ended the call abruptly, not bothering with a goodbye or thank-you.

This was supposed to be a restful holiday after the elections and now it was just turning into a nightmare. His wife Henrietta glanced at him.

"What is it?" she asked. "Can't they manage without you for even a day? How on Earth will they cope for three weeks?"

She scowled, unhappy that he was putting work before the family holiday.

"Look, don't panic, but that was Johnson. He says that Warbeck Hall has been destroyed in a fire."

She gasped.

"What? How did it happen?"

"I don't think we need to worry about all that now, darling. I am asking Justin to take care of everything. We will just go to the summer house at Tintagel when we return. Don't worry."

Angrily, he pushed the button to call Justin.

Somebody would pay for this, he vowed.

Later that evening, Sir Michael had just arrived in St Lucia and was meeting his chauffeur to be driven to the marina where his yacht was moored. His phone, on silent since the earlier call, vibrated insistently.

"What now?" he muttered.

It was Justin.

"Sir Michael, I'm afraid have bad news. Not only did Warbeck Hall pretty much burn down to the ground, but some of the Masters have had terrible accidents. Tony Chan was killed, along with most the board members of his bank, when an earthquake caused his mansion near Beijing to collapse. Phillipe Moreau died of severe burns when the water in his swimming pool at his villa in Cap Ferat somehow heated to boiling point. His daughter Corinne and her two children were also injured. Liese Kaufman was engulfed by a tsunami wave following an earthquake in the mountains above her castle. There have also been reports of injuries and maybe deaths to civilians at several locations around the world. We're just trying to get a full picture."

For once Goldman was speechless. This was awful. So many of the elite wiped out. Just like that. How long would it take them to recover from this?

"What? But, what happened? Who did this? Was it some sort of resistance movement? You aren't trying to tell me that all these events were acts of nature? That would be too much of a coincidence," he stammered.

But, in his heart he suspected that he knew who was responsible.

These incidents were no coincidence. Someone would pay for it.

They would pay very dearly.

4. Roll Call

The ruling World Democracy Party had ordered the migration of the population into the cities and Elizabeth MacKenzie had moved her base to London in her new role as Leader of the Opposition party, the World Alliance. Her constituency was now the Lake District, since Sam Paige had taken Calum's old seat representing the Scottish Highlands. Calum had unofficially taken up his old role of resistance leader, albeit of a very much reduced group of people. Some people, both within the village and rebels against the World Democracy party around the world, still looked to him to resolve issues.

There were only around fifty people who had decided to defy government instructions to move to the nearest big city and instead remain in the village. They didn't know how long this would be allowed and life was certainly going to be difficult, but they were not giving up without a fight.

Calum was calling out the names of all the known inhabitants left in the village, checking off the names on a list as he went.

"Lauren MacKenzie," he called, then he realised that she would not be answering. Faltering, he quickly read Jessie and Hannah's names, a deep dread creeping over him as he worried whether they too had perished in the earthquake and tsunami.

He got to the end of the list. There were four people missing, Jessie, Hannah, Lauren and a man named Vinny O'Neill who lived on the outskirts of the village. Nobody had seen him since the earthquake.

"I need volunteers for a search party," said Calum.

"Maybe the missing people have just been injured and couldn't reach the caves. Except Lauren of course," added Rob. He felt it was a desperate hope, but he had to cling onto something.

A subdued group of people, including Calum, Rob, David, Chloe, Millie and Bill set out to search the village, starting with the last known locations of the missing four.

Millie opened her front door and pushed her way inside.

"Jessie, Hannah," she called, going from room to room, followed by Calum and Rob. Have they taken shelter here when they had called for the children, noticing that the storm had started to rise?

There were no welcome answering voices.

They reached the final bedroom upstairs and looked inside.

Nothing.

David, Chloe and Bill headed to the edge of the village where Vinny O'Neill had lived alone. As they walked up the lane that led to his house, it became evident that a catastrophic force had struck his house.

"Oh my God," said Chloe, as she viewed the ruins of what had been a white, stone cottage. The whole of the upper floor was gone, collapsed in a heap of stones on top of the lower floor, the whole building now just a pile of tumbled stones and broken furniture.

"Vinny, Vinny, are you in there?" called Bill.

David had fetched Shep with him, in case he was able to detect life, where none was visible in the rubble. He unclipped the leash and Shep ran over to the heap of rubble sniffing the stones and the broken furniture.

They started to carefully lift stones and unrecognisable pieces of wood and metal aside carefully, looking beneath each one for any sign of Vinny.

Suddenly, there was a volley of barks and Shep was standing, his ears up and tail wagging intently, staring at a heap of wreckage in the middle of the pile.

They rushed over to the site, trying not to disturb anything.

"Vinny, are you here?" shouted David.

As they looked where Shep was focussed, they could see a heap of wood and clothing.

"Oh, no," said Chloe. She gently pulled away blocks of wood and stones from the heap of clothing and a shape emerged.

It was Vinny. He was stone cold.

"Poor guy, he must have been in bed when the earthquake struck," said Bill. "He wouldn't have stood a chance; the whole bedroom must have collapsed onto the ground floor. He must have been dead for hours."

"Let's get him loose and do what has to be done," said Chloe.

Between them they retrieved the body from his ruined house and wrapped it in blankets.

They carried the bundle back down into the village with heavy hearts.

Calum said some prayers and the villagers joined in, as they shovelled the dirt on top of Vinny's body. They also buried Lauren, after winching her body from the crevasse.

Calum felt that he had said too many funeral prayers these last two or three years, for people who had died way before their time, a lot of them close friends and family.

It never got any easier.

And they still hadn't found Jessie or Hannah.

It was midnight and the inhabitants of the Manse were trying to sleep. James and Shaun were talking quietly in their room, too wound up to sleep.

Rachel was wide awake, thinking of Jessie and worrying about what could have happened to her. Could Balthazar have taken her again? He had done it before. That would be awful. But, the alternative was just too terrible to consider, that she might not have survived the storms and tsunami, buried somewhere underneath a yet undiscovered rock fall, or swept out to sea.

She glanced over at her sister, Joanna, asleep at last after lying weeping for some time. She was grief-stricken that Jessie was missing and that her favourite teacher, Miss McKenzie was dead.

What an awful day.

Downstairs, Calum poured himself another whisky. He knew that this would not solve his problems, but at least it was taking the edge off his pain. Realistically, he couldn't see any way that Jessie could have survived the storm. They had searched the village painstakingly, including sifting through the rubble of all the collapsed buildings and all along the shoreline where she had last been seen.

Was there an outside chance that Balthazar had taken her again? Even that awful possibility would be preferable to Jessie being gone forever.

Tears streamed down his face as he contemplated life without his beloved Jessie.

He didn't think he could cope.

5. The Reckoning

Edward Vanderbilt presided over a very tense and angry meeting in his summer mansion on the side of Zürichsee, where he had been staying since the evacuation of America.

"Three more slaughtered," thundered Michael Goldman. "That's only five of the Supreme Masters left. I want those responsible *eliminated*."

Goldman was furious that more of his elite brotherhood had been killed and indignant that his holiday had to be cut short because of world events.

"What's the connection between earthquakes, tsunamis and boiling swimming pools?" asked Vanderbilt. "Any ideas?" he added, looking around at the small group of survivors.

"How do you know it's not the work of Balthazar and his mutants?" asked Marta Petrov. "You claim they were all killed in the attacks in the US, but this is exactly the kind of paranormal behaviour that they were exhibiting before. What if some are still alive? And what if more of them are being created in the polluted heartlands of America?"

"I thought that we had reports that the base where they were last known to be hiding was flattened by the nuclear blasts?" said Katsu Mori. "How could they have survived that?"

"I don't know," said Petrov. "But, I guess we have to assume it's possible right now. I think we all accept that the deaths of the elite and the others killed around the world were no coincidence."

"Especially occurring all at the same time," said Goldman.

"So what next?" asked Ricardo Fabbiana. "We have to regroup, replenish our elite. And we need to find the mutants, if indeed they survived and destroy them, beyond any possible doubt this time."

"I will issue instructions to the Hickam Field Air Force Base, Hawaii to visit Nellis and check for survivors. If they find anyone, they will be told to eliminate them."

"Good," said Sir Michael. "Let's hope that's an end to it. But, somehow, I doubt it. These mutants continue to haunt us. Genetically-modified food seemed like such a neat depopulation idea at the time. We should never have believed the scientists when they said it was fool-proof. *Idiots*."

Vanderbilt shook his head, exasperated at the negativity being shown by his brotherhood.

"Well, I think we need to focus next on restoring the Master Elite without delay. There is work to do and we need to be at our full strength," he said.

"So, who are the candidates?" asked Fabbiana.

"The bloodline in China goes next to Marcel, Tony Chan's eldest son. Then, in France there is Phillipe Moreau's eldest daughter Corinne, who was burned in the attack on her father. But, I understand she will make a good recovery. Liese Kaufman had no children, so the line goes to her younger brother Max. Matheus Araripe's daughter Rosa is Chief Executive of the board of the Araripe dynasty of companies and Sahil's son Gaj Kapur, were already earmarked to take over after the original firestorm at my house. I think the path is clear. I suggest Michael gives them the good news, whilst I mobilise the unit from Hawaii."

The surviving five, between them the most powerful force in the world, departed, each intent on the business at hand.

The bloodline could not be denied. It would never die.

6. The Skies Wept

Rob had arrived at The Manse in the pouring rain just after breakfast, together with David and Chloe. A hung-over Calum met them at the door, rubbing his red-rimmed eyes.

"Any word?" he asked as soon as he saw them.

"No, sorry, Calum," said Chloe. "And Rob has heard nothing from Hannah either. Unless the Genies teleported them out of here, we might have to prepare for the worst. The storm was so severe that day and they were last seen running along the harbour side. I'm so sorry Calum," she added, as she saw his devastated face and drooping shoulders.

She gave him a hug, motioning to David to put the kettle on.

"Tea?" she asked trying to be cheerful.

"I think something stronger is called for," grunted Calum. Rob nodded and embraced Calum, his own face flushed, his eyes red.

David gave up and got the whisky bottle and glasses from the kitchen.

As they were sipping their drinks, there were sounds of the kids getting up and dressed.

Rachel was the first to appear.

"Has Jessie been found?" she asked, her eyes unnaturally bright, the tears close by.

Calum shook his head and enveloped her in a bear hug, as they both wept.

"Here," said David, handing her a glass. "I think we can make an exception for once. You've had a terrible shock."

Rachel took a sip and immediately spluttered, the liquid burning the back of her throat.

"Steady," said Chloe. "You have to move the whisky around in your mouth first, then slowly swallow."

She tried again with a little more luck, as first Joanna, then James and Shaun appeared, fully dressed.

Joanna looked at Calum hopefully.

"Is there any news of Jessie and Hannah?" she asked, then as she saw Rachel and Calum's moist eyes, burst into tears herself.

James put his arm around her, looking pale and shocked.

"Right, I'm making toast and coffee, you have to keep your strength up," said Chloe, heading for the kitchen with David in tow. "And you're not sitting there drinking *that* stuff all day either," she added.

Calum and Rob exchanged glances and despite their grief, raised their eyebrows in unison, as Chloe left the room.

"There's no answer from Hannah's phone," said Rob. "At first it was ringing out, but now it's just dead." His voice cracked.

"It's the same with Jessie's phone, completely dead," said Calum. "She never goes anywhere without her phone being on and by her side."

"I just can't believe they're gone," said Rob. "Why didn't they take shelter when the tsunami burst over the harbour wall?"

"They mustn't have had time," said Calum. "It was all so sudden."

"It was on the news that there have also been storms and earthquakes around the world and many deaths," said Rob. "We know that the Genies have some terrible powers and that they can cause firestorms, shockwaves and earthquakes. I think we must assume that they were responsible for the attacks and destruction around the world."

"That's what I thought," said Calum. "Even though the news reports said that the Genies had been destroyed by missile strikes in the US, I think that is just propaganda. They *must* have survived. I just don't think the World Democracy Party want to admit that there are forces that they can't control."

"So, do you think the Genies may have taken Hannah and Jesse?" asked Rob, his expression hopeful.

"I just don't know, mate," said Calum. "But, although it would be terrible for them to have fallen into the hands of Balthazar and his evil followers again, it would also be fantastic if that meant they were still alive."

They fell silent considering the awful alternatives. Chloe couldn't think what was worst. She had been a captive of the charming Genies before and would not have wanted to repeat the experience. She was sure there would be a punishment waiting for Jessie, for daring to escape from them the last time too.

The rain battered down on the roof of The Manse, echoing their tears and grief, the wind howling around the eaves, as if in a shrill lament for the dead.

7. The Basilica of Saint Jean

The pilgrims toiled up the two hundred and sixteen steps to the Basilica of Saint Jean, part of an ancient shrine built high into a cliff face in southern France.

Father Lemuel paused, his chest heaving. He really was getting too old for this sort of exercise. Wiping his damp forehead, he continued upwards. It would all be worth it when he reached the cool interior of the basilica and met with the other pilgrims for their daily prayers.

Another priest caught up with him, his face flushed with exercise, but still bounding up the steps, full of the energy and enthusiasm of youth. He pushed his damp hair from his eyes, as he slowed down to speak to Father Lemuel.

"Bonjour, Father Ferdinand. It's okay for you, running up the steps like a young gazelle. I need to take my time these days, even to worship."

"Sorry, Father Lemuel, I will walk with you," said the young priest politely, slowing down his pace to match the older priest's. "Who is leading the service today?"

"It's Bishop Sebastian, apparently," replied Father Lemuel. "He is new around here and I haven't met him yet. It will be interesting to hear what he has to say about recent events."

"Do we know where he is from?" asked Father Ferdinand. "He's not one of the usual local clergy, is he?"

"I don't know," replied the older priest, conserving his energy for the climb. "I've heard nothing about him."

At last, they reached the top and entered the relative darkness of the basilica to find many pilgrims already there. The other members of the congregation were an unusual mixture of older people, traditional church-goers and younger members of various ages and dress styles.

One man stood alone towards the front of the congregation, staring fixedly at the altar, his eyes glazed.

My God, he looks like he is on something, thought Father Lemuel.

Bishop Sebastien stood behind the altar, looking out over the congregation. He was indeed new around here and in fact had been created a bishop only the week before. He was part of a new force within the church, sweeping all before it and evangelising congregations. He expected to be in the forefront of this drive.

"In Nomine Patris et Filii et Spiritus Sancti," he began, making the sign of the cross.

"Amen," said the congregation loudly, their voices echoing around the walls of the cathedral.

"Who is that chap at the front?" whispered Father Lemuel to Father Ferdinand. "You see him, the one with the dark clothing?"

Father Ferdinand peered to see.

"I have no idea," he whispered back, as Bishop Sebastien said the introductory prayers and the congregation murmured its answers. The congregation was motioned to sit, and the sermon began.

"My brothers and sisters in Saint John," he said in his strong, clear voice. "You will recall that Saint John received a revelation from Our Lord Jesus Christ and he was told what would happen and that he should write this down for all to read. John saw seven angels and they attacked the Earth, bringing a hail of fire and a fall of blood, killing the creatures of the sea. Then a great 'star' fell from heaven upon the rivers and waters of the Earth, killing many who drank the water. And, do you remember the name of the star that fell to Earth causing such devastation?"

The crowd fell silent, waiting for someone to answer.

"I will tell you," said the Bishop. "The name of the star was Wormwood and *it has already fallen onto the Earth poisoning the land, water and human life*. That is the name of the nuclear missiles that have rained down upon America these last few months. *The revelations of Saint John are coming true and are in fact happening now,*" he finished with a flourish.

There were gasps from the congregation. Could it be true? Were the events predicted in the Bible's Revelation of Saint John starting to happen today?

The young man at the front was named Zacharias Garnier and he didn't seem surprised by Bishop Sebastien's words. In fact, he nodded vigorously and exchanged intense looks with others whom Lemuel had never seen before.

"Saint John, save us," proclaimed the Bishop.

"Amen," exclaimed Zacharias, echoed by some others of the congregation.

"Saint John, bless us."

"Amen," came the answer.

"Saint John, pray for us."

"Amen."

Lemuel glanced at Ferdinand.

"What is this?" he said. "Who are these strangers?"

Ferdinand shook his head perplexed. He had never seen them before. The morning service at Saint Jean was usually a quiet, devout affair.

The strangers pushed their way to the front of the basilica and echoed every word from the bishop with loud 'Halleluiahs' and 'Amens'.

"And a white horse did appear. Its rider had a bow and he brought pestilence to the land and we have seen the great sickness that the poisoned food has delivered to the world population. Next another horse appeared, bright red and its rider took peace from the world so that people would slay each other. We have seen war, violence and nuclear attacks. Next, a black horse and rider carrying a balance or scales would bring famine to the earth and we have seen our food supply poisoned and become toxic and many of the population die because of lack of good food. Finally, the fourth horse was a pale horse and its rider's name was Death with power to kill with sword, pestilence and famine."

As the bishop took a breath, the regular congregation were shocked by the tone of the sermon and its content. However, the newcomers were fired up, their 'Halleluiahs' becoming louder and louder.

"The Lamb opened a fifth door and there appeared all of those who had been killed. Many have died in the wicked war, by nuclear missiles, poisoned water and earth. The sixth seal caused a great earthquake, the sun turned black and the moon red like blood and the stars fell from the sky. My brothers and sisters, we have seen great earthquakes in recent days, we have seen strange signs in the sky and massive turbulence in the sea. Missiles have rained like bright stars from the sky."

"And yet, in all this death and destruction, the angels of God did call out for no harm to be done unto the earth until the people of God were marked on their foreheads. And so was our survival prophesised. Only the faithful have been allowed to survive the awful war, pestilence, famine and death visited upon the earth. You, my brothers and sisters are the faithful whom God has loved enough to save. Now, we must show ourselves to be worthy."

"Worthy, *yes*," chanted the now large group immediately in front of the bishop swaying, beating their breasts and yelling 'Halleluiah.'

But, *what* was being visited upon them? This was fundamentalist stuff; the like of which Lemuel had not heard in the church for fifty years or more. Was this really God's word?

Or was it a gross heresy, emanating from somewhere else entirely?

8. Evangelisation

Edward Vanderbilt shook his head as he picked up the phone to call his cabal. The Hickam Field hazard containment team had arrived at Nellis Air Force Base a few hours ago and checked out the whole base, including the vast underground complex

There was no sign of the gene mutants. That either meant that they had not survived the nuclear pounding. Or, they had moved on somewhere else and yet again, it was going to be like finding a needle in a haystack. Until they struck again, that is and, with no bodies found at Nellis and the recent attacks, he was now quite sure that they *had* survived.

With an angry grunt, he picked up the phone to begin telling his comrades.

Calum glanced at the television, which had been on the news channel all morning. The volume was low as he had a humdinger of a hangover and was still sick at heart over the loss of Jessie. Rob, Chloe and David had all stayed overnight, all trying to comfort one another. These were dark days.

But, what was this? The scene on the television seemed to be a church service. Turning the volume up, he shushed the others.

"Not sure what's happening here, but it looks unusual," he said.

"We go now to our correspondent in France, Jean Leclerc. Jean, can you tell us what is happening now?" the UK presenter was saying as the shot cut to a local reporter.

"Yes, Elaine, we are here inside the ancient Basilica of Saint Jean, where an extraordinary movement, or cult, seems to have taken over," he whispered as a service was ongoing. "The basilica was originally run by the Roman Catholic Church, but in recent days, a new group of worshippers has appeared. They seem to be worshipping Saint John. I'll just let you listen in for a minute to the sermon by the minister here, Bishop Sebastien."

The bishop was in the middle of a passionate sermon.

"I tell you, my brothers and sisters, the first angel blew a trumpet and there was hail and fire mixed with blood and a third of the Earth was burnt up. We have seen this with the hail of nuclear missiles that struck our brethren in America. The second angel caused fire to fall into the sea and it became blood and many creatures and ships were destroyed. We have seen the watercourses and seas poisoned by the toxic chemicals that have spewed from the intensive farming that was carried out, without regard for human or animal life or the environment. The third angel caused a star named Wormwood to fall and the waters and many people were poisoned. This predicted the fall of the Wormwood nuclear missiles which have rained down, poisoning the Earth. The fourth angel put out the light of the sun, moon and stars so that the world suffered in darkness. We have recently been plunged into darkness many times, when the power networks have failed. Locusts were sent down and they had the faces of men and women and their king is the one of the bottomless pit, where he has been cast. This my dear brethren foretells the appearance of the Genies in our midst. They look human but are horribly malformed and sick and have awful powers. They can fly like locusts and they apparently live underground. And I can tell you, my brothers and sisters, that their king from the bottomless pit is none other than the evil Balthazar."

23

Calum and his friends gasped as they realised that the bishop was saying that the Genies were one of the plagues sent to Earth by God. And, God help them, Balthazar was the *Evil one*.

"What the hell is this?" muttered Rob. "Have we not had enough dark days, without people starting to believe that the tales of the Bible are coming true? What next, the evil witch and trolls under the bridge?"

"Yes, my brethren," the bishop continued. "The predictions made by our patron Saint Jean again prove to be accurate. We are heading for Armageddon, the *Apocalypse.* Have mercy on us all."

Some of the congregation gasped, others intoned an "Amen".

The correspondent hurriedly backed out of the church, delivering a final statement.

"I never thought that I would see a day when such superstitious, mediaeval tales would be stated as fact. Back to you, Elaine."

Calum was up out of his chair as soon as the report ended.

"What are you going to do?" asked David.

"I need to speak to Renée Mercier in Paris. Although she no longer leads France, she is still the Leader of the Opposition World Alliance Party there and she may know more about this group. I have to find out what's going on here."

He went into the kitchen to use the phone in there.

"At least this is providing a distraction from the loss of Jessie," said David.

"I don't think it will help much though," retorted Rob. "Nothing seems to help much."

"Sorry, mate. I didn't mean to imply that it is so easily fixed. It must be awful," said David.

Chloe gave David a look.

"How about another coffee?" she said, getting up.

"I've drunk enough coffee to keep the whole of Scotland awake. I need something stronger," Rob grimaced.

Chloe gave up trying to be sensible and fetched the whisky bottle and some glasses. A little something to numb the pain was probably all that she could do for him right now. She couldn't imagine how she would feel if it had been David that had been lost. Shuddering, she poured the drinks.

Calum swept back into the room looking flustered.

"Renée has been called into an emergency government session. Her PA seems to think it is something to do with the situation at the Basilica. What concern is it of government if there are a few crazies starting a cult?"

He sat down, grabbing a glass and filling it with the straw-coloured liquid.

"I can see how they have come to the conclusion that this is the End Times though," he added. "All of those events spoken of in John's Revelation can easily be correlated to what has been happening in the past couple of years."

"What?" snarled Rob. "You are joking right? No way is all that stuff in the Bible true. It's just scare stories to keep the masses in their place. You can't still believe all that stuff you were told as a kid?"

"I'm not sure," said Calum. "I didn't think a lot of it was the *literal* truth, but I feel there is *something*. God, a 'Higher Power,' whatever you want to call it. Some of it may be *based* on truth. I just don't know. But, it would be so easy for these guys to whip up popular support for their movement after everything that has happened. Is still happening."

Rob shook his head.

"I've heard it all now, mate. I thought you were the scientist, the rational one. Work with the facts and the actual research, not rumour and propaganda, isn't that what you have always said?"

"But, we are in different times, Rob. Nothing seems so certain any more. Even life itself," he added gazing at a large photo of Jessie hanging upon the wall.

Behind Calum, Chloe looked over and shook her head slightly at Rob. If it helped Calum to believe that there was some higher purpose to life after his loss, maybe that was a good thing. Anything that helped him cope. She moved a little closer to David, grateful for his warm company.

What do we have left when our loved ones are taken? But, she thought that we must carry on and the secret was having supportive family and friends around. She had no intention of letting Calum or Rob drown in their grief.

The phone rang and Calum jumped up to answer it. They could hear his agitated voice from the kitchen. They wondered what was going on now that was causing him such consternation.

"Surely you don't believe all that nonsense based on Bible teachings?" said Rob quietly.

"Some people believe in it, Rob," said Chloe. "Just don't upset Calum now, okay? I know you are grieving too, but you have a different way of dealing with it."

After a few minutes, Calum returned.

"I don't believe this," he said. "That was Renée. She said that these cult groups are springing up everywhere around the world like wildfire, even in the

UK. They are calling themselves the Revelation Army. They say that the End Times are upon us, the Apocalypse talked about in the Bible."

"Oh, for goodness sake," spat Rob in disgust.

"Renée says that cult leaders are coming out of the woodwork, largely from established religions, especially evangelical ones, but involving all the major religious groups. The Pope has been asked for a position statement."

"Oh, well, that should produce some interesting nonsense then," said Rob.

Calum ignored him.

"There was something else on the agenda of the emergency session. She said I didn't hear it from her if it gets out. But, apparently it soon will anyway. There have been massive crop failures around the world, especially in those countries where most of the agriculture was based on GM crops. The worst-hit countries include the US, although the information from there is patchy, coming from the few contacts who refused to be evacuated. Also, Argentina, Brazil, Canada, China, Paraguay and India, where GM crops were widely grown. They think that the GM crops and the toxic chemicals sprayed on them have killed the bees and other insects that pollination relies on. GM material has contaminated other crops, which are now dying. So, the crops are failing and there will be huge food shortages in those countries later this year, when supplies start to run out."

"Bloody hell," said David. "What about the UK? Our crops here seem okay."

"The UK, like many European countries, was largely sceptical about GM and there was no widespread cultivation here, just a few research sites. So, there is little effect here. Yet. But, if worldwide populations of insects are decimated, the food supply becomes disrupted. Bees pollinate the crops that feed around ninety percent of the world. We have already seen water-borne contamination spreading via the rivers and oceans into other parts of the world, like Spain and Portugal. If these toxic chemicals continue to spread, the crops could fail here too. And, in any case, food will be severely restricted to just what we can manage to grow in the UK."

"What will become of us then?" asked Chloe. "This evil that has been done in the world, it will never end, will it, until we're all history?"

She looked down at her swollen stomach. What sort of a world would it be for this little one?

9. The Vatican Speaks

The papal valet, Lorenz Pastore, handed Il Papa Nicholas his white cassock and skull cap. It was time for him to address the crowds below in Saint Peter's Square. This was not a regular scheduled appearance, but one prompted by the unusual recent events.

"Thank you, Lorenz," he said as Lorenz helped him with the cassock. "It sounds like there is a good-sized crowd out there today."

The clamour of the crowd below could be heard quite loudly, together with the odd emergency vehicle siren passing through the square.

"Yes, Papa Nicholas, they started arriving early this morning and I think there are quite a few media crews amongst them too."

"Good, good. It's important that as many people as possible in the world hear this message. There is already too much evil and confusion in the world. Time for some clarity I think."

With that, the Pope walked out onto the balcony and the crowd broke into tumultuous applause.

As the sound slowly died down, he started with giving a blessing to the huge crowds below.

"In Nomine Patris, et Filii, et Spiritus Sancti," he intoned, blessing the people.

"Amen," murmured the crowd.

"I'm sure that you all must be concerned with the recent news from France that claims that the End Times are upon us," he began.

"I need to tell you that these claims made by the so-called Revelation Army are false. They are based on superstition and are ill-informed. The Church's teaching is that the Apocalypse of the Bible, like the feeding of five thousand with loaves and fishes and many of the Bible's other stories, is a *parable,* not a record, or a prediction of actual events. By that I mean that it is a simple story told to simple folk long ago by Jesus, his disciples and prophets. This needed to be in terms that they could understand, to illustrate a spiritual lesson that he wanted to teach them. So, there will be no signs in the sky that fall to Earth, analogous to bombs, no plagues, no demons, no poisoned waters of the seas. Only signs that humans themselves create. And it is in the power of humans to stop these bad events. Not the evil one, or some angry God sending plagues and signs upon the Earth. So, I tell you my brothers and sisters to pray. Pray that God will deliver us from these evils that *humans* bring upon us. Pray that we will once again live in peace and harmony, with enough good food to eat and clean water to drink. Let us pray now."

The crowd seemed to sigh as one in relief. The Pope had said that the Apocalypse wasn't real, it wasn't happening and that was good enough for them.

It was what they needed to hear.

The Pope began to recite the Our Father and the crowd joined in enthusiastically.

"And deliver us from evil."

"Amen," breathed the crowd.

The Pope smiled. His work here was done.

He went back inside the Vatican, with a final wave to his flock.

Camarlengo Rafaele and other trusted cardinals were waiting for him.

"Do you really believe what you told them?" asked Rafaele. "That there is no such thing as the Apocalypse, that it is not a real event that will someday happen? What about the second coming of Jesus? Is there to be no truth in any of it?"

"I am afraid that I just don't know for sure," replied the Pope. "But, I have to tell them something and

I don't want them to be afraid. God will look after the righteous. That's all that should concern the people."

"But, what do *you* believe?" asked Cardinal Sanchez. "Surely, the Bible must be our guide on these matters? We cannot discount everything in it as mere parables."

"It doesn't feel right," said the Pope. "I cannot state it any more clearly than that. It's a gut feeling. I don't believe that God would send such devastation upon the Earth to strike good and evil people alike. I don't think he would create an evil force like the Genies."

"But, we have seen this time and again," said Cardinal Riley. "Disasters; earthquakes, tsunamis and famine have stricken good and evil people alike, many times before. This latest disaster is the work of people, not God. He gave us free will to do as we like. Some chose evil."

"Maybe it *is* all true," breathed the Pope. "But, what do we do about it? There is nothing we can do except ask people to pray and live good lives. If it truly is the end of the World, then we can do *nothing* else about it," he finished forcefully.

"Don't you think we should tell the people if you think it might be true?" asked Cardinal Riley. "Surely, they have a right to know that these are the end of their days, as they might wish to put certain things in order first?"

"I don't see how it would help to cause worldwide panic, when this story might not even be true," answered the Pope. "Is that what you are advising?"

"I see your point, your Holiness. Even if it's true, what benefit would there be to the human race to admit it?" said Cardinal Sanchez. "And who knows, if it isn't true we can just put it all behind us, instead of being seen as swept up in superstitious rumours."

"Exactly," answered Il Papa. "And I want all church buildings and facilities out of bounds to this Revelation cult with immediate effect. They will *not* take over our Christianity. Now let's have some lunch, shall we? My head is really beginning to ache with all this."

The crowd of people were not in a good mood. Angry jeers and threats were flung at the double line of soldiers standing in their way in front of the supermarket in the centre of Bonn.

The night before, a crowd of locals had broken into the supermarket and stolen most of the food on the shelves. Now, a sign reading 'Closed Due to Unforeseen Circumstances' was pinned to the door.

"Wir Verhungern! We're hungry! Come on let us in, you *bastards*!"

"My children, they need food."

"Have you no families? Let us *in*."

The soldiers stared on impassively, their automatic weapons held ready for the least sign of attack.

A woman cried out to the nearest soldier.

"Son, you *must* let these people have some food. They are starving."

"Mutter, Sie nicht verstehen; you don't understand. There is little food in here. We have orders to guard what little is left. Go home!"

The crowd went wild then, pushing into the line of soldiers and shoving them back against the storefront.

"Back, back!" ordered the captain. "You must all leave here right now."

The crowd pushed even harder and the soldiers pushed them back, some of them falling over and others falling on top of them. The soldiers raised their riot shields, pointing their automatic weapons directly at the crowd.

"Aim. Fire!" shouted the captain.

The guns fired over and over.

Soon all was quiet again.

Orders had been followed.

In Mumbai, Hanita shook her head in despair. She had cooked the last of the rice yesterday and there were only one yam and two potatoes left. Once they had gone, they had no food left for the family. She looked across at their two children, Anaya and Rohan, happily playing on the floor. How would they ever feed them now?

"Eshan, please can you go out again and see if the shops have anything to eat yet?" she asked despairingly. "We only have enough for today, then we will all go hungry."

"Okay, I will try. But, I am not hopeful. Maybe Guptas will have something, some cans of food, or a little bread. All the large supermarkets have armed guards now."

"Be careful, dearest," whispered Hanita, not wishing to worry the children.

"I will," he answered as he left.

Outside, there were crowds of people milling around the city. Angry-looking crowds. As he walked along in the direction of his friend Gupta's store, he was pushed roughly over onto the ground by a gang of males who were rushing down the street, shouting.

"Hey, watch where you're going," he called.

There was no response. Picking himself up and dusting off his jacket, he shook his head. What was the world coming to when a man could not even walk the streets to buy food for his family, without having to endure this rude, violent behaviour?

After a few minutes he reached the street where his friend's store was. A crowd of people had gathered on the pavement outside. Plumes of smoke wafted around the doorway. What had happened here? Worried for his friend, he hurried to the store and pushed his way through the crowd.

"What are you all doing here?" he shouted, as he got to the front of the store. The shop window was smashed and there were many people inside. Flames licked up around the shelves and there were crashes as the tubs holding the dried goods were smashed open.

"Gupta," he called, trying to be heard above the yelling. Then, a tousled head appeared from behind the counter, timidly looking around for who had called his name.

"Gupta. What *happened* here?" asked Eshan, hurrying to his friend and helping him out of the shop.

"The people, they came for the food. I said I had very little left. I reminded them that the authorities have introduced rationing. Everyone is only allowed a small amount of rice and lentils and a small portion of vegetables. I locked the door, but they wouldn't listen. They broke in and took everything. Now, they are destroying my shop," he finished with a sob.

The shop had been in Gupta's family for as long as Eshan could remember. This was just awful. How could people behave this way? People who probably also knew Gupta and his family. Eshan supposed that hunger makes people desperate. He led Gupta away.

There would just have to be one more for dinner tonight. Even though they didn't even have enough for the four of them. They would manage somehow, he thought.

In London the Tube was full of people. The usual blank stares had given way to angry discussions about the food shortages.

"I heard a rumour that the crops are all failing," said one woman. "My friend in East Anglia is a farmer. She says that there don't seem to have been many bees around this year. And now, the harvest is ruined. The crops just did not produce any healthy fruits."

"I heard that it is all due to the use of GM crops and toxic pesticides killing the bees," remarked a man sitting opposite.

"Well, they'll be sorry they wrecked our environment," said a young woman with purple hair, whose name was Roxy. "Today's march on Westminster will show them what we think. And if they don't stop using all these toxic crops and chemicals, we will attack the forces of capitalism," she added her eyes shining with zeal.

"But, what can we do against soldiers and tanks?" asked an older man. "Last time there were riots, when all this started, they just brought out the military and crushed all dissent."

"We use sabotage and cunning," said the young woman. "We don't have to mount a military counterattack, just use what we have and hit them where it hurts."

The train stopped at Hyde Park Corner and most people swarmed off and into Hyde Park, where the protest march would begin.

"Wow," said the girl with purple hair to her friend, Ali, who had short cropped blond hair. "Look at all the people. This is *great*."

"I know, I can't wait to get down to Westminster, let those corrupt fat-cats know what we think of them," said Ali, scowling.

The park was crowded with people, milling around and preparing to march. Banners and flags were being handed out by local activists.

Roxy took a banner reading "Clean Food, No to GMOs, Stop the Poison."

Ali's read "Save our Food, Save our Bees, Go Back to Nature."

Whistles and drums were handed out and it was a noisy crowd that formed into a ragged line and marched out of the park.

"What do we want?" yelled a caller through a megaphone.

"GMOs out!" was the reply.

"When do we want it?"

"Now!"

They marched past Buckingham Palace and there were many shouts about the Monarchy.

"Hey, Royal Family, what are you eating tonight?"

"Is the Queen short of food? Do you want some of our bread?"

There was laughter at that.

Whistles were blown, as the crowd swept onwards through St James Park towards Westminster.

The crowd were in good spirit, singing and shouting slogans all the way along The Mall and Horse Guards Road. As they came to the end of Downing Street, they were halted in their tracks by a mass of armed police wearing riot gear.

The marchers crowded around the metal gateway and barriers, frustrated.

Jeering, they threw insults at the police.

"Are you proud of yourself, traitors?"

"I bet *your* family aren't starving!"

Pushing against the barriers trying to break through, the crowd jostled each other. People were getting crushed.

A voice crackled through a megaphone.

"You need to clear this area. I am warning you of serious consequences if you don't clear this area *now*!"

The crowd just jeered in reply and renewed their assault on the barriers.

"This is your final warning! Clear the area for your own safety!"

A few stragglers at the back of the crowd broke away, scared and started to head back up Horse Guards Road. But, most of the crowd were angry at being ordered off a public road in their own city.

An order was given. The police formed a line and raised their weapons. They began to fire. People began to drop to the ground, but the guns were not silent until every single one of the protesters had fallen.

There *must* be obedience by the population on the streets of this country.

Prime Minister Paige had ordered it.

11. Gathering Storm

Calum could not believe what he had just seen with his own eyes. The news report had just shown unarmed people being shot on the streets of London.

"*Bastards*!" he hissed. "How could they shoot unarmed civilians? On the streets of our own capital?"

"I'm afraid this is getting to be a habit," said Rob. "The army and police being used against their own people, I mean. Disgusting! They only wanted to protest about the food shortages. Their families are probably half-starved. Who can blame them for taking to the streets in protest?"

"We only have enough food here because we have been growing our own crops," said Chloe. "What will happen when the problems hit this area? When the bees fail to turn up in the spring to pollinate our crops? When the poisons have spread around all of the oceans and rivers and nothing is left alive there?"

"We have enough crops and seeds for this year and next," said David. "We need to protect our land from pollution, that's all. There must be a way."

"And when the bees die off? What then?" said Chloe. "There are already reports that there are less bees this year."

"It's not an immediate threat, Chloe," said Calum. "The GM pollution has killed most of the bees and polluted crops and land across America and other countries that grew a lot of GM crops. That included mainly North and South America, Canada and China. There was little cultivation of GM crops in Europe and it will take a while for the pollution to spread to us."

"But, the GM pollution has already spread to the coasts of Spain and Portugal, as well as some reports from Eire," said Rob. "It is only a matter of time before it hits the UK."

"Obviously we have to be prepared for that," replied Calum. "But, the shortages in the UK are currently mainly of the products that were formerly imported from the Americas. We still have home-grown crops. But I guess these are under pressure from elsewhere in the world and the need to export to countries that are experiencing shortages. Do our engineers have any ideas on how we might preserve unpolluted areas where we can grow safe food supplies?" he asked David and Chloe.

"Well, we would need to feed in unpolluted water and protect the land from air-borne pollution, whilst maintaining an adequate amount of sunlight," said Chloe.

"How about hydroponic agriculture?" said David. "If we can source pure supplies of water and nutrients, we could grow the crops in huge greenhouses and control all of the inputs. We would need to include insects and bees for pollination."

"That's sounds good. Why don't you two do a bit of research and see what you would need? Then we can try to source everything and set it up before things get critical here too."

Chloe and David went off, in deep discussion about the techniques that might be used to guarantee a clean food supply for the village.

"If we can get a workable method up and running here, we can pass the word around our contacts in other countries," said Calum, feeling more positive than he had for a while.

Little did he know that things were about to get much worse.

The next day started with bright sunshine and a blue sky. Calum rubbed his eyes. He almost felt positive again until the dull ache of his loss caught up with him. He could almost smell Jessie's Amber perfume in the room. Wait, he *could* smell it.

He looked around. Had she left a bottle of it around? He had thought that the girls had taken all of Jessie's perfumes and toiletries. He couldn't see a stray bottle. At that moment, there was a knock at his door and Rachel came in with a steaming mug of coffee.

"Morning, Calum," she said, drawing back the curtains. "It's a lovely day. What have you got planned for today?"

The kids had been great. Although they too felt Jessie's absence keenly, they had been constantly keeping him company and trying to keep his spirits up.

"Not sure, sweetheart. I need to catch up with a few old Alliance friends, see what the food supply is like for them."

"Do you think we will run out of food?" she asked worriedly. "They seem to be running short in the cities."

"I think they must have been diverting some supplies to countries with shortages," said Calum. "But, we have plenty of our own crops here. We'll be fine."

Later, as he switched on the computer and prepared to contact his friends around the world, there was a knock at the door.

He heard Joanna shout, "Door, I'll go," and settled down to load the video conferencing software.

There was a short, mumbled conversation and then Joanna called him.

"Calum, it's for you."

She had closed the door and was waiting at the bottom of the stairs as he came down.

"Calum, they are soldiers. And they're *armed*. They wouldn't say what they wanted," she whispered.

"Okay sweetheart; don't worry. Go and sit with the others."

He opened the door to see six armed soldiers waiting. He could see a large flatbed lorry idling at the end of the lane. There were four men dressed in waterproofs and wellies standing around it.

"Calum O'Connell?" said the first soldier, obviously of a higher rank from the stripes on his sleeve, but Calum had no idea what they denoted.

"Yes, that's me, how can I help you?"

"The new legislation on food security states that all food growers must surrender their crops for redistribution by the State," replied the soldier, his face a mask.

"What? I have not heard anything about this," said Calum angrily. "What right does the State have to take our food?"

"As I have already told you, the legislation requires that we take all food into central storage for redistribution. If you had obeyed government orders, you would be living in the city now and you would have known all about this," he added. "Anyway, do you have a licence to grow these crops?"

"We don't need a licence to grow our own crops to feed ourselves."

"Yes, you do. And you don't have residence permits to live in this area either. You will all be resettled, according to government orders."

He nodded to the men around the lorry, who drove off towards the food storage barns.

Calum was furious and tried to stop them, but the soldiers restrained him. Then, the senior one took out metal cuffs and tried to put them on Calum. He angrily pulled his arms away, until the soldiers forced him into the cuffs.

"We can add resisting arrest to your list of crimes if you like," said the soldier.

"Get off me! I have committed no crime. Just tried to feed myself and my family and friends that's all. I've got kids to look after!"

Calum struggled to get free, but four of the soldiers dragged him down the lane. As they reached the harbour road, he saw that there were two large coaches parked on the seafront. As they pushed him into the nearest one, he saw other villagers already aboard.

Bill nodded to him as he was pushed into a seat next to him.

"It looks like they have finally caught up with us then," he muttered to Calum.

"Yeah, the bastards," growled Calum. They wouldn't even let me go back for the kids. And they say it's now illegal to live here, we need residential permits, or some nonsense. Not to mention a crop-growing licence."

"I know, they gave me the same story. It's just crazy that nobody can grow food to feed themselves without government permission now. They took all my spare food supplies."

Just then there was a noisy disturbance at the coach doorway.

"Get off me you bastard! You have no right to just bundle us into a bus and *abduct* us!"

The tousled figure of Rob in full angry flow was propelled struggling along the coach by soldiers, until he was pushed into an empty seat behind Calum. He was followed by David and Chloe, David's arm protectively around Chloe, who was protecting her bump with folded arms.

"Watch out you idiot," he snarled at a soldier who tried to hurry them along. "Can't you see that my wife's *pregnant*."

"I can see that and don't call *me* an idiot," said the soldier coldly, indicating two seats.

David and Chloe sat down heavily.

"You okay?" asked Calum, looking worriedly at Chloe.

"I'm fine, really. I just don't take too kindly to oafs shoving me around. Especially not when I'm this size."

"Where the hell are they taking us?" asked Rob, still flushed and angrily.

"I think our rejection of government orders to move into the city has finally been detected. I assume we are being relocated to somewhere that they will issue a permit for. The annoying thing is the loss of all our food. Even if we can escape these thugs, we won't have any food. Unless we can manage to steal some in the city."

The final passengers were being led onto the coaches. The four kids were among them and they rushed to where Calum was sitting.

"Calum, what's going on? What do they want? Are we being taken away from Gallanvaig?" The questions came thick and fast. Joanna was a little tearful, but the other three just seemed angry at being taken from their home.

"I think we are being resettled in the nearest city. Inverness, I suppose. That's where the other villagers went. We'll be okay, don't worry. As long as we stick together."

"But what if Jessie comes back?" wailed Joanna. "She won't know where we are."

"We'll find a way to get a message to her," said Calum, his voice breaking. He didn't think she *would* be coming home.

The coaches started up, armed soldiers on each one.

They began the journey through the mountain passes to Inverness. The last time they were there, it was full of Genies. He hoped they had gone for good, but somehow, he doubted it. Although he had put a brave face on it for the kids, Calum was worried.

What awaited them in Inverness?

12. Inverness

As the buses crossed the Kessock Bridge, Calum could see the harbour area, with its boating industries and the conurbation beyond that which was Inverness town. The last time he had been here they had been held prisoner by the Genies and forced to wait on those who were sick and bring them food.

Not to mention bury those who died.

His heart sank as they were once more driven into its centre as prisoners. Then, it had been the Genies, now it was government authorities. He didn't know which was worse.

Rob whistled.

"Would you look at that? A welcoming party," he said.

Calum looked out the other side of the coach at the town hall, all gothic sandstone and spires. A crowd of people waited outside, some of who began to cheer and wave as they drew up alongside. He was puzzled.

"What is this?"

"Out," said the soldier who was guarding their coach.

The party trooped off and Calum was delighted to see a few of the former villagers of Gallanvaig who were amongst the welcoming party.

Chloe pointed excitedly.

"Rachel look, it's your friend, Duggie."

Rachel hadn't seen or heard from Duggie since he had left Gallanvaig with his family. After the Democracy Party won the election they introduced legislation requiring all people to move into the towns and cities. Duggie had been her boyfriend in Gallanvaig and had been studying for an environmental degree with her, instructed by Jessie and Rob.

Rachel eyed him coldly. He saw her and smiled and waved. Unbelievable. After not bothering to contact her for weeks. She turned the other way.

The soldiers led them towards the town hall. They filed in, as a few of their former neighbours yelled greetings.

"Calum, great to see you mate,"

"Rob, we'll have to meet up soon, yeah?"

There were a few calls out to Ellie and Mick from the Harbour Inn, who most villagers had known well.

But, Calum thought it was mostly curiosity that had brought their former neighbours out to see their arrival. All their close friends had stayed with them in Gallanvaig and this lot had decided to leave according to Democracy Government law. Most of them just stared silently as they went into the building.

An officious-looking man in a crumpled suit was waiting inside.

"You will all register at this desk. Then you will be allocated a residency permit and accommodation. You will be taken to the bank where an account will be set up for your wages. Since you have broken the law by remaining in a restricted area without a permit, you will forfeit the usual financial bonus offered to settlers. Tomorrow you will be assigned to a job and will start work. Welcome to Inverness."

This last was stated in a cold, automatic tone which Calum was sure had been used on many settlers who had arrived in Inverness before them, in an equally emotionless way.

He already strongly disliked this jumped-up official.

The woman at the desk looked up as he approached.

"Name?"

"Calum O'Connell."

"Ah," she muttered running her eyes down a list on her computer. "*Your* residency permit will have attached conditions."

"What are you talking about?"

"No meetings of more than four people, eight o'clock evening curfew, no exit permit to leave Inverness."

"What? You are joking right?"

She stared at him unsmilingly, handing him a printed paper. "You need to go to the accommodation desk. Next." She was already looking past him to the next in line.

Giving her a dirty look, Calum went to the desk indicated and stood in front of another officious-looking man. Whatever he was doing was clearly very important as he didn't look up for nearly a minute.

"Excuse me," he said finally.

"Residency permit," barked the man, holding out his hand without making eye contact.

Muttering to himself, Calum handed it over.

He took ages reading the print and finally handed it back to Calum with a plastic card.

"Cameron Barracks. Wait for the bus outside. Next."

Disgusted at his brusque treatment, Calum went to the back of the hall to where the others were gathering. As they waited for the bus, they compared notes. They had all been assigned to Cameron Barracks.

"Not another bloody army camp," snarled Rob. "I don't have fond memories of the last one."

"It *is* an army camp," answered Bill, joining them. "I remember going to an adventure training course there as a teenager."

"Yes, it was the barracks for the Queen's Own Cameron Highlanders, until they were moved to Fort George, I think in the 1960s," added Millie. "More recently it was used for military training courses and civilian adventure training. I did some army training there once. Sturdy old buildings; all towers and arches and a parade ground."

"I guess that's why we're going there then," grumbled Rob. "They don't want us escaping."

The subdued group were ushered back onto the buses. It has been some time since they had been held prisoner and they had thought those days were long gone.

The next stop was a large bank where they all disembarked. Although it had obviously once been a Bank of Scotland Branch, the sign had been covered over and a new sign proclaimed, "World Bank - Inverness East Branch."

"Even the banks have been taken over," grunted Calum. "And can you guess who will be the main beneficiaries of any money held in your account?"

"That will be the World Democracy lot, the Elite, whatever you want to call them," said Chloe. "How long do we have to put up with this? I do *not* want to give birth in this place."

"It will be okay darling, we'll get out of here just as soon as we get a chance," whispered David.

"Well, we have three months and counting," said Chloe.

"Papers?" growled the bank assistant behind the glass screen at the counter.

Calum slapped his residency permit and accommodation card on the counter.

With a cold glance the official studied the papers and typed the information into the keyboard on his desk.

Without a word, he got the output from a nearby printer and dumped the papers back on the desk.

"Next."

"Oh, for goodness sake, you could at least be civil, we aren't criminals you know."

"I think the authorities would disagree with you there, Mr O'Connell. Which is why you are to be held at Cameron barracks."

Calum snatched up his papers in disgust. What was wrong with this people? Had they all been brainwashed?

He wouldn't be surprised, after their recent experience of the poisoning of the drinking water supply by the elite.

As soon as they were all back on the coaches, they were on the way to their new home.

Soon they drove through a gateway with an arched sign proclaiming, 'Cameron Barracks.' Inside the gate, several armed soldiers stood to attention and opened a barrier, as the soldier on the first coach showed them a pass.

The coaches stopped in front of a large imposing building where an arched doorway stood between two conical-roofed towers. They were ushered off the coaches and into the building.

"I will need all your papers," said a stern voice and a stocky, older soldier appeared with a clipboard. Soon, the formalities were over and they all had been allocated rooms in the old, Scottish Baronial-style building.

"Well, at least we'll be comfortable," said Rob looking around the large room with attached bathroom which he had been allocated. Everyone had gathered there once they had discovered their own rooms.

"The old guy said we get fed at six thirty," said David.

"Can't wait," said Calum. "I'm sure that will be delicious."

The others burst out laughing. It was good to see the kids laugh for the first time since the military had showed up in Gallanvaig.

"How do we pay for our food?" asked Joanna. "Or is it included?"

"I don't know sweetheart, but I hope it's included," said Calum. "Since we don't have any money."

"Oh," said Joanna. "In Gallanvaig, we just had to go into the garden to get fresh veggies. When can we go back?"

"We don't know, sweetie," said Chloe. "As soon as humanly possible. They can't watch us all the time."

"Well we are in a secure barracks, I think the general idea is to stop us escaping," muttered Rob.

"Okay, so after we eat, let's see if we can get outside to do a tour of the grounds. Test out the security around here," said Calum.

"Yep, count me in," said Rob.

"Me too," said David and Bill together.

"Let's not go in too big a mob,"" said Calum. "We don't want to raise suspicion already. How about just me and Rob go? If we aren't challenged, we can go out in greater numbers tomorrow."

There was a tentative knock at the door.

Rob glanced at Calum, who shrugged. Rob went and opened it.

It was Duggie and he looked more than a little sheepish.

"Can I come in?" he said.

Rob motioned him in.

He looked at Rachel briefly, then started to talk rapidly.

"Look, I didn't want to leave Gallanvaig. Why would I? Rachel was there. I was happy. I had everything I wanted. I was studying for a degree. Why would I want to leave?"

"You did though, didn't you," said Rachel, not looking at him.

"Rachel, I'm so sorry. I know I've hurt you and that's the last thing I wanted to do. But, Mum and Dad, they were insistent that we had to leave. They said that Calum was a rebel, a radical and that I shouldn't listen to him. And that the rest of you were just as bad. I didn't agree, but what could I do? There was no way I could contact you after we left. The authorities took my phone and there are no landlines in our building. We have been put in these barracks too. They don't trust us because we were with you Calum. We are guarded all the time."

"What even during the day, when you go out to work, or study, or whatever you do?" asked Calum, his heart sinking.

"Yes. They are letting us study at the University here. I opted for Environmental Science. But, it's not like you were teaching us in Gallanvaig," he added, looking despairingly at Rob. "The professor says that climate change is a lie, there is no such thing, so we can continue to use fossil fuels and nuclear power. Apparently, there is no problem with water or air quality, or any problems with the animal feed now. We have been advised that to get a balanced, healthy diet we should be eating meat and fish. But I don't *want* to," he added.

"What do your parents say about all this?" asked Chloe.

"They have changed. I can't get through to them. They used to be very anti-animal exploitation. But now, they just parrot everything that the authorities are saying. And the television programs here are *dire*. The only stations you can get are state televisions channels. One for news and one for entertainment. But they are full of propaganda and lies. Most people here just seem to swallow it, as if this is the best entertainment ever. One of the programmes is just a group of people sharing a house. They spout all sorts of rubbish whilst pretending to pair off, or just argue all the time. But, nobody can see that they are just promoting the messages that the state wants us to believe. They are turning us all into mindless *zombies*."

"But, *you* have seen through them," said Rachel slowly. "That's good, yeah? It means *you* haven't been brainwashed."

"I think they are *drugging* our food," he whispered. "I refused to eat anything they gave us after I noticed how lethargic and indifferent I became after eating. But nobody believes me."

"I do," said Calum. "It doesn't surprise me at all. I have noticed how weird everyone is here. Nobody seems to care. Nobody has any human empathy. Everyone is *numb*."

"We *have* to avoid eating their food," said Rob. "How have you been surviving, Duggie?"

"I know a few places where crops are still growing wild," said Duggie. "I pass them on the way to classes every day. I can show you."

"Okay, good," said Calum. "So, nobody eats tonight. Just push the food around your plate and dump it under the table when nobody is looking. Then, tomorrow we can get clean food."

"What about your parents?" asked Chloe.

"They eat everything they are given," said Duggie. "I tried to tell them, but they think I'm mad. They won't listen to me anymore."

"That's sad," sad Chloe. "But, at least *you* have realised what is being done to everyone."

"I knew they were lying when I went to classes and they were spouting lies and propaganda about the environment."

"Well, thanks for visiting us and letting us know," said Calum. "Will you get into trouble?"

"No, they don't bother us in the evenings. We do what we like. But we can't go out of the barracks. Most people are happy just watching the crap they put on the telly. Rachel, please can we talk in private for a while?"

Rachel shrugged, but followed Duggie as he went out of the room. Calum could see that she was softening towards him after he had explained his failure to contact her since leaving Gallanvaig.

"Don't go too far, sweetheart," cautioned Calum.

"It's okay, Calum," said Duggie, turning as he opened the door. "There are common rooms in each wing of the barracks where we can socialise. It's only down one floor. We'll be fine, honestly."

"Well, that didn't surprise me at all," said Rob. "The elite are still drugging the population into accepting whatever they are told to do. And feeding them a diet of mindless trash on television to blank out their independent thought processes. I am convinced more than ever of the need to live beyond their grasp. We were quite right to stay in Gallanvaig. I wish we could have stayed under the radar."

"I suppose it couldn't last forever though," said Calum. "There was no point in all those new laws about residency in unlicensed areas if they weren't going to eventually enforce them and catch up with the rebels. I need to establish some communications whilst we are here. I need to check what is going on with our other rebel communities around the world."

"Well, why don't you start now?" asked Chloe. "They haven't taken our mobile phones yet."

"You're right and there's no time to lose. And if anyone else needs to get any messages out, now is the time to do so."

Calum went back to his room to begin trying to contact people. The others lounged around lethargically. There didn't seem to be anyone left to contact. All their friends had stayed with them in Gallanvaig and were now here with them in the barracks.

There *was* nobody else.

A bell, which they later discovered was the dinner bell, rang.

"What the hell is that?" asked David.

"Could it be a meal bell?" said Chloe. "Remember years ago, in little hotels where you all had to eat at the same time, they used to ring a gong for dinner. Maybe it's like that."

"Fascinating," muttered Rob. "Summoned by the bell to sit and play with some food that we daren't eat. Looking forward to it already."

"We have to keep up the pretence that we don't know what they are up to," said Bill. "Then, when they think they have drugged and brainwashed us enough, they might eventually give us a bit more freedom and we can get out of here."

"Where's Calum," askes Joanna looking worried.

"He was ringing his contacts," said Chloe. I'm sure he will be right here when he hears the bell."

Right on time, the door opened. It was Calum slipping his phone into a pocket. He was determined to keep communications open as long as possible.

"Ready? Everyone seems to be making their way to dinner. I think we just need to follow the crowd."

"Well, you've never been known for that before," said Rob.

"Ha, ha, first time for everything. Let's keep them guessing."

As they walked down to the dinner hall, Calum quietly told them what he had found out from his contacts.

"Many of them report that rebels are being rounded up and taken to the cities. Some protested against food shortages and were shot by the militia. Some have gone into hiding in underground bunkers. But, some good news; Renée Mercier, the French leader of the World Alliance Party and her team took advantage of a disturbance caused at a meeting of the Revelation Army. Apparently, the militia had to be called in to quell a pitched battle between the new cult and traditional worshippers fighting for control of Notre Dame Cathedral in Paris. Renée and the others managed to transfer to a secret underground bunker before the army caught up with them. Renée has gathered a considerable party of people, some ex-military and weaponry and is now offering to help us."

"That is great news," whispered Rob, aware of eavesdroppers. "But, how can they help us here in Inverness?"

"Rob, they have military helicopters. If we can give them a grid reference of somewhere they can pick us up, they will rescue as many of us as that we can gather at the rendezvous."

"Wow," said David. "They would risk their own lives for us?"

"Renée said that we are all in it together. We cannot allow them to win, otherwise we will be submitting to a life of dictatorship and control."

"You know there are military underground bases in Scotland too," said Millie. "If we could reach one of those which we could defend, we would be safe. I know there is a large underground bunker, with all the facilities; the Largo Bunker, in Fife."

They were stopped from talking about rescue by their arrival at the dinner hall and busied themselves with getting seats at the communal tables. They took as small a portion of the food from the dishes on the table as possible without raising suspicion.

There wasn't any sign of the military guards who had admitted them here, only a couple of kitchen orderlies putting the dishes of food on the tables. They were able to feign eating by pushing cut-up food to the edges of their plates, as if they just couldn't eat any more.

Later in Calum's room, they gathered and discovered exactly what Duggie had been talking about.

One channel was just transmitting a game show, the point of this one seemed to be to determine which individual knew the most facts about some supposed celebrities, of which Calum had never heard.

"For goodness sake," he muttered, switching the channel.

There was a photo of himself on the screen at that very moment. He groaned.

"Today the army were successful in tracking down the rebel Calum O'Connell, who has been living with some of his followers in a forbidden area without a special residential permit," the presenter was saying.

"I wasn't exactly hard to find, just where I have always been," grumbled Calum.

"It's just propaganda, Calum," soothed Chloe. "They have to justify their stupid laws, show people that they can't get away with breaking them."

"Yeah, make an example," said Bill. "They don't want anyone else trying it."

"I don't see how we can have been breaking the law just by living in Gallanvaig, growing our own crops and drawing our own water. What harm were we doing to anybody else?" said Rachel.

"We were a threat," said Calum. "They make laws to subdue the population, make it easier to control. It has happened from time immemorial. We *weren't* doing anything wrong."

"Well, it *stinks*," Joanna said, frowning.

They all laughed.

"I think we all agree with you on that one," said Rob.

"Okay, why don't you all stay put whilst Rob and I take a walk around the barracks? See how the land lies. Come on Buster."

The dog leapt up from his spot under the window, Shep following, barking excitedly.

"We'll take both dogs, give them a walk," said Calum. "And we have our cover story organised just in case."

Calum and Rob saw only a couple of stragglers returning late from dinner on the way downstairs. When they reached the large front door, Calum tried it fully expecting it to be locked. But, it creaked open at his touch. He looked at Rob, raising his eyebrows.

Outside they let the dogs run free, excited to be running around, after a day cooped up in the coach and the bedrooms.

"So far so good," said Rob quietly.

They strolled around the parade ground and through a small wooded area, until they came to the main gate. There was a barrier and a guard station manned by two armed soldiers.

As they approached, one called out to them.

"Where do you think you're going?"

"Just taking our dogs for some exercise. They have been cooped up all day," said Calum.

"Well, you need to keep away from the barriers and boundary fences. The terms of your residency permit do not allow access to the city without supervision. I suggest you keep to the parade ground in future. The penalties for breaking the conditions of the permit are serious."

Calum and Rob turned back towards the parade ground, calling the dogs.

"Bloody jobsworth," muttered Rob, who had little patience with any kind of authority.

"Well it proves that we will have to be imaginative about planning our escape," said Calum. "Perhaps tomorrow will provide an opportunity when we see what work they have planned for us."

"I wouldn't hold your breath," said Rob. "They are a soulless lot here. I can't see them giving us much opportunity to wander off alone. They aren't thick like most of the Genies were."

Arriving back at the accommodation block they went back to brief the others.

Nobody was feeling too cheerful as they all turned in for the night, exhausted.

13. Dark Work

David was very angry. This just wasn't happening. Chloe, her face red and angry was also shouting at the man at the Job Centre, where they had all been taken after breakfast.

"You cannot possibly expect a pregnant woman to work in such a hazardous place! A nuclear power station!" she yelled. "Do you actually *know* the effect that radiation can have on unborn babies?"

The man stared at her, a stupid grin on his face.

"Well, I'll tell you, shall I? Cancer, growth retardation, reduced IQ, malformations – not to mention *miscarriage and death*. There is absolutely no way I will be working at a nuclear plant."

"You must be *joking*," added David. "We are not going to expose our baby to toxic hazards, no way. You must find something else for Chloe to do. *I* will do your sordid work at the nuclear plant."

"No," cried Chloe. "You will be exposing *yourself* to the risk of tumours and cancer too."

"Look, you will *both* be going to work at the plant," said the man. "Now, go with the guards and wait for your transport. There are other people in the queue."

David and Chloe angrily stormed off, followed by their guard to join Paul and Amir, who had also been assigned to the nuclear plant.

"Have you heard this?" said David as he passed Calum in the queue. "They expect Chloe to work at a nuclear plant. And she is *pregnant*."

"I know, I heard. I'll have a word," said Calum. But, he didn't hold out too much hope. The people here were automatons, without any warmth or empathy.

"I want to see the manager here," he said as soon as he got to the front of the queue. "It is illegal to generate nuclear power. The law says that only sustainable, natural power is allowed."

"Really? Well, things have changed since you were in charge Mister O'Connell. Now, I need to get your details and allocate your work. Then, we will have to see."

"Oh, for goodness sake," stormed Calum. "So, what have you got lined up for me? Not milking cows again, I hope?"

"I have no idea what you are talking about. Here are your details. Report to Inverness Castle."

"And the manager?" persisted Calum.

"Not in at this time. You will need to make an appointment."

"When can I see them?"

"*If* you are granted an appointment, we will be in touch with you at your accommodation. Next."

Furious, Calum strode off, glancing at the card he had been given. It said 'Focus Group Member. Location, Inverness Castle. Hours: Nine to Five, Monday to Friday.'

What the hell *was* that, anyway? 'Focus Group Member?' He strode out towards the waiting coach. Maybe he would find out at the castle.

The kids had already been dealt with. Joanna was disappointed that she still had school, along with her friend Shelley.

"Calum, do I *have* to?" she wailed. "I was allowed to do farm work last time."

"Yes, but that was when we were being held prisoner by the Genies. And you're still only fifteen," added Calum, smiling. "You'll thank me in the end, when you have lots of qualifications and you are a doctor, or a professor, or something."

"Yeah right," she threw back, as she was taken to the school bus with her best friend.

"See you later sweetheart," he replied. "Have a good day."

Rachel was to join Duggie on the university's Environmental Science course. Although, if Duggie was right, he expected Rob would need to do a whole lot of retraining each evening. Shaun would join them, but on the Farming and Agriculture course.

Rob joined him on the coach, which would drop them at their workplaces.

"So, what did they give you?" asked Calum. "Apparently I will be a 'Focus Group Member.' Whatever *that* is."

"I am to work as a *lab technician* at the University. Working with the Environmental Science students. I ask you. I used to *teach* that course. But, at least I can get an idea of the nonsense they are teaching them, so I can challenge it."

"Just be careful, mate, they are nasty pieces. They are trying to break your spirit. Don't let them."

"I know. Don't worry, I'll be fine. I'm going to enjoy sniping from the side lines."

Just then, there was an influx of people. Calum looked up to see Doctors Nazeer, Yasmin, Ian MacDonald and Susan Brady. Seeing him and Rob, they came up the coach and sat near them.

"Not surprisingly, we have been assigned to the local hospital," said Nazeer. "Where I am sure we will be kept busy dealing with the fall-out from a return to the bad old days of what passes for Western Civilisation. Stress, industrial accidents, food poisoning, shootings. What joy."

"At least we will be doing what we trained for," said Yasmin. "Maybe we can do some good."

"Such an optimist still," remarked Ian MacDonald. "You'll learn, when you've been in this business as long as I have."

"Oh, don't tease her, you old cynic," said Susan Brady. "Let her keep her idealism for a bit longer."

The coach was full and set off to drop them off around the city.

Calum stepped off at the imposing red sandstone castle, with its turrets, towers and fluttering flags, raised up on a hill above the River Ness.

"I suppose there could be worse places to work," he muttered to himself as he followed the guard through the barriers and up the driveway. At least he hadn't been allocated to the nuclear plant. Poor David and Chloe.

Then, he went inside to find out what he was supposed to be doing.

14. Games and Subterfuge

"Good morning, colleagues. My name is Anna Harris and I was asked to set up and run this focus group. Firstly, I would like to welcome new members to our Highlands Focus Group meeting," said the woman leading the meeting of around twenty people of different ages. "I see we have one new member today. Please can you introduce yourself and tell us about where you are from and your background?"

"As I expect you all know, I am Calum O'Connell, former World Alliance Leader in the UK. You may not know that I was forced here as a prisoner from my home in Gallanvaig. Where I was living in peace, doing nothing illegal and harming no one. So, what else do you want from me?"

"Well, that will do for starters," said the woman. "Our purpose is to ensure that the new communities that we build here in the Highlands meet the modern needs of this post-disaster world. The idea is that we take in the views of a wide range of Highlands' residents and that is why you are all here. I know some of you are already familiar with our modus operandi, but we will start from the basics for the benefit of our newer members. So, I will introduce our first exercise for today."

Writing on a flip chart, Anna Harris described how they were to break out into small groups of two or three. They were to introduce themselves and their background. Then, they were to brainstorm what they considered were the basic requirements for a prosperous and happy life in the Highlands.

Sighing, Calum joined the other two people who were to be in his group around a flip chart.

"Well, shall I start?" asked a man, who was dressed in casual trousers and a fleece top. "I am Jack Carter. I live in Tain and I am a farmer, with a permit for agriculture and for the pastoral farming of animals for dairy and meat."

Calum sighed, as it was again brought home to him how the high ideals of the World Alliance were being abandoned under the new regime.

The middle-aged woman sitting opposite Calum was dressed smartly and looked very professional.

"I am Daphne Morrison. I live and work in Inverness for the World Bank. Before that I was a banker based in London. I was transferred to Inverness after the election of the new government to help set up the World Bank in Scotland."

"As I have already said, I am Calum O'Connell, former UK World Alliance Leader. I am not here out of choice," added Calum. He couldn't believe he was playing stupid management games with these people.

"Let's start the brainstorming bit then," said Jack, picking up the marker pen by the flip chart. "State what you think we need for life here and I will chip in with anything I think is missing."

"Freedom of movement," started Calum.

"Sufficient food and water," said Daphne.

"To eat food of your own choice and not exploit animals."

"Shelter."

"To live in a place of one's own choosing."

"A fair government and local authorities."

"A government that permits you to live in peace with your family and friends."

"To receive a fair day's pay for work," said Daphne."

"To work at a job of your own choice."

"A reliable source of energy."

"A source of energy that is also sustainable and non-polluting."

"Are you are deliberately trying to be controversial, Calum?" said Jack.

"You know the rules of brainstorming," retorted Calum. "Just write it down."

Jack shook his head but added Calum's comments.

"Having a say in how your community is run," continued Daphne.

"Being able to choose which community you live in in the first place,"

Anna Harris coughed and tapped her pointer on the table.

"Okay everyone, please get ready to present back your findings now. Jack would you like to start?"

Jack stood up and ran through the list of requirements they had generated.

"I can see a certain amount of divergence of opinion there, Jack," commented Anna. "Maybe in the next exercise we can reflect on how some things we might think are requirements are not really compatible with our post-disaster world. After all, the population is severely reduced in numbers. For instance, residing in a place of our own choosing is a nice ideal, but one which we can no longer afford. We simply do not have enough resources to spread them thinly around lots of tiny, remote communities."

She stared at Calum as she said this. He looked back at her coldly.

The other groups had come up with similar lists to those that Daphne had mentioned. Nobody else seemed to think the items Calum had listed were of any importance. What was wrong with these people, he thought. Had they really all been so brainwashed as to accept everything that the corrupt new government had decreed?

"Right, so before lunch, please get back into your groups and consider how we can deliver these essential items. Especially the infrastructures we will need, both mechanical and human."

"Freedom of movement and association first," began Calum, as Jack once more took up the pen. "The energy and utilities infrastructures need to support small communities as well as city-based ones. We need alternative small-scale power generators and boreholes for fresh water."

Jack sighed as Daphne gave Calum a haughty look.

"Shall we do the human resources bit first instead?" he asked. "Maybe we will get more consensus there."

"There really does not need to be a huge human resources infrastructure to support small communities generating their own power and drawing their own water," insisted Calum. "Nor do we need the heavy hand of international, national and local governmental organisations. We need a network of international co-operatives to share experience and best practice."

"Oh, for goodness sake Calum," spluttered Daphne. "You are living in a dream world if you think we want to go back to the hippy, idealistic nonsense that you have peddled for the last two years. We are *sick* and *tired* of power cuts, not having enough water, no new cars, nice clothing, or foreign holidays. We need a change."

"So, you would rather recreate the corrupt, self-serving, oil-hungry systems and infrastructure that we had before? Those systems which caused the mass destruction of most of the population of the world and which has left the earth in the most polluted, poisoned state ever? Well, excuse me if I don't share your enthusiasm."

Anna Harris looked over at them, pointedly.

"Okay everyone, I think we need a break to let all of this sink in properly and think about what is reasonable. Let's go and have lunch and present your findings back afterwards."

She led the group out to the castle's restaurant, where a buffet had been set out for them.

Calum avoided standing with Jack and Daphne. He did not think he could stand one more minute of their opinions. He also did not want to eat anything here as he was quite sure it was all contaminated.

He spotted a younger man standing by himself over by the window, gazing out at the castle grounds.

"Hi, I'm Calum O'Connell. Fancy a stroll outside?" asked Calum. "I could certainly do with some fresh air."

"I know who you are, of course. I'm Marty Jackson. Yeah, can't wait to get out of here."

As they went outside, the guards on the gate looked over sharply, but relaxed when they saw Calum and Marty stroll off around the perimeter of the castle grounds.

"So, how did you come to be in the wonderful Highlands Focus Group?" asked Calum.

Marty looked disgusted.

"I was living quite happily in Pitlochry working for an engineering firm in Perth before all this. Then, I stayed there with my parents after the catastrophe. We were growing our own food and using the local water supply. Then, after this crazy lot was elected, we were forced to come here. We are being kept prisoner in Cameron barracks."

"That's where we are based," exclaimed Calum. "I guess they put all the rebels there."

"You are a friend of Duggie aren't you?" he asked.

"Yes, he was in Gallanvaig with us until they forced us to Inverness. He was friendly with my adopted daughter, Rachel. You know him then?"

"Yes, I met him at the Barracks. Duggie told me all about life in Gallanvaig and the lovely Rachel," said Marty. "So, what next? Do you have a plan to get out of here? Duggie said you'd be bound to have."

"Possibly," said Calum, guardedly. He wasn't sure yet how much to trust Marty. Was he what he seemed, or just spying for the authorities?

"Well, the sooner the better," said Marty. "We have to get out of here. None of the food is edible and they are trying to brainwash us all with the television programmes. Not to mention the so-called 'Focus' group rubbish."

"What's the deal with that then?" asked Calum. "Have you worked out what they are really doing here?"

"They ask a lot of questions about life in Pitlochry and the local area and about the other people living there. I think they are using us to get information about the rebels to use against them."

"Pretty much as I suspected. Well, they will get nothing from me."

As they were called back into the meeting, Calum was determined that he would give nothing away.

He had to protect his friends and connections if they were to survive this.

15. The Battle of Liverpool Cathedral

The sun shone brightly through the stained glass of the cathedral tower, painting the interior, benches and walls with shimmering deep blues, purples and golds. Archbishop Murphy processed up the aisle with his entourage of priests, deacons and altar servers. The Metropolitan Cathedral was crowded, as were most of his services.

Reaching the altar, he began the Mass and the congregation responded.

"In the name of the Father, the Son and the Holy Spirit."

"Amen," thundered the crowd in unison, making the sign of the cross.

As the mass progressed, the congregation were seated for the readings. The Archbishop opened the bible on the lectern.

"A reading from…" he began but stopped dead as there was a sudden commotion.

The congregation turned their heads to the rear of the church.

"Let us *in*," yelled someone, who had shoved his way in with a crowd of other people at the back of the Cathedral. They were all wearing black clothing and had oversized crosses on chains around their necks. They were all shouting and protesting.

The armed guards who had been stationed at the door, raised their guns and pointed them at the intruders.

"Back outside, now," said one. "You will have to leave this building *immediately*."

The intruders pushed back. The riot police immediately raised shields and began to push the intruders from the cathedral.

With many shouts, complaints and groans as people were struck by batons, the crowd were forced from the building. Noises could be still heard outside, as the battle continued.

The mass continued, but the atmosphere was now subdued and fearful, the congregation shocked at the violence and the sudden shattering of the peace inside the cathedral.

"Why did this have to happen in God's holy place?" one woman asked her neighbour.

"They are sinners who want to cause a disturbance and make us doubt our faith," said her friend, shaking her head.

Although they made all the appropriate responses, the two women were no longer really concentrating on the service.

What was the world coming to when there were near-riots in the cathedrals of England?

The Pope was worried. He turned to Camarlengo Rafaele.

"There have been many disturbances at Catholic churches. I do not like to use the armed machinery of state to deter people, but what choice do we have? We cannot allow the church to be dragged down by mediaeval superstitions and over-literal interpretations of the Bible."

"I think you are doing the only thing you can do. I agree with you that we can't allow this. They will chase away all the genuine faithful."

"Let's hope that this awful sect will soon be quashed. Surely they will give up when they find they can't enter any of the church buildings?"

"Unless they just use somewhere else," said Rafaele.

"God help us," replied Papa Nicholas.

16. An Incredible Theory

Calum opened his door in the Cameron Barracks to find Duggie and Marty. He invited them in to join the rest.

"This is Marty Jackson, a friend of Duggie. He lives here in the barracks and is on my 'focus' group."

"I bet that is riveting stuff," said Rob. "Calum has been telling us all about it."

Marty laughed.

"Well, it is definitely more for the benefit of the authorities than the community. It is tough going, that's for sure. They only want to know what we really think about the new regime and to find out about our networks. So, Calum, do we have a plan?"

Glancing at Duggie, who nodded slightly, Calum explained the immediate plans.

"My contact in France will send helicopters for us, we just need to provide a time and place. The question is, when can we get everybody together without raising suspicion?"

"If we are prepared to overcome the guards, it would be best in the evenings," said Duggie. "We would be all together in the barracks and there is a small airstrip in the grounds of the barracks where they can land."

"So, the question is when?" asked Chloe. "I don't want to spend a moment longer than necessary in here."

"Here is the grid reference you wanted," said Duggie, handing a piece of paper to Calum.

"Right, let's go for Saturday night then," said Calum. "That will give us time to let everyone know to be waiting over by the airstrip. And as it isn't a work day, we will all be in the barracks. Is there somewhere we can conceal ourselves so that we won't raise suspicion?"

"Yes, next to the airstrip is an office building. It isn't usually locked, as the barrack gates are guarded anyway," said Marty.

"A few of us will need to deal with any guards who are around," said Rob. "Anyone willing to join me?"

Millie, Calum and David all said they would.

"Okay, I will contact Renée and set it up. Now, let's have that glass of wine."

The atmosphere was relaxed and friendly as they anticipated getting as far away from here as possible.

Later that evening, as the wine was flowing, and the chat had become lively, there was a tap at the door.

"Expecting someone?" asked Rob, glancing at Calum.

"No, not as far as I know," said Calum.

Getting up he cautiously opened the door. A dark-haired, casually-dressed man stood outside.

"Calum O'Connell?" he asked.

"Yes, who's asking?" answered Calum, his hand still preventing the door from fully opening.

"My name is Gavin Routledge. I was formerly a professor of early Middle Eastern Studies and Arabic mythology at Edinburgh University. I was brought here by the authorities from Pitlochry where I had made my home."

"It's okay, Calum, I knew him in Pitlochry," said Marty. "He's sound. He helped with a lot of projects in the town. I told him you were here."

Still a bit unsure of the additions to his group, Calum opened the door anyway. Marty seemed to have been accepted by Duggie and he was just going to have to trust in his judgement for now. But, he intended to keep a close eye on the newcomers.

"Glass of wine?" asked Chloe, always the good host.

Gavin accepted a drink and sat down.

"Calum, I'm going to tell you something that you might find fantastic and unbelievable."

"Well we have heard a lot of weird stuff over the past few years," said Calum. "Try us."

"Well, you know that the Genies are thought to have evolved as a result of consuming genetically modified food?"

"Yes, we had a scientist friend who had lots of theories about how that happened," said Calum. "The genes activated dormant psychic traits and allergies in human DNA, as well as killing many through organ destruction. Sadly, Ben's no longer with us."

"Well, we had geneticists at Edinburgh University and there are couple of them who moved to Pitlochry after the GM catastrophe. Eamon and Tristan have their own theories."

"Go on," said Rob, intrigued.

"I'll introduce you to them later, they are here too. But, I said I would sound you out first. See what you make of it all. I know you were a key player in the anti-GM movement and obviously still wield lots of influence as ex-head of the UK World Alliance. We need to raise awareness of what we think is going on. Firstly, genetic modification can only work on the gene structure that exists. That is the gene structure of the receiving organism and that of the genetically-modified substance that enters the organism. Although GM food has unpredictable results that can include organ deterioration and even death, it cannot produce something entirely new, something that wasn't in the make-up of the two combining DNAs to begin with."

"You're losing me a bit," said Rob. "What's your point?"

"What if the resulting modifications, or mutations if you like, of the receiver's DNA re-activated a trait that was *always there anyway*, but which had long been dormant?"

"What, like suddenly becoming left-handed, or having red hair?" said Rob. "Not to mention psychic abilities like mind reading and telekinesis.

"That sort of thing, yes. But, in this case, re-activating traits that were reported thousands of years ago. In fact, at the dawn of time."

"What traits?" asked Calum.

"So, firstly, I need to back-track to my own academic specialty, which as I said includes Arabic mythology. In mythology there are creatures called 'Jinn' or 'Djinn'. They were said to be created from smokeless fire but have a physical nature. They can be good or evil like humans and angels and were created by God."

"Fascinating," said Rob. "I still don't see where this is going."

"Give him a chance Rob," said David. "This might help us make sense of things. You know how much we learned from Ben about the subject of GM and its impact on humans."

"It was thought that the Jinn lived in dark places and were feared. They can be male or female. They live their lives just like humans do. But, with a few key differences. There are three classes of Jinn. One that can *fly instantaneously* from one place to another. One resembles snakes or dogs and another that travels far and wide. They can also *shapeshift*, appearing as animals, or in human form, or even be invisible. They can move items through the air without touching them. Any of this sound familiar?"

"What are you talking about? This is just a myth, right?" said Rob.

"Maybe if I tell you that the Anglicised form of Jinn that appears in Roman religion comes from the Latin word 'genius' - or *Genie*?"

Chloe gasped. "Oh, my God. So, you are saying that the Genies are reactivated Jinn? And the potential for humans becoming Jinn was in our DNA all the time?"

"That's what Eamon and Tristan believe. They say that the Human Genome Project identified around thirty thousand human genes. Only *ten* per cent are used to code and produce proteins. The other ninety percent is known as 'junk' DNA, with possibly redundant and unknown functions. What are all those genes *for*? When you christened the mutant humans 'Genies' Calum, it seems you were far more accurate than you ever dreamed."

"I'm shocked," said Calum. "You really believe this?"

"Eamon, Tristan and I have studied this for the past three years. It is the only explanation."

"So, if it's true, what can we do to protect ourselves from them?" asked Calum.

"Very little according to the literature. Praying mostly."

"Great," grunted Rob.

"Well, it explains how some humans mutated into the Genies, or Jinn as you call them," said Calum. "And presumably the rest didn't become Genies because they weren't eating GM food, or their genetic make-up was different and maybe less susceptible. But I don't see how it helps. And how does this fit in with the Revelation

Army lot? They think that the Genies, GM sickness, death, nuclear missiles and hunger are all signs of the imminent Apocalypse."

"The Revelation Army, as far as I can make out, is saying that the signs are there that the Apocalypse outlined in the Bible is near at hand. Arabic mythology says that the Jinn will be judged just like humans on the last day. They will be sent to Heaven or Hell depending on their deeds during life. I think all these events are part of the bigger picture. I think that we are approaching a cataclysmic time, an apocalypse, if you like. And yes, all you can do about any of this is try to avoid getting killed - and maybe pray."

"Well, I think I need some time to think through all of this," said Calum. "How about we call it a day. Can you come back tomorrow night and bring your two friends?"

With that they all said goodnight and Calum was left alone with his thoughts.

Was Jessie dead already? If she was and the Apocalypse really was near, would he see her again on the last day, or after it? That's if there really *was* an afterlife. How he wished he knew for sure what the answers were. He shook himself as a shudder ran through his body.

He really must get some sleep and clear his head.

As he drifted off to sleep, he caught a vague waft of Jessie's favourite perfume, Eastern Amber.

"Jessie," he mumbled reaching across.

He fell asleep, dreaming that his arms were around the love of his life.

Calum awoke with an uneasy feeling that he couldn't explain. His stomach felt queasy and his head was banging with the beginnings of an awful headache. And there was something else.

A dark presence was probing his brain. Throwing back the covers, he leapt from the bed.

"Get out" he shouted, his hand on his forehead trying to ease the pain. "Go and bother somebody else."

It was Balthazar and his evil cronies, he felt sure. He *knew* they couldn't have all been destroyed, as had been claimed on the news. Not with the recent killings and destruction that had all the hallmarks of the Genies. Did they know that they were resurrected Jinn? With their mind-reading capabilities, had they heard the professor telling them about the mythology last night?

But, what did that mean, if they now knew they were Jinn? If they knew of their full potential, would there be any stopping them?

Shaking his head, he went into the small kitchen and put the kettle on. Strong, hot coffee might just help him to dispel the intruder in his head.

There was a knock and he opened the door. Rob came in looking worried.

"Calum, did you have any strange experiences last night?"

"Like what?"

"I think our old adversaries, the Genies, are around. I felt them in my mind late last night and briefly this morning when I awoke."

"Well, yes, this morning I woke up with a hell of a headache and I felt something creeping around my brain. It seems to be gone now, though. Do you think the fact that we know what they really are will help us to deal with them?"

"I don't see how. But, we can understand what they are and what they are capable of with the help of Gavin and his friends. It might allow us to be more prepared to deal with them."

"If they are supernatural beings, evil ones if you like, could religion help? What about exorcisms and things? Could it be possible that would dispel them from a place?"

"Not sure I believe in all of that, mate. I didn't think you did either."

"But anything is worth a try surely? What else can we do against possibly invisible, shape-shifting evil Jinn with extreme paranormal powers?"

"What are you thinking? Would you ask a priest or something?"

"I don't know. Might need to be a few of them and they would need to be experienced in exorcism."

"I'm really not sure about this, Calum."

"What about if we had a worldwide effort, led by the clergy, to dispel them back to the dark corners of the earth? Which, according to Gavin, is where they belong."

"If you think it's worth a try, go for it. But, let's not wait for that to escape from this place."

"No, course not. That is still on for tomorrow night. I contacted Reneé last night and she has the grid reference and will send the helicopters. Enough room for as many as we can gather."

There was a sudden tap at the door and David and Chloe arrived with the four kids.

"Did you by any chance feel any strange probing last night?" began Chloe.

"Yes, we both did. We think it's the Genies, or Jinn, or whatever they are. I think we should try to organise a mass exorcism. Rob's not so sure though."

"Calum, you're right, I don't believe in it. But, go ahead, try it. We're all out of other ideas."

"Would that work, Calum?" asked Joanna looking worried. "Are they really evil ones?"

"I gather that's what you might call them," said Calum. "But don't worry sweetheart, you're safe with us."

Even as he said it, he knew it wasn't true. He hadn't managed to keep Jessie safe, had he? He felt so helpless in the face of unimaginable, powerful evil.

They all set off on their allocated jobs, not feeling too positive about it, especially David and Chloe who had to once more work at the nuclear power plant, restoring it to its full polluting, deadly power.

Calum also wasn't looking forward to the sessions at the castle. He had had just about enough of the preaching and snooping of the other participants. But at least he now had an ally in Marty. He was quite sure that they didn't think they could brainwash people like him, but were just trying to find out about their contacts, networks and plans, as Marty had suspected. Anyway, hopefully they would be out of here by tomorrow night.

Anna Harris was being her usual annoying self, lecturing them about the foolish ways of breakaway groups trying to go it alone in isolated villages.

"I am sure you all agree that we will be much safer from the Genies living in larger groups. We can also more easily provide reliable water and electricity supplies, as well as food, in larger communities. We can't afford the resources to provide these things to many small isolated communities."

Calum sighed. How much longer was she going to go on about this? He let her words wash over him as he day-dreamed about their escaping tomorrow night.

He was suddenly aware that the room had fallen silent and everyone seemed to be looking at him expectantly. Marty looked over and shook his head slightly.

"Mr O'Connell? Any comment? You were allocated to this group to contribute, not to fall asleep whilst everyone else does all the work."

"Sorry, I missed your question," he mumbled.

"I was asking for information on other groups who might be struggling to survive in remote locations so that we can help them too. I know you have your contacts around the world. So, where do we look for them?"

Calum shook his head incredulously. Did she think he would just give up that information? Betray his friends and comrades? Maybe she assumed he was already drugged into acquiescence by the contaminated food. Anyway, it simply wasn't happening.

"I don't know what you are talking about. I am unaware of anybody who is not living in the towns and cities. After all, it's the law now isn't it?"

With an angry sound, she turned and put the next exercise on the board.

"You will all complete this before lunch," she snarled. "And Mr O'Connell I need to speak to you in private. *Now*."

She glared at him and strode from the room. Calum glanced at Marty who mouthed 'good luck' as he followed her out.

Going into a room on the opposite side of the corridor, she beckoned him in.

"Mr O'Connell. I am just about sick and tired of your negativity. You never take part in discussions and when you do finally say something, it's usually a criticism of the authorities and our way of life. If you do not start to cooperate, I will have no alternative but to refer you to the city council and you will be reallocated to penal work. And I can tell you categorically, you will not enjoy *that*."

It doesn't matter anyway, Calum thought to himself. I only need to survive here another day then I am out of here.

"Sorry Ms Harris," he said half-heartedly. "I will try to do better from now on."

He hated kow-towing to this awful, arrogant woman, but there really was no alternative. He couldn't afford to be allocated to penal work and possibly have even more restrictions placed on him, not just when they were about to escape.

"Well, we'll see," she said. "I remain to be convinced. Go and join your group. I expect to see something more positive from you after lunch."

Calum joined the others, dreading already the pointless discussions he was condemned to have with the other awful people in his group.

"Ah, Calum, you decided to join us eventually," said Jack Carter.

"Let's hope he is feeling a bit more positive now," added Daphne Morrison.

With a heavy heart, Calum tried to say something positive about the topic, which was how to track down all the itinerant groups who hadn't joined those in the towns yet. But, there was no way he would tell them anything they could use against his friends.

"So, we were saying that we could track these struggling communities using heat tracking from helicopters," Jack said. "Even though their power supplies are unreliable, their communities will still be radiating heat, so we should be able to detect that."

"We may be able to track their vehicles as they move around the area," said Daphne. "Follow them back to their base. We could use 'copters or drones for that."

"Er, I think that there was a group in Alpbach near Innsbruck that had problems with providing enough heat and food in the harsh winters they have there," Calum said.

He knew full well that that particular community had moved down to lower pastures some distance away, over a year ago. It was difficult to survive in the Alps, without adequate power supplies and food. But, he had to offer them something. By the time they found out it was a false lead, he would hopefully be gone.

"Good, good," said Daphne. "I am sure we will be able to help them. The weather is so harsh there."

Jack was making notes on the flip chart.

"Thanks, Calum. Anyone else you think needs our help?"

"Well, communications weren't that great, you know. We were all so isolated, the systems didn't always work."

Calum grimaced inside as he noticed Daphne giving Jack a victorious smile.

"I think there were some groups on the islands just off the coast of Canada. But I can't remember which ones Alan Jackson mentioned."

All the small islands had mostly been evacuated when North America was abandoned to the Genies and the ravages of pollution from the GM crops. Anyway, there were so many islands, it would be impossible to search them all. And even then, all they might find would be a few Genies.

"Ah, I see you're making good progress now, Mr O'Connell," remarked Anna, as she passed their group. "Well done."

She walked away smirking to herself.

She obviously thinks she has won, thought Calum.

Little did she know, but by the time she found out, it would be too late.

That evening, they had gathered in the social room, together with others living in the barracks who had taken up the offer to escape tomorrow. Calum hoped he could trust them all. But, after all, they were all rebels, just like the Gallanvaig community. That's why they had been brought here and kept prisoner. Although the brainwashing seemed to have neutralised some of that rebellious spirit and made people compliant.

"So, we will need to be ready to leave at six o'clock tomorrow evening. It will be dark by then and the guards will be relaxed. Please travel light, there may not be much space on board and we need to get as many people out of here as possible. We must all be at the office by the airstrip at nine thirty. We need to gradually go over there in small groups to avoid suspicion. Then, we wait in the office building until the helicopters arrive. Reneé said they should be here around ten o'clock. Please be ready to board quickly when they touch down and you are given the signal. These things can be noisy. We don't want the guards getting over there before we are all in the air. Any questions?"

"Can we take Buster and Shep?" asked Joanna.

"Of course, I wouldn't leave without them," said Calum smiling. "And that goes for any other pets. Small ones of course, we don't have room for any horses."

Everyone laughed, breaking the tension a little.

"We will be going to a secret underground base in the north of Scotland," he continued. "I'm sure you will understand why we need to keep the exact location secret for now."

He also knew that it was possible that the group had been infiltrated. He didn't want their plans to become known to the guards or the authorities, until it was too late.

"Tomorrow, please do as you would normally on a Saturday. We don't want to raise suspicion. But, make sure you are back in the barracks in time to get ready to leave. We can't wait for anyone once the helicopters arrive."

Everyone nodded and there were no more questions.

"Okay, let's get a good night's sleep and I'll see you all tomorrow. Good luck everyone."

Later, the group of friends gathered in Calum's room for a nightcap.

"So, this thing about the Genies being Jinn," Rob was saying. "We all felt their presence last night and this morning. So, what was all that about? Why are they still hanging around? I thought they had all been killed in the US?"

"Obviously not," said Chloe. "Balthazar seems to be particularly hard to get rid of."

"I guess some of them must have survived," said David. "They were apparently living in an underground base, so the nuclear missiles may not have killed the ones who were underground at the time. And anyway, we only have the word of the authorities that they were attacked and wiped out."

"True," said Rob. "It's probably just disinformation. Telling us what to believe. They must know they haven't killed them off. Those earthquakes and tsunamis were right out of the Genies psychic trick box."

"Well, we can't worry about them now. Let's get out of here first and then work out what we can do against them later," said Calum.

There was a sudden rush of air into the room and a menacing laugh.

"Not so fast, my friend Calum," said a creepily familiar voice.

Oh no, thought Calum.

Balthazar. And his evil cronies.

"I think you have had some news about our origins," said Balthazar, shaking back his hood. "So, what exactly did the professor tell you about us?"

"Do you mean Professor Routledge?" asked Calum, playing for time.

"If that is who you were speaking to last night," answered Balthazar.

"What do you want to know about him?"

"You know very well, Calum. He has knowledge of our origins and purpose. Of our powers and whether we will be victorious in the battle for this world."

God, he was so arrogant, thought Calum. Everything had to be about him and his evil band of murderers. Well, maybe he could use that to his advantage.

"He says that you will succeed in your endeavours, that you will rule this world."

"I *knew* it," crowed Balthazar. "We have already made our mark on those who would destroy us. We have critically wounded some of them and others are dead. They will not readily recover."

"Yes, I am sure you are right. They can do little against your extraordinary powers."

Rob gave Calum a sharp look. What was he playing at?

Balthazar smiled, a slow, creepy smile full of absolute confidence that one day he *would* rule the world.

"Where are the rest of the cabal then? We wish to pay our respects." He laughed."

"We don't know who they are, nor where they are, or I would gladly tell you. I owe them no allegiance. Anyway, I'm sure that you have more idea of their location than we do, with all the power at your disposal."

Balthazar shrugged.

"No matter, I will find them. Anyway, where is your *girlfriend*?" he sniggered. "I haven't seen her for *so* long."

"Jessie is out of *your* reach, that's for sure. As I am sure you already know," said Calum his voice taut.

Balthazar threw his head back and gave a maniacal laugh, showing a mouthful of crooked, blackened teeth.

Calum only just stopped himself from launching at the creep and tearing his throat out. But, where would that get him? Jessie was gone, whether this evil bastard had anything to do with it or not. Chloe looked over at him and shook her head slightly. This wasn't the time to challenge Balthazar and his cohorts.

"I can *feel* her, my friend," crooned Balthazar. "She is around somewhere, but out of sight. But she *will* come back to me soon. Of that I am sure."

This almost drove Calum to fly at Balthazar. He was lying obviously. He was sure that Jessie was dead. If she wasn't, she would have found a way to get a message to him. Although, he wasn't going to let the kids know that. He wanted to keep their hope alive a little longer.

"You just stay away from her. Or you will be sorry."

"Ooh, threats. I love it when powerless people threaten me. You know my power, my friend."

"I am *not* your friend. Now, if you don't mind, we have a busy day tomorrow, so can you please get lost now?"

Balthazar's face went purple and Calum thought he had pushed it too far and he was going to attack him.

Then, he shook his head from side to side, as if trying to clear troublesome thoughts from his head and laughed.

"I could swat you like a fly," he said. "But, you are useful to me yet, so I will let you live. Just for now."

With that, Balthazar and his cronies put their hoods up and swirled away in a cloud of black mist until they weren't there anymore.

With the release of the tension they hadn't even known they were feeling, everyone gasped. Joanna burst into tears of shock.

"It's ok, sweetheart, they are gone now," said Calum, as Chloe put her arm around the girl.

"Do you think they really came here just to check what Gavin said about the Jinn?" asked David. "Why didn't they just find out from probing our minds?"

"Maybe they wanted to hear it for themselves, directly from the horse's mouth," said Calum. "Oh, no, *Gavin*," he said as he suddenly realised that their new friend was now in danger.

As they all rushed from the room, there was a chorus of evil laughter from out of nowhere. Maybe from the ether itself.

It was as if there was a window on their world, through which the Genies could peer whenever they wished.

Calum didn't think the headsets would work anymore at blocking out the Genies.

They were just too powerful now.

Rob banged on Gavin's door, but there was no answer.

"Gavin. Are you there?"

The next door along the corridor opened and a man stuck his head out.

"Are you looking for Gavin?"

"Yes, we believe he is in danger."

The man came out and closed his door quickly.

"I'm Eamon Coleraine - I'm a friend of Gavin. What's the danger?"

"He told us about you, you're one of his geneticist friends. We think the Genies, or Jinn as you know them, are after him. They want to know more about the Jinn and their links to the Genies."

"Oh great," said Eamon. "Wait, I'll get Tris, he may know where Gavin is."

He knocked on a door further up the corridor and it was answered by a tall man.

"Tris, Gavin may be in trouble. Where is he?"

"Last I heard he had gone to see the janitor to see if they have fixed his heating. It's been playing up and it's a little cold for the heating to be off. Why, what's up?"

"Come on, we'll explain on the way," said Eamon leading the way down a flight of stairs to the maintenance office.

Breathless, the group burst into the janitor's office. There on the floor was the janitor. He was lying on his back and his head was at an odd angle. There was blood trickling from his face.

"Oh no," cried Chloe. "Quickly, we need to find Gavin."

"Let's spilt up and check the building and the grounds," said Calum. "And be careful. They know about you two and your Jinn theories."

They rushed off in various directions. Calum headed outside with Rob, Chloe, David and the kids.

As they reached the grounds, they could hear a commotion over in the woods surrounding the barracks.

Wordlessly, they ran towards the sounds. They could hear shouting and scuffles.

"Get *off* me I tell you. You won't get anything from me."

There was a mumbled threat that they couldn't decipher.

As they entered the woods, they saw the crowd of Genies with Gavin. Balthazar had Gavin by the neck and Nicholas was holding his arms behind his back.

Calum and Rob charged straight at them. Catching Balthazar off-guard, Calum knocked his hands away from Gavin's throat and Rob kicked Nicholas's legs from under him. He went down like a sack of potatoes.

Balthazar growled as he recovered his balance and pointed at Calum. And then fire flew from his fingers, engulfing Calum.

With a loud shriek, the kids launched themselves at Calum and threw him to the ground rolling him in the wet grass to dampen the flames. David left Chloe and ran to join them. Meanwhile, in the chaos, Rob grabbed Gavin and made off back towards the building.

There was a sudden crack of a firearm. A large squad of soldiers had run from their part of the barracks and were firing at the Genies, trying to avoid hitting Calum or the kids.

Screaming now, the kids dragged Calum up and ran for the building followed by David and Chloe.

As the firepower intensified, the Genies did not appear to be getting hit by the bullets. They just moved aside from each burst of fire with lightning speed.

Then, with one smooth move, they rose up and disappeared.

19. A New Threat

Calum examined his red, blistered arms. He had sustained some skin burns, but thanks to the quick action of the kids, the damage was superficial.

"I'm okay," he reassured the kids, who had gathered around him looking worried. "It will soon heal. Thanks to you lot."

The friends stayed together in Calum's room, fearing another attack by the Genies. Everyone had stayed in groups and posted guards through the night.

"At least we will be out of here tomorrow," whispered Calum to Rob, as they kept watch.

There was a sudden loud howl from somewhere very close outside, then a couple of seconds later followed a whole chorus of blood-curdling howls.

The others stirred at the sounds.

"What the hell is that?" mumbled Chloe. "Balthazar playing tricks?"

"If I didn't know better, I would say it's a pack of wolves," said Rob. "Are there wolves in Scotland?"

"I'm pretty sure they died out in the UK hundreds of years ago," replied Calum. "Decimated by over-hunting and habitat destruction. Is there a zoo in Inverness?"

Nobody knew.

At the window, David whistled softly.

"I don't believe it. Come and see."

Looking out on the dark barrack grounds, they could see at least fifteen dark shapes. Large, long dark shapes that were lifting their muzzles and howling at the moon.

Wolves.

"They must have escaped from somewhere," said Calum. "We haven't seen them before up here. Do you know if there were wild wolves here Gavin?"

"Not since they died out, around the year fifteen hundred. As Calum points out, due to hunting and tree felling destroying their habitats. There were a few small animal parks, but I've never seen anything outside of those."

"I guess the guards will sort them out, unfortunately. They are beautiful creatures though," said Chloe.

"Well, I hope it's calmed down by tomorrow. We need to have our way clear to the airstrip. Better get some sleep if you can."

Calum and Rob settled down and handed over the watch to David and Chloe.

Gavin seemed unsettled and was in a huddle with Eamon and Tristan, whispering so as not to disturb anyone.

After a while, he went over to Calum and shook him awake.

"Sorry, mate, but there is something I think you need to know."

Calum was alert immediately.

"What is it?"

Talking low, he briefed Calum on their conversation.

Calum gasped.

"It's not so surprising," said Gavin. "Not after what happened with the Genies, or Jinn as we know them to be."

"What's going on?" demanded Rachel, rubbing her eyes.

The others were also stirring.

"Sorry, I didn't mean to disturb everyone," said Gavin.

"Gavin thinks that there is a new danger," said Calum. "Of course, you all know what happened with the Genies, how their DNA was mutated after they consumed GM material. The transgenes altered what was already in their genetic make-up. They regressed to Jinn, as they would have been thousands of years ago. As was still defined somewhere in their DNA. In our DNA too."

"And in the form that they are in all around the world," added Gavin. "Arabic mythology says they exist."

"Do you want to explain Gavin?"

"Well, humans aren't the only beings to be affected by GM material in food. Animals eat GM feed. Birds consume GM waste material draining into watercourses and in plant seeds and plant material that they consume. Domestic dog and cat food often contain GM corn, oils and soy, as well as meat from GM-fed animals. Eamon?"

"Yes, and the transgenes that they consume could equally affect the DNA make up of animals and birds. This hasn't really been considered up to now, as we have been too busy trying to avoid getting killed by the Jinn, or the Illuminati. The thing is, there is no reason why the changed DNA would not cause the animal to change form according to its genetic make-up. That is, its own DNA combined with that of the transgene DNA, whatever that came from. That is an unknown. The effects of all this are untested."

"What we do know is this, "added Tristan. "Wolves are the genetic ancestors of *domestic dogs*."

The room fell silent as this awful truth sank in.

"So, our dogs are turning into wolves," said Rachel in a shocked tone.

"That has to be considered as a distinct possibility," said Tristan.

"Will Buster and Shep turn into wolves?" asked Joanna.

"We don't know," said Calum. "I hope not. I only ever fed Buster food that I would eat myself. As for Shep, we can't know what he was being fed before David rescued him from that farm. But, that was a long time ago and the dogs have been fine."

"How long would it take to show its effects?" asked Chloe.

"We really don't know, this is a totally new field. But, if domestic dogs are being affected only now, assuming they don't still have access to GM food, maybe it takes longer for animals to fully exhibit the characteristics of changed DNA."

"Could other animals start to mutate then?" asked a shocked Calum.

"We can't rule it out," said Tristan.

"That sounds like a ticking time bomb," said Rob.

"I'm afraid we cannot know the full extent of the damage wreaked by this stupid, ill-thought out experiment."

As everyone was too shocked to sleep anymore and the dawn was slowly breaking, they decided to prepare their stuff for leaving later.

But, would anywhere else be safer with this new threat?

20. Leaving Day

There was an atmosphere of pent-up anticipation in the barracks that day. Everyone was eagerly looking forward to getting out of there later, with the help of their French friends.

"Are we being too obvious, do you think?" asked Chloe. "I mean, we are all trying to look busy to deflect attention, when on a Saturday we might normally be having a stroll or reading."

"It will be fine, honestly," said Rob. "Nobody suspects a thing. They pretty much leave us to our own devices at the weekend. But, I must admit, I can't bloody wait to get out of this place. I am just about sick of being told what to do and where to go."

Chloe smiled. Rob wasn't really known for his patience, especially with the authorities.

"Oh well, as least tonight we will be out of here and safe," she said.

Calum and the kids had gone for a walk around the perimeter with Buster, who was busy sniffing the ground under the trees. He gave an excited yap.

"Can you smell something interesting?" said Calum, smiling. "Is it the wolves?"

He glanced around, suddenly concerned about their safety. There might be a big pack of hungry wolves still around. But, there was nothing in sight and the sun shone brightly, enveloping them in a feeling of overwhelming wellbeing. Did wolves come out in the daylight? He couldn't remember, but he didn't think so. Was thinking so enough?

"Maybe we should head back to base now," he said, worried that out here they were exposed to attack from any wild animals that were lurking about. It really wasn't worth taking the risk now that they were heading out.

"We can catch up with our reading, try to be unobtrusive. Can you manage that James?" he added, with a grin at his adopted son.

James pulled a face.

"I suppose I will just have to try," he quipped.

"I very much doubt you'll manage that," said Rachel. "Do you even know what it means?"

James gave her a little dig in the ribs, laughing.

"Hey, Joanna, how about you?" he asked his little sister. "Can you manage to sit quietly all afternoon reading a book? Or will you be wittering on about your latest *boyfriend*?"

"I haven't got a boyfriend," she answered, flushing.

"Okay, so that dude who I saw you talking to outside school yesterday was just some random 'friend?'"

"Shut *up*, James," she answered turning away.

"Ooh, methinks she has something to hide," said James. "What do you think Shaun?"

"Leave her alone, James," said Rachel. "Haven't we got enough to worry about today without all this teasing?"

James fell quiet, feeling a bit guilty at ribbing his sister, when they were still being held prisoner. Shaun gave him a sheepish smile.

"Anyone fancy something to eat?" said Calum, changing the subject.

It was six o'clock and Calum's room was full of friends, all anticipating the moment when they could make their move. There were other groups in several of the rooms on that floor. It was already fully dark on that December evening and a chill wind was gusting around the barracks, whistling through the eaves.

"Okay, time for the first group to leave," he said motioning to them. "Good luck."

"See you on the outside," said Gavin, who was in the group about to leave, as he shook Calum's hand.

Calum had insisted that Gavin and the two geneticists should each join a different group. He didn't want to risk losing all their knowledge and expertise if any group was captured. Their skills were just too valuable. Yet again, he regretted the loss of his friend, Ben to the GM disease. He had known so much about genetic science.

Every twenty minutes, Calum sent the next group out. Keeping a watch on the barracks grounds through the window overlooking the path to the airstrip, he worried that the guards would suddenly appear and stop them. He also hoped that the 'copters wouldn't have trouble landing in the rising gusts of wind.

More than two hours had gone by and another group had just left. There was only himself, Rob, Paul, Amir, Bill and Millie left, who would leave last. Calum had insisted that the four kids go with Chloe and David's group. He wanted to know that they were safe before he left.

The last group were almost at the building by the airstrip and all was quiet.

Until they heard the horrific roar.

21. Horror in the Dark

Calum strained his eyes at the window. The others rushed to peer from the window.

"What *is* it?" asked Millie.

"I have no idea," said Calum. "It didn't sound like wolves anyway."

"Definitely something bigger," said Rob. "What the hell?" he muttered, as the growl sounded again, only louder. "It's beginning to sound like a jungle out there."

"Maybe you're not far wrong," said Calum. "Remember what Gavin and his chums were saying yesterday about the 'junk' DNA in all terrestrial beings and how it could mutate with the transgene DNA? Perhaps transforming physical appearance and behaviour into something already there in the DNA, which hadn't manifested for thousands of years."

"Bloody hell, what are you saying?" exclaimed Rob, hardly able to believe what he was hearing.

"I don't actually know what species that could be until I see it. But, it sounds awfully like a big cat. How many of its direct descendants live quietly and unobtrusively in most of the households on this Earth? That's right, the humble domestic *cat*."

"Oh. My. God," said Millie quietly.

The group who had almost reached the building by the airstrip were running now and they could hear their panicked shrieks. They must be terrified thought Calum, as they had all agreed to make their transfer in total silence, to avoid alerting the guards on the gate.

"Right, let's go," he said making a quick decision. "It's now or never. The guards will probably be making an appearance soon with all this racket and we need to get past those beasts whatever they are. Grab anything you could use as a weapon."

They all looked around frantically and grabbed curtain poles, pokers, shovels and a heavy table lamp.

Calum thought they must look pathetic, but what choice did they have?

They reached the door to the barracks grounds and there they saw a terrible commotion. Several soldiers were crouching behind the wall at the edge of the green, their guns pointed at an area just in front of the trees, from where an enormous roaring emanated.

Calum silently pointed to the wall to their right, in the opposite direction and they quickly made their way along it, keeping in its shadow.

When they reached the end of the wall, they would be forced to run across open ground to get to the office building. Then they would be under threat from both the army and the animals. Whatever they were.

Calum didn't know which was worst.

Reaching the end of their cover, Calum led the way in a brisk run for the building ahead. Then, they heard a shout from their left.

"Halt. What are you playing at? Can't you hear that there are wild animals out here? Return to your building *now*."

Calum ignored the instruction and carried on running towards the building, followed by the others. If they could just get inside they could shelter and would have a place to defend themselves from both the guards and the beasts.

A bullet pinged past Millie's ear.

"Ow!" she shrieked.

"Millie are you okay?" called Calum, stopping.

"I'm okay, keep going," she said. "Only a graze."

Not a moment too soon, they reached the building, where David held the door open to let them all inside.

They collapsed out of breath on the office chairs.

"Nobody must go outside," said Calum. "Not only the soldiers are after us, but some kind of large animals."

"I know, we heard them, mate," said David. "Are you all okay?"

"I think so," said Calum. "Millie are you sure you didn't get hit?"

"A bullet grazed my ear and it hurts like hell. But, I'll survive," she said.

"How long before the French come for us?" said Chloe," anxiously holding her swollen tummy.

"About twenty minutes. Let's hope that the soldiers are kept busy for a while until we can get away."

There was an intensification of the roaring and growling, followed by the horrific screams of the soldiers.

Joanna burst into tears and James and Shaun also looked very upset.

Calum stood up by the door.

"Look, we have to stay inside. We can't go to help those soldiers. If we do, we risk them stopping our escape, or worse, being attacked ourselves by those creatures. We just can't take the risk."

As more screams added to the general horror, everyone fell silent, trying to shut out the sounds and the images trying to enter their minds. Then there were other sounds. Tearing, wet sounds and much grunting.

"Oh, my God. Those soldiers are being eaten alive," said Chloe.

A few people were openly weeping now, wondering if they would even survive the night. Even if the helicopters arrived, would their rescuers be attacked too? How would they get from the building to the helicopters without getting attacked?

Calum took out his mobile phone, which he had managed to keep hidden from the guards and called Reneé.

"Salut, Reneé, Calum here. Yes, we are all here, waiting for the 'copters to arrive. But there is a problem."

"What sort of problem?"

"There are animals loose here in the barracks. I mean *big* animals. Wolves, lions too maybe, believe it or not. Our geneticists say it's a throwback caused by the GM transgenes."

"That would explain some of the odd events in France too. We had some people bitten by huge wildcats. We haven't ever seen wildcats that big here. Also, farmers on the lower slopes of the French Alps have reported huge cattle, seven feet tall, with long horns. They were trying to drive their animals down to the village for winter, but were attacked by these huge animals, which included several young calves. But, these were nothing like the domestic variety. The odd thing is, the huge beasts were *wearing the cowbells that the farmer had fitted to his herd months ago.*"

"Well, can we talk more about that once we're out of here? Can you tell your crews to be careful where they land and not to exit their craft? We will come to them once it's safe."

A few minutes later, they heard the regular throb of several helicopters approaching. Calum went to the window.

"They are landing now on the airstrip. We'll send a recce group out first, check that the animals are still being kept busy by the soldiers. Any volunteers?"

A group of brave people soon stood at the door ready for a signal from Calum.

"Good luck," he said as they ran out towards the landed choppers.

Millie was leading the group and she reached the first helicopter, opening the door and waiting till all the others had climbed aboard. She looked back at the area in the trees. She saw a horrific site of several lions, attacking lumps of bloodied meat on the ground. One or two soldiers were obviously still alive, as sporadic firing came from just inside the door to the main barracks. For the moment they were safe.

But, it might not be long before the lions wanted more food.

Frantically she signalled to Calum to hurry.

He decided that the rest of them should leave together before it was too late. The whole group rushed to the 'copters. Calum helped the kids and Chloe and David aboard.

He was the last to board a 'copter and, as he was climbing up, he sensed a swift approach behind him. He heard a slight grunt and saw a flash of brown out of the corner of his eye.

"Calum!" screamed Joanna from the 'copter.

He grabbed the rail and started to pull himself up, then he felt sharp claws rake his back, triggering instant pain.

He slammed the door shut and collapsed on to the floor.

"Go, go, go," he cried to the pilot, holding his back in agony.

"Let me see, said Chloe. "Rachel, can you get the first aid kit from the crew?"

The 'copters took off one by one as the large animals circled around them, trying to work out where the people had gone.

They had escaped.

104

22. Night Flight

Chloe worked at Calum's back with antiseptic lotion. He winced every time the stinging solution touched his cuts.

"It's not too bad," she said. "Looks worse than it is. The main thing is to make sure it doesn't get infected, so I'm afraid you'll just have to be brave until I get all the cuts sanitised."

Calum groaned. He glanced up and saw David watching over the operation.

"Save me from this torture, David."

"You just take your medicine," said David. "You know it's for your own good."

They were all still in shock with the discovery that lions and wolves were roaming around Inverness. It seemed unbelievable, yet they had seen it with their own eyes.

"Could the geneticists really be right about domestic animals mutating back into ancestral forms, their own DNA mutating, triggered by the transgenes in the GM DNA?" Rachel said, shaking her head. "It just seems incredible."

"I can't see any other explanation," said David. "Apparently there were no nearby zoos or wildlife parks with lions. Although, one around forty miles south of Inverness had a few wolves. The nearest with lions was Edinburgh, but that's like a hundred and fifty miles away. It would have taken weeks for them to get to Inverness. And I think they might have been spotted on the way."

"There were so many," said Rob. "It's *got* to be the explanation. Look at the rapid mutation of the Genies. They are constantly developing new traits."

"I'm afraid it *is* true," said Eamon, coming over from his seat. "When we were waiting for you to board the 'copters, I noticed a couple of the lions had the torn remnants of cat collars around their necks. You know, the kind with their name and address on?"

"Oh my God," said Chloe, looking up from treating Calum's wounds. "This just gets worse. What other animals might be affected?"

"Well, the animals that might pose the greatest risk because of their large numbers would be domesticated ones - and wild animals, birds, rodents and insects of course," said Eamon. "So, cows, sheep, pigs, chickens are all potentially mutating."

"And what is their genetic makeup?" asked David. "What might they turn into?"

"Well, there are already reports of aurochs, the huge ancestors of domestic cattle, in France. The ancestor of the domestic pig is the wild boar. No reports of those yet. Wolves are the ancestors of domestic dogs and lions are those of cats of, course. And the ancestors of birds are - the dinosaurs."

"What?" gasped Chloe. "That's not possible surely?" she added. "The return of dinosaurs? Bu,t they're millions of years extinct."

"I'm afraid anything is possible in this new era of genetic modification. The DNA is still there buried in bird DNA. All of today's birds are distant relatives of Tyrannosaurus rex. T. rex was a theropod, a large family of dinosaurs that stood on two legs and included the largest land-dwelling carnivores that ever lived. As we have seen, mutation triggered by transgene DNA in GM food is happening fast. Much faster than when, for example, birds first started to evolve from dinosaurs. You only need to look at how quickly the Jinn have emerged and continue to mutate in certain humans with the right genetic make-up."

The friends were shocked at the full impact of the threat that they might be facing.

"So, we not only have to contend with murderous Genies, shadowy elites trying to control the world and loony religious cults, we now might be going back to the dinosaur age?" said Rob.

Calum and he shared a look of utter horror.

"I think I need to contact Renée and the rest of the Alliance," said Calum faintly, sitting up and grabbing his phone, headed to the cockpit.

An hour later, they could see the twinkling lights of St Andrews, way below them on the east coast of Scotland.

"Is this where we will be living now?" asked Joanna.

She was feeling unsettled, after two years of relative stability in Gallanvaig, which she had loved. Then, the enforced move to Inverness and captivity. Now apparently, they would be living underground in some dank bunker. She wasn't too impressed. Her friend Shelley put an arm around her.

"We'll be okay," she said. "We always are, aren't we?"

"Well, not exactly," replied Joanna with a grimace. "We've lost Jessie - that wasn't great. Nobody knows where she went. I *miss* her."

"I know you do, sweetheart," said Chloe. "We'll find her soon, I'm sure we will."

Joanna wrinkled her nose.

"But, we didn't manage to save Miss McKenzie, did we?" she replied.

Her mouth set, she went off with Shelley to sit with Rachel, Duggie, James and Shaun.

Things were hard for the youngsters, thought Chloe. They shouldn't have to face all this death and loss. Not to mention the many evils in the world these days.

The 'copters started to reduce height, circling around an area away from the lights of St Andrews, where nothing could be seen below except blackness.

The youngsters sitting over by the window suddenly shrieked and shouted in alarm, jumping away from the window.

"What on earth is wrong with you all?" yelled Rob, startled by the commotion.

Shaking Joanna pointed out of the window. "T-t-there," she stammered. "We saw it - a. monster!"

"What?" cried Chloe, rushing over to the window. "Where?"

People crowded over to the window searching the darkness, their eyes straining to see anything in the blackness.

"There!" shouted James, pointing.

There, just visible in the lights from the 'copter, flying on strong wings, was a huge flying animal. And as it flew along, it turned its head to look at the bright 'copter with beady eyes and opened its beak.

Inside its mouth was revealed a row of sharp, pointed teeth.

The kids all screamed.

Calum rushed out of the cockpit, followed by one of the crew.

"What's going on out here? We heard screams."

"Well, we don't know what we just saw flying outside," said Rob. "But, it looked awfully like a flying dinosaur. With teeth."

"A Pterodactyl," gasped James. "A mutated bird."

"Well, no actually," said Tristan. "Pterodactyls, or Pterodactylus to be correct, were Pterosaurs and were actually flying reptiles, rather than dinosaurs. But dinosaurs and pterosaurs had a common ancestor, the Archosaur. So, Pterosaur descendants include crocodiles, lizards and snakes. There would be plenty of scope for the reincarnation of pterosaurs in the DNA pool around here. And by implication, we might see dinosaurs and other relatives of the Archosaurs. Very exciting for a geneticist!"

"Speak for yourself," said Rob. "I'm not looking forward to meeting any of these mutant dinosaurs, thank you very much."

"Is it safe to go out there?" asked Rachel. "What do these Pterosaur guys eat?"

"We think they ate fish and small birds and animals," said Eamon. "It would depend on what was nearby."

Seeing the youngsters' faces, Eamon quickly added, "I don't think they would be interested in humans. We are too big for them to attack. They would go for prey smaller than themselves."

"Really?" said James. "You know that for definite? After all, these are mutant animals. From what I've read, we don't even know for sure what the characteristics of the dinosaurs were, let alone what mutated animals with dinosaur, or reptile DNA in them might display. And if the mutations include some of the larger, meat-eating dinosaurs, what happens then?"

Eamon looked suitably embarrassed. A hush settled on the group as the 'copters landed one after one.

"I can't see anything out there," said Calum. "Do you have any idea what we are looking for?" he asked Millie.

"The underground base is very extensive, but it's reached from an unobtrusive-looking farmhouse. The pilots have the grid references and they will have put us down in a field as near as possible. But, we will still need to walk a little way. I suggest we take torches."

"Well, be careful," said Calum. "Stick together. We don't know what's out there and I don't want any nasty surprises. Please everyone, take a gun and some ammunition from the box here - not you Joanna," he added, as she reached into the box. "And make sure you have a clean shot before you use it. We don't want any injuries. And take a bag of the supplies that our French friends here have provided."

Calum went and thanked the French crews and they prepared to leave.

People streamed from the 'copters, torches flashing, guns loaded. Calum could feel his nerves jangling.

What would they find in the bunkers?

Were they even still accessible? Would they have been bombed two years ago?

They trudged once more into the unknown.

23. Sanctuary?

As the 'copters took off again on their return trip to France, the group trudged through the field in a rough straggling line of twos and threes, trying to ensure no one was lost in the dark.

Millie was at the front with Calum and the others.

"We should be close now," she said, flashing her torch around the landscape ahead. "We should soon see the farm buildings that are the access route into the bunker."

"Let's hope we find it before the dinos find us," muttered Rob.

Then, there was an unearthly growl.

The kids yelped in shock and Buster and Shep and a few of the other dogs began to bark furiously.

"Okay Buster, calm down," whispered Calum, patting the dog. The dogs would have no chance if mutant dinosaurs were around. He clipped the leash onto Buster's collar and motioned for the others to do the same.

They hurried forward past a wooded area, following Millie's lead.

"There," she said. "That's the farmhouse." She pointed towards a normal-looking building ahead.

Then, all hell broke loose.

A large pack of snarling wolves broke cover from the woods and raced towards them. Calum pointed his gun at them and fired above their heads. They immediately changed direction and backed off to a safe distance, circling around, waiting their chance.

"Quickly everyone, head for that building, Millie make sure we can get in."

Millie dashed to the door. It was locked. She raised her own gun and aimed at the lock, firing off a couple of quick shots. The wolves snarled again but kept their distance.

Millie gave the door a good shove and it gave way.

Everyone rushed inside, immensely relieved to be out of danger for the moment.

That's when the eyes appeared in the darkened room they had just entered.

And the wolves outside moved ever nearer and set up a howling cacophony.

Calum shone his torch towards the eyes in the room. And illuminated a shocking sight.

There was a huge pterosaur standing quite still, staring at them. As it saw the light, it started to panic and darted forward, its toothed beak snapping at them.

There were some squeals of fear and the dogs set off with loud barking, straining at their leashes to get at the creature.

"Buster!" yelled Joanne, horrified that their dog might get attacked.

"Clear, everyone, aid Millie, pointing her gun at the creature. She aimed a quick shot at the head. Its body jerked back, and blood sprayed around, as it fell, lifeless, to the floor.

"Ugh," said Rachel. "That is gross."

"Sorry, buddy," Millie said. "I had no choice."

"Well done, Millie," said Calum. "I hate the idea of killing too, but we can't take a chance on anyone getting injured. It's them or us. How the hell did it get in here through a locked door?"

On a search through the farmhouse to ensure there were going to be no further nasty shocks, they found the answer.

"Ah, "said Millie, as they entered an upstairs room. "There's how it got in. Somebody left a window open in here."

She went over and closed it, anxious that no other creature invaded their refuge.

"Okay, now we can explore the bunker," she added. "I heard it's very extensive, sleeps around three hundred people."

"There should be plenty of room for us for a while then," said Calum. "There are just over a hundred of us so there should be plenty of room for any other refugees that come along."

Going back down to the ground floor, Millie located the entrance to the lower complex which formed the actual bunker, within which would have been housed the Scottish Government, military and support personnel.

"These doors are blast-proof and would protect personnel from nuclear attack," said Millie, releasing the latch and pushing open the heavy doors. "There are two huge floors below ground, which would house the government and all other essential staff, so that they could continue to govern the country in the event of nuclear war."

She led the way down a long, sloping passageway.

"How is it so *warm* in here?" asked Rachel. "It was freezing outside."

"The whole site is heated by stored solar and wind power. In case of war, alternative sources of power would have had to be used, as the military had to assume that power stations would have been taken out of action by missiles. And the air is kept clean by external air intakes with filters for poisonous gases and an extractor system to expel waste gases."

"How is it all still working?" asked Rob. "I mean the Cold War was over years ago."

"The military intelligence people like to cover all bases. With solar and wind power feeding the complex, the whole thing is self-sustaining. There will be extensive dried and canned food and other supplies in the store cupboards and freezers. Anyway, the world situation was still fragile, even before the GM catastrophe. There were issues with North Korea, Iraq, Afghanistan and Syria, among others. We knew they were keeping these bunkers maintained and supplied. They couldn't let their guard down."

"Well, I for one am very glad about that," said Calum. "Out of it we've got a well-equipped base with plentiful accommodation and all the utilities. Shall we go see what our rooms are like?"

He grinned at Millie and she smiled back.

"Come on, slowcoaches," said the youngsters, charging ahead, keen to see where they would be living.

"Easy now," cautioned Calum. "We don't know yet if it's safe down here. Remember our pterosaur friend upstairs. Let's check it out slowly."

But the youngsters didn't slow down much. Calum tightened his grip on the gun.

You could never be too sure.

Walking down the sloping tunnel lined with concrete, Calum marvelled at the forward planning that drove the bunker to be built.

"These walls are really thick," he said, his voice echoing around the tunnel.

"I know," said Millie. "They were designed to withstand missile blasts. They are about two feet thick. We should be very safe here for a while. We need to barricade that door at the entrance to the farmhouse though. I pretty much wrecked the lock."

"Okay that's the first thing on our list once we've checked the whole place out and made sure there are no more unexpected visitors here. Anyone any good at locks?" he asked.

"I can do it," offered Marty. "Let's see what's in the store rooms."

As they reached the end of the tunnel, it opened out into a large hallway, from which led doors on either side.

Millie reached the first door and drawing her gun, opened it cautiously. She shone her torch around. There was a light switch just inside the door and she flicked it down.

Light bathed the room in a gentle glow from several wall-lights.

"Let there be light," she said.

"This place is amazing," said Rob. "All up and running and ready to shelter its new residents."

"That was rather the idea," said Millie. "There may not have been much warning of an imminent nuclear attack and these bunkers had to be ready at all times."

"Well, I'm impressed," said Chloe. "It's going to be a comfortable home, though I would have preferred it to be above ground."

"We can't afford to be visible from the air," said Calum. "We don't know if the government are patrolling the airspace looking for dissidents. My guess is that they are. How else did they find all the remote communities to round them up and into the cities?"

"I think this is a guard room," said Millie, looking around the room. "These locked cupboards will hold weapons ready to defend the bunker should it be invaded."

She tried the door.

"Locked, I thought it would be. But, it's good to know we have a spare supply of arms if we need it."

Checking further down the corridor, they found stores of tinned, bottled and dried food and drinks.

"We won't go hungry anyway," said Rob. "What do we have anyway? Hope it's not all canned meat and fish."

Picking up a few packets he said, "No, we're okay. Pasta, rice, tinned vegetables and fruit. And here's nuts and lentils. I think we're going to be okay." He grinned at Calum.

"Well, as long as your stomach is looked after, *you'll* be okay," said Calum. "You're useless when you're hungry." He smiled back at his friend.

Millie called from down the corridor.

"Wow look at this," she said.

Chloe caught up with her and peered around the door.

"I think we found the communications hub," she said.

"That's fantastic," said Calum. "Wonder how much of this stuff will work?"

"I'm sure it *all* will," said Millie. "It all had to be permanently ready, as I said. This is the emergency communications room. I heard they had all this gear but never saw it before."

"So, what if the telephone lines aren't working?" asked David. "Or the on-line communications? You know, in the event of any emergency – well like this one."

"The system is designed to be resilient and adaptable," said Millie. "So, there are conventional landline telephones, smartphone systems, wireless radio wave systems, as well as internet communications obviously. There are internal public address systems and

117

ones that communicate to a wide area outside to disseminate emergency information and instructions. Social media messaging, either via the mobile phone network or internet, is also an essential part of the infrastructure. There are also television and radio broadcasting systems."

"Why did they need all this *stuff*," said Joanna looking around, her eyes wide.

"The idea is that under emergency conditions, say a fire, earthquake or nuclear attack, one or more of the communications infrastructures may be damaged or inoperable. So, there are always several alternative means of communication. The sustainable supply of solar power also underpins all of that. No reliance on coal or nuclear-powered energy supplies that might have been compromised."

"Well, I think we'll be testing all of this out later," said Calum. "We need to make sure we don't leave a digital trail though. We don't want to lead them straight to us."

"I'm not an expert in how all this works though," warned Millie. "I did my general military training, but my actual experience was in catering. Although, it is supposed to be simple to use in an emergency. No point in sophisticated equipment that nobody around can use."

"I should be able to help with that," said David. "I used to maintain a variety of communications systems at the power plant. It can't be that hard."

They wandered on down the base and Chloe opened an arched door, finding herself in a small chapel with an arched roof and an altar.

"Look," she said. "How about that? They built in services for spiritual as well as physical needs."

"Don't think I'll be needing *that* service," said Rob, scowling.

"Oh, Rob, let up a bit. These things mean a lot to some people and you wouldn't deny them some small comfort in these dark days, would you?" she asked.

"Huh," he muttered, moving on.

Smiling, Calum followed him down a staircase to a lower floor, where they found many bedrooms and shower rooms.

Opening one door off the lower corridor the kids peered in and exclaimed.

"Wow, cool!" remarked James.

"Yes!" said Shaun.

"Cool," said Rachel.

Wanting to see what the fuss was about, Chloe went in. The large room was stacked with books, games, laptops and games consoles, DVDs and music systems. There were large screen televisions and long sofas.

"My goodness," said Chloe. "I know where you lot will be spending most of your time."

"The rec. room," said Millie, smiling. "The military and government types like to play hard as well as work hard. I'm guessing we'll find a cache of beer, wine and spirits somewhere too. The officers like their home comforts."

"Looking forward to finding that already," said Rob.

They set off to allocate rooms for the night and Marty went off to find something to secure the upstairs door.

This felt like a very safe place already.

In a palace just outside St Petersburg, Marta Petrov walked along the long echoing corridor, its walls filled with works of art and gilt carvings.

Her personal assistant met her further down.

"They have all arrived now, Madame," she said, turning to lead the way. "I have put them in the drawing room. Do you wish the coffee to be served straight away?"

"Yes. And lunch at one o'clock please," said Marta, bustling through a large ornate door, inset with gold, that her personal assistant held open.

She entered a large room, with a polished, inlaid wood floor, murals of animals and scenes on the ceiling and gilt carvings all around the walls. The walls were covered in blue Chinese silk.

"Good morning," she said to the gathering sitting around a large, gold-edged, highly-polished table. She pulled out one of the blue and gold ornate chairs and joined them.

"Has Dr Stromberg arrived?" she asked.

"He arrived from Berlin earlier. I asked him to wait next door in the ante room till we were ready for him," said Michael Goldman.

"Yes, well he has a lot to answer for," muttered Edward Vanderbilt. "This bloody chaos is all *his* fault."

"Shall we see what he has to say for himself then?" said Marta.

She returned with the harassed-looking scientist in crumpled tweed jacket and trousers over a tired-looking shirt.

"So, what the hell happened?" started Sir Michael, even before Marta had pointed Karl Stromberg to an empty chair.

"The current crop of genetic anomalies cannot definitely be directly attributed to the AC10 Project," he stammered. "We would have to carry out long term research to determine the exact cause."

"Rubbish," said Sir Michael. "You know full well that there *has* to be a link. Why did Novagentech's supposedly thorough research programme not identify these side effects three years ago?"

"We were operating within the terms of the project outline, which was to target overpopulation," he replied. "The terms were very specific. If you also wanted all potential side effects identified, some of which may take years to materialise, you should have widened the terms of reference, the timescale *and* the budget."

"Don't give us that," said Marta. "You should have realised what the longer-term effects might be. You are the Chief Executive; you have a whole team of scientists working for you. Yet, you let loose a genetic time bomb that might lead to widespread devastation and the possible extinction of humanity."

"I think you are being premature with your bleak picture of the future," said Stromberg. "We don't know the extent of any further genetic mutation, or what effect it will have on the existing life on earth."

"You don't know? You *must* know. You are the scientist," interrupted Gaj Kapur. "Already your ineptitude has led to the death of my father and several other of us. You need to get a grip and tell us how we can put an end to all of this. And fast."

"But, the research just hasn't been done; it could take years."

"Well get it done - and you have a week to do it," said Vanderbilt angrily. "And no excuses. We don't have time for long-winded experiments. Just produce a plan for getting things back to normal."

The scientist was led from the room, still protesting.

"Bloody incompetent," burst out Vanderbilt. "Novagentech was supposed to come up with a coherent strategy to address overpopulation. Instead we have this DNA shambles. Do you know that the internet is awash with rumours that the so-called 'Genies' are reverse-evolved Jinn who appear in Arabian mythology? Ridiculous."

"But, reverse-evolution has obviously been an outcome of the AC10 project," said Corinne Moreau. Her hands and legs were still heavily-bandaged after the boiling water incident that had killed her father, Phillipe. "The Genies exist. Or Jinn, if you like. So, the assumption must be that another outcome is the appearance of reverse-evolved animals. In the Alps, there have been giant Aurochs, or ancient cattle. There have been packs of wolves observed everywhere. And now, we have had reports of flying prehistoric reptiles, as well as small *dinosaurs*, for goodness sake."

"That bloody research team at Novagentech is just incompetent," snarled Ricardo Fabbiana. "Are you sure we can trust them to come up with a plan to fix this?"

"Well, if they don't, they are finished in the research business," said Vanderbilt. "Their funding stream will dry up. And we will have no option but to target these monstrous beasts with the only thing they will understand. Missiles. The extinction of the dinosaurs will be once more."

They all sniggered, but it was short-lived. This was serious. This was a real cock-up. They could not afford to make any more mistakes or make anything worse than it already was.

"I want our genetic team at Edinburgh to be brought in," said Goldman. "We don't have much time and I want a second opinion."

"Agreed," said Marta. "We can't afford to rely solely on the Novagentech team, who have already proved their incompetence. Get them in."

Sir Michael went off to contact the UK research team, who had been successful in many genetic modification and cloning projects.

They would be able sort all this mess out.

He was sure of it.

25. The Revelation Army

Bishop Sebastien donned his robes in preparation for that day's service. He was quite sure about his belief in the Apocalypse, which had already started. It would soon be complete, as foretold in Saint John's Book of Revelation.

There wasn't much time left. He must hurry in evangelising people. To save themselves from Armageddon, they must repent of their sins without delay.

With his servers, he made his way through into the Basilica of St Jean. This was where the movement had started. It was where it would end.

The congregation stirred and stood as they saw him approach. Music flowed through the church from the ancient organ and the voices of the congregation joined in ecstatically, filling the space with a harmonious song of worship.

"Au nom du Père et du Fils et du Saint-Esprit," he began, making the sign of the Cross with the congregation, saying the opening prayers of the Mass with the congregation responding.

Then, he motioned for them to be seated.

"My dear brothers and sisters in Saint Jean. Today, I need to tell you that our time here is short. God has sent plagues, terrors and natural disasters to test our brethren. But, we can overcome these and then we will live with him forever in Paradise."

The congregation sighed in anticipation. By now, those who were of the traditional church had left St Jean for one that more closely followed a path to God that they understood. Those who remained were fully committed to meeting the Apocalypse full-on.

"So, last week I talked about what St Jean said about the plagues that were sent to Earth to punish the wicked. Now, I need to tell you about the false gods and those who only want to deceive you onto the wrong path. I want to highlight the lies that you are being told about the world and the way things must be. You will all be familiar with the laws of the new rulers of this world. Those who say we must all live in the cities, we must continue to use polluting, poisonous energy. They say that to be efficient and control terrorism, we must subscribe to their financial and regulatory systems and have identification microchips embedded in our hands. They tell us that this is so that we can be paid for our work, operate across borders and buy the goods we choose to buy with our own money. I tell you this is all a *lie*. A *smokescreen*. Saint Jean says that the Beast, the Deceiver, will cause all, both small and great, rich and poor, free and slave to be marked on the right hand or the forehead, so that no one can buy or sell unless they have the mark. And the mark is the number of the beast. And the number of the beast is a human number and its number is six, six, six. My dear brothers and sisters, I must tell you that the microchips embedded in all of you have been analysed by technical experts. And they confirm that *every single one of these barcodes* contains the numbers six, six, six. Yes, *you* have been marked out by the Beast as one of his followers."

There were gasps in the congregation, as the full import of the Bishop's words were realised.

They weren't following Christ, or Saint Jean at all, but the evil one himself.

The gasps of shock turned to a rising anger. Who did the new rulers think they were to lie and deceive the people in this way? In such a fundamentally evil way, by forcing the awful numbers into their bodies. Without these, they couldn't live their lives, couldn't buy food and goods, get paid, cross borders; everything that a free

125

human being expected to do. But they weren't free at all were they?

They were servants of the corrupt system and of the evil one himself.

"I can see that some of you are already feeling angry at the way you have been deceived. And you quite rightly are asking, what can I do about this? I tell you that you must rid yourselves of this evil mark which has been injected into your bodies. You must take a sharp knife, sterilised by boiling water and cut it out of your hand. The hand that should be serving God - but instead is serving someone else entirely."

He took his hand from inside his bishop's robes and the congregation gasped as they saw his bandages.

"Yes, my brothers and sisters. I have already rid myself of control by the system and the mark of the evil one. Now, you must go and do the same. Then, I will give you further instruction tomorrow."

He blessed the people, then turned and left the altar.

26. Fighting for Control

Sam Paige combed his well-cut, shining hair and smoothed down his tie. A shot of expensive aftershave exuded from his skin as he left his office to give a live broadcast outside number Ten Downing Street.

This wasn't going to be an easy speech and he didn't want to be subjected to too many awkward questions. But, he must allow the press to ask one or two. He had to be *seen* to be listening to the concerns of the people. His Press Secretary, Phillip Barratt, met him in the hallway.

"Morning, Phil. You have seen a copy of my speech, yes? See any problems or tripwires?"

"No, it all seems fine. But, don't get drawn into any arguments or discussion on the microchips. Just stick to the party line; the chips are to control the borders and stop terrorists from entering our country illegally, thereby protecting the public. Full stop."

"Okay, but rescue me at the end, when I have shown willing to be questioned."

"Don't worry, Sam, I have your back. I've done this a few times before, you know."

He opened the door for Sam and a fusillade of flashbulbs erupted from the media gathered outside. Sam reached the podium which had been set up for him and Phil took his position behind him.

"Good morning, everyone. Today I am making a statement about the cult that has started up in France, known as the Revelation Army and their illegal instruction to the populace to cut out the microchips from their hands. I want to make it clear that not only would this be illegal, it will render any individual foolish enough to follow this instruction an illegal alien. They will be unable to be paid a wage or buy their weekly produce. They cannot cross any borders. The next time their credentials are checked, which as you know is a regular security procedure in the streets and establishments of this country, they will be arrested for failing to produce their identification. The penalties for this crime are severe and they could find themselves in jail for a very long time. Do *not* follow this foolish advice. There is nothing wrong with the implants, as has been claimed, they are keeping you safe from terrorists and protecting our borders. Now, I have time for a couple of questions."

"Prime Minister, can you comment on the reports coming from France that the microchips contain the number of the beast and mark us out as followers of the evil one?"

"Mr Cook, I am surprised at you, an experienced member of the BBC even asking me this question. This is *fake news*. It is a just a load of *rubbish*. What century are people who believe this living in? It's a complete lie. Next?"

"Mr Prime Minister will the government be taking action against the Revelation Army for spreading these stories?"

"We will be charging their leaders with incitement to commit a crime, that of refusing to provide valid identification. As we speak, they are finding themselves in very deep trouble. I repeat; this story is fake news from a crazed cult, without any basis in fact at all."

"Thank you, ladies and gentlemen, that is all the Prime Minister has time for today," said Barratt, bustling Paige back inside Number Ten.

"Well, I think that went quite well," said Paige after the door was shut. "I think I got across the message that people will be in serious trouble for defying the law on this matter."

"You did," said Barratt. "The only trouble is that there has already been a spate of casualties in local hospitals of people who have already excised their chips and caused severe bleeding or infections."

"Well sort it out then," said Paige. "We have laws for this. They have committed a crime, send the police to arrest them."

"Very well. I will get onto the Home Office right away."

Paige bustled off self-importantly. Another crisis resolved. He was quite good at this running a country business, he thought as he reached his office and asked his PA to bring his morning coffee. He could handle any problem that the world might throw at him. Terrorism, cults, war, starvation, riots. Pah!

Who would have thought it, when only two years ago he was a simple builder? He was obviously capable of much greater things, even then. He had been selling himself short, he thought puffing out his chest and taking a shot of whisky from his desk decanter.

Oh yes. He had been very much under-estimated. He would demand higher rewards for his position as head of the country.

This was going to be his year.

In an office in the basement, Barratt picked up the phone. This was a secure, encrypted landline that could not be tapped.

"Goldman residence," said the voice at the other end.

"Is Sir Michael around? It's Barratt."

"Please hold, I'll check."

There were a few minutes silence and Barratt tapped his fingers on the desk impatiently.

"Goldman. What do you have to report, Barratt?"

"Well, Paige handled the media fairly well and I cut him off before he could get into one of his confrontations with the press. But, he is becoming increasingly arrogant and opinionated. He is starting to make his own demands and set conditions. He has demanded a huge pay rise. I'm not sure we can afford to risk it for much longer."

"Maybe it's time to bring in our own PM. I'll get onto to Justin. Things are too critical right now to have any other outsiders involved. You know what to do."

The line went dead. Barratt dialled again.

"Morgan."

"It's time to carry out Directive SP101. You are aware of the details. We require full neutralisation."

Barratt ended the call without any further conversation.

Morgan knew what he had to do.

The hospital casualty waiting room was overcrowded and the patients there were in a state of high anxiety.

"Nurse, nurse can you help me? My hand is bleeding! It won't stop," cried one woman hysterically to a passing nurse.

"Please, take a seat, we'll get you into triage as soon as we can. As you can see we're rather busy tonight. But, the reception desk has clean bandages that you can use to put pressure on the wound to stop the bleeding."

She hurried away to deal with the long queue of people with injured hands. Honestly, these people hack into themselves, then they expect us to wave a magic wand and fix it, she thought. Well, they would just have to wait their turn. She had already done a double shift due to the crisis and was almost asleep on her feet.

The evening news was full of reports of injured people who had removed their microchips, because of apparently fake news from the Revelation Army who had told them that the chips were the work of the evil one.

"For goodness sake," snarled Rob. "Have we gone back to the dark ages of superstition and blind following of whatever church officials say?"

"Apparently," said Chloe. "But the good news is that it's only a minority so far that believes in this Revelation stuff. Although, it *has* spread around the world from its initial roots in France."

They were sitting with the others in the recreation room of the underground base. Dinner had been delicious; the dried and canned goods at the base were found to be surprisingly good.

"I really enjoyed dinner," said Chloe to Millie, who had just sat down from working in the kitchen. "It seems like ages since we ate properly, having to avoid the contaminated food in Inverness."

"My pleasure, it wasn't too onerous, with all the food already more or less prepared. Just a matter of combining things into something edible."

"Well, it was great," said Calum. "Thank you. Wait, did you hear that?"

"No, what?" said Rob.

"Listen."

Calum muted the television. Then, they all heard it. A buzzing noise coming from somewhere above. Outside maybe.

"Quick, let's get to the observation room," said Calum, rushing out towards the upwards sloping corridor leading to the upper floors. Half-way along was a room with CCTV output from cameras covering the outside of the building.

Reaching the room, they hurried in and Calum switched on the CCTV. They immediately had a view from the five cameras outside that covered every aspect and approach to the building.

Calum spotted a movement in the sky to the right of the building, about half a mile away.

"Is that what I think it is? Looks like a drone."

"Yes, I think it is, said David. "Everybody needs to stay out of sight. It might be the authorities looking for their escaped prisoners."

"Is anyone on the upper level?" asked Calum.

A sudden realisation struck.

"James and Shaun went to see if they could see any more dinosaurs," Millie said faintly.

Calum, Rob and Millie ran up the corridor searching frantically for the lads.

Suddenly they heard laughing and rounding a corner saw the two of them standing by the back door, which was wide open. They were having a sneaky cigarette.

"James, Shaun, get inside. Millie, close the door quickly. And lock it," said Calum urgently pulling both back into the corridor.

"Did they see us?" asked Rob.

"We'll just have to hope not, said Calum, leading the lads back to the recreation room.

"Everybody, can I have your attention please?" he said to the others. "We have just had a near miss with a drone outside, which may have been searching for us. These two were outside having a fag, no less," he added with a curt nod at the lads. "Please, can we all remember we are in a state of danger here? Not only is there the threat from wild animals and possible prehistoric beasts, but the authorities that were holding us in Inverness will no doubt be very keen to get us back. So, unless you wish to go back there, I advise you to keep your heads down. Nobody is to go outside or open any doors to the outside whilst this state of emergency continues. Sorry, guys, I don't mean to be hard on you, but there are real dangers out there."

The lads had the grace to look suitably embarrassed.

"Sorry, Calum," said James.

"Sorry, Calum," echoed Shaun. "We didn't realise that there may be drones out there."

"Okay, let's say no more about it. But, in future, if there are to be outdoor expeditions, they will be properly planned and agreed."

He heaved a sigh of exhaustion. The responsibility for protecting them all was once more weighing heavily on his soul.

The chauffeur opened the door of the limousine, which had stopped outside a period mansion in a large, walled estate in a village nestled on the banks of the Thames. Sam Paige stepped out and the door of the mansion was opened for him. He entered without a word of thanks to his driver or the butler.

"Tell the chef I will have dinner in half an hour," he barked at the butler. "And bring me a bottle of the Dom Pérignon. I will take it in the library."

The butler hurried off. His master was known for his short temper with anyone who didn't do his bidding and pronto.

In the library, Sam poured himself a generous whisky whilst he waited for the Champagne. It had been a good day. Another media interview dealt with successfully. Tomorrow he had a meeting with the Cabinet about the ID chips matter. He was quite sure he could sort this out very effectively. No problem at all. He sipped his whisky contentedly.

Later that night, after the servants had all retired for the night, Sam was in his bedroom reading a detective novel by one of his favourite authors. He sipped at the champagne as he read. His eyes began to close as the effects of the alcohol overtook him and he put down the book and drained his glass.

Tomorrow was time enough to continue and he could read another chapter before the meeting. He sank back into the soft pillows and closed his eyes contentedly.

There was a slight noise on the stairs, which Sam didn't notice, as he was already snoring due to the copious amount of food and drink he had consumed before bed.

Then the door opened a crack. The landing outside was dark. The door opened a little more and a man, wearing a balaclava crept into the room. Standing over the slumbering prime minister, he took out a silenced pistol and fired three shots to his head.

Feeling for a pulse and finding none, he hurried from the room.

His work was done.

The breakfast news was blaring out in the bunker in Scotland. Bleary-eyed, Calum arrived in the rec room.

"Why's that on so loud?" he grumbled to Rob, David and Chloe, who were up early watching the television.

"Calum, there's been an assassination," said Chloe.

"What? Who?" asked Calum, instantly alert. "What's happened?"

"I'm afraid it's our friend, Sam Paige," said David.

"He's no friend of mine," growled Rob.

"Okay, okay, Rob, we know," said Chloe. "But, he didn't deserve to be murdered."

"Bloody hell!" exclaimed Calum. "What the hell happened? Where were his bodyguards?"

"Apparently, he ordered them all to leave him to read his book in peace. They all went to bed and he was alone in his room when the intruder got in and killed him."

"That doesn't sound right," said Calum. "There should still have been somebody guarding the entrances. There is always a duty guard protecting the PM."

"Well, not according to the news," said Rob. "Maybe it was an inside job."

"I wouldn't put anything past the people in charge of this country," said Chloe. "It wouldn't be the first time they got rid of somebody who had become an inconvenience."

As the implications of this sank in, everyone shared troubled looks.

"Wonder what old Paige did to upset them?" asked Calum.

"I don't think it takes much," said Rob. "You know how they like to control everything. Well, Sam never was one to fall in with other people's ideas. I'm sure he defied them one too many times."

People started to filter in for breakfast and help themselves to coffee and toast. As they heard the news they became solemn and the dangers of their current position were once more apparent.

These people would stop at nothing.

Sir Michael Goldman arrived in his library at his summer villa in Tintagel, where a video conference had been set up for him. He saw that most of the others were already waiting by their terminals.

"Morning, everyone. Firstly, I can report that candidates for UK Prime Minister are currently being interviewed."

There was laughter amongst the other attendees.

"I'm glad you sorted out that particular matter," said Vanderbilt. "Can't have PMs who go off pursuing their own agendas, can we now?"

"Well, I am sure the replacement, who will be hand-picked this time, will not have the same traits," said Goldman. "Last time we had to pander to the existing power base. This time, we are in charge."

"We most certainly are," said Marta Petrov. "Now, what are these rumours about Calum O'Connell? That bloody man is an absolute nuisance."

"I'm afraid he escaped from custody in Inverness, along with a hundred or more others. They were picked up in helicopters whilst the security forces were otherwise occupied, fighting attacking lions no less."

"Lions in Scotland, eh?" asked Petrov. "I didn't think there were any that far north."

"There weren't before Novagentech released their genetic time bomb into the environment," snarled Goldman. "But I have our Edinburgh people on that. And we have drones out searching for signs of the fugitives. They can't be too hard to spot in those sorts of numbers. Especially when all of the remote communities have been rounded up and detained in the cities."

"Well let's hope you're right," said Vanderbilt. "We already suspect that O'Connell is the source of the current rumours on the internet about the Genies being Jinn and about the other reverse-evolved creatures."

"Well, he's right," added Petrov. "Due to the incompetence of Novagentech."

"Yes, but we can't let the truth of that out into the public domain," insisted Vanderbilt. "We have to maintain calm and civil obedience."

"Well make sure you find them and fast," said Petrov. "We have to silence that man once and for all."

"We'll find them don't worry."

Petrov looked unconvinced and they moved on to discussing the Revelation Army.

"Have we stopped the removal of ID microchips, started by that crazy Revelation Army lot?" asked Katsu Mori, from Japan.

"The hospitals have been instructed to report any individual presenting with injuries due to excision of microchips to the authorities," replied Vanderbilt. "Offenders are arrested as soon as they have been treated. We have many in custody already. It is being sorted out. Meanwhile, the idiot who started it all, Bishop Sebastian, in France, has been arrested and charged with incitement to commit identity crime. It is under control."

"Good. And our seasonal skiing meeting in Austria, are the arrangements made?" asked Goldman.

"Your personal assistants are being sent the details," said Max Kaufman, who was the late Liese's younger brother. "The resort in Austria is preparing your accommodation and they expect us all in two weeks' time. It will be a very comfortable stay in the best Alpine hotels."

They fell to discussing plans for skiing and hunting in Austria over the Christmas holiday.

Their supremacy over the world was assured.

137

They could relax.

Deep in the bunker under Dulce Base, New Mexico, Balthazar read an online document intently. He turned to his followers.

"This all begins to make sense," he said. "Apparently, we are Jinn, otherwise known as Genies. The geneticists think that we evolved back to this state by eating GM food, which mutated our DNA to re-activate the DNA segments that code for the characteristics of Jinn. We are supernatural beings. We were thought to be demons or fire spirits, who inhabited dark spaces."

He threw this arms out to indicate the walls of the underground chamber where they had gathered and uttered a chilling laugh.

"The Jinn were divided into three types; those who can fly fast in the air from one place to another," he indicated himself. "Those in the form of snakes or dogs and those that travel ceaselessly. We have indeed been condemned to travel frequently to avoid our enemies. We can lift objects into the sir. We can take many forms including human form. We can apparently even become invisible."

"Most of this sounds familiar, Master," said Nicholas. "We haven't yet mastered becoming invisible though. But what does it say about our power? Will we prevail against our enemies, who have been trying to destroy us?"

"If we can master invisibility, I don't see how we can fail," crooned Balthazar. "How can they kill what they cannot see?"

For the rest of the day, Balthazar and his elite tried to master the art of invisibility. He knew that they could teleport instantly from one place to another, seeming to disappear to observers' sight. But, what happened was they moved through the air very fast, whilst still being visible at whatever place they were in physically. He needed to utilise the same techniques that they used for teleporting, but with more focus on suppressing the physical form. Balthazar found that by intense focussing on his physical body, his attention could slide sideways. His body immediately became lighter, more opaque. He was nearly there. Excited he renewed his efforts.

At eight thirty-five that night, Balthazar suddenly completely vanished.

But, they could still hear his voice, proclaiming his greatness.

He was truly a god amongst Genies. When he reappeared, he coached his favourites in the technique.

By the end of the night, all his elite followers could do the same trick.

28. Sebastian

The Bishop and his followers were barricaded in the crypt under the Basilica. A member of the congregation who had infiltrated the local police had phoned earlier to warn him that they were on the way to arrest him and any followers who had removed their chips.

So, Vanderbilt's claim that Sebastian had already been arrested was quite premature.

And the faithful were claiming sanctuary within the Basilica and had pinned a note to the church door setting out their claim for refuge within its walls.

Would the police respect the principle of sanctuary and leave them in peace?

Since he had grave doubts that they would do any such thing, the Bishop had sent a deacon to the local village to gather sympathetic locals to witness any attack by the police on the Basilica. Whilst he was certain that they would not respect sanctuary, he thought that they may not wish to violate the Basilica in full view of local villagers.

There was a sudden commotion outside and then loud knocking at the large doors to the Basilica and shouts of "Ouvre la porte! C'est la police! Open the door! It's the police."

Cries of protest from the locals followed. The bishop smiled to himself. With a bit of luck, the police would realise they had been defeated this time and go away, to return another time when there was no disapproving audience present.

He looked across to his worried followers.

"It will be fine, you'll see. They are unlikely to want to break into the Basilica with a local audience."

"Do you think this police state we are living in will even care what people think?" asked a follower.

The Bishop shook his head.

"Have faith, my brethren, have faith. Saint Jean will protect us. Let's pray."

He led them in prayers to Saint John and all the Saints to protect them from all evil.

And after a while it became quiet outside.

Then, there was a tap on the wooden door to the crypt.

"Bishop Sebastian, it's me, Michel."

It was the deacon.

The Bishop nodded to the followers by the door to remove the barricade. Michel entered smiling.

"They have gone My Lord. I have sent the villagers home but warned them that we might need them again later."

"I don't think that we will," said the Bishop. "We are leaving. There is a passage leading from the crypt, down through the mountain to the back road from the village below. It was built and used during the persecution of the church in the seventeen hundreds."

He led them to a side passage from the crypt and at the end was an ancient wooden door, hidden behind a large, decorated stone construction with inset compartments, each containing human remains.

Within the hour, the Bishop and his congregation had travelled downwards through the rocky passageway and reached the road. They separated and left the village in various vehicles, so as not to attract attention from the authorities.

From this time forth he vowed, they would meet clandestinely, as the Christians had had to do in the times of persecution. Saint Jean would continue to protect them.

They must continue to spread the word of Saint Jean so that the people could prepare for the coming storm.

It was written.

Balthazar was prepared for an attack on his enemies. His new weapon would be most helpful. He laughed aloud as he and his followers prepared to become invisible before teleporting to Switzerland. He had a pressing engagement with an enemy there.

A hubbub arose as at the same moment, all twenty of them became invisible. They started to exclaim in victory. Balthazar cautioned them.

"We must remain quiet now," he said. "And so, to Zurich."

Invisibly, they moved at lightning speed through the air to their destination.

Then, Balthazar could see the huge castle at the edge of the lake which was their target.

"There," he said. "The castle. We will emerge within the walls. No locks can keep us out."

With a swirl of air that just felt like a breeze, the party zoomed into the castle's central hall. The walls were hung with shields and hunting knives, as well as the heads of various animals. They flew through the door into the corridor that led to the rest of the castle. There would be no hiding place.

On the way they passed servants busy with cooking or preparing rooms. Nobody saw them. Nobody even sensed them.

Balthazar was ecstatic. The power to move amongst his enemies with impunity was fantastic.

Then, entering a large lounge stuffed with leather sofas, bookshelves and paintings, Balthazar saw the face of the man who had been haunting them, trying to eliminate him and his people.

Vanderbilt. One of the enemies who had been trying to kill him and his followers. Anger seethed through Balthazar.

If he sensed the intruder he did not show it, his attention focussed on reading some paperwork, sipping from a glass of wine on the table before him.

Balthazar instantly moved behind the man, his arms thrown around the man's neck.

Vanderbilt shouted in surprise, knocking over his wine in a red stream over the papers.

Then, Vanderbilt's eyes became larger with huge black pupils. He appeared to be growing. His face and head bulged, his limbs elongated. His mouth turned into a long slit with reptilian teeth. His hands became claws that reached up to grab the hands around his neck with a vice-like grip.

Still invisible, Balthazar shrieked in shock. What was this abomination? The man was changing form. How was he doing that? He tried to free himself from the grip of the monster before him.

"Nicholas," he cried. "Help me."

Distracted by the struggle before them, Nicholas and the others lost concentration and snapped into full visibility and rushed at the being, who didn't even look human anymore.

The thing dropped Balthazar and let out a huge roar, swiping at them all with its claws, snapping its jaws at them.

"Retreat!" yelled Balthazar.

In the blink of an eye, they disappeared, and the monster was left roaring in anger. Footsteps sounded along the corridor. By the time the door was flung open and three of his bodyguards rushed in, Vanderbilt was once more in his usual form. He glared at them angrily.

"How did these intruders get into my castle?" he asked. "You are supposed to be here to protect me. What the hell happened?"

"But, we didn't see anyone go past us," began one. "Nobody could have got through the castle doors. They are locked. We would have stopped them."

"Well they did get in and you failed to do your job," he said coldly. "Now get out of my sight."

He poured himself another glass of wine angrily. He had recognised Balthazar and another of his followers.

The Genies would not get away with this.

Back at Dulce, Balthazar rubbed his neck, which now had a painful, livid red mark around it. He wasn't used to being beaten in physical combat, especially with all his special powers. What *was* that thing anyway?

"Are you okay, Master?" asked Nicholas. "What happened? How did that man become a monster? Can we fight the enemies if they are all monsters?"

"Of course. We just need to be prepared next time," said Balthazar, sounding far more confident than he felt. "Anyway, we are 'monsters' ourselves. The Jinn are scary beings too, remember. We can beat them."

"But, *how* will we beat them? They are so strong and powerful."

"We have extraordinary powers ourselves. We can become invisible, we can teleport and be in different places at the same time. They can't kill what they can't see. We just need to focus next time, stay invisible."

"What are they? It didn't look human. I have never seen anything like that before."

"Neither have I. But, maybe it's connected with the unusual animals we have been seeing on our travels. It said online that they are reverse-evolved domestic animals becoming dinosaurs. I don't understand it. But, there are many strange things in the world now. We just need to adapt to beat them at their own game."

Nicholas looked troubled. He didn't understand any of it and wasn't sure they could beat monsters like they had seen at the castle. Not to mention the huge beasts that had been roaming around the countryside. Not sure at all.

But, he wouldn't say anything to the Master.

That would just be foolish.

Vanderbilt was in a video conference with the other Elite.

"I tell you, they got in, walked right past my guards and attacked me in my own library. They were Genies, or Jinn, or whatever the hell they are called now. I know this seems incredible, but I think they were invisible when they first entered. That's how they managed to evade detection. I have my guards checking it out on the CCTV."

"I thought the Genies had all been eliminated," remarked Marta Petrov.

"We thought they had been killed at Nellis base. But, some must have escaped. The slaughter of our Elite, the earthquakes, tsunamis and now this attack on me has all their hallmarks. Anyway, I think I recognised Balthazar, what I saw of him after he became visible just before he fled with his cronies."

"So, we need to sort out the problem once and for all then," said Corinne Moreau. "We need to be sure they will not get in the way of our purpose here."

"There is one other little problem," said Vanderbilt. "I was taken by surprise and slipped back into form. They saw me."

Everyone fell quiet for a moment.

"Oh *great*," said Marta. "Now it will be all over the Internet that we are some kind of monsters."

"I'm not so sure," said Vanderbilt. "The Genies are pretty much outcasts from society themselves. Who would believe anything they say? That's even if they have access to the media in whatever dark cave they are living in. And even if they do manage to spread rumours, we'll just spread the word that they are up to their usual deceptions. It will be fake news. Nobody will believe such an unlikely story. The propaganda was very well-delivered throughout the early twentieth century."

"Just the same, it's careless," said Marta. "We need to be on our guard. They may try to provoke us into showing ourselves again. That must never happen."

"We all agree with that sentiment, Marta. Of course, we do. No need to worry."

"Look, everyone be careful," said Corinne. "Now that we know they are still out there we must be on our guard."

Below, in the cellars of the castle, Frank Hogan fast forwarded the CCTV footage, trying to find the point at which the intruders must have entered the castle. The feed from the main hallway showed nothing. He had viewed it for an hour up to the point at which Vanderbilt was attacked in the library. There was nothing. That was the only way they could have got into the castle. And all the doors had been locked. It was as if the intruders had simply been picked up and put back down inside the castle. He shook his head. He turned to the footage from the library to see what that showed. He could see

147

Vanderbilt sitting at the large library table, reading something and drinking wine. Forwarding it, he tried to see exactly when the intruders had turned up in the library and how many there had been. How had they got out anyway? They couldn't have got past himself and the others who had been guarding the entrance.

Then, he paused the film. He had spotted a disturbance around Vanderbilt. It wasn't clear what was happening. He played it at normal speed. Vanderbilt suddenly jumped and shouted out, grabbing at his neck. What was wrong with him? A heart attack?

Then, Vanderbilt seemed to get angry and threw very long arms in the air. Had his arms always been so *long*? Were those *claws* on his hands? His head appeared to be getting larger. His mouth seemed to be full of sharp-looking teeth. Hogan gasped. As the struggle continued and moved closer to the camera, it suddenly showed the full face of Vanderbilt. His jaws opened and shut, baring long teeth, like a reptile. His eyes seemed to consist of large black pupils.

He wasn't human. He had just *shapeshifted*. Hogan continued looking at the footage, unbelieving.

Then, suddenly there were at least fifteen people struggling with the changed form of Vanderbilt. Where the hell had *they* come from? In one frame they weren't there, but in the next one, there they were. Vanderbilt's claws, which Hogan could now see were around the neck of the man standing nearest to him, suddenly fell away as the others rushed at Vanderbilt. Vanderbilt bared his teeth and swiped at them with his long limbs and sharp-looking claws.

The people surrounding him suddenly disappeared again. In the next few frames, Vanderbilt gradually returned to the form that Hogan knew him in.

What the hell was he?

A cold chill sneaked down his back and he shivered. Panicking, he switched off the machine and hurried to his quarters.

He had to pack a bag and get out of there.

And fast.

29. Flight from Zurich

Vanderbilt finished his meeting. He called for his butler and ordered coffee.

"And get one of the guards to come and give me an update," he barked.

Hogan was already at the front gateway of the castle. He ordered the doorman to open it up.

"Where are you off to?" he asked.

"Oh, just out for some fresh air," said Hogan.

"What's with the rucksack?"

"Just my waterproofs. I plan to go for a run and it looks like rain. Don't want to squelch back."

The doorman laughed and swung wide the gates onto the causeway leading up to the castle across Zurichsee lake.

Hogan went out and started to run. He was glad he had given that cover story, he now had an excuse to get away as fast as possible, without the man getting suspicious.

His car was in the underground car park at the side of the castle.

When he got to the start of the causeway, he looked back. Good. The gate was closed and again and the doorman nowhere in sight.

He changed direction for the car park. He reached his vehicle and started the engine.

It wasn't until the car was moving down the causeway towards the access road that the castle doors opened again and two guards rushed out.

Yelling, they gesticulated at him.

He accelerated the car and moved onto the access road as fast as he dared.

In five minutes, he would be on the autobahn.

By the time the guards had mobilised he would be well out of reach.

He hoped.

The airport carpark at Zurich was busy. Hogan parked his car and hurried towards the check-in desk. He would get a flight on the first plane that was leaving, wherever it was going. He needed to put some distance between himself and Zurich. He didn't feel safe here anymore.

The check-in desk was very busy. As he approached, he noticed two uniformed guards standing behind the desk monitoring all departures. They were checking each person's ID chip with a reader. It was unusual for the guards to check every person's ID, they usually only checked one in every group of travellers.

Could Vanderbilt already have put out an alert on him? How could he know what he had seen anyway?

He decided he couldn't take a chance. About twelve people were before him in the queue. He quickly turned and putting his collar up, headed out of the queue and walked towards the coffee bar, as if he had just decided he would have a drink whilst he waited.

Then, cup in hand, he checked the guards at the desk, who were busy with a long queue. He headed for the exit.

Outside he quickly returned to his car.

He would just have to go overland.

Calum had instigated a regular watch for drones via the CCTV system in the control room. He had also decided to lead a team out to reconnoitre the grounds to check if it could be cultivated to provide fresh food.

He was outside with Rob, Douglas and Annie, the farmers and Millie, who was interested from her culinary view, as well as providing an armed guard.

"This ground looks pretty healthy," said Annie. "The soil is good, if a little sandy. There is a good amount of clay in it too."

They were in the field adjacent to the farmhouse, which masked the location of the secret bunker.

"Look at that," exclaimed Douglas. "Someone has already had that idea."

He pointed at an area where green shoots and plants poked through the topsoil.

"We've got potatoes, parsnips, Brussels sprouts, cabbages and kale. And look at the next field. Those are apple and pear trees. And I think I see raspberry and strawberry bushes that should bear fruit next year."

"We're going to be pretty self-sufficient," said Calum. "That's great. This place was obviously well thought-out. The fact that it looks like just a farmhouse provides perfect cover for all this crop growing."

"We're going to need a bit of help doing the harvesting," said Annie. "But, I think we can provide you with fresh vegetables for tonight's meal, Millie."

Millie smiled broadly.

"That's fantastic. I'm not sure a continued diet based on the dried and canned fruit and vegetables in the base's store would go down too well for much longer."

"I'll send out the kids to help you gather what you need," said Calum. I'll also get the control room to monitor you closely, so they can warn you if there are any drones around. You've got one of the radios from the control room?"

Douglas nodded.

Calum returned to the bunker feeling more positive about surviving there.

He called in to see David, who was manning the control room.

"All clear, mate?" he asked.

"No sign of anything. It's all been very quiet," he replied.

"Can you do another couple of hours? I need to send the kids out to help with getting some vegetables picked."

"No problem."

"Any news on the replacement PM?"

"There's been nothing on the news since the report yesterday on Sam's death."

Calum headed to find the kids. They would be in the rec room taking full advantage of all the games, no doubt.

He was right, he could hear them from down the corridor as they played some virtual reality game with lots of shrieks and laughter.

"Hey, you lot! How about keeping out of trouble for a while? Annie and Douglas could use some help picking some veggies for your meal tonight."

"Sure, Calum," said Rachel, taking off her headset. Duggie who had been on her team, removed his as well.

"I'll help."

In the end, all five of them went off to help.

"Just make sure you stay alert out there, OK? Listen to whatever Douglas and Annie tell you and no messing around."

"Okay Calum," they all promised, the boys still embarrassed about nearly being seen by the drone yesterday.

Douglas showed the kids which vegetables to harvest and brought boxes for them to load up. He kept the radio in his pocket, making sure he didn't miss a warning call.

After a while the kids were getting hot and a bit giggly. Douglas smiled at Annie. They surely deserved a bit of fun, after all they had been through.

He was just about to say that he thought that they had probably collected enough for today, when there was a blood-curdling yowl from the far end of the field, where there was a copse of trees just the other side of a drainage ditch.

"Grab the boxes and follow me back inside," he said quietly, taking Annie's arm. As they moved towards the farmhouse door, which was closed but not locked, Annie saw movement out of the corner of her eye. Two shapes were hurtling from the trees into the field and heading right for them. She glanced at the house; they were only yards away from the door.

"Run!" she called. Everyone broke into a run for the door. James reached it first and flung it open, turning to make sure his sisters, Duggie and Shaun were behind him. They rushed in after him, panicking. Douglas and Annie were a little slower.

The shapes were gaining on them and James could now see that they were wildcats.

"Joanna, go and get help," he said, before looking around frantically for anything he could use as a weapon. She rushed off, shocked at seeing the wildcats chasing Douglas and Annie.

James and the others grabbed lengths of wood that had been chopped for the fire and brandishing them rushed back outside to help Douglas and Annie.

As the couple were almost at the door, the wildcats caught up with them in a growling, leaping mass of brown fur. James and Shaun moved to each side to head them away from Douglas and Annie, swinging the wood at them. The cats turned on them, snarling. Douglas and Annie took the opportunity to rush inside and shouted to the kids to follow them. Rachel and Duggie were also waving their arms and the wood at the wildcats, but all the kids were reluctant to injure them. They were so beautiful.

Then, Calum and Rob rushed out, rifles drawn. Calum fired a shot above the heads of the struggling group. The wildcats took fright and veered away, across the field. Rob fired again above their heads to keep them moving away.

"Are you all ok?" said Calum.

Everyone nodded, shocked but uninjured.

"Right, back inside," he said, throwing an arm around a shaking Rachel.

Later, Calum told everyone that in future whenever anyone needed to go outside, they would not only be monitoring the CCTV for drones and intruders but would also use armed guards.

Today was a close call and he didn't want to take any further chances. It was a dangerous world out there.

Hogan drove fast, but not above the limit, along the Swiss autobahn. He kept an eye on the following traffic, unsure whether Vanderbilt could have tracked him.

Was that black limousine the one that had been behind him five minutes ago? He wasn't sure, as it had now disappeared. He checked the number plate. There was only one way to find out.

He indicated to turn off at the next exit.

Checking the rear-view mirror, he felt a cold chill in his heart when he saw that the limo was also indicating. Was it just a coincidence? Or something more sinister?

At the top of the exit slip road, he turned right. The sign said 'Nancy, Parc Naturel Régional de Lorraine.'

Driving briskly, he checked his mirror. The limo was still behind. It *could* still be a coincidence. He came to a turn off for the Parc Naturel and right at the last moment, wrenched the steering wheel around and took the turning with skidding wheels and squealing brakes.

The limo followed.

Shit. This was no coincidence.

He was in real trouble and even worse, he now seemed to be in the middle of nowhere. Green fields, forests and hillsides whizzed past as he sped along, now unconcerned about keeping a low profile. They were after him. There was no mistake. There was little other traffic on the road, just the odd car or tractor.

He took many tight turns onto side roads, the limo always screeching after him. Suddenly he reached the end of a lane, which opened out into a parking area with a huge expanse of forest behind it. There was no room to pass the limo on the single-track lane, even if he could turn the car around in time.

Shit, shit, shit.

He screeched to a stop, grabbed his rucksack from the passenger seat and dived out of the door taking evasive action just in case they were armed. What was he saying? Of course, they were armed. Vanderbilt's goons always were. He knew that. He had his own gun in his pocket.

How many of them were there, how many?

He heard the limo pulling up at the car park. Then, bullets started to ping around him, ricocheting off tree trunks and fence posts.

Running in a zig-zag, avoidance pattern for the line of trees, he didn't stop his headlong flight until he was in the forest. Then, he ran from path to path, always taking the direction away from the car park and off the main track, up into the hills.

After what seemed like hours, but was probably minutes, his heart was pounding. His chest felt tight. He had to stop. Listening for any sound of pursuit, he strained his ears.

Then, he heard it. A jabbering, squawking sound. And screams.

What the hell?

Taking his gun out, he detoured back a little way behind the tree line, so that he could see the paths below. He couldn't see anything for a minute, but oh, the sounds.

Then, he saw it.

There were three men, all dressed in black. They were firing guns sporadically. But what was attacking them, making them miss the mark? It was a huge flying creature with a massive wingspan, maybe ten feet wide. It flew around the men, making snapping movements at them with a large beak. Which had teeth. Then, he saw that two more beasts were flying to join in the fray.

He stood rooted to the spot for a moment. Then, he shook himself. This was his chance to escape, whilst they were occupied with the creatures. Whatever they were.

He crossed back to another trail through the trees, this one descending by another route and looped his way around the attack below, roughly in the direction of the car park. He thought. He hoped.

After fifteen minutes, he came out of the forest and could see the car park in the distance along a riverside trail.

Thank God.

He started to run and didn't stop until he had reached his car and threw himself back inside. He gunned the engine, thank goodness they hadn't had time to immobilise it.

With shots and screams in the distance, he exited the car park and sped back along the single-track road, hoping he didn't meet anything.

He reached the main roads again and headed northwest on the motorway.

He decided he would try to reach the United Kingdom. He was an American, but after the US was evacuated, he had travelled to Zurich with his boss, Vanderbilt, together with the rest of his retinue.

He thought that the World Alliance Party would be very interested in what he had found out about the people who he now knew were behind the World Democracy Party. Since the US was evacuated, the US leader of the World Alliance, Alan Jackson, was pretty much discredited by the fact that the US was left a polluted ruin by GM crops and nuclear missiles and had to be abandoned. Hogan had no idea where Jackson was now. But, the UK Alliance leader, Calum O'Connell had impressed him whenever he had seen him on television. He seemed like a sincere, principled man. He knew his boss, Vanderbilt, hated him. So, that was a good sign.

So, he headed for Calais.

Would he be able to evade border checks to reach England? He couldn't allow his chip to be scanned if there was an alert out on him.

How far did Vanderbilt's influence stretch?

He was afraid he knew the answer to that.

31. Haven for the Persecuted

Bishop Sebastian looked around with satisfaction. The large barn in the foothills of the French Alps was warm and smelled of hay. The journey had been uneventful and the faithful had been gathering here all day, keeping in touch by phone.

The farmhouse and outbuildings were unoccupied, the farmer having decamped to winter quarters in the valley. This place would be the home of the local Revelation Army for a while.

When everyone had eaten and settled down to rest, he stood up.

"My dear brethren," he started. "We have truly travelled through troubled times, but by God's grace, we have reached this haven. Just like the Christians in former times, we are being persecuted for our faith. But, we will not give up the fight."

The congregation gave a huge, enthusiastic chorus of "Amens" and "Halleluias."

"Saint Jean said that 'If anyone worships the beast and its image and receives a mark on his forehead or on his hand, he shall also drink the wine of God's wrath, poured unmixed into the cup of his anger and he shall be tormented with fire and brimstone in the presence of the holy angels and in the presence of the Lamb. And the smoke of their torment goes up for ever and ever; and they have no rest, day of night, these worshippers of the beast and its image and whoever receives the mark of its name. So, I tell you my brothers and sisters, you have truly followed God and rejected Satan by removing the mark of the devil from your hands. As Saint Jean tells us, you will be in that number who 'have been redeemed from mankind' for you are spotless.'"

The congregation rose at this and shouted 'Halleluiah.'

"Saint Jean explains that seven angels would 'pour out on the earth the seven bowls of the wrath of God. And the angels poured out bowls causing foul and evil sores on those who bore the mark of the beast. The sea became like the blood of a dead man and every living thing in it died. The rivers and fountains became blood for the evil ones to drink. The sun could scorch them with fire. The earth was plunged into darkness and foul, demonic spirits like frogs issued from the mouth of the beast. The evil ones cursed the God of heaven for their pain and sores and did not repent. My brethren, we have seen all these signs in recent years with the rendering of the good earth to poison with GM crops and the poisoning of the rivers and oceans so that all the life within became sick and died. We have seen the people afflicted by the GM plague, with sores and pain, who died in agony. We have experienced the darkness caused by the lack of electricity in the days where no sun shone, or wind blew. We have seen the evil spirits, the Jinn that were sent as punishment that issues from the mouth of the monster that was genetic modification and pollution. All these signs were sent as punishment for the evil ones who turned their face from God and followed the evil one. That, my brethren is why we must adhere to the path of righteousness and always follow the Lamb. This is the ONLY path to redemption."

Revelation Army congregations around the world were also going into hiding, continuing their journey along a path that they believed would bring redemption and freedom from pain and plague and God's wrath.

The evil one must not win.

161

Hogan had avoided all major border crossings by skirting around on country lanes and minor roads. Now, he was facing his biggest challenge; crossing the English Channel to reach England.

He had decided to head for the small port of Wimereux. He could see from the maps that there was a small harbour, which looked to have moorings for small boats. Its biggest advantage was its proximity to England. It was unlikely that there would be border guards, as it wasn't big enough for the passenger ferries that operated from Calais and Boulogne.

But, he was tired. He must rest for a while, not to mention use some facilities. He indicated to exit at the next motorway service station. As he parked his car, all seemed quiet. It was late in the day and most commuters had already reached their destinations. The restaurant had few customers, but he didn't want to risk being seen in the open, so after visiting the facilities, he bought some snacks from the shop and went back to his car.

He would just have a short nap.

Sometime later, he awoke with a start. It was dark. What had woken him? He looked around and saw a truck that had just parked nearby and whose occupants had exited for the services, no doubt slamming the doors as they went. That was probably what had woken him. He looked at the truck. It was a beat-up old farm wagon with lots of bumper and window stickers.

"Stop polluting the Earth - end nuclear power" was one, together with 'Save the Whales,' 'No to GMO' and 'Vote World Alliance.'

He sat up suddenly interested in the occupants. It sounded like they wouldn't be big fans of the World Democracy Party. Could they help him? He decided to see who they were before deciding.

He opened one of the snacks he had bought earlier, suddenly ravenous. He couldn't remember last time he ate, probably it had been breakfast in the castle. That seemed like another lifetime now he was a fugitive from the authorities. All he had had since was a cup of coffee at Zurich airport. No wonder he was starving. He bit into the baguette hungrily, watching the door of the café.

He ate everything but was still hungry. He would just have to get more when he reached England. *If* he reached England.

The door of the café opened and out came two people, a man and a woman. They were casually dressed in crumpled clothing that looked like it could use a good wash. As did the people. He cranked open his window a little, so he could listen.

"À quelle distance de Monsieur Lambert? Je veux obtenir les fournitures agricoles et rentrer à la maison avant minuit," said the man.

Hogan quickly translated in his head as best as he could.

"How far is it to Monsieur Lambert's? I want to get the farm supplies and return home before midnight."

"Il est environ vingt kilomètres maintenant," answered the woman reaching the truck and unlocking it. "It's about twenty kilometers now."

So, they were farmers. Not guards or politicians. Or Democrats.

He opened his door as they were getting into the truck.

"Excusez-moi?" he began in his best French. "Parlez vous Anglais?" He knew that his primitive schoolboy-level grasp of French would not get him too far.

163

"Oui. How can we help you?" said the man. "You need directions?"

"I wondered if you could tell me where I could get a boat to England from the coast nearby?"

"You can catch a ferry at Calais or Boulogne," answered the woman.

"I kind of wanted to stay under the radar," answered Hogan with a shrug.

"Ah," said the man. "Someone is maybe looking for you? Is it the authorities?"

Hogan didn't answer. How much could he trust them?

"Don't worry the authorities are no friends of ours," he said, spitting on the ground. "We try to keep well away from them. When they came to the farm recently and tried to round everybody up to take them to Lille, we set the dogs on them. If they return, they better bring more people. We won't be going anywhere without a fight."

"Oh, good for you," said Hogan feeling reassured. These people wouldn't report him. And he had to take a chance on somebody. "Is there somewhere that they have small private boats I could hire? Where there are no questions asked?"

"We have a friend, Jean Dumont, who keeps a boat moored at Wimereaux," said the woman. "As you are obviously a fellow Résistance member, we can take you to him if you like?"

"That would be very kind of you," said Hogan. "I would be most grateful."

"Okay, but you had better leave your car here," said the man. "I'm sure the authorities know what vehicle you are driving. I am surprised they haven't picked you up before now."

"Oh, they tried, believe me," said Hogan. "But the local wildlife had other ideas. Huge winged creatures attacked them."

"Ah, we have seen lots of odd creatures ourselves," said the woman, "Creatures that shouldn't even exist today. Small dinosaurs even. Pah. We had to chase them off our land."

"I know. It's the GM food that has caused it. I overheard my former employer talking about it."

The man opened the back door to the truck and Hogan grabbed his rucksack and locked his car. Not that he supposed he would ever see it again. It was provided by Vanderbilt anyway. He could get other transport when he reached England.

Jumping into the car, he held out his hand to the man who was sitting in the passenger seat.

"Frank Hogan, I'm obliged to you both."

"Alexandre Perrin. And this is my wife, Marie."

She reached over to shake his hand before starting the truck and moving back onto the highway.

"What did you do to upset the powers-that-be anyway?" asked Alexandre. "Apart from refusing to go and live in Lille, we have insisted on growing our own organic crops and refuse to succumb to the government pressure to return to livestock farming. Those things are apparently crimes these days. Imbéciles."

"Well I saw a little too much for my boss's liking about what he is really like," began Frank, not really expecting them to believe his incredible story.

"Ah, a bully, eh?" said Marie. "Pathetic how bosses must prove their power by bullying their staff."

"Well, he's that and more," said Frank. "I'm sure this will sound incredible, but I had to check the CCTV at my boss's, castle after some intruders got in - and I saw him change into a reptilian monster. It had an elongated face and many sharp-looking teeth. Oh yes and big, jet-black eyes."

He shuddered at the memory.

"I know it's hard to believe but I saw it. And I have a copy of the video clip right here." He patted his rucksack.

"Oh, I don't find anything too hard to believe these days," said Alexandre. "With the way the earth has been polluted and laid waste. The waters have been poisoned and people and animals mutated and killed. It's not so hard to believe that your boss turned into a monster."

"But, he didn't mutate, or devolve as they are calling these conversions to prehistoric creatures," insisted Hogan. "I saw him change right back into human form again afterwards. He is a shape-shifter. The type that I used to scare myself with late at night, reading science fiction when I was a kid in America. I never believed the stories were actually based on truth."

"Well we are living in a whole new age now, where nightmares are coming true," said Marie. "It's not much of a stretch from prehistoric monsters to shapeshifters."

"Well, when I saw what he was on the CCTV, I did a runner. I think he has put out an alert on me. They know what car I was in. I was certainly followed by three of his goons, who were themselves attacked in Lorraine Parc Naturel, by the flying creatures I mentioned."

"What will you do when you reach Angleterre?" asked Alexandre.

"I want to blow the whistle on the evil that is behind the so-called Democracy Party and the GM corporations which caused a whole lot of death and devastation. Not to mention the destruction and evacuation of my beloved homeland. I need to ensure this new information on who is really behind it all reaches the right people."

"Bastards!" spat Alexandre.

"I thought I would try to find Calum O'Connell, who used to lead the UK World Alliance Party. He strikes me as an honest man, a man who has principles and sticks to them. Such a man is hard to find in politics."

"I think maybe we can help you there," said Marie. We have contacts in the British Résistance who will know how to contact him. We will contact them and get them to meet you when Jean drops you in England."

"That is fantastic, thank you," said Hogan, quite overwhelmed at how helpful the couple were being. "I owe you, big time. If there's ever anything I can do for you in return just say."

"Just spread the word about what those bastards really are," said Alexandre. "Make sure they get what's coming to them. That will be reward enough. Many French people don't take kindly to being told what to cultivate, or where to live, I can tell you."

"Here we are," said Marie as she pulled the truck onto the front drive of a small white-painted house, with a red tiled roof, on the outskirts of Wimereux.

"The home of our good friend Jean Dumont," said Alexandre. "Wait here, I will explain who you are, so as not to alarm him. The hour is late, we have had many hostile visitors recently."

Hogan had no choice but to wait. He was pretty sure he could trust these people, but what if they were going to betray him to someone in authority?

"Don't worry," said Marie, seeing his anxious face in the mirror. She turned around from the front seat. "Jean is a good man. He will help you, I am sure. Even if there is a personal risk to himself. He is a brave man."

"Thank you," said Hogan, not quite knowing what else to say. They had already done so much for him.

The door opened, Alexandre came out and beckoned to them. Marie got out and Hogan followed. A man stood behind Alexandre, inside the hallway.

"Jean, this is Frank Hogan. As I told you he is fleeing from the monsters in the World Democracy Party and he needs to get to England, so that he can make people there aware of who, or should I say what, is behind all of our troubles and we can beat them. He is un Americain."

"Pleased to meet you," said Frank offering his hand. "Thank you so much for helping me."

"It is the least I can do. These bastards in charge have to be brought down somehow and if you have information that will help that, I am only too pleased to play my part."

"I appreciate it," said Frank, shaking his hand.

"Okay, we should leave then, whilst it is still dark," said Jean. "Do you have luggage?"

"Only this," said Hogan lifting his rucksack.

"Good, then let's go."

Bidding farewell and thanking his new friends profusely, Hogan got into Jean's car.

"Bon chance, mon ami, good luck!" called Alexandre and Marie.

Waving, Jean and Hogan drove away.

Hogan was nervous. The evil facing humanity was immense and he was one man. What if they didn't believe him? What if Vanderbilt's goons caught up with him before he managed to tell anyone his story?

What would the passage to Britain bring?

32. To England

Jean parked his jeep at the small marina on the outskirts of Wimereux. It was very quiet at this hour; the whole place was deserted.

"Follow me," he said and led Hogan along the quay, where several medium-sized yachts and boats were moored. He stopped in front of a blue and white painted boat with black lettering on the side: 'La Jolie Fille.'

"This is mine," he said proudly. "It's not exactly luxury, but she sails very smoothly. I have had some good trips with her."

Hogan nodded approvingly. It looked like it would do the job anyway. The crossing to England wasn't far and the boat looked sturdy enough.

"Allons, mon ami."

Busying himself preparing the boat for its sail, Jean moved around confidently, untying the mooring ropes and starting the engine.

Hogan wandered down into the cabin and found it very comfortable. There was a long seating area that obviously converted into beds and a galley area, with a small two-ring cooker, sink, kettle and fridge.

"Bathroom's down there," he said, pointing to a door. "Help yourself to a beer and snacks," Jean added as he went on deck. "Could you bring me one up?"

Hogan got a couple of beers from the fridge and some bags of snacks and took one up to Jean.

"You're lucky," said Jean, opening the beer as he steered the little boat away from the quay. "It's a calm night, very clear, lots of stars. We will have a smooth crossing."

"That's good, I'm not a great sailor," remarked Hogan.

Jean erupted into good-natured laughter.

"And I don't have any seasick pills," he said grinning.

Hogan relaxed on deck, drinking his beer and chatting to Jean, as he sailed the boat into the English Channel. The boat started to rock a little from side to side as the sea currents hit. But, it wasn't so bad, thought Hogan. In fact, it was making him drowsy. It had been a long day. After a few minutes, Jean noticed he wasn't replying to his questions. Glancing inside the cabin, he saw that Hogan had gone inside and was fast asleep, his breaths exhaled in little cold clouds of air.

Let him sleep. The man had had a hard day from what his friends had told him. And what would he would have to face on the other side?

Hogan was in the castle at Zurich and he was walking along the main passage from the entrance to the rooms on the ground floor. Someone came out of a room to the left as he passed it. Startled, Hogan looked back. It was Vanderbilt. There was some reason he should be nervous around him. What was it? As he racked his brain, the man seemed to change in slow motion from a man into a reptilian monster. It reached for him with its long talons, its mouth wide and lined with horrible teeth and making an awful growling noise. He screamed.

"Wake up Hogan, wake up," cried Jean. "You're just dreaming. It's just past two in the morning and we are approaching the English coast. I daren't land at any of the ports, too many guards. But, we can take the dingy and row to that beach where I will leave you."

Hogan shook himself awake. That was some nightmare. Except it wasn't. That evil thing really existed. He grabbed his rucksack and followed Jean onto the deck. Jean had already dropped anchor and the boat rocked steadily in the slight current.

"Come," he said, opening a small gate that led to a ladder and a dingy already waiting in the sea.

They reached land in a few minutes and Jean handed him a piece of paper.

"Here is the number for the contact who will meet you. You have a mobile phone? Good. Ring her once you are ashore. I can't risk coming with you. Her name is Yvette Colbert. She is a cousin of Marie Perrin, who you met earlier. You can trust her. She is expecting you. Go through the caravan park by the beach, no one will question you. They are used to strangers coming and going at all hours. Then, turn right when you reach the main road. There is a pub along there, the Black Cat Inn, which won't be open at this hour, but that's maybe for the best. The place is called Winchelsea. Ask Yvette to meet you there. And good luck, my friend."

"Thank you so much," said Hogan. "If you ever need a favour don't hesitate. Here is my number."

He handed Jean a card, who reached into his pocket and exchanged it for his own card.

"Likewise. The truth must be told. Goodbye, and bon chance, mon ami."

"Au revoir," said Hogan, shaking his hand, then climbing from the dingy into ankle-deep water and wading towards the beach.

He turned around when he reached the shore. Jean was paddling his dingy and was almost back at his boat. He didn't look around.

He had been lucky to meet such good, helpful people. Now, he had to tell the world what the things lurking in the shadows of power really were.

171

33. Yvette

Hogan walked through the caravan park, a little apprehensively. He didn't know what he would say if challenged. Why was he up and about so late? Ah, maybe an assignation. Yes, that was understood in all languages.

But, Jean had said there would be no questions in such a place.

He was almost at the gates of the park leading onto the road, when he saw a shadowy figure approaching.

It quickly resolved into a man with a large dog on a leash, which started to bark as soon as it saw him.

"*Ssh, Max*. You'll wake the whole place," admonished the man. "Sorry," he said to Hogan. "He's harmless really. He's been making a fuss to go out for the past hour, so since I was awake anyway, I finally gave in."

"No worries," said Hogan, with a forced smile. "Nice dog."

He was a large sheepdog-cross of some kind and now started to wag his tail.

"Well, goodnight, enjoy your walk," said Hogan.

"And you," said the man, but he seemed to stare at Hogan a little too long for his liking.

He hurried on to the road and turned right. The sooner he was out of there the better, before the man decided to question him further.

The road was little more than a sandy lane and he hurried along looking for the pub. After a few minutes he could see buildings up ahead, a few houses and then at last the Black Cat Inn. He went onto the car park and sat on a wall, in the shadow of the building where he couldn't be seen from the road.

He dialled the number carefully. It was a mobile number. It was answered on the third ring.

"Yvette," the answering voice said.

"Hi, Yvette, my name is Frank Hogan and I'm a friend of Marie Perrin, your cousin. I think she may have told you to expect me."

"She did," said the accented voice. "Where are you?"

Hogan explained as well as he could, with his limited knowledge of the area. Yvette seemed to recognise where he was and said she would be with him in around twenty minutes.

He settled down to wait, keeping an eye on the road.

It was just after three thirty in the morning and there was no movement or sound, just the odd shriek of a gull and the hoot of an owl in the nearby woods. He pulled his coat more tightly around him. It was a cold December night and the sea wind blew around him, freezing him to the core.

Eventually, he heard a motor in the distance and he ducked back further into the shadows. He hoped this would be Yvette. He didn't want to stay out here exposed for much longer. Not only was he tired, cold and uncomfortable, he feared that early morning traffic might start soon.

A car came into view. It was a medium-sized saloon and it seemed to be slowing down as it approached the pub. Was this Yvette? Hogan ducked further into the shadows. It might also be Vanderbilt's goons still searching for him. The car turned onto the pub car park and a hooded figure in the driving seat opened the passenger door. Hogan felt his stomach lurch in anticipation of a possible fight.

"Get in," said the accented female voice. "Quickly."

Hogan left the shadows and got into the car, hoping that this really was his contact. But, what choice did he have but to trust her?

The car drove back onto the road and accelerated away from the coast.

"Yvette, I presume?" asked Hogan.

The woman threw back her hood. Hogan examined her with interest. She was young, around thirty, with dark brunette, shoulder-length hair. And very attractive, he thought.

"Oui, I am Yvette, from the British Resistance movement. We work closely with our friends in Europe to beat this evil government, who are mere puppets in the hands of the people in the shadows."

"Frank Hogan. Pleased to meet you. I understand you will be able take me to Calum O'Connell?"

"Oui. It will take some time though. O'Connell is thought to be in Scotland, on the east coast. I must contact him again when we reach the area to check on the exact location. It will take at least ten hours. And it is possible we may have to detour if there are any road blocks reported. You may as well get some sleep."

"Thank-you. It is very good of you to take me all that way."

"No problem, it is my pleasure to oppose this evil rule in any way that I can."

"Can I ask you about this Resistance movement? Is it widespread across Europe? I never heard of it whilst I was working for Vanderbilt in Zurich."

"And who is he?" she asked sharply.

"Vanderbilt is one of the most powerful people in the world. An American, nothing much happens in the world without his and his evil cohorts' approval."

"And you *worked* for him?" she asked.

"Yes, to my shame now. I did not know what he was. You might find this hard to believe, but I recently discovered that he can change *form*. He changed from what looked like a human into a reptilian monster with huge jaws and teeth. And he did it right on camera."

"Mon Dieu! A shapeshifter. I have heard of such things, but I never saw one."

"I know. It's hard to believe. But, that is why I must meet with Calum O'Connell. He always seemed like an honest person with principles and I know he was a leader of the Alliance Party here. I hope he will be able to use this knowledge against Vanderbilt's evil. I am just one man. I can do nothing alone. But, this evil must be stopped."

"And you say there are more like Vanderbilt?"

"Well, he is part of a small, secretive group of people from all over the world who meet regularly. We never knew what their business or motives were, but it was obvious that they were a very powerful group, who had their fingers in all sorts of pies. Our role in security was to protect and serve them. Now, I'm wondering if they are all reptilian under their human disguise. I have no evidence. But, I suspect that they must be."

"Then, it is imperative that we get you to Calum O'Connell, who will know what to do about this. He is still UK leader, as far as we in the Resistance are concerned. It was only the corrupt lies of the Democrats that lost the Alliance the election. Sam Paige was just a puppet leader in their control. Now, everyone with open eyes regrets putting those corrupt creeps into power. I think I will need to request back up, though. It is vital that you reach Scotland and Calum's group safely. Too much depends on it."

Yvette pressed a button on her hands-free phone.

"Pierre? Yvette. I need some security for a trip to Scotland. Can you organise some armed personnel to meet me at the usual place near Brighton? Okay, Merci. Au revoir."

"It's sorted," she said to Hogan. "We will be safely escorted to Scotland. Also, I will be bypassing the capital, just in case you wonder why I am taking a roundabout route. There will be too much security on the orbital roads."

"Thank-you, I appreciate the trouble you are going to."

Hogan settled back in his seat, impressed with the extent and the organisation behind the Resistance. He felt he was in safe hands for the moment. Drowsy from many hours on the road since Zurich, his eyelids began to droop.

Calum was warm, enveloped in a loving embrace, the feeling of familiar arms around his neck. The heady smell of amber wafted around the room.

"Jessie? Sweetheart?"

No reply.

His eyes flickered open, slowly taking in his surroundings. The unfamiliar layout of his bedroom confused him for a moment. Where was he? Then, it all came back. He was in the bunker near St Andrews in Scotland.

But, Jessie? He looked around frantically. He could have sworn she was here. He could still smell her perfume. But, she was gone, wasn't she? Taken by the wild tsunami at Gallanvaig. As he again remembered what had happened, a heavy feeling of sadness enveloped him, replacing the previous feeling of warmth and love.

He got up and showered then went down to the dining room.

"Morning, Millie," he called out to the bustling sounds in the galley kitchen.

"Morning, Calum," she replied, cheerily.

He wished he could feel so happy again.

Just then, Rob came in.

"Morning," said Calum. "Coming to check the CCTV, make sure there were no incursions during the night?"

The group had got into a morning routine of checking the communications room equipment for any breach of security around the farmhouse that concealed the bunker beneath, before having breakfast, or venturing outside. There never was much, just a few wolves and the odd small dinosaur. Once, a couple of lions.

Calum couldn't believe that he now thought these incursions to be minor. There were much worse things around though.

They went up and ran the CCTV recording. At one thirty-three, three wolves appeared in the field. They gradually crept closer to the farmhouse and ran around the yard for a while, sniffing the doorways and as they watched, a wolf jumped up at the window, its face immediately magnified by the camera above.

"Ah!" cried Calum. "Bloody thing. That scared the life out of me."

Rob laughed. "This place had got you spooked hasn't it?"

"The wolves and lions are bad enough, but dinosaurs and the risk of military drones catching us unawares, it's all getting a bit much," said Calum, smiling ruefully at himself. "I'll be fine once I've had a good strong coffee."

"Are you okay?" asked Rob. "Anything bothering you?"

"Well, I had the same dream that I have been having most nights. It starts where I think I can feel Jessie's warmth with me in bed. Then, I can smell her perfume, strongly. Then, I wake up and of course she isn't there. It's very unsettling."

"That is odd. I have had some feelings that Hannah is close. I sometimes feel like she never went away. Once or twice, out of the corner of my eye, I sometimes see a shadow, like the shape of her. Then, when I look properly, there's nothing. What do you think is going on? Is it just grief do you think?"

"Well, grief can be a strange thing," said Calum. "When I lost my ex, Siobhan, to suicide years ago, she sometimes came into my mind unexpectedly. But, I don't think I ever thought she was physically near. Not like now."

"Well, I have no idea what is going on," said Rob. "Maybe it's just Balthazar messing with our heads. Maybe he did take them after all."

"Well, at least they would be alive then. But, I don't hold out much hope really. There's been no contact since they went missing and Jessie has always managed a call or a message before."

The phone rang suddenly, making Calum start.

"Hello? Ah, good morning, Jeff. Really? Do we know anything about him?" He whistled in surprise. "And you say Yvette is bringing him here? Good. Yes, give her this number. Fine, thanks Jeff. I'll await his arrival with interest. You too. Bye."

"Was that Jeff Colman?"

Jeff was an Alliance Party member who they had met several times in London and who kept in close contact with Calum.

"Yes, and he had something very interesting to tell me. Apparently, some security guy who was guarding someone very powerful in Zurich turned up near Winchelsea beach. He says he has something very important to tell me about the man, which has a bearing on the current situation. He is on his way up here and wants us to help him."

"Sounds intriguing," said Rob. "When will he arrive?"

"Later today, they hope. Depends on if there are any checkpoints. Apparently, the guy in Zurich is keen to get him back. Yvette Colbert is bringing him here and she has armed security with her."

"Good. She might need it if this guy knows something so significant about those in power."

Calum switched off the viewing screen and they went to get breakfast and tell the others.

Yvette pulled up at a remote service station near the Scottish border, the security escort parked next to her. Hogan was asleep, lying back in his seat, breathing deeply. She examined his face. He was quite attractive, a little older than her she thought, but nice. He had olive skin and dark hair, the lashes on his closed eyes were long and black. As if sensing her scrutiny, his eyes flickered and opened.

"Morning," said Yvette, looking away quickly. "We are stopping for a short break. We can use the facilities and get something to eat. The security guys; Mike, Dana and Ron, are in the next car."

Hogan sat up and checked the security car. He had been asleep when they had met up with them near Brighton, exhausted by his shock in Zurich and his long drive to the French coast. He saw that there were two men and a woman getting out of their car.

"Morning, Yvette," said the first one. "Time for breakfast?"

"Oui, but let's keep it short. We don't know if anyone will be chasing our friend here. Let's get back on the road in ten minutes, yes?"

"Ok, no problem."

As he stood aside to let Yvette and Hogan walk in front, Hogan saw a flash of a shoulder holster and a gun. Good, he thought. He had his own gun too and felt much safer in the company of people like himself, used to protecting themselves and their charges against all odds. Although, he supposed he was now the one who was being protected.

He detoured to the men's washrooms and one of the security guys went with him, the other two went with Yvette into the café.

As he washed his hands, the security guy, whose was apparently Mike, was in the cubicle. The door to the washrooms opened and two men came in, immediately staring at Hogan.

Drying his hands, he made to leave but the newcomers stood in his way in front of the door.

"Excuse me."

The men didn't move. Hogan reached inside his jacket quickly for his gun, at the same time calling Mike, who burst from the cubicle, his own gun already drawn.

The nearest man grabbed Hogan and the other tried to grab Mike but was rewarded with an upper cut from Mike's gun and dropped to the ground groaning. Hogan shook off his attacker and knocked the gun out of his hand.

As it clattered to the floor, the man backed away, his hands up.

"Don't shoot," he pleaded.

Mike grabbed the man on the floor and searched him, removing the belt from his trousers. He pushed the second man to the ground impatiently and bound the two men's hands together with the belt, knotting it tightly behind their backs.

"Let's get out of here," Mike said to Hogan, pushing open the door. "Who knows if they have friends around?"

They went quickly to the café and met Yvette and the others coming out.

"We have food for you," she began.

"We have to leave. Now," said Mike. "Two goons just attacked us in the toilets and they might have colleagues. They are out of action for now, but I don't know for how long."

Yvette and the others immediately made for the cars and Hogan got in beside her. She started the car and they set off with a squeal of brakes, the security car close behind.

"That was close," said Hogan. "Your guy did a great job though. I'm glad he's on my side."

"Let's hope the rest of your boss's goons don't catch up with us," muttered Yvette. "We might not be so lucky next time."

"How far do we have to go now?"

"We just crossed the Scottish border. It will take around three hours until we reach where Calum is staying. Here is some food," she said handing him some sandwiches from the dashboard shelf.

"Thanks. What about you?"

"I'll eat as we go," she said. "I don't want to waste any more time, as you are obviously being followed. If we can keep ahead of them, we can avoid further confrontation."

"How are they tracking us anyway?" asked Hogan handing her a sandwich.

"Well, your mobile phone is switched on, I guess?"

"Yes, of course," said Hogan, feeling a bit stupid. He took out his phone and switched it off. He should have swapped the phone on his journey. But, he had been a bit preoccupied with the chase. Still, he had been careless.

"And you have the ID chip, yes?"

"Yes, but that's just identification data, for crossing borders and accessing money."

"It contains a tracking device too. The Revelation Army aren't as mad as you think, removing their chips as the mark of the evil one. We Resistance members have already removed ours. So, it must be you."

She pointed him to the glove compartment and indicated a knife.

"Heat that with a match first to prevent infection, Then, I'm afraid it's going to hurt a bit. Here take a few sips of that first."

She pointed to a bottle of French brandy in the back of the car.

Hogan recoiled in shock at the way he had been tagged for tracking, like a dog. There was nothing else for it. He would have to cut it out. He followed the instructions, taking three deep gulps of the brandy. He winced in anticipation, as he aimed the knife at the chip, just visible beneath the skin of his right hand.

As the knife bit into his hand, he moaned in agony.

"As soon as it's out, use the towel there to staunch the bleeding," instructed Yvette. "Can't have you bleeding to death before you give Calum your news."

As he moved the knife around trying to get under the chip, he glared at her in disgust. Was she being deliberately flippant? When he was having to cut open his own hand?

At last the chip came free and he opened the window, hurling it out.

"Good. Now we can relax a little. As far as they are concerned the trail went cold in a field just across the Scottish border. They will have no idea where you might have gone from there. Are you okay?" she added, looking at his ashen face.

"I'll survive," he muttered, wrapping the towel tightly around his hand and taking more deep gulps of the brandy. If she was going to be so unconcerned about him, she could damn well provide him with some anaesthetic.

"Ha! You men. So brave when you are squaring up to each other, but little babies when you have to endure any real pain."

He stared at her, deciding she could be very annoying. But, oh so pretty.

With a grunt he settled down in the seat, taking sips of brandy as he tried to get comfortable. Very soon, the warm buzz of the alcohol relaxed him. He fell sound asleep, snoring loudly.

Yvette laughed.

"Sleep baby, sleep. Soon you will feel better. Then, maybe we can get to know each a little, no?"

Smiling she drove onwards, waiting for the time when she could contact Calum.

Calum was outside the bunker with David and Chloe. They were showing him the hydroponic system they had rigged up to grow fruit and vegetables in one of the large greenhouses on the farm. This would control all the inputs to feed the plants and prevent any pollution from GM reaching them. They had the water pump hooked up to the solar power system at the farmhouse.

"That looks really great," he said. "So, we can guarantee clean food for ourselves, no matter what pollution drifts in on the oceans or from the rainfall?"

"Yes, it's a completely closed system. The plants are organic, from the bunker's stores. The government and essential staff wanted only the best for themselves if the worst happened. The water is from a spring up the hill and we are distilling it to make it even purer."

"That's great, we will be self-sufficient. Thanks, you two."

His phone rang, he took the call, leaving David and Chloe to finish setting up the hydroponics system.

"Hello, Calum here. Ah, Yvette. I have been expecting you. Where are you?"

He quickly gave her directions and the postcode for her navigation system.

"Don't think you have come to the wrong place, you'll just see a farmhouse. I'll be waiting for you."

He ended the call and called to David and Chloe.

"Our visitors will be here soon. Just going to get the welcome party sorted."

He called in to see Millie's team to let them know there would be extra people for lunch. Then, he called together the other members of the community, who he wanted to hear what this Hogan had to say.

"Rob, would you come out with me to meet our visitors so we can make sure they don't get attacked by wild animals as they arrive?"

Rob nodded and followed him outside. Calum was keen to hear what secrets Hogan had discovered working for this elite group and what their aims were.

They heard cars approaching and Calum and Rob stepped back inside the farmhouse door. The armed guards on duty drew their guns and waited by the gates. Then, as Calum watched from inside the farmhouse, the familiar face of Yvette driving her car appeared in the lane outside the gate, followed by another car.

"It's okay, that's Yvette," nodded Calum to the guards, who hadn't yet met her.

As she parked in the car park and opened her door, Calum greeted her with a hug.

"It's great to see you again, Yvette," he said. "I hope you can stay for a few days, see what we are doing up here?"

"I'd love to, but it depends on if we have any emergencies down south," she replied. "It's good to see you too, mon ami."

Hogan got out of the car. The escort car also parked, the security guards followed him.

"You must be Calum O'Connell," Hogan said striding towards Calum, his hand outstretched. "Good to meet you at last."

"And you must be Frank Hogan. I'm very pleased to meet you. Welcome to our latest refuge. We are all looking forward to hearing your story. I'm sure you must all be hungry, but would you mind briefing us first? We can have lunch after," said Calum, pointing out the way. Hogan nodded and followed with the others.

They joined the community waiting in the meeting room and waited for Hogan to brief them over coffee.

"Okay, I think you are going to find this a little hard to believe," he began once they were all settled.

"Try us," said Calum. "Why don't you start with your background? What were you doing before the GM sickness?"

"I was a security officer at Nellis Air Force Base. A lot of the work was classified and I didn't have the highest level of clearance. But, I still saw some weird things. One day, we were called out to an intrusion through the perimeter fence. Whilst we were searching for the intruders, we passed by some large hangars. There were some strange craft inside. I'm not sure if they were research projects, or alien, or what. But, they rushed us away from there pretty quickly and told us to search another area."

"Oh, my God," said Chloe. "David, you remember me telling you about when Jessie and I escaped from the Genies at Nellis? I said we saw strange craft inside a hangar? We always thought it was a UFO."

"I remember you telling me," said David. "And I confess I ribbed you about it for days after. Thought you had just mistaken an experimental vehicle for an alien craft."

"Yes, you did," said Chloe. "But, Jessie and I knew what we had seen."

"Anyway, after the GM sickness started, my family got sick. I was working long hours at the base, helping to keep the Genies out. We had to sleep and eat there for days on end. Next time I got leave, I arrived home to find all of my family dead."

"Oh, Frank. I am so sorry," said Chloe. "That must have been awful."

"It was. We had no idea what was really going on outside the base. We were totally isolated from all of that. But, when I went back into work the next day, we were told that, from then on, we would be living on base

186

for our own security. I didn't argue. After all, whatever was out there had already killed my family and friends."

"So, how did you get involved with this elite group at Zurich?" asked Rob.

"Well activities at the base slowly wound down until we were just camping out there. There wasn't much to do. There was nobody left to guard the base from. Then, the food was running out and people were going AWOL. I was just about to join them when I had a visit from one of the top bosses, a Jack Clark. He seemed very preoccupied. He told me that my job was being transferred to an Edward Vanderbilt, who had a top job in world politics. He didn't specify exactly what the guy did. The next day, three guards arrived to escort me to my new post. I didn't complain. It was work and Nellis was obviously through. So, I went with them to a high security mansion in Washington DC."

"What did you make of Vanderbilt?" asked Calum.

"At first, he seemed okay, though he obviously didn't suffer fools gladly. But he had some high-powered friends, all with huge chauffeur-driven cars and they met regularly all over the world. They seemed to have a finger in all sorts of pies. I don't think much happens that they haven't engineered. Later, when things got bad and we were told we had to evacuate America and move to Vanderbilt's castle in Zurich, he just gave us the information coldly, as if we were compelled to go, as if we had no choice. I thought he was a cold fish, not much empathy for those who had lived in the US their whole lives. I mean, he was obscenely rich. He had properties all over the world, so he was used to spending his time in various countries. He used to spend a lot of time in Zurich, but we were always left behind to guard his Washington place."

187

"He had a hard life, then," grumbled Rob. "And it doesn't sound like he was very grateful for his fortune either."

"But, wait till you hear the rest of it. The thing that brought me here. Two days ago, the castle at Zurich had intruders. Vanderbilt got attacked and he was angry with us. He demanded to know how they could have passed us, when we were supposed to be guarding the place. We were all completely baffled. The guards on duty had been in the entrance hall and around the perimeter all morning. Nobody came in and nobody went out. Then, I was assigned to check the CCTV to see if the point of intrusion could be identified. There was nothing. Until I went right to the moment of the attack to check if it had caught who had done it and how many there were. One minute, Vanderbilt was just sitting there alone, reading and drinking wine. The next, there was an attack, but I couldn't see anybody else. I didn't know if he was having a heart attack or fit. Then, Vanderbilt got angry and threw what had become long arms in the air. There were claws on his hands. His head elongated, his mouth was full of teeth. His eyes had large, black pupils. He looked like a *reptile*."

There were a few gasps from those in the room.

"Are you sure that's what you really saw?" asked Rob. "I mean, had you been drinking or were you sleepy? Could you have dreamt it?"

"It was morning and I had just had coffee, so I was wide awake. And I can categorically remove all doubt from your minds. I have the proof right here."

He held up the data stick and inserted it into his laptop.

"I lifted this footage off the CCTV system just before I fled the place."

He clicked on the file and pressed 'play.'

The shocking footage, showing Vanderbilt's transformation, played out right before their eyes. It could no longer be denied just who, or more accurately, what, was really running the world.

"Do you think that Vanderbilt's cohorts are all reptilian, too?" asked Calum. "It would certainly explain a lot about the indiscriminate, heartless nuclear bombing and the use of toxic GM food on the human race, without a thought for the inevitable consequences."

"I think we have to assume they are all the same. The rest of them were all cold with us staff members. I heard them laughing once, after a nuclear missile strike in the US. I think they were trying to wipe out the Genies at the time, from what I overheard. They didn't predict the full effects of GM food on humans and the Genies' uncontrolled development of supernatural powers. They were a threat to the Elite's world order. One of the household staff clearing up after a party that night discovered the remains of a red liquid in their glasses. It was supposedly wine, but he swore it smelled like blood."

"Oh God, that is *disgusting*," gasped Chloe.

"Are they some kind of Satanists, killing people and drinking blood?" said Rob. "We know they make sacrifices, because James Cameron saw it with his own eyes when he pretended to join them. And he was killed for his refusal to go along with it."

"I don't think so," said Hogan. "I think that they are from somewhere else in the universe. The spaceships that I saw at Nellis; did they arrive in those? They spoke with an odd accent which I couldn't place, wherever in the world they were supposedly from. They have a reptilian form and they can also appear as humans. But they aren't human, so are they from another planet?"

189

"Are you serious? You really think they are *aliens*?" said Calum.

"It's the only explanation that seems to fit, now that I have seen what they are with my own eyes. They for sure didn't want me spreading the word around. Their goons chased me for hundreds of miles. Thankfully, they were stopped by dino-birds in France. And when the others caught up with us in England, Yvette's security here managed to help me escape."

"They weren't so tough," said Mike, patting Hogan's shoulder. "We made a good team. If you ever need a job over here let us know."

"Well, I think it will help keep you safe if we get this news out right away. And I think we're going to be needing extra security up here, from what you've told us," said Calum. "So, if you could, we would appreciate you sticking around. All of you. They might come after you again, but I am more concerned about the local forces finding us. We escaped from them already. They already sent drones to search the area, though thankfully I don't think we were spotted."

"Suits me," said Hogan. "It's not like I have anywhere else to go, anyway. I would be glad to join you."

The security team and Yvette nodded.

"I have nothing much to go back for either," said Yvette, glancing at Hogan speculatively.

Chloe noticed this and smiled.

"And we still have the Genies to worry about. It sounds like you have experienced their latest paranormal power, that of invisibility," added Calum.

"That is all we need right now," groaned Rob. "Shapeshifting aliens running the Earth and invisible Genies. Happy days."

34. Plotting Destruction

In a cellar below a chateau in the Loire valley, the elite group were gathered. Corinne Moreau had welcomed them to one of her homes earlier. She was enjoying being at the top of the power structure in France. Although, it had been a shame about her father, Philippe, who had been scalded to death at his mansion in Cap Ferrat.

There were many benefits to becoming the most powerful person in France, she thought. She turned her attention to Vanderbilt, who was speaking.

"So, we are agreed? The Genies must be eliminated as soon as possible."

"I thought we had agreed *that* at least a year ago," said Marta. "It's what do you say, a no-brainer, yes?"

"Obviously," said Vanderbilt. "But, first we need to devote more resources to finding out their location. And, since the CCTV seems to prove that they can now become invisible whenever they like, that might be difficult."

"So, there must be some marker or something that that we can search for? What do the scientists say?" said Max Kaufman, also now very powerful in Germany since his mother Liese was killed in the earthquake and flood at her castle on Lake Geneva. Which was now his own home.

"There is nothing specific," said Vanderbilt. "The specialists in Eastern mythology say there are localised signs of Genies or Jinn, but that's no use when we have the whole world to search. But, we do suspect that they are still in the US. They seem to prefer it there. They have mainly chosen to live in underground military bases. So, we can send in drones carrying thermal sensors to detect body heat. These could be focussed around former military bases. We know that there are still small pockets of people living in the States who refused to leave. But, large communities living in military bases should be easier to detect."

"Then, let's do it," said Marta. "We cannot afford to have these mutants constantly attacking us and trying to wipe us out. It is distracting us from our purpose here."

Everybody agreed. Vanderbilt contacted the military's Chief Commander to give the order.

"So, we are all set for our Christmas break in the Alps?" asked Vanderbilt.

"The hotels are booked. The private jet is on standby for tomorrow. Everything is prepared," said Max Kaufman.

Vanderbilt nodded. "Excellent."

Then, the group fell to more enjoyable activities. By candle light, they enacted an ancient ceremony wearing white hooded robes, the drumbeats echoing through the underground crypt.

The highlight was as usual, a drugged human, who was soon to be dispatched to supply them with energy and life blood.

The screams of the dying human echoed around the cellars, as they thrashed around in their agony.

The chanting stopped. It was done.

Then, the feeding began.

Jessie was confused. She had been with her friend, Hannah, running along the promenade at Gallanvaig. Why had they been running? Oh, yes, the earthquake and the huge waves that had been threatening to top the harbour wall. But, where was Hannah now? Where was *she* for that matter? But, this wasn't Gallanvaig. It was dark and there was an odd odour. She couldn't hear the sea, which was a constant background sound in Gallanvaig. Had the Genies taken her again? She opened her mouth to call for help.

"*Calum*," she cried, but it came out as a faint squeak.

Where was she and what the hell had happened?

36. Putting the Pieces Together

They were all gathered in the lounge the next day and Calum was trying to make sense of everything that they now knew.

"Well, I've sent a briefing to all our contacts and put it on-line about what we think are alien powers that have probably been manipulating humans from the shadows. I have outlined their apparent reptilian nature. That might distract them for a while, though I'm not holding my breath on that one. It might at least stop them trying to gag Hogan, as the story is already out. I thought it might help to gather all our thoughts on this. So, say these alien shapeshifters were behind the intelligence organisation, AC10. They were probably behind the development of GM food and the covert feeding of this poison to humans, to cull the human population. We don't know why they might have wanted to do this, although AC10 thought that it was connected to overpopulation and limited resources. That was what Sarah Norris told us anyway. The Genies, or Jinn as we now know them to be, are humans devolved by the mutated transgenes in the GM food switching on the genes that control Jinn characteristics. They are continuing to mutate, developing more and more paranormal powers. Some of them may still be dying from GM poisoning, from what we have heard. As observed by Chloe and Jessie when they were captured, they are still consuming GM food, to develop even more powers. The aliens want to kill the Genies, who are a threat to them. Genetically modified DNA is mutating the DNA of wildlife and pets and they are devolving to ancient forms as wild animals and dinosaurs. The aliens may be behind the continued drive to control and manipulate the human population into slavery, doing the work they tell us to do, for the wages they tell us we can have, in towns and cities, where they tell us we must live. Humans are being controlled, tracked and manipulated in everything they do."

"What a nightmare," said Chloe.

"Well, I'm not giving in to them," said Rob. "A load of shapeshifting, lizard aliens. No way."

James and Shaun laughed. It was just all so ludicrous.

"Have we any idea how long they have been here?" asked David.

"Well, they all seemed to have families here and sometimes talked about their ancestors here. The ruling elite pass on their rule to their children. A few of them have been killed recently in Genie attacks and their offspring have taken over. So, I'm guessing they could have been here for hundreds of years," said Hogan. "Or even thousands of years."

"Where did they come *from*? And *why* did they come here?" said Chloe.

Rachel had been sitting quietly, taking all this in. Then, she cleared her throat.

"You know, I have been thinking about all of this and I was reading something a while ago," she began.

"What do you mean sweetheart?" asked Calum. "About shapeshifting aliens and stuff?"

"Well, that was in the book yes," she said uncertainly. "It was by a pretty off-the-wall author that got a fair bit of criticism, but I like all that stuff, you know?"

"We know you do, love," said Chloe. "Go on."

"Well the book said that aliens came here thousands of years ago. It said there are traces of their civilisations all over the earth, if you care to look. Like the Nazca Lines in Peru. These are huge carved lines forming the shapes of birds, spiders, monkeys, flowers and humans. The largest figures are a thousand feet long. They are thought to have been created before 500AD. They can only be properly seen from the air. *But, the first aircraft were not flown until the early Twentieth Century."*

"Yes, I've heard about the Nazca lines. They are a mystery," said Calum. "But, that doesn't necessarily mean that aliens created them, sweetheart."

"But, that's not all," insisted Rachel. "There are *loads* of signs. Nobody knows how Stonehenge, or the great pyramids were created; all those huge blocks of stone that were transported and placed on top of one another, before mechanised transport, or lifting equipment was invented. And I also read that aliens were said to have interbred with humans to produce hybrid creatures."

"Rachel, my dear, you need to be a little more discerning in your reading," started Rob. "Those sorts of books are cheap thrills for the masses."

"Wait, let's hear her out," said Chloe. "After all, we have just heard Mr Hogan here describe how he saw a human change into a *reptile*. And we have seen the footage for ourselves."

"It's Frank, please," added Hogan.

"Okay, Frank here strikes me as a very reliable witness and we saw the film of something very strange happening in Zurich. We have seen the Genies teleporting and flying through the sky. Not to mention feeling them doing that creepy mind-reading thing. Go on, Rach."

"Well, I would need to get the book from my room to check the details again. But, it said that an ancient, reptilian extra-terrestrial race called the Annunaki lived in underground bases on Earth. They came from space and, as part of their mission to rule the

Earth, they interbred with humans. The resulting hybrids had the traits and physical characteristics of both reptilians and humans. The hybrids would help to overcome humans by living amongst them undetected, promoting the mission of the reptiles and moving into positions of power and influence. They are apparently cold-blooded and unemotional. Like lizards. That was what made me think of the book, when Frank talked about Mr Vanderbilt turning into a reptile and that he was very cold."

"Well, thank you Rachel, all that is fascinating. We just need to decide how much of it might be true," said Calum.

"Well, I for one support what the young lady is saying," said Hogan. "It seems to fit very well with what I observed, working with the elite group around Vanderbilt.

"Can you get some copies of the book run off in the comms room please Rachel? I think we need to study what it says a little more closely. Frank, would you read it please? And Rob too, as our resident sceptic, to keep our feet on the ground?"

Everyone laughed. But, the atmosphere was sombre as the full implications of the startling revelations from Hogan, taken with Rachel's comments about her book sank in.

The elite party arrived at the luxury private castle in Lermoos from Innsbruck airport to a storm of controversy. They had all gathered in the huge hall set out with comfortable sofas and a bar. They were watching the television news, drinks in hand and canapés being served to them by the waiters.

The report on the news was showing a film that the broadcasting company had received earlier that day from an unspecified source.

"So, our source tells us that a race of *reptilian aliens* invaded the earth thousands of years ago and is now in positions of power around the world. They have huge wealth and power and have engineered every major world event in memory. Our science reporter John Garfield is in London for us. John?"

"Thanks Dan. Our source has produced evidence that proves conclusively that the aliens are not coming. They are *already here*. Yes, an alien, reptilian race is already here on earth. We have been sent a film clip that shows a human-looking male transforming into a reptilian being."

The presenter then cut to footage of Vanderbilt's recent transformation in Zurich.

Vanderbilt snorted into his schnapps.

"You careless bastard," exclaimed Marta Petrov. "You have blown our cover. This is going to cost us time and money in rubbishing it and coming up with a cover story. Not to mention giving the conspiracy theorists oxygen."

"Look, my dear, don't panic," said Vanderbilt. "We will merely get one of our Democracy Party prime ministers to issue a denial, ridiculing this as fake news. Film clips can be faked. There is no proof of anything."

"Don't patronise me, Vanderbilt. This is a major gaffe. You are going to have to learn to control yourself better in future."

"Let's not fight amongst ourselves," said Gaj Kapur, one of the newer members of the Elite, who had taken the place of his murdered father, Sahil, who died in a firestorm caused by the Genies, at Sir Michael Goldman's mansion. "We need to stand together through this and decide what to do about it."

"So, we get the new UK Prime Minister, Alexandria, who is about to be announced, to deal with it at her first and, I must say quite timely, press conference in London tomorrow," replied Vanderbilt, already looking bored with the whole matter. What was wrong with these people today? They were usually so sure of themselves, confident in their total control over events.

"Good idea," agreed Michael Goldman. "There is no point arguing about spilt milk. I can speak to Alexandria's team and get something in her speech. Problem solved. Now, can we get onto our plans for the hunt tomorrow please?"

Marta Petrov was still fuming. Vanderbilt really was a condescending, patronising and extremely annoying *shit*. How dare he talk to her like that? She tossed her head and stormed out of the room, slamming the door, as the others started to discuss what animals they wanted to hunt tomorrow and where they might go to find them.

Vanderbilt looked up after she left and sniggered. He took another gulp of his schnapps.

"Females are such annoying, illogical creatures," he said. "You just can't reason with them."

"Stop winding everyone up, Vanderbilt," snapped Rosa Araripe, the Brazilian magnate who had taken over from her father Matheus, also killed in the Genie firestorm. "You're really not helping."

"Yes, do shut up, Edward" said Corrinne Moreau, the French daughter of Phillipe, who had died in a boiling swimming pool. "At least women don't keep poking everyone else, trying to get a reaction. At least *we* can work together, instead of trying to score points all the time."

"I'm pleased to see that at least the newer members of our Elite are showing some common sense," said Goldman. "Right, try not to bicker amongst yourselves whilst I go and speak to Alexandria's team."

Alexandria Fortescue was a trusted member of the Elite's operations who, together with her husband Justin, had been instrumental in infiltrating Calum O'Connell's group in Gallanvaig and identifying Sam Paige as the most likely candidate for the Democracy Party willing to stand against Calum. She also helped to groom Paige, both before and after his election as Prime Minister and ensure he was briefed in what he must do. Unfortunately, he proved unable to follow orders.

Unfortunately for him, that was.

The next day, Calum and the others were watching the news after lunch, when a breaking news story was announced.

"We are just getting reports that, after the tragic death of Sam Paige, the replacement UK Prime Minster is about to be announced and will shortly give a press conference outside Number Ten Downing Street. We go directly to our reporter Daniel Garside, who is there now."

"Thanks, Karen. Yes, the announcement is expected any moment now and the new Prime Minister will be just over there to give his or her first press conference. Ah, I can see the press secretary, Phillip Barratt, coming out now."

The camera zoomed to Phillip Barratt, who was now standing at the podium outside the open door of Number Ten.

"Good afternoon, ladies and gentlemen. I am pleased to announce that the Democracy Party of the United Kingdom has reached a decision on a successor to Sam Paige. The new Prime Minister of the United Kingdom is Alexandria Fortescue, who will now make a short statement before visiting Buckingham Palace to seek the Queen's approval."

"Oh typical," snarled Rob. "She proved to be one arrogant person when she was in Gallanvaig, just like the rest of the World Democracy lot. We can expect even more of the same controls over the movement and lives of ordinary people, I'm sure. I didn't like Sam Paige, but at least he was one of the ordinary people."

"I didn't like her either, Uncle Rob," said Joanna, wrinkling her nose. "She was really snotty about Gallanvaig and our life there. A right stuck-up madam."

Everyone laughed, but Joanna was right. Alexandria Fortescue and her friends were arrogant people, who had infiltrated their community with their own agenda and as soon as they had got what they wanted, someone who was one of the villagers but who was willing to betray them, they had poisoned the villagers and returned to London.

Barratt stood aside as Alexandria Fortescue came out of Number Ten and stepped up to the podium.

"Good afternoon. I am most honoured to have been asked to lead the party and this country, of which I am so proud. My policies, should the Queen approve my forming a government, will be to tackle terrorist attacks from those who have refused to join our settled and successful communities in the towns and cities and who insist on wasting resources in rural outposts. They will be brought back into mainstream society as soon as possible. I will also defend our country from attacks by the Genies, putting in place improved defences against them and increasing our armed forces. I will ensure that the country has a reliable source of energy that is not dependant on unreliable factors. I will make the United Kingdom once more a country to be reckoned with on the world stage. There is just one matter we must deal with straight away to allay people's fears. Yesterday, there were some ridiculous reports claiming that the world is now run by *shape-shifting lizards*."

Alexandria paused and smiled.

"However, the only evidence that has been presented was a shaky film clip that would have shamed a science fiction B movie. This film was obviously computer-generated, using technology readily available to anybody. Our technical experts have now confirmed this. It was *fake news*. There is no need to worry. Everything is under control. Thank you, everyone."

She got into a black limousine waiting nearby and headed off to the palace.

"Well, that's it, we have our third female UK Prime Minister, Alexandria Fortescue. She has hit the ground running with her plans to increase national security, address energy shortages and tackle terrorism and fake news. She will now visit Buckingham Palace to seek the Queen's approval, then she will make her first speech as Prime Minister at four o'clock today. Back to you, Karen."

Calum switched off the television.

"Well, *our* experts confirmed that the footage was genuine. I know who I believe. Some people won't believe until a shapeshifter appears before their eyes. I think we can expect action against non-conformers to be stepped up even more than in Sam Paige's government," he said. "It sounds like they will go all out to conquer any remaining independent communities. They will probable restore even more nuclear and coal power stations. And the threat of the Genies and 'tackling terrorism' is just an excuse to put in place more military forces to suppress the people."

"Yeah, what terrorism?" remarked Rob. "The worst terrorists are those in charge and the Vanderbilts of this world. Even the Genies just have their own agenda to create more of their kind and otherwise largely leave ordinary people alone."

"Though the Genies are evil, too," said Chloe, holding her tummy. She was having one of her cramps and the baby was kicking like crazy. "They don't care who they hurt or kill in pursuit of their goals. As Jessie and I found out when we were forced to be in their company."

Later that afternoon, the community tuned back in to hear the new Prime Minister's first speech.

The action being streamed from the House of Commons was typically puerile. A Member of Parliament was making a droning speech about the Bank of England and interest rates and how the control of these should now be transferred to the new World Bank, which was to replace all regional and national banks. The speech was punctuated by 'boos' and 'hear hears' and frequent jeering.

"The bill also introduces a new World currency and a standardised interest rate, all controlled by the World Bank," he was saying.

The Speaker of the House interrupted.

"We have reached the time limit for this debate. Now we will vote. The full question is on the order paper and concerns the transfer of financial powers from the Bank of England to the new World Bank."

The members stood and headed for the lobbies to vote.

Soon the clerks came back and announced the results. The House had largely been bored into submission and the last thing members wanted was for the bill to be rehashed and then to have to sit through all this tedious business again. It was bound to be approved eventually anyway.

"The 'Ayes' have it," stated the Speaker. "Now, the next business is the first speech of our new Prime Minister, Alexandria Fortescue."

Alexandria stood up from her despatch box and shuffled papers onto the top of the box.

"Thank you, Mr Speaker. I am honoured to have been asked today by the Queen to form a government. Later, I will be in discussions with members of Parliament to form a Cabinet that reflects the important work that we still need to do. Meanwhile, I will make a short statement on my priorities for the next five years."

There was some general cheering and 'hear hears and only the odd 'boo.' The House was largely giving the new Prime Minster a chance, before starting to demonstrate the full force of their support or opposition, depending on whether members sat on the World Democracy or the World Alliance side of the House.

"Firstly, we need to urgently combat the terrorist threat that is ever-growing in these turbulent times. There have been attacks in our towns and cities by the Genies, or Jinn as they are now being called. Whatever they call themselves, they have been a force for evil, responsible for attacks on the innocent and powerless in our country. This will be met with the full force of our military. I intend to increase our defence budget by five billion pounds. There will be an increase in defence personnel of ten thousand."

"Where's *that* money going to come from?" muttered Rob.

"We also have seen continued defiance of the law that centralises our scant resources on towns and cities. There are criminals who insist on setting up communities in far-flung outposts, using up resources inefficiently and depriving those of the law-abiding population of adequate resources. I will fund a renewed drive to move these criminals into properly-resourced town and cities without further delay. The budget for our national security services and police forces will be increased accordingly."

"Of course, we will have to make sacrifices elsewhere to pay for our increased security. The budgets for health, education and the environment will be frozen at their current levels."

There was a chorus of boos at this from the Alliance side of the House.

"In recent years we have seen unrealistic expectations that solar, wind and hydroelectric power can fully supply the needs of the United Kingdom. Whilst this is an admirable aim, it has proven inadequate to provide consistent, unbroken energy supplies. Therefore, whilst we will of course continue to provide a percentage of sustainable, green energy, we will back this up with more reliable coal and nuclear power, so that never again will power cuts interrupt our normal life. I will provide the budget to re-open, or build new, adequate power stations to fully supply our network. I will now take questions."

As the audience in Largo Bunker shouted at the television in unison, Calum switched off the set. He had heard enough anyway.

Things were obviously going to get worse for them.

Much worse.

38. An Impossible Problem

The hunting team had just returned to the hunting lodge in Lermoos. They had had a very successful hunting trip and the results were heaped in a pile in the courtyard, ready for the restaurant team to remove and prepare. There were many black grouse and a few roe deer and chamois deer.

"Well that's improved my mood," grunted Vanderbilt. "I'm looking forward to sampling some of these tomorrow."

"The grouse won't be ready then, but I'm sure the chefs can do prepare some venison," replied Max Kaufman, who owned the hunting lodge.

Max saw his housekeeper enter to take their damp outer clothing away.

"Hi, Klaus. Have the teams from Roslyn and Novagentech arrived yet?"

"Ja, Herr Kaufman. They are waiting in the main lounge. I have lit the fires in there."

"Thanks Klaus. Shall we go through and take refreshments whilst we hear their reports?" he suggested.

Angus Maclean, the director of Edinburgh University's Roslin Institute had been brought in to present a summary of his scientific team's findings.

"First of all, I want to thank Sir Michael Goldman for giving us this opportunity to showcase the ground-breaking work of the Roslin Institute. We were asked to come up with a strategy to remove GM contamination of the environment and to address the mutations that have been appearing since the release of Novagentech's G517 soya into the food chain and the environment. The main issues we were asked to address were contamination by the weed-killer glyphosate, the contamination of the environment by GM material and finally, the mutated or devolved animals which have been recently observed. So, we first looked at the issue of glyphosate in watercourses and drinking water. Glyphosate is a weed-killer designed to be used alongside the GM crops. Several research projects have demonstrated an association with cancers. We compared and thoroughly tested the potential treatments to remove Glyphosate from water. We discovered that glyphosate is easily destroyed in water by chlorine and ozone treatment. Chlorine is already used in all treatment works. An ozonation step could easily be added. This two-step process would be ninety-nine percent effective in removing GM from the water. All that would be left is a trace amount of glyphosate perfectly safe for human and animal consumption. These two chemicals could also be pumped into watercourses that are heavily contaminated with glyphosate."

"What will all of this cost?" barked Marta Petrov.

"That depends on risk assessment. For example, what level of glyphosate contamination should be set to trigger the treatment in watercourses? Obviously, it would be prohibitively expensive to treat all watercourses. But, treatment of a limited set would not be too prohibitive, providing you can obtain a plentiful and cheap supply of the chemicals. I suggest you may wish to limit the treatment to watercourses in towns and cities, where the population is now required to live. But, that is obviously your decision."

"Okay, what about the contamination by GM material?" asked Sir Michael.

"The only sure way to remove GM-contaminated plants is to destroy the plants completely. The optimum method has been shown to be by burning. This would ensure that all GM material is destroyed."

"So, any areas where GM crops were grown must be burned?" asked Vanderbilt. "In the case of the United States, the land was pretty thoroughly destroyed by nuclear missiles and the rest was abandoned. But, there were several other countries who were cultivating GM at the time. All of these will need to identify their contaminated land and destroy the crops on it."

"Yes, the other major countries involved included Canada, South America, South Africa, Australia, India and China," continued Maclean. "The levels in other countries, particularly Europe, were very low and the sites were pretty much limited to pilot trials. However, these will need to be identified and destroyed to ensure complete removal of GM material from the world's environment. We also suggest that the US still needs to be completely purged, as it had the highest levels of GM crop cultivation in the world. The GM material and glyphosate will continue to migrate outside of US national boundaries into other territories. Contamination of the world's watercourses and oceans will continue as GM material and glyphosate flows out from US watercourses."

"So, what are you suggesting?" asked Vanderbilt.

"The only sure way is destruction of all contaminated land. This could be by local burning. But, with the wide extent of the likely contamination and the risk to personnel operating on the ground, carpet bombing with incendiary devices or nuclear missiles may be advisable. Then, all watercourses out from the US must be treated as we have described to prevent contamination reaching the rest of the world."

"So, the United States is to be wiped from the map?" asked Vanderbilt. Although he felt no real allegiance to the US, he had lived there for most of his life and his ancestors before him. It was a shock. His loyalties lay elsewhere entirely.

"I'm sorry to say that it must be," replied Maclean. "Of course, you will need to ensure complete evacuation of the population first. I understand that some rebels remained there even after being instructed to leave for their own safety."

"They were warned of the dangers," said Vanderbilt. "That would the least of our concerns." He stopped as he saw the shocked look on Maclean's face. "Of course, we will take all possible to steps to make we find everybody and get them out, by force if necessary. Now, what about the other little problem with mutating animals?"

"Well, once the GM material is removed from the environment and the food chain, there should be no further mutation. As far as the existing animals which have already mutated, we know that these are causing some serious problems. The only method of dealing with this is a cull of mutated animals. They cannot be allowed to breed and proliferate the problem."

"Okay, well thanks you for your work on this Mr Maclean. We now understand what we need to do. Your team will of course be required to assist in implementing the measures you suggest," said Sir Michael.

"Of course," replied Maclean. "We would be delighted to help."

"Hold on a minute, what about Novagentech, what do they have to say?" asked Vanderbilt. "Do you agree with this approach?"

Colin Pearson, Novagentech's chief executive, who had been sitting at the back stood up and came forward as Maclean sat down.

"Thank you for asking us to look into this, Mr Vanderbilt," he began. "However, our conclusions are very different to Professor Maclean's. Firstly, the issue of glyphosate. Glyphosate is a very effective weed-killer that has prevented the loss of huge amounts of crops from destruction by weeds. It has ensured a continuous, reliable and safe food supply for millions of people in the world over many years. It has prevented starvation. There is absolutely no scientific evidence of any dangers from this substance, nor is there substantiated evidence of any carcinogenic effect."

Maclean stood up and began to protest.

"You have had your turn, now it's *mine*," insisted Pearson. "I am surprised that a scientific institute like Roslin would repeat *fake news* started by green activists about the 'harm' caused by GM food and glyphosate. At Novagentech, we take our work seriously and all products are intensively tested before being released into the environment or the food chain. GM crops have reduced world hunger and increased crop yields by engineering a built-in resistance to pests. Nor is there any actual *evidence* that GM caused the mutation problems. All you have is circumstantial evidence. No scientific research has been done to prove the cause was GM material."

"But, surely, this is old news now," said Gaj Kapur. "It is conclusively accepted that GM caused the problem."

"But, where is your actual evidence?" asked Pearson. "There is none. The GM soya we produced to address world hunger and ensure high yields of soya to feed animals did exactly what it was designed to do. You wished it to also be toxic to a certain percentage of the population to address diminishing world resources and we achieved this. It delivered exactly what you ordered. No less, no more."

"Unbelievable," snorted Maclean. "There have been many scientific studies that showed genetic engineering to be responsible for continuing genetic mutations in both GM crops and neighbouring non-GM crops. It is obvious that the same would happen with living beings, in fact it been scientifically proved several times with rat experiments. Not to mention the biggest GM trial in history, on humans."

"I am not aware of any such peer-reviewed trials," said Pearson. "Now if I may finish my presentation without further interruption?"

Maclean sat down muttering to himself.

"As I was saying, there is no substantiated, scientific evidence that genetic engineering causes mutations, either in the case of the Genies, or in the mutated animals. So, there must be another factor in play here. I suggest further research is needed to determine if there is another environmental cause. Finally, the mutated animals. I must agree with Professor Maclean that a cull is the only way to deal with this problem. Thank you."

"Thanks, Mr Pearson," said Vanderbilt. "Well, we seem to have a significant dispute as to the causes and cures for our current situation. But, we have total agreement on a cull of mutated animals. I suggest we start that immediately. We need help from the world's armies. I will organise that. As to the issue of glyphosate and GM material, what is the opinion around the table? Do we raze America to the ground? Do we spend a huge amount of money pumping ozone and chlorine into watercourses? What do we think? I myself am a little reluctant to destroy my former homeland."

"I don't think we can take a chance," said Goldman. "If there is still a risk from these substances, let's do as Maclean suggests and treat drinking water and watercourses to destroy it. We should also destroy the contaminated land. We have nothing to lose, even if, as Pearson suggests, it's no longer a threat."

"I agree," said Corinne. "I don't think we can leave this to fate. Let's follow Maclean's advice."

Everyone, apart from Vanderbilt, was agreed.

The water would be chemically treated. The GM crop-growing areas in the US, Canada, South America, South Africa, Australia, India and China would be destroyed by incendiary bombs from above. The added advantage was that the Jinn might finally be destroyed in the fires, as the drones they sent to the US had been unable to find any trace of them.

And fire would rain from heaven.

The first angel blew his trumpet and there followed hail and fire, mixed with blood, which fell on the earth and a third of the earth was burnt up and a third of the trees were burnt up and all green grass was burnt up.

"How are you guys getting on with Rachel's book about the aliens?" asked Calum. "I can't believe I just said that," he added smiling.

"We've been studying it," said Rob. "It *is* interesting. It claims that 'gods' existed on earth thousands of years ago and were said to have interbred with humans. The book claims that Sumerian clay tablets were excavated in 1850, by an Englishman, Henry Lanyard at Nineveh, near Mosul, in present-day Iraq. These were translated by an expert in Sumerian, Zecharia Sitchin. His translation claims that gods lived among the Sumerians, the Annunaki, who came from another planet called Nibiru. They came to earth to mine gold in Africa to transport back to their own planet. Apparently, evidence of gold mining *has* been found in Africa from at least one hundred thousand years ago."

Rachel and Hogan nodded.

"I found one piece of information most intriguing," continued Hogan. "The tablets said that at first the Annunaki used their own workers in the mines, but they rebelled. The Annunaki then decided to create a race of slaves to carry on the work. They mixed their genes with those of native humans in a test tube to create a new sort of 'human.' This was *thousands of years* before humans would develop in vitro fertilisation. And, around two hundred thousand years ago, there *was* a very sudden change in homo erectus to become homo sapiens, with hugely increased intelligence and language. Scientists claim there was a missing link in the evolution of homo sapiens, but *no evidence has ever been found."*

"Yes, and the Sumerians were highly knowledgeable about astronomy, mathematics and energy fields, knowledge which is said to have been given to them by the Annunaki and which they used to

214

construct the pyramids and monoliths with their astronomical implications," said Rachel. "It has been claimed that the Annunaki were reptilian, being much taller than humans and emotionally cold, but highly intelligent. Many civilisations around the world have stories of lizard gods, for example Quetzalcoatl in America, the Nagas in India and the Phoenician Agathodemon, to name but a few. And the Bible has references to an evil serpent."

"But, wasn't all this so long ago that it cannot be proved now?" asked David. "How can we ever know if these were just old legends to scare each other around the cave fire, or whether they were accounts of real events?"

"Even if Henry Lanyard could have somehow faked the Sumerian tablets in 1850, which would be difficult if he had no knowledge of the Sumerian language, how did he come up with the idea of creating a hybrid being in a test tube? Over a hundred years before this became an actual scientific technique? All I know is what I saw," said Hogan. "This theory about Annunaki being reptiles and ruling the world fits with what I saw at Zurich and my experience of Vanderbilt's group, the Elite from around the world. I saw a huge, reptilian being emerge from its 'human' shell. Unless you have any other theories, David?"

"No, no, I don't," said David. "Sorry, I'm just trying to get my head around all of this, that's all. It sounds bonkers."

"It is hard to believe," said Calum. "But, we have seen so many weird things in the past few years, things we would have said were impossible before the GM catastrophe. Humans flying through the sky, teleportation, simultaneous apparitions in multiple locations. Possibly the ability to cause earthquakes and tsunamis and use them to attack enemies. The reappearance of extinct animals; dinosaurs, for goodness sake."

"I am probably the most sceptical person on the Earth about supernatural phenomena, UFOs and stuff," said Rob. "I keep trying to find a reason not to believe it, a logical explanation. But, I must admit that it this all starting to worry me. It's the only thing that fits all the facts that we know and have seen. And, like David, I can't think of another explanation. Things are just getting pretty weird."

"Who are you and what have you done with our Rob?" joked Chloe.

"But, what do they *want*?" asked David. "If the Annunaki have been here for thousands of years, looking for gold, surely they have taken all that they need by now?"

"The book says that the Annunaki interbred with humans over thousands of years and there are now hybrids that have a large percentage of reptilian DNA," said Rachel. "That is how they can so easily shapeshift. There is an Elite bloodline that has high levels of reptilian DNA, descending directly from the Annunaki. They carefully maintain the purity of the reptilian bloodline by interbreeding. They are said to be in positions of immense power; royalty, heads of global financial corporations and industry. That is why intermarriage between power groups like European royalty is so popular. Go back just a few generations and they are all related."

"The book also describes a theory about the widely-differing politicians who come to power in every country of the world," said Hogan. "How come leaders with totally different viewpoints and principles end up implementing the same policies? Because *they* aren't running the show. I saw enough of Vanderbilt's gang to recognise their immense power and lack of empathy with humanity. It's the Elite bloodlines in the background who are manipulating the world to be what they want it to be. They want to control humans."

"But, how many of these Elite bloodline, shapeshifting people are there?" asked David. "And what can we do about them?"

"Nobody knows," said Hogan. "It doesn't say in the book and I don't see how anybody can know for sure, except for the Elite. I'm sure it's constantly changing anyway. They must be continuing to crossbreed all the time."

"Well, knowledge of what they are and what they are doing is something we can use against them," said Calum. "We need to open everyone's eyes to what they are and fight back. They can't fight all of us without our consent. They need the military, who are hopefully mostly human. We've beat them before and we can do it again."

But, he felt much less certain than he sounded. Did they have their own bloodline military, who would obey at all costs? Had they bred a race of super-solders as well?

What could they really do against an all-powerful, hugely rich, soulless group, who had a world of power at their fingertips?

40. Hail and Fire

Later, Hogan and Yvette were sitting together in one of the lounges.

"You really believe all that stuff about aliens having been here for thousands of years, interbreeding with humans and controlling the world from the shadows?" she asked.

"I can't think of any other explanation," he said. "Knowing Vanderbilt and the other Elite leaders, I can believe that they are all cold reptilians. They showed no sympathy when discussing various catastrophes that had befallen Earth. The GM crisis, the earthquakes, tsunamis and all the restrictive new legislation being introduced around the world to control what humans can do, where they can live, how essential services will be delivered. I *saw* Vanderbilt change into an evil looking reptile. I think they must all be the same. I am worried about a future with them in control."

"We should make the most of every moment then," replied Yvette, gazing at Hogan. We don't know how long we might have left."

He gazed at her and then leant in to kiss her gently on the lips.

"I have wanted to do that ever since I first met you. Whatever the future holds, we can face it together."

"I would like nothing more, chéri," said Yvette, smiling at him. "Maybe things are not as bad as we think, eh?"

Calum was busy sending reports to the World Alliance leaders and onto the websites that he had maintained for the past few years to inform and mobilise people. It was essential that everyone knew exactly what was going on and who the enemy were. Only then would the human population have a chance of fighting back. He just hoped that it wasn't too late.

Drones buzzed in the air above Texas state. Their on-board speakers and amplifiers boomed out a message over the fields and towns.

"This is an important message for all residents. In twenty-four hours' time, this area will be destroyed by incendiary devices for reasons of public health. The area is not safe for human habitation. Repeat; this area will be destroyed tomorrow. Please make your way immediately to the nearest seaport or airport, where there are ships and planes waiting to transport you to safety. The government of this territory will take no responsibility for those who refuse to leave and are subsequently injured. This is your final warning."

A shower of leaflets repeating the same message was released from the drone, which flew on to the next area to be targeted.

The same scenario was being repeated at contaminated sites around the world.

Hail and fire would begin to rain on the Earth.

In the grounds of Dulce Air Force Base in New Mexico, Balthazar looked up in surprise. He was unused to there being any movement around there, just a few birds and the odd dino-type creature, which they usually despatched if it threatened them. And sometimes ate. This was different. It sounded like a voice coming from the sky. What was going on?

Wait. The voice was saying they had to leave or be destroyed by fire. How *dare* they? This was their home. Now, he saw it. It was a small plane, no it wasn't big enough for that. But, that was where the threats were coming from. He focussed hard on the object. It's engine stuttered, then stalled. Then, it exploded in a flash of flames and smoke.

There was peace once more.

In the reservation at Pine Ridge, Makawee loaded her gun. She was practising with tin cans for hunting elk with her father. Three cans in quick succession pinged and shot off the wall. She was getting good at this. She would bring honour to her Sioux family. There was a sudden noise in the distance. She narrowed her eyes against the sun and looked up towards the sound. When the flying object came closer and she had heard its message, she put her gun aside and ran home to tell her family. She slammed the door as she ran into the trailer.

"Father! I heard a voice from the sky."

"How many times have I told you Maka? Don't slam the door. What are you trying to say? Slow down."

"There was a voice from the sky! It said we must leave; the government has ordered it. Tomorrow they will destroy this land with fire. They say it isn't safe to live here. We must go to the nearest airport or seaport."

"Look Maka, we didn't give up after Wounded Knee, even though they slaughtered our families, women and children. We have fought the authorities many times over injustice and we have won many battles. Even three years ago, when we were ordered out of our country because of a problem of the government's own making, we stayed in our homes, where we have lived for hundreds of years before they came and took our land. So, why should we move now? They will find out just how strong we are."

"But, Father, I am afraid. What if they kill us with these fire bombs?"

"Then, those of us that Walk On will find eternal peace and be free of suffering with the Wakan Tanka in the sky," said her father.

"We should go to the caves in the mountains, replied Makawee. "There, the fires cannot touch us. Please Father."

"We'll see. I'll talk to your mother," he replied. "Now, go and wash up before dinner."

Queues began to form at airports and ports around the contaminated areas and evacuation started immediately. Some wanted to leave, but many stayed. After all, they had refused to abandon their homeland before and had survived. What was so different this time?

The next day, Makawee and her family watched the plains from a cave high up in the Badlands. All the local people had taken cover there, as many had heard the voices from the sky.

At three o'clock in the afternoon, they saw a huge flight of planes approaching over the plains of their land. When they reached the fields where their livestock, fruit and vegetables were, the planes opened their doors and dropped missiles onto the land. When the missiles struck, there were loud explosions and flashes of flame. Their land was soon burning fiercely, their crops and livestock gone in an instant. The fires caught some of their trailers which also began to burn.

Their food supply and homes were destroyed. The land was spoiled for years to come.

Where would they live now?

Balthazar and his band had taken refuge in the underground base and could hear the bombs hitting the land around the base with dreadful regularity for around an hour.

What would be left when they finally emerged?

Balthazar was angry. How dare they desecrate his land once more?

He vowed his revenge - there would be no hiding place for his enemies.

The pumps on the US warship Aurora, docked in the Gulf of Mexico, were working overtime, pumping ozone and chlorine into the bay. The crew weren't sure why they were doing this, but they had been ordered to pump chemicals into all the waters around the US, especially those that flowed out of the US into the oceans.

They assumed that there was some sort of problem with the water quality, but they weren't sure why the water companies couldn't handle this as usual. Still, it was their job to follow orders and that's what they would do.

The water bubbled and frothed as the chemicals did their work.

But, could they treat every single drop of water on earth?

And, if not, would there be more uncontrolled mutations?

"This is the World Broadcasting News at One. We have some breaking news today about areas of land around the world that are said to be contaminated," the newsreader was saying. "Yesterday, those still living illegally in those areas were ordered to leave immediately and transport was provided for them. Today, the military have been destroying all plant life on land that may still be contaminated with GM material. A military spokesperson has told us that this operation will continue through today and tomorrow until all traces of GM crops have been wiped out. The Prime Minister is about to make a statement on this and we join our political editor, Richard Galsworthy, outside number Ten now."

"Thanks Karen. We are just waiting for a statement from the Prime Minister on the ongoing operation to destroy GM-contaminated land. We understand that thousands of people living there illegally were evacuated yesterday. Here is Alexandria Fortescue now."

"Good afternoon. As you know, there have been many continuing mutations since the great GM disaster around the world and the scientists have linked this to GM contamination remaining on land used to cultivate the crops. There is also pollution washing into watercourses from those areas, flowing into rivers and seas. Therefore, various governments affected by this have ordered a clean-up operation which has been mounted by the military. Here in the UK, there are only a few areas where GM crops were grown. These were mainly at research test sites. All nearby residents have been cleared from the areas concerned and the contaminated land is being burned to ensure the destruction of all harmful material. There is also an ongoing military operation to treat the waters flowing from these areas that may be contaminated by GM material. We have decided that these actions are necessary to ensure public health and safety. Please cooperate with any instructions issued by the military in your locality. Thank you."

Alexandria turned and went back into Number Ten Downing Street, not waiting for any questions.

"Huh. Now they decide that GM is harmful and must be destroyed," snarled Rob. "When it has already decimated the world population and contaminated huge areas of land and water. Not to mention conferring paranormal powers onto a load of psycho mutants and resurrecting the dinosaurs."

"Well, at least they are admitting it now and doing something about it," said Calum. "Although I bet that this elite is behind the military involvement. Governments wouldn't normally go straight to the military in pollution incidents, it would be left to the environmental teams."

"It smacks of the involvement of Vanderbilt and his cronies," said Hogan. "They always did have a direct line to the military. They have their own private army, doing their bidding. They used to square it with national leaders afterwards. Not that the leaders had any choice in the matter if they wanted to stay in power. And stay alive."

"Well, the good news is that we have the hydroponics working in the greenhouses outside," said David. "We can now control all of the input to our food crops and there should be no chance of accidental contamination."

"Yes, we have planted crops that should produce fruit and vegetables all through the year," added Chloe. "We will be self-sufficient even after the dried and canned food here run out."

"That's great news," said Calum. "Now, I just need to know that we have plenty of Brussels sprouts and potatoes to go with the nut roast for our Christmas dinner in three days' time."

"Oh, yes," said Chloe. "You won't go hungry. All the trimmings will be on your plate. Millie has it all in hand, eh Millie?"

"It is all under control," said Millie. "I will need some help with the peeling though," she smiled, looking at the youngsters.

"No worries," said James. "We're dab hands at peeling spuds now."

"In fact, you're beginning to look like a potato," laughed Joanna, dodging a paper ball thrown by her brother.

"Cheek," he said. "And don't think you're getting out of it, Missie."

Laughing the youngsters departed for the rec room. where they spent a lot of time these dark winter days.

Outside was too just too risky.

"Calum," began Joanna, as she ate her breakfast toast.

"Yes Jo," he said patiently, looking at her solemn face.

"You know that, in Gallanvaig, we always went and got a tree from the forest nearby for our Christmas tree?"

"Yes, sweetheart. You kids and Jessie used to spend hours making decorations and hanging them on the tree in the Manse."

Of course, this was the first Christmas for years that they had not spent in Gallanvaig. And this time without Jessie. He felt a sudden surge of unbearable grief and almost sobbed. He turned away quickly to the book he was reading, not wanting to upset Joanna.

"Well, do you think we will be able to find a nice tree around here?" she asked. "It wouldn't be the same without it. And we will all make decorations again. We left all our old ones behind in the loft at the Manse. And it's Christmas Eve tomorrow. We always put the tree up on Christmas Eve."

"I know sweetie," he said. "I'll have a word with Rob and a few of the others. See what we can come up with. We'll get you a tree, don't worry."

He gave her a hug. She looked so lost there, maybe also thinking about a Christmas without their beloved Jessie too.

Joanna rushed off to find the others and make a start on decorations.

"What about this area here?" said Rob, pointing at the map. "It's a national forestry area, just further up the coast. Shouldn't take us too long. We can take the trailer, get a nice big tree."

226

"Okay, we had better go today so the kids can decorate it tomorrow. I want to try and keep everything as normal as I can for them. They deserve a normal Christmas."

"Well, I can't go," said Millie. "I will be busy preparing this feast you demanded. I can lend you some guns though."

"Don't forget there may be drones around, looking for rebels who refuse to move to the towns," said David. "Not to mention dinos, wolves and big cats. Is it worth it just to get a tree?"

"I promised Joanna. Anyway, it's Christmas," said Calum, shrugging. He knew it was potentially dangerous, but they couldn't live out their lives life underground. They had to come out into the sun sometimes. Otherwise, what was the point?

Calum, Rob and David got the guns from Millie and set off up to the ground floor. Calum checked the CCTV on the way up and saw nothing unusual.

"Okay, all clear," he reported. They went through the farmhouse that formed the ground floor, hiding the military base below ground. The Jeep and trailer were in the barn opposite and they loaded axes and ammunition in the back.

Chloe came out to wave them off, leaning in the window to kiss David.

"Be careful out there," she called as they drove down the driveway.

"Won't be long hun'," called David. "Save us some lunch."

The drive along the coastal road was uneventful and the scenery was picturesque. The sea was a lovely coral blue and the mountains in the distance were outlined against a watery, winter blue sky. Soon they could see the tall firs and pines of the national forest park in the distance.

"I think we can find Joanna and the others a great tree in there," said Calum grinning, turning into the car park and looking for a forest track.

"There," said Rob, pointing. "It's a forestry workers' access route. Might be a bit bumpy, but the jeep should cope just fine."

Calum drove slowly onto the rough track and the jeep bumped along, disturbing birds and the odd squirrel along the way. He stopped in a clearing surrounded by several large fir trees.

"These would fit the bill nicely," he said.

They got out and unloaded the guns and axes.

"So, who's the tree-felling expert?" asked Rob, hefting an axe in his hands. "I've only ever trimmed a hedge in my garden."

The others laughed.

"I did a bit of tree felling on the farm," said David. "Here, let me."

Rob handed him the axe and they picked out a suitable tree. David took steady swings at its base with the axe.

"Should we be getting out of the way, lumberjack?" joked Calum. "This isn't gonna drop onto my head is it?"

"If you're just going to stand around mocking, at least go get me a cold drink," returned David. This was hot work even in the chill winter air. The axe was heavy and the strain of swinging it into the big tree was starting to make his arms ache.

The others wandered back to the jeep to open the cool box.

"This do you?" said Rob, holding up a can of beer.

"Looks wonderful," said David, swiping his arm across his forehead.

Then, he continued to strike the tree at the base, making a larger and larger cut. He reached the point where the centre of gravity was no longer going to allow the tree to stay upright and with a quick shove, he stepped back quickly.

"Timber!" he called.

The other two looked up from unloading the beer to see the large fir tree whump to the ground in a cloud of tree and forest debris.

"Hey, well done," said Calum. "You made that look easy."

"Hmm," said David, rubbing his arm muscles. "Not sure I want to apply for the full-time job though."

Laughing, Calum offered him a beer. "You have earned this," he said.

"Let's get it loaded first, then I would love a cold beer," said David.

Between them, the three of them dragged the tree onto the trailer and tied it securely on. Then, Rob got the beers and handed them around.

As they took long draughts of cool beer, there was a sound at the other side of the clearing and a disturbance in the trees. Calum put the beer down and picked up his gun, suddenly very alert to the potential dangers.

"Ssh," he motioned the others and indicating the far trees. They picked up their own guns, ready for whatever it was.

With a loud roar, the tree foliage parted and a large animal, about two metres tall and several metres long, ran towards them. It stood on two legs with two shorter forepaws held in front. Its tail was long and thick. But the scariest bit was its reptilian, crocodile-like head, which had two rows of sharp looking teeth. It growled again, Calum shouted "Run!"

All three of them rushed for the jeep, Calum and Rob got there first and flung open the doors. David reached the back door just as the animal did.

Calum frantically reached back and flung open the back door.

"Get in, quickly," he yelled.

But, David was blocked from the door by the animal, who stood between him and the jeep, its head on one side, teeth bared, staring at him. David took a step back and raised the gun.

That wasn't going to work; there was every chance he would hit the jeep, or one of the others at this range. He would just have to lead it away first.

His heart beating fast, he took another step back, then another. The animal looked puzzled, then took two quick steps forward, growling. It snapped its jaws at David, who then turned around and ran for his life.

As the animal ran after him, it was gaining on him by the second. Shit, it was fast thought Calum. He opened his door, grabbing his gun and Rob followed.

"David, climb the tree," yelled Rob, pointing.

David saw that it was his only chance; the animal would be on him in a minute. He reached the tree near the one he had just felled and jumped up, grabbing a branch. The animal arrived at the tree and jumped, snapping at his heels.

Calum took aim and shot at the animal. Rob followed it up with another shot, which hit home.

The animal roared horribly and continued to snap at David's heels. David's arms were aching. He was hanging onto the low-hanging branch for all his life. But, the earlier work had taken its toll and his arms were weakening. He was going to fall. That beast would be upon him, even wounded as it was.

Would the others be able to stop it?

Running towards the animal as it snapped at David, Calum fired another shot and the animal roared again, its leg buckling. But, it was determined, Calum gave it that. With its one good leg it continued to jump at the tree trying to reach David.

"David, pull yourself higher," shouted Rob.

"I can't," said David weakly, his grip nearly broken.

"Oh my God, he's going to fall right into its jaws," said Calum, picking up the axe lying by the fallen tree on the way.

Just as they reached the tree, David fell from the tree with a moan and Calum swung the axe at the animal, as it dived towards David.

He caught it on its scaly back, drawing blood just as it closed powerful jaws on David's arm.

David screamed in agony and Rob turned his gun around and hit the animal around the head a few times. It let go of David's arm and limped a few steps. Calum pointed his gun at it and pulled the trigger.

The animal fell straight down with a heavy thump as the bullet entered its head.

Calum and Rob ran to David's side and Calum looked at the wound. The teeth had pierced his jacket and shirt and there was blood oozing from several deep-looking teeth marks.

"Quick, get the first aid kit from the jeep," he said to Rob.

They cleaned the wound as best as they and applied a thick bandage. They helped David into the back of the jeep with Rob applying pressure to the wound to stop the bleeding.

"We need to get back and get the Doc to look at that," said Calum, starting the engine and hurtling off back up the uneven track, the jeep rocking from side to side.

"Careful," said Rob, being thrown from side to side. "I need to keep the pressure on this arm."

Calum slowed down a little and then drove as fast as he dared back to the bunker.

Doctors Ian MacDonald and Susan Brady had cleaned David's wound and set up an antibiotic drip. He was now sleeping, absolutely exhausted by his experience.

"You never know what bacteria these dinosaurs might be carrying," said Susan. "There might even be mutant bacteria, unknown to present-day science. In which case, the antibiotics might be ineffective."

"Thanks Doctor, just what we needed, mutant bacteria," growled Rob. "Surely antibiotics kill all bacteria?"

"No, there are some bacteria that are resistant to antibiotics," said Susan. "And if there was a virus, antibiotics cannot help."

"We just have to watch and wait," said Ian. "Hopefully, there will be no infection of the bite and if there is, the antibiotics will be effective."

"What if it isn't?" asked Chloe, looking on distraught.

"Then, we will need to try to identify what is causing the problem and research treatment methods. But, I must warn you, if it is a mutated virus or bacteria, there may be no known treatment for it."

Calum put his arm around Chloe as she paled and stared, panicking, at David.

"Come on, why don't you sit by David and keep an eye on him?" said Calum. "Let the doctors know if he awakes, then they can check on him."

She nodded.

He led her back to David's bedside.

"The next few days will be decisive," said Susan. "He may get symptoms at any time over a week or two. Then, we will should be able to tell whether an infection has taken hold of his body. Until then, we should let him rest."

As Calum and Rob left the treatment room, Joanna rushed towards Calum in tears. He put his arms around her.

"It's all my fault," she sobbed. "If I hadn't gone on and on about a Christmas tree, this wouldn't have happened. What will happen to him?"

"The doctors are treating him with antibiotics and keeping him under observation for a couple of weeks, sweetheart," said Calum. "I'm sure he will be okay. He's being taken good care of. And you mustn't blame yourself, it isn't your fault. It could have happened here on the farmland, or anywhere."

"But, it didn't, it happened when he was getting me that stupid tree," she wailed. "I don't even want to see it."

"Now, you know David would be upset if you didn't put that tree up, after him working so hard to cut it down for you and all. And the others have made all those decorations and lights. Come on honey, let's put it up together."

He led her down to the lounge where the tree was waiting to be wedged into a large holder and decorated.

Her sister and brother and Shaun were waiting in the lounge with their artwork and some of the other youngsters.

Rachel put her arm round her sister and James gave her a hug.

"Come on, Sis. You need to put the fairy on the top of the tree. Look, I gave it a sparkly dress and wings."

Joanne smiled weakly as she took the fairy. It had always been Jessie who made the fairy for the tree in

Gallanvaig. She thought that Jessie would want them to carry on the tradition.

Calum and Rob heaved the big tree upright and into the container and checked it was steady.

Joanne picked up a shiny, gold paper chain and began to drape it around the branches of the tree.

"That's my girl," said Calum. "Now, who wants hot chocolate?"

Later, Calum and Rob were describing the dinosaur that had attacked David to Gavin, Eamon and Tristan from Edinburgh University.

"I did my masters in Palaeontology," Eamon said. "Let me show you some pictures of dinosaurs and see if you can pick yours out of a line-up."

"Well, it was certainly the perpetrator of bodily harm to David," said Rob. "Though I guess I shouldn't joke when we don't know if he will be okay."

Eamon fetched his reference books from his room.

"You reckon it was around your height, Rob? About six feet, two meters tall?"

Rob nodded. "It stood on its back legs and had two short front paws."

"And how long overall? You said its tail was long and thick?"

"I reckon it was around ten to fifteen feet long, say four metres," said Calum. "Big teeth in a long jaw. An evil-looking thing. And boy, could it move."

"Since it attacked and bit David, we can assume it's a carnivore. It is likely to be one of the dinosaurs historically found in the United Kingdom, where the relevant gene pool would still exist," said Eamon.

He flicked through the book and then turned it around.

"Was it this one?" he asked showing a picture. "This is a Proceratosaurus, thought to be around four metres long."

"It could be," said Calum "What do you think, Rob?"

"It looks quite like it. But, the jaw is wrong."

"How about this one, the Sarcosaurus? A bit smaller, it would have been about three metres long."

"I think its jaw was longer and flatter," said Rob. "And this is definitely smaller than ours."

"This is the only other one that fits the bill then," said Eamon, turning the book around at a new page. "The Eotyrannus. It would be four to five meters long. It may have had feathers on its head and tail."

"That's *it*," said Calum. "What does this mean?"

"Well, the reverse evolution, or devolution that was triggered off by the genetically modified transgenes in the food supply and which Gavin has linked to the Jinn or Genies reappearing from the human gene pool, appears to be progressing fast. We have seen some devolution of small birds to raptor-like creatures with teeth, like pterodactyl and the bird we discovered when we arrived here. Also, some larger animals like cattle have regressed to primitive forms, like the Aurochs. Dogs have regressed to wolves and domestic cats to wild cats and lions. But, we have seen nothing that has regressed this far back yet. Ordinary wild birds becoming birds with teeth isn't such a huge leap in devolution as that of birds to reptilian dinosaurs, like the Eotyrannus. The process of devolution is speeding up enormously. The GM material is continuing to mutate and affect the DNA in every living thing. We don't know where this might end. I fear it means we may one day see the return of species like the Tyrannosaurus Rex."

"You're joking," said Rob. "How are we supposed to co-exist with beasts like that? They would annihilate us."

"I'm afraid they just might," said Eamon.

Max Kaufman was enjoying the role he had taken over from his sister Liese, though it was a shame the way she died in the earthquake and resulting flood caused by the Jinn. Together with taking over her role as head of the Kaufman banking dynasty, the power he could now wield and the respect which he was shown were very gratifying. He particularly enjoyed the control he had with the rest of the Elite over the world's population and their lives. Today was going to be especially rewarding with their planned celebration of the eradication of the contaminated GM land and waters. And it was Yule, always a special time for the Elite.

He put his skis away in the lodge hallway cupboard and went to join the others. Going down into the cool basement, he could hear the others already gathering, talking and laughing. Reaching the stone-walled cellars, he grabbed his robes from the rail.

Thick wax candles guttered in wall sconces, not quite chasing away the shadows. The drummers were already starting a rhythmic beat as they all donned their robes. Then, the ceremonial assistant entered, carrying something wrapped in sacking. Something that was moving and squealing.

The Elite fell silent, then commenced their ceremonial dance around the small bundle on the central table, their eerie chants and the drumbeats bouncing off the stone walls. Shadows moved around the extremes of the room and monstrous creatures with animal heads and humanoid bodies seemed to lurk there. Deep growls and howling added to the dark atmosphere of the cellars.

237

Then, the chanting stopped, the hooded, robed figures came to stand around the altar and a dagger was handed to Max. He was still relatively uninitiated in the ceremonies of the Elite and he was tasked, together with the other newer members of the Elite with taking a lead role in a certain number of the sacrifices before he could become a full member. He didn't mind that, he quite enjoyed it.

He looked upon the struggling bundle and raised the dagger high, saying the sacred words. Then, he thrust the dagger downwards with force and a dark red liquid oozed from the bundle. The mewling ceased after a few seconds and Max handed the bundle back to the assistant to be prepared.

The celebrants then moved up the stairs into the upper lounge, shedding their robes on the way and convivial conversation resumed.

"Did you do the Grubigstein ski run today, Max?" asked Vanderbilt.

"Yes, the weather was favourable. I managed a decent run down," answered Max. "Did you go hunting?"

"Yes, we got a couple of boars and a deer," replied Vanderbilt. "The chef is preparing those for New Year. Will you be joining the shooting party on Boxing Day?"

"Of course," said Kaufman. "I am looking forward to it."

They took seats in the lounge with the others and the waiters circulated with metal chalices containing the thick, red liquid that would sustain them. Then, they brought the finest wines and aperitifs before dinner.

"So, we celebrate the successful elimination of the GM contamination and the end to this morphing of animals back to dinosaurs," said Goldsmith, holding up his glass.

"Prost," said Max draining his glass.

"Saluti," said Fabbiana.

"And cheers to you all," said Vanderbilt.

The waiter came in to call them to dinner and they all went through to the dining room. It had been a good trip so far.

And they had sorted this problem with the GM once and for all.

Balthazar and his band came up out of the underground military base at Dulce, New Mexico to a scene of apocalyptic destruction. The ground was scorched to ashes, all their crops were destroyed. No signs of life could be seen. Balthazar angrily shook his head.

"They will pay for this," he vowed. "They have destroyed too many of our homes now."

"Yes, Master," said Nicholas. "We will make them pay. But, where do we grow our crops and keep our animals now? Everything is gone."

"Send Inola, Nashoba, Megedagik and Shappa to scout for good land where we can make a settlement," said Balthazar. "They are good at that. We will start over. The rest of us will go out and take our revenge."

The four native Americans teleported off to find new land. Balthazar and the rest of his elite prepared to take revenge on their enemies, who had once more driven them from their land.

They pulled their hoods over their heads and closing their eyes, they saw in their minds exactly where their enemies were. Then, they teleported to the place, invisible to human eyes. They were instantly standing outside a lodge, surrounded by snow-covered mountains.

"Master, what do we do if they should change shape again?" asked Nicholas. "They may all be able to become the big lizards."

"They are no match for us. Now that we know what they are, we can fight them with our powers," said Balthazar. "Now focus on their destruction," he said.

Pointing his hand at the lodge, he closed his eyes and a spark of flame flew from the ends of his fingers, then it became an inferno as it struck the wooden, flower-laden balcony of the lodge.

The others followed his example and they called up quakes and the mountains shook as rocks came tumbling down. As the power of the quake grew, the deep snow on the slopes started to cascade down the mountain side with a thundering roar, clouds of snow flying up into the air. Rocks and snow collided with the walls of the lodge and Balthazar and his band flew straight up into the air, as the walls started to collapse. The flames had taken hold and were now licking at the inside furniture.

The doors flew open and a crowd of people ran out.

"What the hell is going on?" shouted Vanderbilt over the noise of the tumbling rocks and snow.

"Avalanche," shouted Kaufman.

"Where are the flames coming from?" yelled Goldsmith. "Get your staff to go back in with fire extinguishers."

Kaufman turned to his housekeeper.

"Sort it out," he barked. The man and his staff ran back into the lodge, grabbing the fire extinguishers from the hallway.

"It smells like a Jinn attack. And we need to find shelter," yelled Vanderbilt, just as a huge rock bounced down from the mountain and hit him in the back, knocking him flat.

Goldsmith and Kaufman hauled him up and the group ran towards the village. Maybe there would be shelter there.

There was a huge roar of maniacal laughter from many voices in the skies above them. Enemy eyes watched the party as they made their way to the village.

They would not escape.

As the party ran along the road to the village, rocks bounced down from the mountainside all around them and thick blankets of snow scudded down the mountainside in an unstoppable avalanche, engulfing the path ahead. Goldsmith and Kaufman dragged Vanderbilt, who was unconscious, off the road and into a roadside stone barn, normally used for cattle and winter silage. It looked sturdy enough.

"In here," called Goldsmith to the party ahead, who had stopped and were trying to work out a way around the deepening snow.

They all headed for the barn and huddled inside. Most of them were without coats and it was freezing cold.

How long would they last here? They were vulnerable to further attacks by the Jinn and risked hypothermia in the alpine winter temperatures, especially overnight.

Then, they had another problem, as there was a blood-curdling growl and a huge shape appeared from the gloom of the barn's shadows.

Bishop Sebastian donned the gold robe that he always wore for the Christmas celebration masses.

Christmas Eve midnight mass was one of his favourite occasions, the candlelight, the procession with the baby to the crib, the shining faces of the little children, the anticipation of the adults for the feasting the next day.

He sipped his sherry before going through the passageway between the farmhouse and the little chapel in the farm grounds. It would have been used by the farmer, the family and the farmhands for masses on Sundays, the village church being too far away.

He met one of his priests, Father Zacharias Garnier, in the chapel doorway. Zacharius was carrying the statue of the baby and half a dozen altar boys carried candles in large brass candlesticks.

"Are we ready?" asked Bishop Sebastian with a smile.

"Everything is prepared," said Zacharius.

The Bishop moved into place in the procession and they walked into the chapel and along the aisle to the crib at the front.

The congregation stood up as they saw the Bishop's procession. They began to sing a Christmas carol 'Once in Royal David's City.'

The Bishop placed the baby in the crib next to Joseph and Mary and knelt to say a prayer with the congregation.

Then, the mass began. The congregation joined in with prayers and singing. There was a joyful atmosphere.

Soon, it was time for the Bishop to make his sermon. Usually, it was light-hearted and joyful over the Christmas season.

But, today was different. There wasn't much to be joyful about. Not with the devastation of the earth, poisoning of the land and waters and the return of mighty dinosaurs due to human stupidity.

"Brothers and sisters. Welcome to our celebration of the birth of Our Lord Jesus Christ, here in our little chapel. This is an important feast day in the church calendar, a day when we welcome the arrival of the baby Jesus into the stable at Bethlehem. A saviour for the world, who will enable forgiveness of our sins by his later death on a cross. But, this year, things are a little different. Due to human failings, the earth has been devastated. Evil forces are at work, manipulating the governments and institutions. Corruption and greed are everywhere. And for simple families, there is only hardship and suffering. There will be no big feasts tomorrow here or in many other ordinary family homes this year. Food is scarce and what there is will be very simple fare indeed. There will be no expensive presents underneath the tree. The earth is again being walked by monstrous dinosaurs and haunted by evil Jinn. No, there is little to celebrate. And yet, we know from the Revelation of Saint John that there is hope. There will be a small band of people of the light, who will survive these hardships. For, he said that although the earth would be scorched by fires, the people sick from plagues and the waters poisoned and the old earth and heaven destroyed, there was a future. He said, 'I saw a new heaven and a new earth, for the first heaven and the first earth had passed away and the sea was no more.' And again, he said, 'neither shall there be mourning, nor crying, nor pain any more for the former things have passed away.' So, my brethren did Saint John prophesy a new world, where people would be judged on what they did in their lives. The good people of light will live in the new heaven and earth with God and the evil ones will be banished for ever. So, I say to you, live a good life, for we have little time left. We have seen the signs and we should look forward to eternal life with God.

243

Very soon now, my brethren. This is the Word of Saint John."

"Alleluia, amen!" answered the congregation.

The dinosaur was big and powerful-looking, with a long body and thickly-muscled back legs that propelled it forwards and smaller front legs. Its jaws were long and rounded at the end. Its back was mottled, and it emitted a weird sort of growling sound.

Kaufman grabbed the only weapon he could see, a log from a pile which was chopped ready for the winter fires. He brandished it at the animal and it backed away a little, still growling.

"Grab Vanderbilt, we need to get out of here," he hissed to the others.

Vanderbilt was still lying against the wall where they had placed him. As Gaj Kapur and Marcel Chan grabbed him and started to drag him towards the barn door, he stirred and flailed around. As he hit out at what he thought were enemies who had attacked him, he became agitated and instantaneously, his face began to change. The long snout of a reptilian appeared and his whole body elongated and became scaly with a long tail. He growled back at the dinosaur and rushed towards it.

"Vanderbilt, you were warned about your public displays," began Marta angrily. "Come on we need to get out of here."

But, Vanderbilt's rage was not extinguished. He continued advancing on the animal which started to look panicky in the confined space, as Vanderbilt snapped at it with his huge jaws, his powerful lower limbs carrying him swiftly towards the dinosaur.

The dinosaur made an odd yelping sound and fled towards the open door, brushing past Kaufman and Chan.

Vanderbilt uttered a throaty, victorious laugh as he morphed back into human form.

"Vanderbilt, you should know better than to change in a public place," scolded Marta. "You have already presented us with problems recently. We don't want to have to do any more damage limitation. People will really start to get suspicious."

"Yes, yes, my dear," crooned Vanderbilt. "I get the message. But, did you expect me to just sit there and let our dino friend eat you all?"

"I don't think it was ever going to do that," said Kaufman. "I was into dinosaurs in a big way when I was a kid. I knew all about the different ones, especially those that once walked our beautiful land of Austria. There were only ever two species found here and if this is from the local gene pool mutated backwards, then it must be either Rhabdodon or Struthiosaurus. Both were herbivores. From its markings and size, I would say it was a Rhabdodon. So, it wouldn't have done you much damage, maybe stepped on your toes, or breathed grass in your face, or something."

He started to laugh.

Vanderbilt stared at Kaufman, a junior member of this very Elite club. He was angry at being challenged and made to look a fool. His face and limbs began to elongate once more.

"Vanderbilt, no," shouted Marta.

With an angry growl, Vanderbilt snapped back into his human form. Kaufman was an irritating little man, but it would wait.

He would get him one day.

"So, what's the plan?" asked Chan. "We can't stay here, we must find proper cover somewhere."

"I'm calling my back-up team to bring the helicopter," said Goldman. "They will get us back to safety. We can go to my place in Cornwall, Conneaux Castle. It is well-fortified."

There was a noise from outside and Kaufman went to the door.

The dino was long gone, but, standing outside was Balthazar and several of his cohorts.

"Hello, Kaufman," said Balthazar. "You look so much like your sister. Pity about what happened to her, in that earthquake and all."

"You leave my sister out of this," snarled Kaufman, striding towards the group.

Balthazar moved his head from side to side then straight forward and a bolt of lightning emanated from the top of his head and flew at Kaufman. Kaufman was struck and collapsed, clutching his chest.

Hearing the commotion, the others ran out of the barn.

"So, we meet at last," sneered Balthazar. "You aren't so scary in real life, I don't think. You have caused us some inconvenience at our home in America."

The Native Americans around him nodded and muttered in agreement.

Vanderbilt saw who it was and immediately became angry at their recent attack on his castle in Zurich. His eyes became totally black and he became a long-limbed, snapping-jawed reptile once more, advancing on Balthazar. Balthazar lifted his arm and pointed at Vanderbilt. A huge flame flew from his fingers and hit Vanderbilt, who snapped back to human form in shock and dropped to his knees crying in pain.

Laughing, Balthazar and his band lifted into the air and became invisible, as they teleported away.

They would deal with the rest later. It would keep.

Calum was up early on Christmas morning. It would be a busy day and he wanted to check how David was doing in the sick bay. Susan and Chloe were with him and he was sitting up in bed.

"Happy Christmas mate," said Calum. "How are you feeling?"

"I'm okay, now that my arm has been stitched up," he said. "Hurts a bit, but Dr Susan here says there seems to be no infection."

"Well, we are keeping him on antibiotics, just in case. And he had a tetanus injection too," said Susan.

"He's not a very good patient," said Chloe. "Keeps insisting he wants to get out of bed and back to work. Just take the opportunity for a rest, it's Christmas Day after all."

"Well, if you're good, maybe Susan will let you out in time for Christmas dinner," said Calum, grinning.

He went off to find the others in the big lounge. Although it was still early, most people were up, excited at the prospect of Christmas Day celebrations. Under the large tree, presents were heaped up and people were excitedly opening them.

"Happy Christmas, sweetheart," said Calum, handing Joanna a parcel from his pile under the tree. "It's not much, but it's the thought that counts, right?"

"Thank you, Calum."

She tore open the paper and exclaimed when she saw what it was.

It was one of Jessie's favourite necklaces.

"Calum, this is beautiful! But, it was *Jessie's*. Are you sure?"

"Yes, there's no point holding onto all her jewellery. You may as well get some pleasure from wearing it sweetie. She would have wanted you and the others to have something of hers, I'm sure."

"Here, fasten it for me please."

She turned around then as Calum did the clasp, turned around her eyes shining. "Thank you so much for this and for everything you and Jessie have done for us. You know, taking us in and everything when we were living rough in the Lake District. We never really thanked you properly, we were just kids."

Tears sprang to Calum's eyes. He was fond of these kids and so was Jessie. Or she had been, he thought correcting himself.

"You're very welcome. It's been a pleasure looking after you all. Though I can't say the same for James and Shaun when they start with their terrible jokes." He grinned at the lads and they knew he was only joking, pretending to punch them as they dodged, laughing.

"At least our jokes are better than yours, Calum," said Shaun.

"Yeah, at least ours are, like, funny," added James.

"Matter of opinion, mate," said Calum. "Here you are, happy Christmas, you two, hope you like these. And good morning, Rachel, sweetheart. Here's your present, happy Christmas."

The lads opened their parcels to find books and video games.

"Ah, thanks Calum, that's great," said James, giving Calum a hug.

"Yeah, thanks Calum, this will keep us busy after that big lunch Millie is making," said Shaun.

"Well, I think you lot are helping her," said Calum. "There's lots of vegetables to peel, you know."

"Yeah, yeah, we know," said James, pulling a face.

"No worries," said Shaun.

Rachel opened her present to find one of Jessie's silver bracelets.

"Oh, Calum, are you sure? This is one of Jessie's favourites."

"Well, I'm sure she would want you to have it then," said Calum. "It's no use to anyone sitting in a box in the cupboard is it? Enjoy it sweetheart."

Rachel gave him a big hug.

"Here's your present," she said handing him a brightly wrapped parcel with shiny bows.

"Wow, good gift wrapping," he said impressed.

There was a handmade printed bandana from Rachel and a home-made friendship bracelet from Joanna.

The boys had bought him bottles of whisky and wine.

"Thanks guys, I will enjoy a glass of the whisky later. And these are beautiful," he said to Rachel and Joanna. "It must have taken you hours to make them."

He gave them all a hug.

Douglas McDunne, his wife Annie, son Jamie and his partner Yasmin came in, wishing everyone a merry Christmas.

"Is everyone here," asked Douglas. "Shall we start?"

Douglas had been a lay deacon when he ran the farm outside Edinburgh and he always led a Christmas Day service.

"Yes, I think everyone's here now," said Calum. "Thanks Douglas."

Douglas stood by the big fireplace, with its blazing fire of local logs that the kids had collected in the week before Christmas.

Douglas said the opening prayers and then gave a couple of readings about the story of Christ's birth in

Bethlehem, in the stable among the cattle and shepherds. Then, they all joined in a Christmas carol, Calum playing his guitar and the kids singing lustily.

The kids really enjoyed Christmas, thought Calum. They must have some good memories from their childhood. He remembered many wonderful, snowy Christmases with his parents and siblings in Dublin. And the singing and the feasting after the Christmas morning mass and the games they played after lunch. And more recently, the times he had with Jessie, the love of his life. His eyes filled with tears as he sang one of favourite carols, one she had loved and always enthusiastically joined in with.

Watching him, Chloe gave him a quick hug.

"I miss her too," she whispered.

Then, the service ended with a blessing from Douglas.

"Happy Christmas everyone," he cried. "Is it too early for sherry?"

Everyone laughed.

"Well, I am having one anyway," he said. "Annie?"

"Oh, yes please, dear. I always have a sherry on Christmas morning."

"Now, who's for a quick walk in the snow before lunch?" said Calum. "We should be safe if we keep within the farm grounds and take the guns."

What had it come to, he thought to himself, having to take weapons on such a wonderful, festive day, one that should be full of hope and peace.

They all bustled about collecting coats and scarves. The walking party went outside, wrapped up warmly. It was quite cold now, the east coast winds blowing the snow into their faces.

Calum and Rob walked at the front with guns at the ready and David and Chloe were at the back. They must be vigilant for wild animals and drones, thought Calum, as they strolled around the farm boundary and the surrounding meadows and footpaths.

But, the walk passed by undisturbed and they arrived back at the farmhouse, rosy-cheeked and ready for lunch.

"I guess it was too cold for the dinos," said James as they warmed themselves by the fire.

"Yeah, perhaps they don't like the snow?" said Shaun.

"Well that's a good thing for us then, isn't it?" said Chloe. "It gave us a nice peaceful walk. No sign of the drones either."

"Maybe our reptilian friends are too busy celebrating," said Calum.

"They don't really celebrate Christmas, not as we do anyway," said Hogan. "They all used to disappear down to the cellars of whatever mansion we were staying in. No idea what they used to get up to down there. But, we did hear drums and singing, or chanting sometimes. Weird. We on the staff had our own Christmas party. We were happy enough, plenty of food and drink were provided for us."

"I don't suppose they would be followers of any earth-based religion, anyway," said Rob. "Not if they came from another planet. Maybe they worship the Great Alligator in the Sky, or something."

Everybody laughed.

"I can't believe you have changed your views on aliens and reptilian shapeshifters so quickly," said Calum to his old friend. "You were always the most sceptical one."

252

"Yes, well, there have been lots of strange things happening in the past two or three years. It's the only thing that makes any sense to me."

Douglas had handed around the sherry and everyone was soon feeling very festive.

"Hey, kids, I need you now," said Millie, grinning as she poked her head around the doorway to the large lounge. "Time for some spud bashing."

With a collective groan, the four kids got up and followed Millie to the kitchen.

Laughing, Douglas topped up everyone's glass.

"Despite everything, it's a great Christmas," he said. "I mean, we're all together, we have food and shelter. And even sherry," he added, brandishing the bottle then filling up his own glass.

"Wonder if the reptiles are enjoying Christmas?" said Calum. "After all, they have lots of money, food and beautiful properties to spend it in."

"Who knows?" said Hogan. "They were never really happy unless someone else was suffering somewhere. Usually at their own hands. Nasty bunch."

"Oh, well, let's not think about them now," said Chloe. "Plenty of time to worry about them after Christmas. Let's just enjoy the celebration together."

The talk turned to Christmases past and plans for the day's traditional celebrations.

Why worry about the reptiles when they were so far away in Zurich?

The helicopter circled around above the field next to the stone barn in Lermoos. Then, as it landed, Goldman led the others towards it and the haven of his security team. All aboard, they headed for Goldman's summer home in Cornwall.

253

Balthazar watched remotely. He could see them as they flew through the sky and he could see that Vanderbilt and Kaufman were with them. So, he hadn't finished them off then. That would have to be put right. And he saw exactly where they went.

Oh yes, his enemies would finally be eliminated. Soon.

The butler opened the front door as the helicopter landed on the north lawn. Goldman climbed out and led the others to his summer home, Conneaux Castle. It was a lovely old place, a stone castle, with battlements and an outdoor swimming pool. He loved being here, usually on a summer break. Not so often at Christmas time, though. But, his Surrey mansion, Warbeck Hall, where they usually spent Christmas, still hadn't been rebuilt after the fire, so this would be his year-round home for a while.

"Johnson, hello, happy Christmas" he greeted the butler. "Will you make sure we have rooms ready for all my guests here? They will be staying over Christmas and New Year. A last-minute thing. Our accommodation in the Alps had a problem."

"Of course, we are just finishing getting the rooms ready now. We already started work, after getting your call. Meanwhile, I'm sure your guests would like Christmas dinner? I understand that you didn't have time to dine in Lermoos?"

"No, we didn't and that would be great," replied Goldman, leading his party into the castle and into the drawing room, where the staff could serve aperitifs before dinner. The staff bustled out, fetching what luggage had been grabbed into the castle and delivering it to the spacious bedrooms.

This was perfect thought Goldman. He could control events here more easily than at Lermoos. No unexpected visitors here, with the security team in residence.

He might even be able to arrange a shoot for Boxing Day.

"This place is beautiful," said Vanderbilt, rubbing his chest, which was still sore from the burns inflicted by Balthazar and company. "You should invite us down here more often."

"I will be doing so," said Goldman. "As long as my Surrey residence is being repaired after that awful fire. Now, who's for canapés? How are you feeling now Kaufman?"

"I'm okay, a bit sore where that thunderbolt hit me. There's a nasty blister developing there."

The staff brought in drinks and handed around the snacks.

This was better, thought Vanderbilt. He could enjoy Christmas here.

Balthazar gazed at the remote site in his mind's eye.

His enemies certainly had some fantastic houses. But, it wouldn't protect them. Oh, no.

"Let's go," he said to his band of Jinn.

As one, they lifted into the air and moved silently across thousands of miles in mere seconds.

The Christmas dinner table was loaded with good food and the friends all sat around, happily chatting and laughing. David had managed to persuade Susan that he was fit to join in and he arrived with Chloe, to Joanna's delight, who rushed over to give him a hug.

"Uncle David, I'm so sorry you got hurt just because I insisted on having a real tree."

"Think nothing of it, sweetheart. Just one of life's hazards these days. Anyway, it was only a scratch. I'm okay. Just don't send me out for Easter eggs."

Joanna giggled., as David ruffled her hair.

"Millie, you have really excelled yourself today," said Calum. "This is all delicious."

"Well, I did have some help from these four," she replied, indicating the four youngsters. "And Ellie, Mick and Shelley helped too."

Ellie and Mick had run the Harbour Inn in Gallanvaig and were used to providing pub meals every day. Shelley, their daughter, was a friend of Joanna.

"Oh, you were the head chef," protested Ellie. "We were just the kitchen hands."

"And we only peeled a few spuds," said Rachel.

"A very important job," said James. "These roast potatoes wouldn't have been half as delicious without us."

"Oh, James, you need to get over yourself," said Joanna sternly. "Millie did all the clever stuff."

Everybody laughed.

"Well, it all tastes better for being a team effort," said Chloe. "Now, if nobody minds, I think I will just go and have a nap. This one is kicking like mad," she added rubbing her stomach. She was huge now.

"Of course, you go," said Calum. "You've got precious cargo on board."

David helped Chloe upstairs. There would hopefully be a new member of their little community in the New Year.

After the clearing up of the remains of the meal, everyone gathered around the Christmas tree, as was their tradition. Games of charades followed. Then,

Calum fetched his guitar and there were several rounds of favourite Christmas songs and carols, each person taking turns to pick a song and lead the singing.

Calum finished off the evening with a rousing chorus of "Merry Christmas Everyone" with lots of giggling. But, one line struck home with Calum.

'Look to the future now, it's only just begun.'

But, what *did* the future hold for them in this corrupted paradise? With reptilian monsters running the world and mutant Jinn and dinosaurs roaming the earth?

And without his lovely Jessie by his side.

Balthazar landed outside Conneaux castle with his followers. They had multiplied themselves using their power of multi-location that enabled them to manifest in different places at the same time. There was another party of Jinn by the gates and another on the battlements of the castle. Yet another two groups hovered over the castle ready to unleash an attack.

The voices of many Balthazars boomed around the castle.

"Goldman! I order you to come and face your enemy! Come outside, *now*."

The echoes of the voices bounced around the castle walls, creating a strange turbulence and an odd timbre to his words.

The castle doors opened, Goldman appeared, shielded by security staff.

"What do you want?" he cried. "Go away. Get off my property."

There was a multitudinous chorus of mocking laughter from the Jinn, that turned even Goldman's reptilian blood cold. Goldman's mouth fell open and he rushed back inside. His staff closed and bolted the doors.

Inside they readied themselves for a battle. Goldman had fought many battles in his time, but never one quite like this.

Balthazar and his horde of robed clones then disappeared at a signal from him.

They reappeared in the castle entrance hall, right beside Goldman and his staff and his band of Elite, who were all grabbing guns and missile launchers.

"Naughty boy," exclaimed Balthazar. "That was plain *rude*, closing the door in our faces. Well, I think it's time you learned some manners, eh friends?"

The Jinn muttered agreement and spread out and surrounded the party in the castle.

Battle commenced.

Missiles blasted holes in the castle walls, as the Elite tried to destroy the Jinn. The Jinn replied with thunderbolts and flames, their hands moving so fast, that it seemed like the worst thunderstorm that Goldman had ever seen. Balls of flame bounced around the hallway, hitting several of the castle party. The Jinn moved so fast that the bullets and missiles were doing more damage to the fabric of the castle than to them.

Angrily, the Elite started to snap into their reptilian shapes, snapping and clawing at the Jinn.

The Elite's growls of anger and frustration at the Jinns' ability to produce fire and thunder, whilst dodging every missile fired their way, resounded around the castle hallway. Goldman was becoming more and more angry. But, with the multi-location of the Jinn, the Elite were outnumbered.

"Retreat!" called Goldman, and the Elite started to fall back towards the inner hallway leading to the main part of the castle. They had to escape. The security staff moved into place between the retreating Elite and the Jinn.

However, they were no match for the Jinn, even with all the firepower at their disposal. But, it gave the Elite space to escape into the inner castle. Meanwhile, those they had left behind in the hallway to fight their battle were gradually overcome, until all lay dead or grievously injured.

"We have unfinished business," growled Balthazar. "This way, my friends."

He led the way into the inner castle and there was now no resistance. There was no sign of the Elite. But, Balthazar could smell them. Oh, yes.

They moved along the wide internal corridors, past works of art and stag's heads. Then, as sure as a tracker dog, Balthazar went straight towards his prey.

The Elite had taken refuge in a large annexe to the castle, connected to it through a glass-roofed corridor. This was obviously a later addition to the castle and was out of character. They reached the end of the corridor and Balthazar turned the handle on the connecting door.

Locked.

Roaring with anger, he directed a bolt of fire straight at the door. The thick oak door erupted in flames and Balthazar kicked it open, as the lock parted from the burning wood.

Inside the Elite were staring to panic. Never had they faced an opponent that posed them so much of a threat. Humans were so weak, and they preferred a one-sided fight. But, these mutants were something else.

Damn those bloody scientists at Novagentech, unleashing this on them.

Goldman opened the exit door onto the garden at the other end of the annexe and they all rushed out into the manicured gardens set out with fountains and ponds.

To face a horde of Jinn who had appeared directly in from of them.

"We meet again," sneered Balthazar.

He thrust out a hand and directed a bolt of fire at Vanderbilt. Vanderbilt, already weakened by the earlier attack, fell to the ground, his shirt on fire. Kaufman rushed forward to help him. But, Nicholas and his clones moved to stand directly in front of the blazing figure.

"No, you don't," he sneered, throwing a forcefield around Vanderbilt and then a bolt of fire at Kaufman. Kaufman yelped in pain as his clothing started to burn.

Goldman and the others tried to make a run for it, but the clones moved to block their every escape attempt. Frustrated, the Elite snapped into their reptilian form. Goldman snapped his huge jaws at one of the clones, who moved aside, but he was caught off balance and he fell to the ground. Goldman leapt on the clone and started to tear at his throat.

Balthazar let out a furious cry of rage and directed a bolt of energy at Goldman, which hit him on the scaly back and caused him to spring up and away from the clone. The clone, however, did not move.

"How dare you kill one of my own?" stormed Balthazar. "You will pay for this."

Balthazar was ready for a fight to the death and sent another fire bolt at Goldman. This time, it hit him. His reptile form roared in rage as his clothes caught light and his skin started to burn.

The clones and the Jinn together moved to take revenge on the one who had killed one of their number.

This time he would not escape.

As huge flames rose up from the prone body of Goldman, the rest of them made a bid for escape, whilst the attention of their attackers was elsewhere. They made for the helicopter which was still on the north lawn, its pilot aboard, anticipating the need for a quick escape.

As they approached the 'copter, Balthazar suddenly roared as he noticed their flight.

"Oh, no, you don't," he growled, teleporting to a position directly behind the group and throwing fire at them. It caught the rear group of two Elite, Marcel Chan and Katsu Mori, who fell to the ground in agony.

The remaining five had already jumped into the 'copter and it was already taking off. As it rose into the air, Balthazar directed a thunder bolt at it, but in his fury at their escape, he missed and the 'copter rose safely into the air.

"No matter," sneered Balthazar. "I will find you. Once we have made sure no one here survives."

Turning back to his Jinn and clones, they went around the garden checking that all were eliminated.

Nobody was left alive once the Jinn teleported out of Cornwall.

But, Balthazar felt tired.

His concentration lapsing, his clones snapped out of existence, one by one. The same was happening to his fellow Jinn, until only they remained.

Why was he so tired?

The five survivors looked shakily around at each other. How had such a catastrophe happened? They were invincible, surely? They had ruled the people of Earth for many thousands of years. How had it come to this? Half of their leaders lost. Some of them within only weeks of reaching Master status.

Gaj Kapur, Corinne Moreau, Marta Petrov, Ricardo Fabbiana and Rosa Araripe were the only survivors. Gaj, Corrine and Rosa were inexperienced in the ways of the control and manipulation of humanity. The other three were overwhelmed by their situation. They didn't even have the heart to start the succession process. What was the point?

"What do we do now?" said Gaj. "Where do we go? Those Jinn, they know *everything* about us. What we are, where we came from, where we go. Even the common human population are spreading rumours about our nature. Although there isn't much *they* can do about it. The Jinn, though; they are a different matter."

"We have to sort this out," said Riccardo. "There must be a way. We have always prevailed. We will overcome them."

"But how?" asked Gaj. "Those monsters have powers. We just have guns and missiles. They don't seem to be able to harm the Jinn."

"Well, we killed one of their clones, didn't we?" said Riccardo. "We did it in our reptilian form. So, we can use that again against them."

"But, we can only do that at close quarters," said Corinne. "We need to evade their fire and thunder long enough to get close enough to attack them. It just doesn't seem like a strategy that's all."

The pilot flicked the communications switch to the passenger compartment.

"So, where do you want to go?" he asked.

"Let's go to my place in St Petersburg," said Marta. "I have many vicious security guards. The Jinn won't find it easy to get past them. We can set up a protective, fireproof cordon around the palace. Then, we take refuge in the cellars. There is plenty of food and wine down there. And other things to entertain us," she added smirking.

The others laughed cruelly, their spirits already bolstered by the strong Russian woman's plan.

What could go wrong?

44. Boxing Day

Balthazar and his followers had arrived back late on Christmas Day at the underground Dulce military base in New Mexico. They were exhausted and slept for many hours.

Balthazar woke and shook his head. His brain seemed fogged, he couldn't seem to think straight. What was wrong with him?

He got up and went to find his followers. Nicholas was sitting in the canteen nursing a cup of coffee and looking terrible.

"What's wrong with *you*?" asked Balthazar.

"I don't know. I feel terrible," said Nicholas. "You don't look so good yourself."

"I'm not feeling great. But, we had a good day yesterday didn't we, wiping out half our enemies at one fell swoop? And we will get the rest of them soon."

"Yes, I know we will. But, not today eh? I really need to rest. I don't think I'd be up to teleporting and creating fireballs today."

"Okay, it will wait," said Balthazar, secretly pleased that he had an excuse to delay doing anything until he felt better himself, not wanting to admit to any weakness. "We know where to find them."

Two of the local people they had captured and kept as slaves came in with breakfast. Oh well, today could just be a rest day. After all, it *was* Boxing Day, thought Balthazar.

The Elite met for breakfast in Marta's palace dining room. It was a sumptuous feast, the table loaded with fine meats, cheeses, coffee, fruit and bread. They felt a bit better now they had rested, but the loss of five of their number had hit them hard.

"I think we should carry on as usual today. Enjoy Boxing Day hunting and feasting, just as normal," said Marta. "Then, after the Christmas break we can consider what to do next about succession planning. Okay, so we have lost five of our number, but we have destroyed the GM-contaminated land and purified the waters, so there should be no more mutations."

"Yes, we have," said Gaj. "But, though I don't want to put a damper on things, we still have to cope with those that are already here. The dinosaurs, the devolved wild animals, the Jinn. What do we do about those?"

"The Jinn will come to us when they are ready for another fight. We just need to be ready this time. I vote we send out military scouts to locate the main herds of dangerous beasts and then destroy them with nuclear missiles. That way, no genetic material will remain to cause us any problems."

"What if those areas contain people?" asked Corinne.

"What if they do?" said Marta. "That's not our problem. And if this planet continues to present problems, we'll cut our losses and go somewhere else. We still have the ships. They have been maintained and flown regularly over the years. And caused lots of human rumours about UFOs in the process," she added smiling.

"So, are we sure they are fit to go back into space?" asked Fabbiana.

"I will check with our technical team, but as far as I know, yes, that shouldn't be a problem," replied Marta. "Now, how about we start the morning with our traditional Boxing Day hunt?"

There was general enthusiasm for this around the table and they went off to prepare for the day.

Many animals would die before the end of the day.

Calum was in a deep sleep, but he was dreaming. Well, he must be, because he could feel the shape of Jessie next to him and he could smell her heady amber perfume. He slowly woke up, not really wanting to dispel her presence, the feeling that she was with him, but not being able to stop himself.

He opened his eyes. In the light from the lamp on his night stand, he could see that there was no one there.

Well, what had he expected? Jessie was gone forever. She had been consumed by the tsunami that had hit Gallanvaig. He closed his eyes and tried to go back to sleep.

He felt a slight touch on his cheek and his eyes sprang open.

Nothing there.

Damn, he really would have to stop imagining things and move on, he thought. But, how could he? She had been everything to him. He wasn't sure if he could carry on with life without her.

He started to get showered, further sleep eluding him.

Then, he heard a loud scream from outside. Hurriedly pulling on jeans and a sweater, he ran from his room. He could hear someone yelling and followed the sounds. It was coming from the corridor to the farm house, which sat above the bunker.

"What's going on?" he asked, seeing Chloe.

"We think the kids went out for an early walk," said Chloe. "We heard screams and think they must have got into trouble. David, Rob, Millie and a few of the others went out to find them."

Calum's heart sank. He hoped they were okay, he really loved those kids.

Grabbing a gun from the cupboard he ran up the connecting corridor and into the farmhouse, running for the door.

"David, Rob, Millie where are you?"

Answering shouts reached him and he ran towards them, in the direction of the nearest field. When he got there, he was dismayed to see Joanna lying on the ground, the other youngsters around her. Some of the adults were chasing off a pack of wolves, which were running towards the woods at the bottom of the field, Rob, David and Millie in pursuit, firing at them.

"Oh, God Joanna, are you okay?"

She moaned in pain.

"What the hell happened?" Calum asked the other kids.

"We were just taking a walk," said James, shakily. "It was so peaceful yesterday when we went out. Then, these wolves just rushed us from the woods over there."

"You know not to go out on your own," said Calum, angry at their foolishness.

"I'm sorry, Calum," said Rachel "We didn't want to disturb anyone, you were all asleep. We thought it would be okay, like yesterday."

"You know this is a dangerous place now."

Seeing their crestfallen faces, he put an arm around Rachel.

"Okay, the main thing now is to get Joanna safe inside and let Nazeer have a look at her. Come on."

They lifted Joanna between them and took her inside. She had an ugly wound on the neck, where she had been bitten. Damn, did these things have rabies? He had no idea.

Calling for Nazeer, they went into the rec room and put Joanna on a sofa. Nazeer had heard the commotion and had just appeared, his hair wet from his shower.

"She's been bitten by a wolf," said Calum.

"Okay, let's get her into the sick bay so I can have a proper look," said Nazeer taking over. "That will need cleaning and probably a few stitches. Then, a series of injections in case of rabies. And antibiotics. God knows what those things out there are carrying."

They rushed Joanna off to the sick bay with Nazeer and Doctor Susan Brady, who had come rushing in to find out what was going on, in attendance. Leaving her in good hands, Calum came back to see the other kids.

"Look, I'm not mad at you. But, please, *please*, do not take any more risks. There are all sorts of dangers out there, however lovely it looks and however much you want some fresh air and exercise. Just wait for us in future. Okay?"

They all sheepishly agreed.

"Sorry, Calum," said James.

Rachel nodded, distraught at the impact of their 'harmless' walk on her sister.

"Yes, sorry, we won't do it again," said Shaun.

"Right. Well, we can't do anything for her right now, so let's get some breakfast."

Rachel didn't want anything, she said she felt sick. But, the boys went with Calum to the dining area, where Millie, back from chasing off the wolves, was already busy.

People congregated in the dining area, shocked at this latest reminder of their precarious situation, despite the lovely, peaceful time they had had on Christmas Day.

"How long can we go on like this?" asked Bill. "We can't carry on not being able to go out or enjoy life's pleasures. We have to move somewhere else."

"But, move where?" said Calum. "At least we are safe here inside - outside too if we go out properly armed. We don't know if anywhere else will be safer. For the moment, I think we are better staying put. The Elite don't know where we are. We can keep the wild animals out. We have stores of food and crops growing in the fields. It's probably no safer anywhere else, and Gallanvaig, if that's what you're thinking, hasn't got an underground bunker where we can shelter from animals as well as missile attacks."

"I agree," said Rob. "We have to stay where we are safe, for the moment. In time, if things change, we can go back to Gallanvaig, if that's what we all want."

"I would certainly love to go back," said Rachel. "We were happy there.

"Yes, but now isn't the time, sweetheart," said Calum. "We need to wait until it's safe."

He gave her a hug. She was still shaken up by what had happened to Joanna.

Everyone was disturbed by the attack on Joanna and Calum suggested a game after breakfast to try to distract them from the danger they were in.

No-one's heart was really in it, but they all tried to stay positive.

Sometimes Calum felt the responsibility for everyone's safety weigh heavily on his heart.

Joanna had a fever by that evening and Calum, her brother, sister and Shaun were by her side.

"My neck is hurting," she said weakly. "It's so hot. And I feel sick."

"I know, sweetheart. But, Doctor Nazeer will look after you, don't worry," said Calum, stroking her forehead.

Doctor Nazeer came in with her medicine.

"Here you are Joanna, take this," he said handing here some tablets and a cup of water.

Joanna raised herself against the pillow with some difficulty, her face hot and flushed and she was shivering.

Calum followed Nazeer out of the sick bay.

"How's she doing really?" he asked. "I don't like the look of her. Has she caught something from that wolf?"

"I'm afraid she is showing some symptoms that might well be rabies," said Nazeer. "The burning in the wound, the nausea, the fever. As well as antibiotics, I have started giving her the vaccine, which will need to be continued over a month. But, I have to say that if it is rabies, it is often fatal, especially if the symptoms have appeared."

"What? But she's just a kid. There *must* be more you can do."

"I'm sorry, Calum. I am doing everything that can be done. But, you need to prepare for the worst. Rabies is not usually found in the UK, we've been rabies-free since the early twentieth century, apart from a few bats. But, these are devolved dogs that are now wolves, who knows what reverted bugs they may carry in their primitive state? This strain of rabies may be a devolved one and our vaccines might not work."

"Do whatever it takes," he said. "And anything else you need, let me know."

Calum was dismayed. He went to find the others. Chloe stopped him in the doorway to the lounge.

"How is she?" she asked. "Any improvement?"

"She's not great," said Calum in a low voice. "Doctor Nazeer thinks she might not make it."

"Oh, no," said Chloe, tears springing to her eyes. "Is there nothing he can do, with all the antibiotics and stuff we have here?"

"He says it looks like rabies and apparently that is usually fatal. And it might be a primitive strain of rabies that he can't treat. I can't believe it. She is so young, hasn't even started out in life yet. How's David doing?"

"He's fine. I'm so glad there was nothing too serious. But, I'm so sorry about Joanna. Let's hope the doc has got it wrong this time."

Calum wasn't too hopeful about that. Nazeer was the best. He had saved Calum's own life after he was shot by Ben, under the control of Balthazar. And he had saved the lives of many more of their community since.

"I don't think we should tell the other kids yet," said Calum. "Let's wait until we are sure."

Chloe nodded. This was so awful. Every day there was a new horror lurking in the shadows.

She worried about the young one in her belly.

Jessie could see Calum in her mind's eye. But, although she was opening her mouth and speaking to him, no sounds were coming out and he didn't seem to be able to hear her. In frustration she closed her eyes. Where *was* she? Why couldn't he see her?

Marta had arranged for a team of horses for the Elite to ride for the day's hunt. Their hunt guide would take them to nearby forests where wolves and foxes roamed. They were in for a treat today, thought Marta.

Beautiful Russian scenery coupled with the slaughter of magnificent animals. Followed by a sacrifice and a feast.

Perfect.

They had had a good day. The icy winds and driving snow hadn't spoiled their ride in the forests and they had six wolves draped over the cart harnessed to the guide's horse.

Now for some fun, she thought as they rode the steaming horses through the big gates into her palace. The evening was still young, they had many pleasures awaiting them.

The stable hands led the horses away and the wolves were taken to be processed. Maybe she would have her staff make plaques of their heads as souvenirs for everyone, she thought.

Once inside, they changed into white robes and headed for the catacombs under the palace. They had been designed for storage when the palace was built. But, Marta had a whole different use for them these days.

Soon, drumming and chanting started. They were joined by some local, junior members of the Elite, not yet fully initiated. They were to take part in the sacrifice tonight. She laughed at their nervousness, the careful handling of the sharp blades and their reluctance to drive them into the small bundle of rags on the altar, surrounded by guttering candles.

The blade finally struck home and one initiate turned away, looking green under her hood. And one of the others rushed away and vomited in the corner of the room.

They would learn, she thought as they processed upstairs to the banqueting room.

The senior celebrant handed them the cups of red liquid, which would strengthen their spirits against the difficult days to come, when they would have to face the loss of half of the Master Elite and the next battle for supremacy with the Jinn.

But, they felt strong again with the lifeblood inside them and they *would* prevail.

Papa Nicholas was thoughtful. Could these rumours about the Apocalypse being upon them really be true? The Revelation Army was all over the television recently, insisting that the signs and symbols from Saint John's Revelation were evident on the earth today and therefore the Apocalypse must be near.

Of course, the whole foundation of the Catholic Church was the Bible and the events described within it, whose words directed the lives of all Christians. But, they weren't all literally true, were they? Many stories were parables, made simple for the unsophisticated audience of the day, used to drive home a message, not describing actual events.

So, what was he to make of the Revelation Army's claims? Exactly which Bible stories and predictions were true? Which were just parables? Live a good life, or else plagues, fire and locusts will descend from the sky, was that sort of thing literally true? He had his doubts before now.

There was no definitive knowledge of which of the Bible chapters were based on fact and which were stories that illustrated a lesson. But, this talk of Apocalypse was causing unrest and worry within the Christian community. It would have to be quashed once and for all and he was the only man who could do it.

There was a knock at the door.

"Come in," said the Pope.

It was Rafaele.

"It is nearly time. Are you ready for your address, your holiness?"

"Si, Rafaele. I have been thinking about this Apocalypse business. I think it is my duty to put a stop to these rumours, which are causing distress to the Christian community."

"I agree. Since that crazy Revelation Army have been going on about the end of the world, nobody is talking any sense. Everyone thinks it's not worth carrying on with normal religious life anymore. People aren't coming to the sacraments. Your authority is being called into question. People think that the only ones with any knowledge on this are the Revelation Army."

"Okay, then, this must be the subject of my address today. I *will* put a stop to it once and for all."

He followed Rafaele down the ornate corridors of the Vatican to the balcony looking over Saint Peter's Square, from which he would give the Sunday address and say the Angelus prayer. His heart was heavy with dread that his people might not believe him, that they might instead follow the Revelation Army.

But, he was resolute. This had to stop, here and now.

"Cari fratelli e sorelle, buongiorno. Dear brothers and sisters, good morning. Today I want to talk to you about the Revelation of Saint John. You may have heard rumours that the predictions he made appertain to the events of today, that the disaster, fire and plagues described refer to what is happening today in the world. The decimation of humanity by the GM sickness, the destruction caused by nuclear missiles, the pollution of our land and waters. The strange mutants and prehistoric animals that have appeared. All have been interpreted by some as the portents of an Apocalypse. But, I say to you, brothers and sisters, that this story in the Bible is not to be taken literally. It is a parable, written to make it easy for simple peasants to understand that if they do not live a good life and love their neighbours, they will have to suffer in Purgatory or Hell for their sins. But, those who follow the teachings of Christ, will be saved and will enjoy eternal life with God in Heaven. The one who has been spreading false rumours has been excommunicated. Yes, Bishop Sebastian, of the so-called Revelation Army, is no longer a bishop of the Roman Catholic Church. He has preached falsehoods and encouraged illegal actions. In fact, together with his misinformed followers, he is currently on the run from the authorities for crimes against the law. So, you must not be worried about the things he says, which are misinterpretations of the Bible. You must not be distressed about the 'end of the world.' This will not come today. Or even tomorrow. No, you must live a good life and continue to practice the Roman Catholic faith. You should partake in the Sacraments, go to Mass and read the Bible. Only then will you reach eternal happiness in heaven. Now, let's say the Angelus. L'angelo del Signore dichiarò a Maria."

"E ha concepito lo Spirito Santo," the congregation replied.

As the Angelus proceeded with the solid responses of the congregation following the Pope's lead, he felt fairly satisfied with today's address. He got the feeling that this congregation at least had taken what he said to heart.

Now to sort out the troublesome Bishop once and for all.

"He has no idea what's going on, does he?" said Rob. "He's just trying to keep all his followers on side. It must be awful for him to see everyone deserting his church to follow some pretender."

"But, what if he's not a pretender?" said Chloe. "What if the events prophesised in the Bible are coming true? What if this *is* the End of Days?"

"All we can do is deal with the situation as we see it now," said Calum. "And since the biggest threat facing humankind seems to be these reptiles, or

277

Annunaki, or whatever they are called, I suggest we need to tackle that first."

"But, how?" asked David. "They are powerful and have vast reserves of wealth and resources. How can we fight a force like that?"

"For a start, we can mobilise the World Alliance supporters against them. Then, we can attack them. There are military forces that are not in their control. So, we use whatever weaponry we can have access to and attack them on their own ground. Wipe them out. They have been using incendiary devices around the world. This is linked to GM-contaminated land in regions where GM cultivation was rife."

"They are trying to eliminate the mutant genes from the Earth," said Tristan. "One of the surest ways of destroying genetic material is by fire. Maybe they have had enough of mutations and devolved dinosaurs."

"Well, it's a little too late for most of the human population for them to realise that GM is toxic," muttered Chloe.

"We don't want to sink to their level and poison even more of the environment and population with nuclear missiles," said Calum. "So, I suggest that using their own weapon of choice, incendiary devices, might be a better way to deal with them. I'll contact the others and see what we have around the world. Hogan, can you list all the places where these creatures hide out, so we can target the attacks?"

"Yes, no problem. I would be pleased to see them get their come-uppance. Nasty bunch of cold -hearted individuals. And I think they are probably all together. They nearly always are since the world situation changed. Safety in numbers, I guess. But, it should make it easier for us."

"That's the plan then," said Calum. He picked up the phone to Elizabeth MacKenzie, the leader of the Alliance in the UK.

"Hello, Elizabeth. How are you?"

"Fine thanks, Calum. But, where are you? The authorities have been searching for you since you went missing from Inverness."

"You don't need to know Elizabeth, it might put you in danger. But, I need your help. As you will have heard, we have discovered that there is a shadowy elite that is standing in the shadows behind every world power and government, manipulating humanity. And we don't think they are human. No doubt you will have seen the footage of one of them shapeshifting into a reptilian creature."

"Oh, not this again, Calum. You know very well that the government have investigated this and has proclaimed it fake news. Edited footage that any ten-year old could produce. I thought that you were a scientist?"

"So, you won't help us to tackle these people? If they *are* people."

"Certainly not. I have a responsibility to run an evidence-based, challenging Opposition to Her Majesty's Government and I intend to focus on that. Goodbye Calum."

The phone went dead.

"She won't help us," he said.

Balthazar had planned that today would be the day when he would eliminate the rest of the enemies who had been tormenting him. He had already despatched half of them. The rest would not be too difficult. But, he felt so tired. Even though he had taken yesterday off, together with his followers. His stomach ached. His appetite was gone.

Nicholas came in to the room.

"You look terrible, Master. And what's this rash?"

"So do you," replied Balthazar. "What is wrong with us? Have we picked up a bug?"

"I'll get that doctor we brought in last month to come and have a look at you," said Nicholas. "A few of the followers are not feeling too well either. It could well be a contagious bug."

"Okay, tell him I will see him immediately."

The doctor, Tanaya, a local Native American, had been practicing in the area for years and had stayed after the evacuation to look after his patients. He had been easy to capture and bring under their control. He followed Nicholas into the room looking worried.

"Doctor, I want to know what's wrong with me," said Balthazar. "My head and stomach hurt, I am tired all the time and I have this rash."

"Let me see," said Tanaya. "Ah. That's not good."

"What? What is wrong with me?"

"It looks like the early stages of the gene sickness. Have you been consuming GM material?"

"Yes, of course. We need it to maintain our powers. It has never done us any harm before."

"Yes, but if you have been eating it for years you may have built up an intolerance. Maybe it just takes longer in certain people to have its full effect. In any case, I advise you to go to bed and rest for a few days. And stop eating GM food. Then, we will see if things improve."

"But, there must be something you can give me?" said Balthazar. "There is medicine here. Or, we can get whatever you need. Just ask Nicholas."

"What about me, I don't feel good either?" whined Nicholas.

"What symptoms do you have?"

"The same. Tired, sickness. I don't think I have a rash, though."

"Take off your shirt. Ah, there it is, right at the base of the spine. You need to rest too."

"But, we can't just rest," Balthazar stormed. "We have things to do, things that must be resolved."

"You won't be doing anything unless you rest," said Tanaya.

"Okay, okay, maybe just for a couple of days. But, I want you to look at the rest of my followers. Check if any of them are sick. Take him Nicholas."

Nicholas nodded and led Tanaya away to examine the other residents at Dulce. It was going to be a long day for Doctor Tanaya.

47. The Coming Storm

After Elizabeth's refusal to help to overcome the Elite, Calum had been in touch with his old Alliance contacts and they had proved sympathetic to his position and agreed to join forces. Most were getting no support from their Alliance Leaders, who all seemed too scared to go against the majority governments of Democracy party leaders. Many of them had been ousted by people more sympathetic to organised government in the run-up to the elections.

It turned out that there were stores of incendiary devices and military forces under the control of the Alliance and their sympathisers in all the world's major cities. Hogan had identified a list of over twenty places where the Elite lived. It seems that they all had more than one residence, mostly castles, mansions and palaces, all around the world.

The World Alliance rebels agreed that attacks would be made at all the main residences.

Then, only if that failed to find them, Hogan knew several other places where they regularly spent time on holiday.

In the United Kingdom, there was a residence in Cornwall and one in Surrey, both belonging to Sir Michael Goldman, the UK member of the Elite. The Surrey mansion had been visited and was reported to have been destroyed three weeks ago. The local military were travelling to Goldman's castle in Cornwall.

The phone rang in the bunker control room.

"Hi, Calum O'Connell."

"Sir, it's Flight Lieutenant Craig. We have just visited Conneaux Castle, near Tintagel, as instructed. I have to report that we found several casualties there, both in the castle and in the grounds."

"What? What happened?"

"As far as we can tell, the seven inside the castle were either badly burned, or had suffered electrical-type shocks. The five found in the grounds were all consumed by fire. All of them were dead."

"But, who did this?" started Calum, confused.

Then, it dawned on him. The Elite had other sworn enemies apart from those in the Alliance. The Elite had tried several times to eliminate them. Now were the Jinn taking their revenge?

"Okay, thanks for letting me know. Is there any identification on the bodies?"

"We have identified one as Sir Michael Goldman, the castle owner, from photographs. The others, we don't know yet. But, we are on it. The bodies have been taken to the local forensic lab."

"I can send you a list of who some of them might be," said Calum.

Calum hoped that the forces in other countries were having more luck at locating the Elite.

But, it seemed that the Jinn had done part of their work for them already.

"There are ten Masters who lead the Elite," said Hogan. "These cover the most powerful countries of the world. Whenever one of them has died, or been killed, a member of the same family always succeeds them in the Master group. Sahil Kapur, for example, was killed in a firestorm at Goldman's mansion in Surrey. He was immediately replaced by his son, Gaj. The countries are UK, US, France, Germany, Italy, China, India, Russia, Japan and Brazil. It's great that some of them have been killed, especially Goldman. He was a horrible man. But, before long, these will be replaced by others from the same bloodline."

"Then, we have to work fast before they get a chance to replace them. If they are weakened, this will be a good time to hit them again," said Calum.

He picked up the phone.

"Renée, hello. Calum here. How is the search going?"

"Bonjour, Calum. We have checked the three residences that you gave us. All are currently deserted apart from a few service staff."

"Same here, except some of the Elite were found dead at a castle in Cornwall. We're not sure who yet, apart from Goldman was one of them."

Renée exclaimed.

"Fantastique, that is great news. So, we just need to find the rest. I have heard nothing from the others yet."

"Okay, let me know if you hear anything."

"Renée has drawn a blank in France," he said pressing another button.

Twenty minutes later, Calum knew that the Elite had been found at none of the residences on Hogan's list.

"Any ideas?" he asked Hogan.

Marta was furious. The housekeeper at Conneaux Castle had been in touch to report that a military team had visited the castle and taken away the bodies of the security team and the five masters had been taken away. Obviously, their enemies were seeking them and would now discover which of them lived and who died. And they obviously had lists of their properties.

They had hurriedly evacuated the St Petersburg palace and she was angry at leaving it behind, although she had left a team of staff to look after it.

Who knew what those idiots would do to her home when they arrived?

The 'copter rose high in the air.

"Well, we can't go to any of the usual places. They know where we live," she said.

"Where then?" asked Gaj.

"My cousin has a castle in Umbria, Italy," said Fabbiana. "It has no other known association with me. I have never stayed there. But, I know he will accommodate us for as long as we wish. It is fortified, standing on a hill above a wide valley, so any approach by land or air will be seen. And it has extensive, underground caverns that can be used to hide for weeks, if needed. They were used in the wars."

"Sounds perfect," said Marta, as Fabbiana went forward to give the new destination to the pilot.

Balthazar shook his head to clear the fuzziness he had been feeling all day. But, he couldn't rest until he had eliminated his enemies. As he focussed on them, a vision started to form. There was a large castle and he saw that his enemies were arriving there by helicopter.

Ah, now he had them.

But, could he fight them, feeling so weak?

All the residences of those now known as Annunaki would be destroyed by fire, even though the reptilian shapeshifters did not appear to be in residence. That way, they would have nowhere to hide when they did surface from whichever hole they were hiding in.

Units of fighter jets set off from all major airbases in major cities of the world, loaded with incendiary devices and with specific targets in mind.

Three hours later, all known residences of the reptilian elite had been destroyed.

The phone rang in Fabbiana's family castle and he picked it up.

"Quello che è successo? What happened?"

He listened for a while, his eyes growing black and his shape beginning to change in his anger. He slammed the phone down.

"Bad news," he announced to his companions in the great hall of his family's castle. My castle outside Rome was destroyed by fire. The staff were ordered to leave first by a voice from a drone. They say there is nothing left," he added with a grimace.

As he spoke, mobile phones began to ring. One by one, his companions were also given the news that their castles, palaces and mansions had also been destroyed by fire.

In a blind rage, the five surviving masters began to change. Their eyes first became totally black, then their faces became elongated and reptilian, their legs muscular and scaly. Unearthly growls erupted from the group and pottery and glasses were swept from tables and helves, as they searched for a target for their fury.

Who had done this to them?

Gaj and Corinne recovered first, slowly reverting to human form. The others followed.

The phone rang again. Fabbiana answered it and, after a few moments, he smiled.

"So, we have a trail to follow, eh? Get the military on this straight away."

He replaced the phone and turned to the others.

"My house manager says that he got video footage of the aircraft that attacked my castle. He says that the markings and numbers are clearly visible. Now we have them."

The others looked up, smiling.

"So, tell your contacts to investigate their origin then," said Marta. "We will hunt them down."

"Already done, Marta," said Fabbiana. "Just relax. We will know soon enough."

"I don't think our mutant Jinn friends have the intelligence for drones or flying military jets, do you?" she asked. "Although they certainly hate us enough to want to destroy our homes."

"I agree," said Corinne. "They are way too primitive a force. I would put my money on the runt of the Alliance resistance."

"That's a diffuse mob," said Gaj. "We don't know where to start looking for them. People like Calum O'Connell escaped from the incompetent local militia and have gone to ground. They could be anywhere."

"Another thing," said Marta. "Who else knew everything about our homes and their localities?"

"Well, nobody but us and our families know anything," said Fabbiana. "Apart from people who need to know, like staff, security guards and so on."

"And, who escaped from Vanderbilt's castle in Zurich?" said Marta. "No doubt with the footage of Vanderbilt's party trick, that appeared on television and which we have claimed is fake? Who would have known about all our homes from our meetings, always with security in attendance?"

"*Hogan*," said Corinne and Fabbiana together.

"So, who is he working with? He didn't arrange this little firebombing party on his own, that's for sure," said Marta. "When we get the id on the planes, we will know more about who he is in league with."

"And then we can plan our vengeance," said Fabbiana.

287

48. Protecting the Vatican

Luca was on guard outside the Vatican apartments when he was given his orders. He was to travel immediately, with thirty colleagues. to the French Alps.

He donned his travelling uniform, quite unlike the ceremonial blue, red, orange and yellow uniform, cap and halberd that he usually wore whilst on duty around the Vatican. He packed his weaponry into a holdall, along with a change of clothing. He looked out of his sleeping cell window when he heard the loud throbbing of a Chinook landing on the heliport at Vatican City. Running from his block towards the transport, he met many other guards, also called into active service.

This must be something important then, he thought. He did not have any details, just the order to mobilise and take weapons, ready to neutralise a problem when they reached their destination.

But then, that was all he needed to know.

With the thirty Swiss Guard on board, whose job was to protect the Pope and the Vatican, the 'copter lifted off.

Luca shared a chat with one of his colleagues who was in the next seat as they drank coffee.

"What do you know about our mission?" asked his friend, Elias. "They told me only to mobilise for a neutralisation mission."

"The same," answered Luca. "But it is good to be on the move, doing something useful rather than prancing around in that ridiculous uniform, posing with tourists for selfies."

"I agree, I don't care what it is. I have been waiting for an opportunity for a real military exercise."

"Except, I don't think it *is* an exercise," said Luca. "The way we were mobilised with no notice and an armed squad smacks of an urgent problem that needs to be addressed, I think."

"Good," said Elias. "At last, some action."

They were soon approaching the white-covered slopes of the French Alps and the 'copter was hovering above a snow-covered field. The squad commander came out of the cockpit.

"When we land, speed is of the essence," he said. "You will follow my lead and when we get to the target, you must ensure that nobody is left to tell any tales. Understood?"

Everyone muttered a reply.

The 'copter touched down and the rear doors opened admitting an icy blast of alpine air.

"Go, go, go," yelled the second-in command.

They ran off in formation, following the lead of the Squadron commander. The squad moved forward up a dark, icy lane at the foot of the mountain. Luca could see twinkling lights in the distance. As they approached, he could see a collection of farm buildings.

The commander gave a signal to surround the farm and then slowly tighten the cordon to ensure nobody escaped.

Luca's pulse raced. This was what he had joined the Swiss Guard for, to fight and protect his Pope. He was wound up, ready for action, as they burst through the doors of the farmhouse and a large barn simultaneously.

The automatic fire flashed from many guns and there were shouts and screams as they hit home. When the firing stopped, they went in to inspect the damage.

Nobody was moving. There had been eighty-five souls in the converted barn and six in the main farmhouse.

Luca was dismayed to see that one of those in the farmhouse was wearing the robes of a bishop and another two the dark robes and white collars of priests.

"Mio Dio!" he cried. "What have we done?"

He was shoved roughly back in the direction of the 'copter as the second-in command did his final checks and the photographer collected her evidence.

"Back to the 'copter," yelled the Commander. "We are done here."

Luca crossed himself. He had signed up for active service to protect his Pope. Not to kill bishops and priests.

He was shocked into silence, as were his colleagues at what they had been ordered to do.

Why would the Vatican consider priests and a bishop a threat to the Pope?

49. It's in the Blood

Doctor Rick Chester couldn't believe his eyes. He had been assigned to a team analysing the corpses found at Conneaux Castel in Cornwall and to try to identify them. The cause of death of both the group of seven in the castle entrance hall and the five in the grounds was extensive burns.

The team had already sent off dental scans to police forces for comparison with people recently missing and Chester was analysing blood samples from the victims.

The samples from the victims found inside the castle were found to be unrelated, their DNA ninety nine percent the same for all of them, with the other point one percent, defining their physical and unique characteristics, being different.

However, the samples from the five bodies found in the garden were presenting Chester with a problem. He had been unable to match the DNA with that of human DNA, with only a thirty percent match.

Chimpanzees shared ninety six percent of DNA with humans, for goodness sake. Fruit flies shared sixty one percent. Even a *banana* shared around sixty percent of its DNA with humans. Who were these people?

If they *were* people.

He called up his senior, Daniel Taylor, for a second opinion.

"What's up?" said Daniel, poking his head around the lab door.

"I want you to check the DNA analysis from five of the victims of the Conneaux Castel massacre. There is something I can't explain."

"Okay, let's have a look."

Dr Taylor studied the printouts.

"Well, these sequences here look like normal DNA; adenine and thymine, cytosine and guanine pairs. But, my God, these sequences here and here. I don't recognise any of these. You say these came from Conneaux Castel? You're sure there has been no contamination?"

"There definitely hasn't. I prepared the samples myself, taken directly from the bodies. I have already repeated the analysis twice. There is no mistake. This is like no other DNA that I have ever seen."

Clutching the reports, Taylor rushed from the room to his office. He dialled the number for Flight Lieutenant Craig, who was leading the investigation on cause of death, identification of the victims and subsequent return of the bodies to their families.

"Lieutenant, we have a problem. The blood samples for five of the victims do not appear to be human," he said his voice wavering a little.

"I want you to seal off the mortuary forthwith," said Craig. "Nobody is to enter. My team will arrive later to remove the corpses for further analysis and identification."

"But, you don't understand, these bodies are not human," he insisted.

"We have the highest skilled scientists in the country and the best technology available. We will take over from here," said Craig. "Now, go and order the mortuary to be sealed off please."

The phone went dead.

This was unbelievable.

Calum lifted his phone as it rang.

"Calum O'Connell. Ah good morning, Lieutenant Craig."

"Mr O'Connell, there is a development with the bodies from Conneaux. They seem to contain DNA that isn't human."

"What do you mean, is it animal?"

"It's like no other DNA that we know of on earth. No earthly animal, plant or insect has DNA like this. I can't explain it."

"We need to preserve the bodies for further analysis," said Calum. "Can you get them put in a freezer somewhere, with high security? We need to keep this under wraps until we find out what we have here."

"Already in hand, Mr O'Connell. I have a team going to collect the bodies from the forensic lab. We will put them on ice at the base here. Let us know what you want to do next."

Calum put the phone down. Seeing his shocked expression, Rob put his book down.

"What's happened now?"

"It seems that we might have more evidence that our Rachel's book about the Annunaki and them being reptilian shapeshifters might be more than just a conspiracy theory," he said. "Analysis of the bodies found at Goldman's castle in Cornwall has shown that they are not human. There is a mismatch with human DNA."

"My God, it's all true," said Rob. "I couldn't totally believe it even after we saw the shapeshifting Vanderbilt on Hogan's video."

"I told you," said Rachel quietly from the corner of the room. "Now, what do we do?"

"The plan is the same," said Calum. "We need to destroy them and stop their interference in world affairs for good. They have controlled things for far too long. We just need to find them first."

"Well, we've already destroyed all the residences that Hogan knew about. Where do we look now?" said Rob.

"I think they will show themselves sooner or later," said Hogan. "They can't resist interfering in world affairs. We just need to be ready."

"Well, we can mobilise the military under our control very quickly," said Calum. "We just need to know where to send them."

Joanna tossed and turned, her face was flushed. Her bedclothes were thrown onto the floor in a heap. Calum felt her forehead. She was burning up.

Nazeer came in with medication.

"How is she?" asked Calum. "She feels so hot."

"Well, I've been giving her the rabies vaccine and antibiotics to treat infection. But, I don't think this is a modern strain of rabies. She isn't responding at all to treatment. I think it's an unknown strain. I have sent a blood sample to the lab to see if they can provide a more appropriate vaccine. But, without that, there isn't much more I can do."

Chloe arrived.

"Oh, she looks terrible," she gasped. "Is she showing any signs of recovery?"

"I'm afraid not yet," said Nazeer. "I was just saying, the rabies strain that Joanna has isn't the modern one that our vaccine treats. If we can't find an effective one soon, I don't hold out much hope. I am sorry."

Chloe looked hopelessly as Calum.

"She is so young. How can we fight these primitive diseases that the modern human race has never been exposed to?"

"We need to develop a whole new set of treatments," said Nazeer. "Unfortunately, what we don't have is unlimited time or resources. These vaccines take years of research and development before they can be put into practice."

"How's my sister?" asked Rachel, coming in, followed by James and Shaun.

"Yeah, how's she doing? Oh, she doesn't look too good," added James.

"Your sister is very poorly," said Calum. "But, Nazeer is doing everything he can. She's in good hands."

"But, what's wrong with her?" asked James.

"We think its rabies, mate. But it's an old form of the disease. We don't know if the modern treatment will work."

"Is she going to die?" asked Rachel. "Rabies is pretty serious, right?"

"We don't know yet, sweetheart," said Calum. "We hope not."

He put an arm around Rachel as she started to cry.

What was he supposed to say to her? What could he say to her brother and Shaun?

He felt so helpless.

Bishop Sebastian threw off his hood and looked at his travelling companions. He had just heard the news about the killing of the entire congregation that had been in hiding in the French Alps. Luckily for him, he had been giving a Christmas service at a local village church.

His companion in the driving seat, Father Zacharias Garnier, turned to him.

"My Lord, you say we can't go back to the farm. What has happened?"

"I have just got a message that several of my priests and the German bishop, Karl Eckstein have all been shot at the farm. They are martyrs, killed for their beliefs. We must be ready to die for our convictions too. But, we have work to do on earth first. We must build a new congregation. We must make people understand that there is little time left to repent of their sins. The signs are all around. The local farmer who has been supplying us with vegetables told me that a military force attacked the farm and shot everyone there. We don't know if they are still around or if they are searching for us. We must flee immediately and find somewhere to hide.

"But, who can we trust?" said Father Marc Roussel, another of his faithful followers, from the back seat. "How do we know who attacked us and who might be on their side?"

"Well, the authorities have issued a warrant for my arrest for wilful damage to the ID chip that was in my hand. So, it might be the government. Also, the Vatican have been outspoken about their view that we have misinterpreted the Bible. The Pope has said that Christians should ignore our message and continue to follow the mainstream church."

"But, the Pope would surely never order our deaths," said Roussel. "I mean, 'Thou shalt not kill' and all that"

"To be honest, I wouldn't put anything past the Vatican. We are a huge threat to the established church. Christians are deserting the church in large numbers, waking up to the fact that all the signs of an apocalypse are already here. Despite these obvious signs, the Pope is denying it and he is losing credibility. Would he kill to protect the church? I don't know, but I think it would be foolish to trust anyone from the established church. I suggest we look elsewhere for sanctuary."

"So, where shall we head?" asked Garnier.

"As we can't trust the authorities either, I suggest we contact some of the rebels. I met the leader of the World Alliance in France, Renée Mercier, a few times and she appeared to be very reasonable. I understand that she is in hiding at a rebel camp with military forces loyal to her. Let me just call her. Meanwhile stay off the major roads."

Five minutes later, the call had been made and a military copter was on the way to a rendezvous point five miles away.

"Madame Mercier is very brave. She stands up against the corrupt government of this country and has agreed to help us. Even though the government has issued a warrant for our arrest and the Vatican would like to silence us."

He gave the grid reference to Garnier and they headed for what they hoped would be safety.

50. Carnage

The herd of Allosaurus charged through the Rhine valley. Towering at three meters tall and ten meters in length, they thundered along, sweeping aside trees and buildings in their path. A group of wolves, disturbed from bracken by their approach, yelped and ran for their lives. One by one, the Allosaurus caught and consumed them, before continuing their destructive path.

Then, the air was displaced by the whine of jet engines, as a Wormwood nuclear missile, launched from a navy vessel in the Mediterranean and guided by GPS, screamed towards its target. As it hit home, the herd of Allosaurus exploded in a hail of blood and flesh, falling into the resulting crater on the banks of the Rhine.

All human and wildlife in the immediate area, around two kilometres in radius, was obliterated. Immediately beyond that, there were casualties due to blast and fire damage. The resulting residual radiation would contaminate the ground, air and water courses and rainfall for thousands of years, causing further deaths, birth defects and cancers.

Around the world, there were similar attacks on areas where dinosaurs had been observed and many were once more wiped out.

On the slopes of the Tibetan Plateau, a herd of Velociraptors worked together to hunt their prey. They were undisturbed by human life and continued to chase and kill wild yak and antelope.

On the plains of the Australian Outback, a herd of Savannasaurus grazed peacefully, birds wheeling around them, feeding on the insects they attracted.

And, at the foot of the Annapurna mountains in Nepal, a Tyrannosaurus Rex roared as it chased after a snow leopard.

It seems that the reach of the Annunaki wasn't total after all.

Later, the television news programme was showing footage of the attacks around the world that had destroyed so much wildlife and laid the foundations for many painful illnesses and deaths for years to come.

The news feed switched to a report from a plain in Peru, where a BBC reporter was presenting an item from an airborne helicopter.

"As you can see, the ground below us has been destroyed, apparently by nuclear explosion. We understand that there was a large herd of Tyrannosaurus Rex living on this plain until yesterday. Now, all that is left is this huge crater and the shattered corpses of many animals. There have been similar incidents of nuclear explosions at many locations around the world. It is unclear who has fired these missiles, but they appear to be targeting the dinosaurs. For safety reasons, we are being told that we must leave this area now. Back to you in the studio, Karen."

"Oh, hell, what are the Elite up to now?" spat David. "More death and destruction?"

"I can't believe that those bastards are still nuking the world with their filthy missiles," said Rob. "I thought we had destroyed all of their homes."

"Yes, but only some of them died and we think they were probably killed by the Jinn, not us," said Calum. "It looks to me like they may be targeting areas where there are dinosaurs. Look at all the bodies they are showing in the affected areas."

"Could it be their clumsy attempt to destroy the mutants that they have themselves created?" asked Chloe.

"If it is, it's a stupid way of achieving it," said Calum. "All they are doing is polluting huge tracts of land and making them uninhabitable for thousands of years. Don't they care about the pollution affecting everybody, including themselves? Surely reptiles are not immune to radioactive fallout?"

"Do they even consider the effects of their actions?" said Rob. "They seem to react like spoilt kids, wanting their own way at all costs to the populations and the environment. Hogan, you were right about their lack of empathy. How could they do this to people if they had a shred of compassion for their fellow residents of planet Earth?"

"We have to find and destroy them, before they destroy whatever is left of the human race," said Calum. "Any ideas Hogan?"

"I think there was a database that the Elite maintained," he replied. "It was supposed to list all their relatives and their locations, I never knew why. But, suppose we could access it, we could maybe find out how many of them there are and where they might be hiding. We were never allowed to access it, but we had the responsibility of doing the security backups every night. And I still have my password for their server. If they haven't changed it, that is."

"What are we waiting for?" said Calum. "Go to the Comms room and hack a database. You too, Rob. I know you did a bit of hacking in your time."

"I was a misguided, bored teenager at the time," he muttered following Hogan.

"Yeah right," laughed Calum.

"Let's hope they didn't delete my user, or change my password," said Hogan sitting down in front of a computer. "The database is on the Dark Web, inaccessible except through using specific software and networks. They were paranoid about their secrets being uncovered."

He keyed in a series of commands and downloaded software. Then, he keyed in more lines of command and soon was at a login screen.

"Now we'll find out how security conscious they really are."

He keyed in a user name and then a password.

The cursor blinked for a few moments as a timer scrolled around.

Then, the message 'User name and password not known.'

"Damn. They deleted my user."

"Not surprising if they're as paranoid as you say about security," said Rob.

"Wait, I used to sit next to a colleague, Jack Lynch when we did the back-ups every day. And I couldn't help knowing his user name and password. He knew mine too. Hold on."

He typed again into the login screen. The timer appeared.

Then, a new screen appeared.

'Back-up data now? (Y/N).'

"I'm in," he said.

Rob sat down next to him.

"Let's see if we can crack this," he said.

Calum headed off to check on Joanna, a feeling of dread in his heart at what he might find. He opened the door into the sick bay to find Nazeer bending over the prone figure of Joanna.

"I was just going to call you," he said. "She has taken a turn for the worse. Her temperature is sky-high. And she's been fitting. She has been refusing food and drink, so I have inserted a drip. But, it doesn't seem to be helping."

"What about the vaccine you were hoping to get from the lab?" asked Calum, in desperation.

"They reported that the strain of rabies virus she has contracted is unknown. It isn't a virus that we have a vaccine for. And it may take weeks to develop a working vaccine. We just don't have that long."

"So, what can we do?"

"I'm really sorry Calum. But, unless the lab can work a miracle, there isn't anything else that I can do for Joanna. Do you want to tell her brother and sister?"

Calum nodded, too choked to answer and he went off to find the others.

Soon, they were all around Joanna's bed, together with Chloe and David, who had fully recovered.

"How is she doing?" asked Rachel. "She's so pale."

"Nazeer tells me that she's not doing too well. They don't have a vaccine for the rabies strain that she has caught from the wolf. It might take the lab ages to develop one. There isn't anything else he can do."

"Will she die?" Rachel, tears springing to her eyes.

"I think we have to accept that she might," said Calum putting his arm around her.

James sat by the bed with Sean, too stricken with worry about his sister to say anything.

Chloe put her arm around him.

"I'm so sorry, James," she said.

There was nothing else to do but sit and watch, keep Joanna company and play her some of her favourite music that Rachel went and fetched from Joanna's room.

As the music started to play, Joanna smiled, just once.

Then, her face went slack, as the alarms on her monitors started to beep.

Nazeer came running, together with Doctor Brady, who was about to take over for the night.

Nazeer started to resuscitate Joanna alternating chest compressions with mouth to mouth.

But, after twenty minutes of effort from both Nazeer and Doctor Brady, they had to admit defeat.

Joanna was gone.

Jessie walked along the dark passage, searching from side to side trying to work out where she was. Had the Genies taken her to one of their underground lairs again? She couldn't tell. But, if they had, where *were* they? She had seen nobody for what seemed like days. And those days had been dark and black. No daylight shone here. The only highlight had been when she imagined being back with Calum. But he wasn't here either.

Then, up ahead she suddenly saw the dim flash of something. As it approached, she could see that it was a figure, dressed in pale clothing.

Apprehensive, she shrank against the walls of the passage, trying to hide herself in case this was a Genie trick.

Then, the figure came into view and a familiar voice spoke.

"Jessie! Am I pleased to see you!"

52. A Friend in Need

"Hannah!" shouted Jessie in recognition, rushing forwards to embrace her friend.

After a few moments of greetings, they drew apart.

"Where are we?" asked Jessie. "I don't remember anything after the huge waves and the earthquake in Gallanvaig. I have been trying to contact Calum. But, I think I must be dreaming about him. I can see him, but he doesn't seem to hear what I am saying."

"I have been doing the same with Rob. I miss him. I don't know where we are. I don't remember either. But, nobody whom I have tried to talk to seems to hear me. It has been so scary," she added, touching Jessie's arm, as if she couldn't quite believe that Jessie could see her. "But, it's been permanently dark. Are we underground?"

"That's what I was starting to think," said Jessie. "I thought maybe Balthazar had been back and taken us to one of his underground bases. But, there has been no sign of him. Or of anyone, for that matter."

"Shall we go and find out?" said Hannah. "I was going the other way until I heard you coming along behind me. And I think I could see light up ahead."

Smiling for the first time in ages, Jessie linked her friend's arm and they went forward together.

53. Grieving and a Celebration

Calum sat in the large lounge with the youngsters, Chloe and David. He wept inconsolably. Chloe put an arm around him.

"Sssh, it's okay, she said gently.

"But, it's *not*," he groaned. "I feel so guilty that I failed to protect one of our youngest. I should have kept her safe."

"You can't protect everybody all of the time, Calum, mate," said David. "You have done so much for us all. I don't think many of us would still be here, if not for you taking us all along with you, giving us hope and working out a plan to cope with all the crap."

Rachel nodded through her tears.

"Calum, none of us four would be here, but for you and Jessie taking us with you when you found us in the Lake District. We wouldn't have survived for long alone, with the Genies around and the military trying to lock everyone up. Joanna knew that and she was so grateful. She *loved* you and Jessie."

"Yes, she did," said James, also looking distraught. "We all owe you a huge debt for what you did. It's awful about Joanna, I still can't believe she's gone. But, I'm sure she wouldn't want you blaming yourself. After all, we disobeyed you and went outside, when you had told everyone not to go out without telling someone. If it's anybody's fault, it's mine. I'm the eldest, I should have known better."

"Well, it won't do any good for us all to keep blaming ourselves," said Chloe. "I think we have work to do. Let's arrange a celebration of Joanna's life. Come on you three."

She gathered them around her and they went off to plan a funeral.

Rob came into the lounge, looking pleased with himself.

"Success. We managed to break into the database. We have access to all the names and addresses of the Annunaki."

Calum looked up, his eyes filled with tears.

"What the hell is wrong?" asked Rob.

"Joanna died," he replied, flatly.

"No! That's terrible," said Rob, throwing his arm around Calum's shoulder. "Was it the rabies? I thought Nazeer would be able to treat it. He has always worked miracles."

"Well, not quite always. There wasn't much he could do for our friend, Ben. But, I didn't think she would die either."

"I can't believe it. She was part of our family. We need a stiff drink."

"I feel like all of you are family," said Calum. "We have been through so much together. But, the four kids; they were so young and scared when we rescued them. I thought I could protect them forever. But, apparently not."

"Oh mate, it wasn't your fault," said Rob, handing Calum a large whisky.

"Why do I feel like it is, then?" he said, taking a big gulp of whisky.

It was going to be a long night.

The kids wouldn't listen to any suggestion that they should take down the Christmas decorations in respect of Joanna's death.

"She *loved* Christmas. She would want us to carry on celebrating Christmas and New Year as normal," said Rachel. "And she loved celebrating New

Year. Oh, and it's New Year's Eve tomorrow. Could we have the ceremony then?"

"I don't see why not," said Chloe. "What else would she like, do you think?"

"Well. She loved the traditional Hogmanay," said James. "Pipers and fiddles, a ceilidh, that sort of thing."

"Oh, yes, she would love that," said Shaun. "And she always loved the nip of whisky that Calum used to give us. We should have that as a toast."

"What about music?" asked Chloe. "Can you get together her favourite songs to play, Rachel?"

"Oh yes, she loved her music. I'll go and make a start. We should have candles too. She loved candle light."

"Okay, how about you guys go and find some nice candles? It would be nice if everyone could have a candle each. I'll put some words together. You could all say something too, if you can want to. I'll go and let Calum know what we plan to do."

With a definite sense of purpose and with Joanna in mind, they all went off to make the preparations for a fitting send-off.

"Calum, the kids are really keen on making the ceremony for Joanna exactly what she would have liked," said Chloe. "They are planning music and candles. They would like a Hogmanay theme as it is New Year's Eve tomorrow. You know how Joanna used to love that. And, they want whisky," she said with a wry smile.

"Oh, that's great," said Calum. "I'm glad they are coming to terms with it a bit. But, I think it might hit them hard afterwards, when they realise they really

307

won't see her again. Also, we need to think about where we bury her."

"Oh, I never thought of that. I guess we need to be aware of wild animals and scavengers." She pulled a face.

"How about the walled garden at the back of the farmhouse, where all the herbs and salads are growing? That would be a lovely area for her and the walls will keep out the scavengers."

"Oh, yes, she loved going to collect the herbs for Millie. I'm really going to miss her. She was always so cheerful."

"Me too. But, this sounds like a good way to say goodbye," he added, wiping away a tear.

"Will you play your guitar then? I'll go and ask Douglas, Annie and Jamie if they will play the fiddle and bagpipes, as they normally do on Hogmanay."

"Except that this year will be a lot sadder," said Calum.

Snow fell thickly, as New Year's Eve dawned and the mood in the farmhouse bunker was sombre, as everyone got ready for the ceremony. Rachel was putting on a kilt with a crisp white blouse. She got the music mix she had made and headed to the large lounge.

In the middle of the room was Joanna's body, wrapped in a tartan blanket.

Rachel stopped short when she saw the bundle. The scene brought it home to her what exactly they would be celebrating today. Her little sister's life, whom she would never see again.

She grabbed a tissue from the box and went to join James and Shaun, who were both dressed in traditional kilts, jackets and white shirts.

"Okay Sis?" asked James, putting an arm around his younger sister.

She nodded, not trusting herself to speak aloud.

Shaun touched her shoulder, a bit choked up himself.

"Here, help give these out, will you?" said James handing her a box of candles.

"Okay, I'll just set the music up first," she replied, connecting the music player to the speaker.

Calum came in with Rob, both wearing traditional dress and carrying a case of whisky between them.

Chloe was showing everyone to a seat and giving them a copy of the service and songs. Each one had a picture of a smiling Joanna, taken last Christmas in front of the Christmas tree at Gallanvaig. When she had been happy. When Jessie was still with them.

Douglas, Annie and Jamie were setting up their equipment for the ceilidh and there were random snatches of reels as they tuned their instruments. Douglas played a short blast on the bagpipes and everyone jumped.

Chloe nodded to Rachel who stared the recorded music playing. It seemed a bit strange to be playing such lively pop songs at a funeral, but Joanna loved her music so much.

Eventually, everyone was seated and had a lit candle. Calum nodded to Douglas who would lead the service.

He stood up in his deacon's robe.

"Dearest friends, we are gathered together to celebrate the short life of Joanna Collins, who was taken from us, another victim of the cruel GM conspiracy and the mutant animals that caused her death. But, we are not here in sorrow, although that will come, we are here to celebrate the life of a lovely, young girl who never had a bad word to say about anybody. Well, maybe she made an exception for the odd evil person, but you know what I mean."

Everyone smiled. Joanna had been a very sunny person, always kind, unfailingly seeing the best in people.

"Our reading is from Matthew. 'Then, were little children presented to him that he should impose hands on them and pray. And the disciples rebuked them. But, Jesus said to them, "Suffer the little children and forbid them not to come to me; for the kingdom of heaven is for such.'"

"Jesus was saying that little children were not to be excluded from hearing his message. Children are innocent and theirs is the kingdom of heaven. Joanna was an innocent child and I am sure that she will enjoy eternal life in paradise. Now, we will sing The Lord is My Shepherd."

Calum picked up his guitar and started to play, with everyone joining in, a bit uncertainly at first. but increasing in volume as they became more confident.

"We will now say the Lord's prayer. Then, we will sing one of Joanna's favourite songs, Wild Mountain Thyme. Our Father."

Everyone joined in, the candles flickering brightly around the room. Calum thought how much Joanna would have loved all of this. He took his guitar up as the congregation said the 'Amen.'

Then, they all joined in with the song about going with a loved one to pick wild mountain thyme. It seemed somehow appropriate. With a final 'Let us go, Lassie go," the congregation prepared for the final, painful part of the ceremony.

As the skirls of the bagpipe started up and the fiddles joined in with an old Scottish lament, Calum, Rob, James and Sean lifted the wooden door on which was placed the body wrapped in the blanket. And to the lilting sounds of the highlands and glens, they carried Joanna outside, with everyone following behind with their candles, guttering out as the chill wind hit them.

The procession approached the graveside, which had been dug the day before, with a lot of difficulty, as the ground was quite hard,

And they lowered the body into the grave, accompanied by the musicians.

"Eternal rest give unto her O Lord,"

"And let perpetual light shine upon her. Amen," replied everyone.

And handfuls of earth were thrown into the grave by everyone in turn. Rachel sobbed into a tissue and the lads frequently wiped tears away

"Come on, we don't want everyone catching a chill. Let's get that whisky sorted out," said Chloe, putting her arms around Rachel and James. Sean put his arm around Rachel, who was shivering with the cold.

Everyone went sadly indoors, leaving Calum and Rob to finish work on the grave. When it was filled with soil, Calum planted the simple, wooden cross that he had made and inscribed with Joanna's name and her birth and death dates. Rachel had made a wooden angel and he placed that at the head of the grave next to the cross.

When they went back inside, their hands were freezing, even wearing thick gloves. David handed them a glass of whisky without a word.

This had been one of the most difficult days since the start of the GM crisis.

Il Papa studied the two sets of photographs, a frown creasing his forehead.

"I don't understand," he said to the Camarlengo.

"What is it, Your Holiness?" asked Rafaele.

"The photograph does not match. Bishop Sebastian, that thorn in our side, he isn't at the scene here. So, he isn't dead. Look."

He pointed out the characters in the photos to Rafaele.

"See this one was taken at one of the Revelation Army's crazy services by the press. This is Sebastian. But, this bishop here at the scene of the elimination in France, it's not Sebastian. He is younger and dark-haired, instead of balding. Who the hell did they kill?"

"And, more importantly, where is Sebastian?" asked Rafaele," realising the mistake that the Swiss Guard squad had made.

Pope Nicholas slammed his hand on the desk.

"I want him found. Get Messina's squad on it. They will root him out."

Cardinal Roberto Messina smiled. He had known that sooner or later, the Vatican would need his help. The call from the Pope's office had been a nice surprise though, a vindication of his rich experience over the years. He knew how things worked around here and he got what he wanted by fair means or foul. But, usually foul, he thought to himself.

He had been unsuccessful in the election of the new Pope when his friend, Papa Giuseppe was forced to retire. He had been frustrated at being forced from a frontline role into the background, whilst that idiot Nicholas bumbled his way around the Vatican.

Now, Nicholas had made mistakes and needed his help.

Well, he would give it, but he would make sure that the debt was paid back in full.

He left his office and headed for the Papal suite. His hair was bouffant and perfumed, his shoes polished to a shiny black finish. The expensive Italian suit was immaculate and teamed with a spotless white shirt. He didn't believe in wearing full ceremonial robes unless he was on duty. And he wasn't much, these days, but, that was all about to change. Oh, yes.

He entered the Pope's office without knocking and Nicholas looked up in surprise.

"Ah, Roberto," he said seeing who it was. "We need you to find Bishop Sebastian, who seems to have eluded our team in France. And obviously, he needs to be rendered harmless. He has caused us too much trouble already."

"Of course," said Roberto, smoothly. "But, I have a favour to ask. I have been kicking my heels lately, with no active role to play in the Vatican. I would like to move into a more active role if I am successful in this mission. Say, Camarlengo?"

He looked slyly at Camarlengo Rafaele, who looked up in shock, as he made his request.

Surely, the Pope would not accede to this unreasonable request? He himself had been a faithful attendant to the Pope since his election. He was certain that the Pope would repay his loyalty.

"Well, I am quite prepared to consider a more active role for you, Roberto. I don't want to waste your considerable talents. But, I already have a Camarlengo. How about Cardinal Secretary?"

"That isn't a role that appeals to me, Your Holiness," said Messina shaking his head. "If I am to play a key role in trouble-shooting for the Vatican, I must have a more appropriate role than Secretary. I don't think it would be in the job description of a secretary to hunt down your enemies and neutralise them," he added loudly.

"Sssh, be discreet," said Papa Nicholas. "Someone might *hear*."

"So, what is it to be?" asked Messina.

"Very well, you will take over the role of Camarlengo, should you be successful in eliminating Sebastian."

Rafaele gasped.

"But, Your Holiness, I have served you well and Papa Giuseppe before you. This is unfair."

"No-one is above taking a humble role now and then," said Messina, smiling. "you have had your time at the right hand of Il Papa. Now it is *my* turn."

"You must find Sebastian first, though," said Papa Nicholas.

"Of course," said Messina. "As soon as I have dealt with him I will contact you to make the arrangements for my promotion."

He glided out of the room to start contacting his friends in the Mafia, who were experts at tracking people down.

And eliminating them.

Today Camarlengo, tomorrow Pope, he muttered to himself.

"I'm sorry, Rafaele. I used to think I had high moral, Christian principles. But, since I have been Pope, all that seems to matter is the Vatican and its reputation. And continuing our leadership of the world's Catholics. I must put the church first and if that means being in league with that rat Messina to get rid of the threat of the Revelation Army, then so be it."

Rafaele ran from the office, almost in tears.

What is happening to me? thought Papa Nicholas.

Calum scratched his head.

"But, there are millions of names here."

"Just over three hundred million, to be exact," said Hogan. "Together with their locations around the world."

"If you think about it, if the Annunaki came to Earth thousands of years ago and produced hybrids with humans, there could well be many of them by now," said Rob. "Do you think they all know that they have Annunaki blood in them?"

"Who knows?" said Calum. "You said that when one of the Elite dies, their role passes to their eldest child," he said to Hogan. "So, they keep this database to document the succession lines. Maybe they don't know, until they are called into service?"

"Possibly," said Hogan. "Anyway, there are many of them, too many to trace them all and destroy them, I guess?"

"I don't think we would have the resources to go after this many people," said Calum. "The military forces loyal to the Alliance are not large in number. We will have to focus on the current Elite, the ones in power right now. Find them and eliminate them. At least we know that some of them were already killed by the attacks on their homes. Probably by the Genies."

"Can we search this data?" said Calum. "Find out how many in the UK for example?"

"Yes, there is a search function. Just a second. Okay, you want to know how many in the United Kingdom?"

"Yes," said Calum.

"Here you are. There are three million Annunaki in the UK."

317

"Hold on," said Rob. "That must be virtually the *entire population* post-GM crisis. There was a census around the time of the general election and I'm sure that was the figure."

"But, that would mean that everyone in the UK is Annunaki," said Calum. "That's impossible. Is it possible to search on names?"

"Yes. What name."

"Try mine," said Calum, quietly.

Within a few seconds the name 'Calum O'Connell' came up. 'Current address: Unknown. Age: Thirty-five.'

"Bloody hell," he swore.

"What about mine?" asked Rob.

The query returned a positive record of Rob Moore, Current address: Unknown.

Soon everyone gathered around had a positive return on their names, all with the current address unknown.

"My God," said Calum. "Does this mean we are all Annunaki?"

"Well, we are obviously not in the Elite group of them," said Rob. "Last time I checked I wasn't obscenely wealthy."

"So, how do you explain the fact that all our names, in fact, probably the names of *everyone in the world* are on this database?" said Calum.

"I think there are sub-groups within the data," said Hogan, slowly, studying the screen. "For instance, your name, Calum, is marked with a 'Category: P.' Now, let's try someone who we know is Elite Annunaki, like Vanderbilt."

The return came back.

'Edward Vanderbilt. Category: M. Current address: N/A. Current Age: N/A. Status: Deceased.'

"He's dead?" said Hogan.

"He could have been one of those who were killed at the castle in Cornwall. I don't think they have all been identified yet, although the investigating team have been given the names," said Calum. "Do you have photos of the current Elite?"

"Yes, I think there are some on my camera," said Hogan. "They didn't much like having their photos taken, but I took a few in Zurich."

"I'll email them to the investigation leader, Flight Lieutenant Craig, later. Now, what do these Category letters mean?"

"Well, I reckon that 'M' must be for Master. I think that the Masters and their direct bloodlines come from this grouping."

"How many are marked as 'M?' asked Calum.

"Hold on," said Hogan, tapping in a query. "There are just under thirty thousand of them."

"Bloody Hell. Thirty thousand full-blooded Annunaki?"

"Looks that way, according to the database."

"We all seem to be marked as 'P," said Rob. "What does it mean? Person? Population? Pleb?"

"It could stand for any of those," said Hogan. "I am guessing it identifies us as ordinary people. Humans."

"So, *why* are we on their database?" said Chloe. "I am feeling really creeped-out by all this."

"We know that the Annunaki, interbred with humans to produce more intelligent humans hundreds of years ago," said Rachel. "So, do we have *their* DNA merged with *our* human DNA?

"We know that the DNA of five of the bodies found at Conneaux Castle wasn't human. The team working on it said there was only a thirty percent match with human DNA," said Calum. "So, what if all of those in the 'M' category have pure Annunaki DNA and are either Masters, or potential Masters and are in the direct bloodline?"

"What if that thirty percent match with human DNA is only there because that segment of DNA *came from the Annunaki* into human DNA, by interbreeding?" said Eamon.

"Yes," said Tristan, excitedly. "And that means that the original human DNA before the Annunaki arrived is the other seventy percent."

"My God," said Chloe. "We *all* have some alien DNA. That means we are all *part Annunaki.*"

Later that evening, Calum filed his regular report on-line, describing their findings about human and Annunaki DNA and the supposed history of Annunaki interference on Earth. He was up until the early hours, answering queries from his Alliance contacts, the public and the media.

In the darkened room, with Calum hunched over the screen, a shadowy figure stood behind him. It moved forwards slowly and laid a hand on his shoulder.

Calum looked behind him quickly.

There was nothing there. He must have imagined it. Again.

His imagination was running away with him these days.

He was tired. Time to sleep.

56. A Shock

Jessie and Hannah stumbled along the tunnel in the dark.

"Where the hell are we?" said Jessie. "Didn't you say you saw light up ahead before?"

"Yes, it was very bright. But, I can't see it right now. Perhaps there is a bend in the tunnel and it's not visible from here."

As she spoke they felt their way along the tunnel walls and turned around a slight bend. Then, they both saw it.

"It's light!" said Jessie, joyfully. "We're getting out of here into the fresh air at last."

"Bring it on," said Hannah," as they increased their pace, linking arms.

The next thing they saw was profound and amazing.

The light was so bright it was blinding after so long underground. And there were people walking towards them

"Oh, no, I hope this isn't Genies," said Hannah. It wasn't.

"Hello, darling," said a voice. Jessie couldn't see their face because she was blinded by the bright light, after weeks of darkness, but she knew that voice. So very well. She rushed towards the figure and threw her arms around it.

"Mum! What are you *doing* here?"

Figures approached Hannah too and she was suddenly crying with joy to be reunited with them.

Another figure approached Jessie.

"Dad! You're here too. But, where are we? I thought that you were *dead*. In fact, we buried you, Calum and I.." Her voice tailed off. "Oh, my God."

Messina was in a back room of a quiet tavern in Rome with a group of people.

"We must find this man," he said, handing around photos. "He is a Bishop, named Sebastian. You may recognise him as head of this new cult, the Revelation Army. He is a serious threat to the Catholic Church and he is to be eliminated immediately he is found."

"And where do we expect that he might be found?" asked one man.

"He was last known to be in France, in the Alpine region. But, he could have travelled further by now. You should start there and keep your ears and eyes open. The Revelation Army are not known to keep a low-profile."

"And the reward?" asked a dark-haired man.

"Will of course be generous, as usual," said Messina. "You know the Vatican. Money is no object."

The man in question, together with the two priests, was currently taking tea with Renée Mercier and her team in an ex-German World War II bunker, South of Calais.

"This bunker was built by Hitler during World War Two, as part of the Atlantic Wall defences against invasion by Allied forces from the United Kingdom," she told her guests. "It is well-equipped with everything we need. We have access to military equipment here, as well as a good communication network."

"But, why do you need to hide underground?" asked Father Roussel. "You are a politician, surely, not an army commander?"

"You may not realise it as a man of God, but the atmosphere toward anyone with a different point of view to the Democracy Party government is not exactly friendly. Several political enemies of theirs disappeared or died in mysterious circumstances. We needed to be able to operate in freedom from their tyranny."

"That is terrible," said Bishop Sebastian. "But, we too have known the evil that humans can do. My own congregation were murdered at our base in the Alps a few days ago. And, I'm afraid to say that I suspect the one person who should be above suspicion and evil acts, the Pope himself. We are too much of a threat to the Church. They don't like their power base being threatened and have been trying to silence me for some time."

"We must protect you then," said Renée. "You will need guards if you ever venture outside the bunker. But, I wouldn't recommend it. Government forces patrol this area in helicopters and using drones."

"Well, the government has never threatened us. I think the threat will come from Rome."

"Still, stay inside the bunker, where you are safe," said Renée. "Now, Jean will show you to your quarters. I will see you at dinner."

"Thank you. We do appreciate your protection and hospitality," said the bishop.

Later, in the room allocated to Bishop Sebastian, he and his two followers gathered together.

"We must pray for the Pope. He has been taken over by the evil one. Let's pray for his guidance back to the right path. Then, we should continue our evangelisation of the message of the Revelation to the world. I will ask Renée for access to the broadcasting studio tomorrow."

Roussel and Garnier smiled and knelt to pray with their bishop.

Meanwhile, the Italian team had arrived in France and had split into teams, each taking a different region.

Lorenzo had been allocated the Normandy region. He had contacted the French Milieu, or underworld. He had a network of Milieu contacts in France, which had often proved useful for cross-border Mafia operations.

"So, Jean, have you heard any rumours of the Revelation Army Bishop going to ground on your patch?"

"Non, mon ami. I have heard nothing. But, I will put out a few feelers, see what the latest is. If he is here, it will not have gone unnoticed."

"Good man," said Lorenzo. "I'll be in touch."

He ended the call and picked up his glass of French brandy. He raised his glass to his Italian team.

"Saluti," he said. "Enjoy your meal."

They sat down to eat the fine food in the luxury hotel where they were staying.

After all, they were being paid a king's ransom for this job. They might as well enjoy themselves whilst they were there, he thought grinning.

Rafaele was at his desk in the Vatican. He felt a deep sense of betrayal, after all his faithful service to that ungrateful man. Frowning, he picked up the phone.

"Cardinal O'Neill," said the voice on the other end.

"Buongiourno, it's Rafaele at the Vatican. I need to speak with you. In confidence."

As the Camarlengo explained the situation to Cardinal O'Neill in Dublin, O'Neill gasped in shock. After a few moments, he replied.

"Yes, of course I will help. That is truly shocking. What is he thinking? Okay, I will meet you at the usual place in Rome tomorrow."

By the end of the morning, Rafaele had also secured the support of Cardinal Riley of the United States, currently living in Rome, Cardinal Antonio Sanchez from Spain and Cardinal Antonio Bertoni from Italy.

He would show the Pope that he couldn't just turn his back on loyal friends and servants.

Not on his watch.

"So, what does it mean?" asked Rachel. "What effect will this alien DNA have on us? Will it kill us? Or make us evil like them?"

"I don't think so," said Eamon. "After all, it's been part of our make-up for many years. According to your book, you said that they came here thousands of years ago and bred hybrids with humans. So, if it was going to harm us, it would have done by now. I think what we should be asking is; why they interbred with humans and why they came here in the first place."

"According to your book, Rachel, Zecharia Sitchin was a historian. He interpreted ancient Sumerian writing that he said recorded that the Annunaki came here thousands of years ago. They engineered modern day humans to help them to mine gold for them, as well as rebuild their bases and structures here on Earth." said Hogan.

"Yes, his theory was that they needed gold to repair the damaged atmosphere on their own planet, Nibiru," said Rachel. "His research showed that their Earth bases were destroyed in a great flood."

"What, like the one that Noah escaped, with his family and all the animals in the ark?" asked James.

"Yes, and that may well be the source of that particular Bible story," said Hogan. "They generally were using humans as slaves to accomplish what they couldn't, due to their small numbers. But, humans were a multitude on Earth and in their engineered form were obviously very useful to the Annunaki."

"So, the Elite have always used humans as slaves, just as the obscenely rich Elite now use their workforces and military however they wish?" said Rob. "Nothing changes. Is there even such a planet as Niburu?"

"It seems that opinions on that differ," said Hogan. "Rachel's book says so, but we searched on-line, and some scientists have cast doubts on his theory."

The phone rang and Calum picked it up.

"Ah, good morning, Renée, how are you? What? You're joking?"

"Non, Calum, no joke. I really have the Bishop of the Revelation Army seeking sanctuary with me at our base. And he claims that his congregation in the French Alps was butchered. He only escaped because he was taking a service in the local village at the time. He says that the attack was probably by order of the Vatican. A farmer neighbour saw soldiers, he thinks they were Swiss Guards. And, as you know, they provide security forces for the Vatican."

"What? That doesn't seem very Christian. So, *why* does he think the Vatican would order his and his congregation's deaths?"

"He thinks he was becoming too much of a threat to the established church and Catholicism," said Renée. "People are starting to desert traditional church services and move to the more startling, but actually quite believable, Revelation Army ones. Calum, he is not a nutcase, as he has been painted by the media. He comes across as very down-to earth and genuine. I think he may be right about some things."

"What, that we are facing an imminent Apocalypse?" said Calum. "I would certainly believe that it could be caused by the lunatics in charge, with their nuclear missiles and drones. Not to mention the Genies, who love to throw fireballs and start earthquakes. But, the one in the Bible? Do you really believe it?"

"Well, it doesn't really matter who, or what causes it, it seems like we could be approaching the

328

destruction of the Earth and all life on it, if something isn't done."

"Do you have any ideas? It seems that the Alliance is powerless right now. We are all hiding underground in fortified bases."

"That is true, we found it necessary to protect ourselves. All of the Alliance leaders around the world are facing similar persecution and unexpected deaths."

"Mind you, the Elite or Annunaki, or whatever, are also facing death," said Calum. "We know that several of their Masters were killed in Cornwall recently. And since their homes were destroyed by the Alliance, there have been no sightings of the rest. We haven't seen or heard of the Genies since they probably killed the Annunaki either. And that was ten days ago. Where are they all?"

"I guess that the Annunaki are hiding out somewhere, recovering from the Genie attack. And trying to find replacement Masters to fill the gaps, I should imagine. As for the Genies, who knows what dark hole *they* are hiding in? But, I wouldn't care if I never saw them again."

"Okay, well take extra care of your guests, the Vatican is a powerful force and has friends in all sorts of dark places. Look after yourself too, Renée," said Calum. "Au revoir, thanks for the update."

He replaced the phone and explained the conversation to his companions.

"I know I was brought up in the Catholic church and Mam would have a heart attack if she heard me saying this, but there are some dark forces in the church," he said. "After all, power corrupts and absolute power corrupts absolutely."

"So, we can't trust the Pope now?" asked Shaun. "Is the Catholic church finished?"

329

"Should we all become followers of the Revelation Army instead?" asked James.

"I think we may all be on the same page actually," said Douglas. "The Catholic church teaches us to lead a Christian life, so that we may have eternal life after our death and so does the Revelation Army. After all, the Revelation is one of the books in the Bible. So, their beliefs are already part of the Christian church. We all want the same thing, to live a good life and have an afterlife. They just have a different approach, that's all. It's a matter of who has the power. I think Calum has a point about absolute power too. The actual quote was 'Power tends to corrupt and absolute power corrupts absolutely.' It was made by John Dalberg-Acton, in response to the First Vatican Council in the late eighteen-hundreds, which stated that the Pope is infallible. He could not accept that a man could be judged differently to any other common man, just because he was Pope. I'm sure that there are many good people in the Vatican. But, obviously, where there are humans, there will be some wrong-doing and corruption. Even in the Vatican."

"You're right of course," said Chloe. "I never subscribed to the theory that the Revelation Army were all nut-jobs. Too much has happened that is parallel to the story of the Apocalypse in the Bible. Although obviously, such a group will attract those who want something new and immediate."

"And we have other things in common too," said Calum. "The Genies hate us and the Annunaki want to control us. There's nothing like a common enemy to unite people. We should remember that the Revelation Army in the United Kingdom might need our help too."

Lorenzo's mobile phone rang. He put down his glass of wine and picked up the call.

"Any news of our man?" asked his Mafia boss.

"No, boss. The local network has heard nothing. No rumours, nothing at all."

"Well, get on it. Il Papa is impatient for results. Where are you anyway? I suppose you're holed up somewhere, keeping warm with plenty of liquid refreshments?"

"Just about to head out on our mission, boss," said Lorenzo, hurriedly pulling on his coat and jerking his head towards his team.

"Well, I expect results in the next twenty-four hours."

The phone went dead.

"Bastardo," he snarled, putting the phone in his pocket with his gun. "Come on you lot, we have work to do. The boss's orders are that the bishop must be found today. And I won't be the one to tell him we failed."

Muttering complaints and curses, they departed in their hired car.

This was like hopeless, looking for a needle in a haystack.

59. The Plotters

Rafaele's guests were arriving and he had arranged for them to use one of the private suites at Domus Sanctæ Marthæ, as was his prerogative as Camarlengo. He didn't want to risk the Pope seeing his visitors. And he knew that the Pope was busy all day in the Vatican, meeting visitors at audiences.

The last to arrive was Cardinal Antonio Sanchez, who had travelled from Spain late last night. Cardinal Seamus O'Neill from Dublin had arrived the night before. American Cardinal Dermot Riley and Cardinal Antonio Bertoni were based in Rome.

"Hola, Antonio," called Rafaele as he bustled in, dumping his overnight bag in a corner. "Coffee? How are you?"

He poured a coffee for Sanchez.

"I'm good, thank you, Rafaele. Now, what is all this I hear about the Pope and murder?"

"Well, as I said on the phone, he sent a team of his Swiss Guards to slaughter the leading members of the Revelation Army. Everyone at their hideout in France was killed. Unfortunately, Bishop Sebastian, their leader, was not with them at the time. But, Il Papa has now enlisted the local Mafia to hunt him down and have him eliminated. And the price for that is that their henchman, Cardinal Roberto Messina, will get my job."

"Unbelievable," said Sanchez. "What is he thinking? It is against all the church stands for."

"He feels powerless to stop the defection of our congregations to the Revelation Army. He thinks that they are a major threat to the Catholic Church.

"I think you're right there," said Bertoni. "Here in Italy, we have seen a steep decline in church attendance. And I think the Revelation lot have benefitted from people's confusion and search for easy answers."

"I agree," said Riley. "I have noticed that the services we run for American ex-patriates have been very poorly attended recently. So, what do you suggest we can do about it?"

"I've tried to talk to him about it, to get him to tackle this in a Christian way. But, he has changed since he became Pope. He was so dedicated, so humble, before. But now, I don't recognise the man. He is obsessed with clutching onto his power."

"Power corrupts," said O'Neill. "Even in Ireland, which has always been known for its many devout followers of the Catholic church, we have seen a sharp decline in church attendance. But what can we do?"

"I think it's time to take urgent action to save the church from this evil. We need to remove him from the Papacy. Immediately. Do we all agree?"

"Of course," said Sanchez. Everyone else agreed. "But how?"

"If we are all certain of this course of action, then I think it is time to call in our own eliminator."

"What, do you mean have the Pope murdered?" said O'Neill, shocked.

"Doesn't that make us as bad as him?" asked Sanchez.

"No, I think we are justified in acting to immediately remove what has become a toxic reign by Nicholas. He needs to go, but we cannot just sack him, or we would have to admit to what he has done. It would finish off the Catholic Church completely. So, we have to be subtle."

Rafaele went to open a side door off the office. A woman dressed all in black entered.

"This is Sofia Rizzo. She can help us."

Rafaele drove his car late at night into Vatican City, his passenger concealed under a blanket in the boot. The guards waved him through and he parked in his personal space near to the Portone di Bronzo entrance to the Apostolic Palace.

"Stay out of sight, I will be back soon," he muttered, getting out and locking the car.

He ran up the steps and through the heavy bronze doors, nodding at the Swiss Guard standing there. It was ten minutes until the guard changed at midnight.

Rafaele walked along the echoing corridors of the Apostolic Palace, his footsteps echoing as they fell on the marble floor. It was the only sound in the night-deserted building. He approached the Papal Apartments and stood for a moment, listening. Good.

Then, he suddenly turned around and rushed back to the entrance.

"Elias. I thought I heard a noise; like breaking glass beyond the papal apartments. I am afraid, can you go and check please? Don't worry, I will watch the door until you return."

Elias drew his weapon and rushed off in the direction of the Pope's personal apartments.

Rafaele quickly went back outside and opened his car boot. His passenger leapt out and followed him back into the building. There was just time to conceal her in a side passageway leading around the building before Elias reappeared.

"Are you quite sure you heard something, Your Eminence? I have checked all around the Pope's apartment and he is quite safe, asleep in his room. All the doors and windows are secure. Nothing seems to be out of place."

"Ah, I'm sorry, it must have come from somewhere outside. Late night revellers, no doubt. Sorry to disturb you. Good night Elias, sleep well."

"It's fine, always best to check, Your Eminence. Good night."

Rafaele went through the door to the side passage where his companion was waiting. He put his finger to his lips. They mustn't give anything away to Elias, who would raise the alarm in an instant and flood the place with Swiss Guards. In any case, he would be off duty soon and the matter would be forgotten as a false alarm.

They reached his own offices and he unlocked the door.

He took a paper diagram from his desk.

"I cannot accompany you any further without suspicion falling on me. Here, this is where we are. This here is the Pope's apartment, where he will probably be asleep. He will certainly be alone.

"Okay. Don't worry I will find my own way out," said Sofia, resting her hand on the slim box hidden underneath her jacket. "The money will be transferred to my account?"

"Of course," said Rafaele. "And thank you for your help and discretion."

She slipped away into the darkened corridor, the lights on night-time setting to save power.

She headed towards the Pope's suite.

Outside the door, she checked around, then quietly opened the door into the outer sitting room. She took out the box and opened it on a polished table. She took out a hypodermic syringe and filled it from a small bottle of liquid.

The poison it contained was a tincture of aconite root, the effects of which were to cause breathing difficulties, slow down the heartbeat and eventually cause death. The poison was hard to detect post mortem and the cause of death mimicked a heart attack.

It was perfect for her mission.

She cracked open the door to the inner bedroom and peered inside. She immediately heard a loud snoring. The Pope was fast asleep, on his back, his mouth wide open.

Sofia crept towards him and then dripped the toxin into his mouth. She needed to administer enough to kill.

The Pope's eyes sprang open, as he sensed the bitter liquid running down his throat.

The last of the toxin reached its destination and she clamped a hand over his mouth.

His struggles did not last long, as his pulse and heart rate weakened. Finally, he became unconscious. She took away her hand and felt for a pulse.

There was none.

Her work was done.

61. Death in Rome

Lorenz Pastore, the papal butler, carried the breakfast tray with coffee and croissants into the papal suite, humming a popular tune he had heard on the radio that morning.

With a quick rap on the door of the bedroom, he entered calling out.

"Buongiorno, Papa Nicholas."

He placed the tray on a side table and drew back the heavy curtains, letting in the bright sunlight.

Then, he stopped as there was no reply. He looked over at the Pope.

Nicholas's face was contorted in pain, as he had struggled in vain to breathe. His mouth was open. He wasn't moving.

Shocked, Lorenz hurried to his side and shook him.

"Papa Nicholas, Papa Nicholas," he cried.

Nothing.

He felt for a pulse.

Then, he ran out of the room yelling for help.

Rafaele examined the body. It was his duty as Camarlengo to determine whether the Pope was dead.

"Papa Nicholas," he said, shaking his shoulder. "Are you all right?"

No response.

"Call the doctor," he said to Lorenz, who had slumped into a chair by the bed, shaking. "Lorenz! The doctor, please" he repeated, as Lorenz stared at him, still in shock.

Lorenz stood up unsteadily and went into the office next door to phone the doctor.

Rafaele picked up the phone by the bed and dialled the number for the Dean of the College of

Cardinals, who helped to ensure the Church continued to run smoothly in any gap between Popes.

"Dean, it's Rafaele. I have bad news."

62. Broadcast from an Outcast

Bishop Sebastian looked at the television screen in the bunker in shock. The report was about the sudden death of Pope Nicholas. He turned to Fathers Zacharius and Marc.

"Although I know he saw us as a threat and probably was behind the slaughter of our congregation in the Alps, he was the *Pope*. He believed in the same thing as us. Just not on the same page with his interpretation of events. What a shock. Had he been ill, I wonder?"

The report from Rome said that the Pope had apparently died in his sleep. The cause of death was not yet known.

"It is now more important than ever that we provide a lead to the Christian population of the world," said Zacharius. "Now that the figurehead of the Catholic Church has gone, it will be weeks before a replacement can be found. We must reach out to people."

"I agree," said Marc. "People need guidance through these difficult times. And I don't somehow think they are going to get it from Rome."

"Well, it doesn't feel right to capitalise on the death of the Pope, but I agree we need to give guidance. I will see Reneé about a broadcast to our followers."

"Good. And maybe this is God's will, you know. Pope Nicholas pushed things too far with his attacks on us," said Marc. "After all, he broke one of God's commandments; 'Thou Shalt not Kill.'"

"Yes, I am sure he did," said the Bishop. "Indirectly at least. Okay, can you contact all our priests and let them know that we will need to step into the vacuum and give leadership and comfort to our congregations? I will speak to Reneé and organise my broadcast as soon as possible."

Reneé nodded her agreement.

"I am shocked at the Pope's death. He has been leader for such a short time after Papa Guiseppe's resignation. But, of course you must guide your people. Jean here will set things up for you in our communications suite. You go with your broadcast as soon as you're ready."

The Bishop left to prepare his sermon. He scribbled a few notes that would help him later that evening.

Jean set up the technical system and soon, nodded to Sebastian that everything was ready. The Revelation Army priests had alerted their congregations that an important broadcast would be made that evening. The public media had been briefed. Everything was set.

The Bishop cleared his throat and sat down on the seat in front of the camera. The red recording light came on. Glancing at his notes, he began.

"My dear brothers and sisters in Christ," he said, gazing straight at the camera. "You will have heard the terrible news of the death of the Pope last night. We can only pray for his soul. And, I think he may need those prayers, because I am sorry to say, he had become corrupted by the enormous power that he wielded. The devil had infiltrated his mind and turned his thoughts to evil and murder. We know that for some time he had seen the Revelation Army as a threat. Because, my people, we have spoken the truth about what is going on and the Catholic Church has refused to acknowledge that the Apocalypse is already upon us. Because of that, the Pope sent his forces to attack our number in France and there were deaths. I myself only escaped by chance and have had to seek refuge."

"Bloody hell," said Rob, watching in Scotland.

The friends had heard about the broadcast to be made by the leader of the Revelation Army after the sudden death of the Pope and had gathered together to watch.

"He has just openly accused the Pope of sending people to murder the Revelation Army leaders. I hope he has proof."

"Reneé reckoned that Bishop Sebastian was positive that it was the Vatican who killed his followers. A neighbour had seen the Swiss Guards, who apparently arrived at their hideout and killed everyone there," said Calum. "Unbelievable, I know that a man of God should resort to murder to get rid of perceived threats. But, there is certainly a threat to the established church from the Revelation Army. The Vatican is just too traditional, clinging to old ways of doing things and shunning new ideas."

"Yes, but *murder*, Calum," said Chloe. "I am shocked that it has come to this. Surely the church should be pulling in one direction in these hard times, not breaking up into rival splinter groups."

"You know, it may all be part of what the Revelation Army have been saying all along. Could it really be that the Apocalypse is happening? I mean the floods, fires, tsunamis, sickness and mutants and war. Is it all true?" said Calum. "I know that Reneé has been very impressed with the Bishop anyway. And she doesn't impress easily," he added.

The Bishop was winding up his broadcast.

"And so, I say to you dear brethren, live good lives. There isn't much time left to repent of your sins and make your peace with God. Please pray and make sure you love your family and your neighbour. Our communities must stick together in these difficult times.

342

Be assured that my clergy will be there to support you in these dark days. Seek them out, attend their services. God protect and bless you all."

The screen went blank.

"Calum, do you really think that the world is going to end?" asked James. "I mean, what should we do?"

"If it is, there isn't a thing we can do about it, mate. Just do as the Bishop says and live your life well. After all, none of us know how long we have left. That at least is true."

He gave James a hug then switched off the set.

"Come on," he said. "Time for some relaxation. David, why don't you open that bottle of good whisky that you found the other day? Let's have a bit of a celebration of life on Earth."

They all settled down, chatting away about the latest developments and how nobody really knows how long they have left to live. Losing Jessie had proved that.

Whether this *was* the Apocalypse or not.

63. Call Off the Dogs

Rafaele was in a meeting with the College of Cardinals.

"So, there is nothing else outstanding that needs immediate attention?" said Cardinal Salvatore of Italy. "No more documents to sign off?"

"No, I don't believe so," said Rafaele. "We can't take any major decisions anyway until a new Pope is elected. Everything else will tick over until then."

"Very well. I will make the arrangements for the election of a new Pope. Thank you Rafaele."

Rafaele went straight to his next meeting, which was a little less formal. And in an unusual setting. He pulled on a thick overcoat and a hat and went from the Vatican into the town. Looking around, he pulled his hat further over his forehead, as he shouldered through a door. There weren't many customers in the bar and he quickly saw who he was looking for.

The dark-haired man didn't look up as he sat down beside him.

"You realise that everything has moved on?" started Rafaele bluntly. "With the death of the Pope, your instructions have changed. Your team must call off their search in France. Oh, don't worry, you will be paid for what you have already done. But, of course, the promise of the job of Camarlengo must be rescinded. That will be in the gift of the new Pope. Whoever that may be."

Messina growled a profanity.

"I suppose you are pretty glad to see the old Pope dead?" he spat. "After all, it will be to your own benefit. You get to keep your precious job. In fact, I shouldn't be surprised if you had something to do with it."

"Don't be ridiculous. The Pope was an old man with a weak heart. He died of a heart attack."

"If you say so. Well, I will send you my bill. And don't expect any help from me the next time the Vatican have an annoying problem that they can't solve."

Scowling, he drained his glass and swept out of the bar.

Rafaele breathed a sigh of relief.

That was surely one very nasty man.

Hyde Park was thronged with people. They had gathered in front of a huge stage. There was an atmosphere of anticipation as the buzz of voices resounded around the huge park.

Then, a man in a long, black robe walked onto the stage and took the microphone.

"Welcome, brethren to today's service of the Revelation Army. We have gathered here to give comfort and guidance to our congregations. We know that you will be stunned by the recent death of the Pope and some of you will be seeking guidance and help. I now present the Revelation Army Bishop of Westminster."

The crowd roared its approval.

The Bishop strode onto the stage to the microphone.

"Brothers and sisters, can we first bow down our heads and say a prayer for the Pope, who has passed away recently?"

There was a massive movement of bowed heads as the crowd readied itself for a prayer.

"Dear Lord, please have mercy on the soul of Pope Nicholas. He has been accused of violence in his life, even murder, against members of the Revelation Army. Please have mercy on his soul and grant him eternal rest."

He looked up at the crowd.

"Amen," came the roar, although some were muttering that the deceased pope didn't deserve their prayers after what he had done.

"In the past few weeks we have seen increasing hostility by the Vatican towards the Revelation Army. Even though we only spoke the truth about what is going on today and how it was foretold in the Bible. But, the Catholic Church refused to listen and denied that we are approaching the Apocalypse, near the end of times."

The crowd murmured, turning to each other. Was he saying that they were all going to die?

"Not only did the Vatican refuse to listen to our message, it sent killers to slaughter our congregation and bishops in France where they were gathered peacefully to pray for humanity."

Angry shouts went up.

"They can't kill us all!"

"Murderers!"

There was a general hum of raised voices after that. After a couple of minutes of looking on and smiling, the Bishop raised a hand. The hubbub gradually subsided.

"My brothers and sisters, the Bible tells us that, at the end of the world, sinners will be swept away into the place called Sheol, or Hades, for all eternity. This will include the wicked Jinn, who have preyed on humans and murdered and enslaved them. It will include the evil, corrupt Elite that sit in the shadows and manipulate humanity to their own ends, robbing the Earth and its people of its riches and resources. I say to you, all of those will be swept into Hell."

"But, the people who have lived good lives, they will go to a place of light. For the Revelation promises a new Heaven and a new Earth. For thus it was foretold by John; 'Behold, the dwelling of God is with men. He will

346

dwell with them and they will be his people. He will wipe away every tear from their eyes and death shall be no more, neither shall there be mourning nor crying, nor pain any more, for the former things have passed away.' And he described a city of light, where there was no more darkness and where there was a tree of life and all kinds of fruit. I say to you, that can be *your* inheritance, if you live a good life here on Earth. Let us pray."

As the people joined him in a series of prayers, the camera cut away and went back to the studio.

Calum snapped off the television.

"You know, the Revelation Army are only preaching what's in the Bible. I don't see how the Vatican can object to any of it. That is supposedly what they also believe."

"Or, would they prefer that it was some distant, never-to-become real, future world that they can threaten people with?" said Rob. "So that they can maintain their earthly power over people's lives and never have to deal with what it's all about in the first place?"

"It must be scary for the church to realise that everything they have been preaching and praying about for millennia is actually going to happen for real," said Chloe.

"Well, what did they expect?" said Rob, showing his usual contempt for organised anything. "They've been wittering on about it for long enough."

"They must be desperate to hold onto power to order the murder of Revelationists though," said Calum. "It's against everything the church teaches. And it probably means they won't reach Heaven themselves, because they will presumably be heading for this Sheol place they mention. They always called it Hell in my day."

"Well, anyway, whatever it is called and whenever we are going, I suggest we need to eat something in the meantime, to keep body and soul together," said Millie, smiling. "Come on kids, help me peel some vegetables, will you?"

They all got up and tramped after Millie without protest.

They were good kids, thought Calum. Especially after what happened to Joanna.

64. Revenge of the Jinn

Balthazar was in a bad mood. The unfinished business of destroying the enemies, who had tried to kill him and his followers, irritated him like a constant thorn in his side. He flung open his door.

"Nicholas," he called down the corridor and, after a minute, Nicholas came slowly along the corridor from his own room. He looked pale and sweaty.

"What is it, Master?" he asked.

"We have wasted too much time pandering to this sickness. I want to go after the rest of our enemies *now*" he stated.

"Very well Master, I will get the others together," said Nicholas. "How are we travelling?"

"The usual way, through the air," said Balthazar, tiredly. "Bring the Native Americans, they are good at this."

Nicholas hurried off to do his Master's bidding. Balthazar was never very patient when his instructions were not carried out to the letter or were not completed quickly enough. He didn't want to cause his Master to become any angrier than he already was.

Besides, he really didn't feel well he thought, as he wiped his damp forehead with the back of his hand.

Not well at all.

Within half an hour, all the most powerful Jinn were gathered at the exit of the bunker.

Balthazar's door opened. He came out, looking around for his favourite followers.

He saw that Inola, Keezheekoni, Megedagik, Nashoba and Shappa were all waiting for him, together with Nicholas and his twelve Elite Genies.

He nodded. It was good. They would attack now.

349

He went out of the bunker and rose into the air, followed closely by his band of Jinn. Within minutes they had teleported to the place he had seen in his mind. He thought it was in Italy, but that didn't matter because he knew exactly where to go.

The castle rose up out of the mist enveloping the low-lying land around it. It looked ghostly, like a haunted castle. Some of the Native Americans started to mutter. They were very superstitious.

"What's *wrong* with you," snapped Balthazar, as he landed outside the castle.

"Spirits are here, this place is evil," said one, looking nervously at Balthazar, who was famed for his rages.

"Well, even if there are ghosts here, you surely aren't going to tell me that you, Inola, a mighty Cherokee, are afraid of a few dead people who can't possibly hurt you?"

"It's bad luck," she muttered, turning away. She couldn't afford to look weak in front of Balthazar. The original twelve followers were already jealous of the fact that Balthazar greatly valued the superior psychic abilities of the Native Americans.

"Look if you can't hack it, go back to the bunker," he snapped.

"No, it's fine," she insisted, setting her face like stone.

"Right, let's stop messing about and go in then," he snarled. He focussed on becoming invisible and disappeared within a few seconds. Everyone followed suit and they went into the castle.

Gaj Kapur, Corinne Moreau, Marta Petrov, Ricardo Fabbiana and Rosa Araripe sat together in the great hall of the castle around a huge fireplace, set with burning logs. The dogs lay in front of the fire asleep.

"So, my investigators have discovered that the aircraft spotted doing the fire-bombings were military. Supposedly under our control, although records show some gaps on the day of the firebombing. They think somebody flew them without authorisation. I have asked the Commanders to check on the whereabouts and movements of all our aircraft. It may take some time and I don't think we have that right now. In any case, it will be difficult to prove who took what aircraft out unofficially that day. I think we can assume it's the Alliance and their sympathisers. Most of their leaders have gone to ground, so they may be behind it. And I would put money on Mr O'Connell being behind it. Wherever he is."

"That man again," spat Marta. "Can't the military do their bloody job and find and eliminate him?"

"They have been looking," said Fabbiana. "But, he could be anywhere, although he seems to like Scotland. We have had patrols regularly searching for him in all the likely places. But, it's a big country."

"So, what now? Any success in locating the Masters to replace those killed?" said Marta.

"We have identified the next in line. They are Eleanor Goodman, Sir Michael's daughter. Edward's son, Mark Vanderbilt, Katsu Mori's nephew Sora, Johnny, the son of Max Kaufman and Tony Chan's youngest son Chao. But, I'm afraid we have had no luck in persuading them to take on their responsibilities. They all say the risks are too great after what happened to their predecessors."

"Well, they cannot refuse," snapped Marta. "It's their *destiny*. Have them all brought here forthwith."

"But, if they don't want to," began Gaj.

351

"Look it's not a matter of choice. They *must* take over and soon," said Marta. "Have them brought here. By *force* if necessary."

"Very well," said Fabbiana.

There was a sudden noise outside the door and it flew open. They all looked up. There was nobody there. But, they felt a movement in the air that caused them all to rise to their feet, looking around nervously.

Then, the attack began.

The Jinn snapped into visibility with a hail of firebolts and the rapid teleportation of objects in the room as missiles. Inola and Keezheekoni hurled fireball after fireball at the group in the room, who were forced to dodge around to avoid them.

Megedagik was adept at creating forcefields of energy that rendered the victim paralysed.

Shappa caused the air to electrify and thunderbolts to crack around the heads of the Elite.

Balthazar and his twelve closest followers concentrated on lifting heavy missiles and smashing them at their victims.

Infuriated by the multiple attacks, the Elite started to change into their reptilian shapes, their long snouts appearing from the flat faces, filled with snapping teeth. Their heavy tails appeared and swept from side to side, trying to knock the attackers off their feet. Fabbiana and drew a pistol and aimed it at Balthazar.

"Oh no, you don't," he snarled, throwing his arm out, causing the gun to fly from Fabbiana's hand and up to the ceiling where it struck a beam and broke into two pieces, dropping to the floor.

Fabbiana growled, now fully reptilian and crashed toward the nearest Jinn, sinking teeth into his neck, clamping his jaw tight. The victim was too close to Fabbiana for the others to use their fireballs or missiles and they could only concentrate on attacking the others.

The attacked Jinn moaned, losing blood from the jugular. He slumped down and Fabbiana let him go with a grunt of disgust.

Immediately Shappa fired a blue thunderbolt directly at Fabbiana, hitting him in the chest, causing him to sink to the floor wounded.

Responding to the commotion, the Elite's military guards crashed into the room, weapons drawn, firing at the strangers.

"At last," growled Marta. "What kept you?"

She dodged a fireball from Inola and moved behind the guards, shouting to the others to retreat.

But, Balthazar had seen her intention in her mind, although she tried to keep him out.

He suddenly appeared right in front of her as she tried to leave the battle.

"Leaving already my dear," he crooned. "Surely that is a bit rude, when we have only just arrived?"

Marta tried to push past, but Balthazar threw a bolt of raw energy at her and she fell backwards.

The guard nearest her moved to stand in front of her and Balthazar had to turn his attention to him, as he pointed his gun straight at Balthazar and fired. As Balthazar moved to avoid the bullet at the speed of light, Marta took advantage of the distraction to rush from the room, closely followed by the others, although they were not all untouched by the attack.

The Jinn were now fully occupied fighting the guards.

It was an unequal fight. The guns were no match for the Jinn's fireballs, teleportation and thunderbolts. Soon all the guards lay dead, or mortally wounded.

"Ok, let's finish the job," said Balthazar, rushing out of the door the Elite had used. There was no sign of them and he snarled at the empty hallway.

Then, a noise from outside made him jerk his head up and he snapped into invisibility to move through the solid walls back outside the castle.

In the cold winter air, a helicopter could be seen rapidly rising through the mists, above the castle ramparts.

Balthazar howled his anger and his followers hurled fire and thunder after the chopper, but it was already out of reach.

With a disgusted roar, the Jinn disappeared as quickly as they had appeared earlier.

The five Elite settled into their seats in the chopper for the journey. The co-pilot, John Masters, came into the passenger cabin.

"Where to?" he asked. "Do you have co-ordinates for us?"

"Well, we can't go back there," said Marta. "And all our lovely mansions have been destroyed by those Alliance idiots. Any suggestions?"

"We can go to my Mother's summer house near Rio de Janeiro, it's on an otherwise uninhabited island," said Rosa Araripe. "It would be easy to defend as there is only access by boat, there's no landing strip. We hardly ever went there as the business grew and my parents became very successful and had little time for holidays. It's impossible that Hogan knows about it, if that's who's behind the destruction of our homes. Father would never have been there with his guards."

"Perfect," said Marta. "Can you give the location to John?"

"We might need to refuel on the way," said Masters.

"Fine," said Marta. "I'm sure we can leave it to you to arrange that."

Masters bowed and went back to the flight controls with Rosa to program in the location.

"You may serve the champagne now," said Corinne to the butler. "And some nibbles too. I think we deserve a little celebration of our latest victory over the Jinn, don't you?"

They all agreed that they did indeed deserve a little treat now and the butler went to get the chilled champagne and glasses.

Then, all hell broke loose.

Suddenly, the Jinn materialised in all their numbers within the passenger cabin.

"Hello, my dears," said Balthazar. "I must say, you seem to be in a hurry to go somewhere, just after we arrived to visit you too. Someone should teach you some manners. Oh yes, we can do that," he snarled, grabbing Gaj. He quickly produced a machete and held it to Gaj's throat. He was taking no chances with these reptilian shapeshifters.

Gaj whimpered helplessly.

"Now, I'll tell you what the rest of you are going to do," crooned Balthazar. "You will all go and sit back in the galley and if you even think about changing into alligators, or whatever you are, this guy gets it. In the neck. Literally," he finished with an evil chuckle.

There was a shocked silence. He had them at checkmate. Unless they were prepared to risk the life of one of their own. And they had lost so many already.

Sullenly, they got to their feet and were shoved back into the cramped galley, designed for staff to chill and serve food and drinks.

The Jinn tied them all to their seats.

"Now, you can serve that lovely-looking champagne to us instead," said Balthazar, the blade still held at Gaj's throat. He guffawed and his followers joined in, a throaty evil chorus of mirth that didn't seem at all funny.

"Watch them closely," he said to Inola and Nashoba, as the rest strolled back into the passenger area, dragging Gaj with them. The terrified butler brought the champagne, his hands shaking as he poured the drinks into tall flutes.

"Tie him up," commanded Balthazar of Nicholas, pushing Gaj into a seat. "Now, bring us something to eat," he snarled at the butler.

The butler scurried back to the galley, hoping to get instructions from the Elite there. But, they were under close guard by the Native Americans.

Loading food from the fridge onto plates he took them forward and handed them around.

The butler disliked his bosses quite a bit. He knew what they were, although he would never dare reveal it. The punishment would be too great. And the wage was more than anything he could hope for anywhere else. But, these Jinn; they were animals. Pigs. They stuffed the delicate, gourmet food into their mouths, laughing and talking as they did, spitting chewed food around the cabin. Anything that wasn't to their liking was spat out onto the floor. Disgusting.

Balthazar was quite enjoying himself, being waited on by a butler and fed nice food and drink. But, these people would suffer before the day was out. They would pay for their constant attacks on his people.

Oh, yes.

Jessie and Hannah sat on the lush, green grass at the feet of their parents, asking many questions about where they were and what would happen to them.

"So, are we all really dead?" asked Hannah.

"We are what people on Earth call 'dead' yes," said her dad, Graham. "But, as you can see, it's not the end for us. And it's not the end of this Earth-like place," he said waving his arm to take in the scenery around them.

The sky was a deep, deep shade of blue, bluer and brighter than they had ever seen it before. The trees and grass were deep green. The sun shone a pure yellow-gold above. The flowers were like none that Jessie had ever seen before. Bright, vivid colours, colours that she had never seen in nature before. Reds, blues, oranges, purples, every colour of the rainbow and more. Brightly-coloured butterflies flitted around the flowers, drinking in their nectar. And the heady fragrance was so, so sweet, better than any perfume on Earth.

The mountains that swept down to the seashore in the distance were majestic and spectacular. The sea was a deep azure blue, flecked with pure white, as it broke onto a sandy beach.

And was that really Scamp, the little black and white dog that had been her constant companion as a child, lying contentedly next to her, breathing gently in his sleep? But, he too had been long gone, in her life on Earth anyway.

"Can dogs live here then? I thought they didn't go to Heaven? *Is* this Heaven? Is God here?" asked Jessie her questions tumbling out, one after the other. She had *so* many questions.

Her mum, Veronica, laughed.

"Yes, darling, they can. That was just wrong. False information spread around by people with vested interests. But, never mind that now. All animals of every kind live here. Just like on Earth. As to where this is, some people call it Heaven. Some say it's Paradise, or the Kingdom of God. Others call it Nirvana, Zion, Elysium, the Elysian Fields, Valhalla, or Avalon. It depends on which culture people are from. But, from what we have learned and can understand, it's an alternative Earth. It's a more perfect Earth, present in the same timeframe, but in another dimension."

"So, is God here?" insisted Hannah.

"That depends on one's culture and religion, Hannah," said her mother, Norma. "To Christians, there is a supreme being called God. Hebrews and Judaism have Yahweh, Jehova or Elohim. The Rastafarians have Jah. There are many, many names for the Higher Being. But, they all refer to the same entity. As to whether the entity called 'God' is here, well, there *is* a higher being of light here that is called The One. We have glimpsed Him sometimes, when He allows us to."

"The thing is, sweetheart, we can't always see God, because God exists at a higher level of vibration than we do," said her dad, George. "We can only perceive beings at our own vibrational level. That doesn't mean they are not all around us. They are. You might understand these beings as 'God' and 'angels.' When you were on earth, you would have thought they were ghosts. Not there, just shadows, or an imprint of former inhabitants left in the fabric of a building. But, they are just present at a different vibrational frequency, that's all."

"We don't fully understand it, you see," said Veronica. "They are explaining it to us, bit by bit. But,

358

as you can see, it's complex. We humans have limited understanding of spiritual matters."

"Who do you mean by 'they'?" asked Jessie.

"The elders here, who have been in this place for many Earth years. They are wiser and more experienced in the ways of Heaven than we are. We are learning so much from them."

Jessie suddenly had a shock to the core of her being, as she realised something that should be impossible.

When her and Hannah's parents spoke, their mouths did not move.

And when Hannah or herself asked a question, neither did theirs.

66. What Are We?

Jessie nudged Hannah as her mum was explaining about the elders and what they had been telling them.

"Watch their mouths," she whispered. "They are communicating *without speaking*. And so are we."

Hannah looked at her in shock, her mouth falling open.

"Oh, sweetheart," 'said' Veronica, smiling. "We can do all kinds of things here that would be considered impossible on Earth. We forget now that it's a shock to newcomers. But, it's quite normal, everybody can do it. Even you, as you have just realised."

"But how, why?" stuttered Jessie.

"These are things that you could do once, before you were born to your Mum and I back on Earth," said George. "When you were an angel and first lived here."

"What? We *came* from here in the first place?" said Jessie.

"Yes, we all did. We just forget where we are from, what we are, what we can do. Young children know, they can still remember. But, adults just tell them not to be so silly, that humans can't do those things."

"So, *what* are we?" whispered Hannah.

"We don't know," said Veronica. "Except we do know that God, the One, created us in his own image. And God is a being of light, existing at a higher vibrational wavelength. So, we think that maybe we will eventually be raised to a higher state of vibration, to be with God for eternal life, as the Bible says. We just don't understand everything yet."

"We think we will become again what we always were, before our Earthly existence," said George. "We will be Beings of Light."

"Wow," breathed Hannah. "That's mind-blowing."

"Indeed," said Norma.

"I've noticed something else," said Jessie.

"What is it darling?" asked Veronica.

"Well, you look younger than you did on Earth. And healthier, less tired."

"Yes," said Hannah. "You all do."

"Our earthly bodies are temporary vessels," said Graham. "When we die, we don't need them anymore, just our consciousness and soul survive. But, it helps us to communicate with each other effectively if we are in our Earthly forms, forms that our family and friends recognise. We could leave them behind if we wished. But, we can pick up our earthly bodies at their most healthy, in their prime if you like."

"That is so incredible," said Hannah. "So, we will never grow old?"

"No, sweetheart," said her mum, Norma. "This is truly a paradise. No sickness, death, wars, or natural disasters. Just beautiful landscape, sea, mountains, animals living as free as we are."

"What about those we left behind?" asked Jessie. "I miss Calum so very much. Sometimes I have visited him, but he cannot hear or see me. Occasionally, he seems to sense me, when he first wakes up. But, he quickly dismisses it as his imagination and grief. Will I ever be reunited with him?"

"And I with Rob?" added Hannah.

"Well, everyone who has lived a good life will end up here eventually," said Veronica. "So, it's pretty certain that, yes, you will see them again."

"What happens to the others?" asked Hannah. "Those that haven't lived a good life?"

"We don't fully understand," said Norma. "But, we know that there really is a place called Hades, or Sheol, or the Pit. We knew it as Hell. You have to have been really evil, but if you have, that's where you go at the end of your Earthly life."

"I can think of some people who are headed there, then," said Jessie. "The Jinn for a start. Really evil, psychopathic killers. And the World Democrats and the Illuminati, who have culled people on a huge scale with GM food and nuclear missiles. Not to mention sacrificing children and trying to poison people by adding fluoride to the drinking water. I hope that they won't be coming here."

"I very much doubt it," said her dad, Graham. "If anyone deserves to go to Sheol, it's those characters. This is a place of sanctuary and peace."

"Good," said Jessie. "Now, is there any way I can let Calum know that I'm okay?"

Calum awoke with a start. What the hell was that? He threw back the covers and went to the window, as he again heard the loud, thundering noise coming from outside.

At first, he couldn't process what he was seeing. The trees lining the farm's fields, separating them from the grasslands beyond were shaking. There was a deep rumbling sound and the ground seemed to be shaking. Was it an earthquake?

Pulling on jeans and a sweatshirt, he rushed to Rob's room next door, just in time to see Rob flying out, his hair dishevelled.

"What the hell's happening?" said Rob. "I heard a huge sound and the ground's shaking."

"I know," said Calum. "Come on let's go and see."

They made their way towards the access tunnel to the farmhouse above the bunker. On the way, they were joined by other members of the community, all awoken by the disturbance. Among them were the kids.

"Oh no, you don't," insisted Calum. "You three stay right here until we find out what's going on. You too Chloe, with the little one. It might be dangerous out there."

Grumbling, the kids dropped back and went into the rec room.

Calum, Rob, David, Millie and a few of the others grabbed guns from the weapons store on the way up.

Calum opened the door and was first outside. The noise out here was immense, a constant pounding of the ground and the trees were swaying back and forth.

"What the hell?" he started.

Just then, a herd of enormous animals came into view. They were huge and had long necks and some had armoured bodies. The rhythm of their running was causing the ground to shake and the trees to move. They roared, a massive sound, as they approached. Were they coming this way, or would they move off towards the grasslands?

They couldn't be allowed to come this way, the farmhouse, their protection and sanctuary, might be trampled and destroyed. Calum yelled at the others with weapons.

"Fire to this side of them!" he yelled above the thunderous sound. "Don't aim for them, try to deflect them away from the farm!"

They set up a volley of missile fire across the animals' flanks, cutting off the route towards the farm. The mighty beasts started to veer away, roaring their anger, towards the tree line.

"It's working!" yelled Rob.

They kept up the fire until they started to run out of ammunition and the last of the animals had disappeared beyond the trees. They could still see them in the distance, charging away from them, roaring their displeasure.

"What the bloody hell were they?" gasped Rob, sinking to his knees, dropping the hot weapon.

"The huge ones were Tyrannosaurus Rex. I think I also saw Stegosaurs and Megalosaurus," said Eamon. "That's from my vague memory of my palaeontology course. The devolution process is speeding up massively now. We have already seen the regression of the DNA of local species to that of a hundred and fifty, a hundred and sixty million years ago."

"Come on, let's get back inside," said Calum, worried that the beasts might return when they were out of ammunition. "We're going to have to set up some kind of protective barriers against them."

"Good luck with that," said Rob. "How are you going to keep ten tons of prehistoric monster out if it wants to come in?"

"We could rig up some kind of electric fence," said Eamon. "You know, the kind they put up to keep sheep in a field. I don't think they would approach that, not once they have had a shock or two from it."

"Let's see what is in the barns," said Calum. "You all go back in and David, Millie and I will check it out. I still have a bit of ammo left."

It turned out that there were large reels of electricity cable in the barns. With the others' help, David set to work on an electric fence powered by the solar power system supplied by the panels on the roof of the farmhouse and barns.

He hoped that the charge would be enough to discourage the massive animals.

Would they even feel it?

"You know, I think we need a plan to join forces with the Revelation Army lot," Calum was saying later in the rec room. "After all, we have common enemies. The Jinn. The Illuminati. Defending ourselves against the dinosaurs. We might not agree totally with them but Reneé certainly thinks that Bishop Sebastian talks a lot of sense and I trust her judgement. And they have scooped up a lot of the congregations from the other mainstream churches. They have the numbers. I think our existence here is too precarious."

"Sounds like a good idea," said David. "After all, we are pretty much barricaded in here. It's not safe to go out, with the constant drone searches by the authorities and the threat from the dinosaurs and the Jinn. I vote we contact them."

Everyone seemed to agree.

"As long as I don't have to join one of their happy, clappy services," growled Rob.

"Don't worry, I can't see them thinking that *you* are worth converting," grinned Calum. "They will see that you are beyond redemption. Anyway, I'll get Reneé to ask the Bishop who we should contact over here. The sooner the better. I'm getting to feel a bit claustrophobic in here."

"I agree," said Chloe. "And I'm going to need proper medical facilities when this little one is ready to make an appearance. Nazeer, I know that you and your team are brilliant at what you do, but you only have basic medical supplies and equipment here. There's nowhere around here. What if it's a complicated delivery?"

"You're right," said Nazeer. "We do need to identify a fully equipped delivery suite soon. After all, you're not too far off now and the baby could arrive early."

"Then, let's get things moving," said David, looking worried.

"Don't worry, darling, I'm not ready to deliver yet," said Chloe, putting her hand on his shoulder.

"She's going to be in good hands, mate," said Nazeer.

"I know," said David. "Doesn't stop me worrying though."

"I used to be a midwife," said Yvette, suddenly. "It seems like an age ago now. But, I could help."

"That would be great," said Nazeer. "Let's get onto the Bishop and find out if they can help us reach the nearest facilities."

Calum came back from talking to Reneé and Bishop Sebastian.

"The Bishop has given me a couple of contacts around this area," said Calum. "When do you think we need to move to the medical facilities?"

"Well, Chloe has a month or so to go," said Nazeer. But, the baby could decide to make an early appearance anytime now. I would like to move Chloe to a safe house with easy access to facilities as soon as possible."

"Right, I'm on it," said Calum, going off to speak to his contacts.

The phone was picked up on the third ring.

"Hello, Father Caspian here."

"Hi, Father, my name is Calum O'Connell and we need your help."

"I know who you are, Calum," said the priest. "You were the boss around these parts until recently. And a much better one than the current lot too. How can I help you, my friend?"

"Thank you. We need to get to a medical facility with a birthing suite. My good friend Chloe is due next month. We also have a bit of a problem with the dinosaurs around here. I want to move our community to somewhere safer, where there is more protection, more people. And we might need a bit of help on the way, as we seem to be in demand by the authorities, who have been searching for us."

"Not a problem, we can provide safe accommodation within our community and an escort for the journey here. How many of you need to travel?"

"There are around a hundred of us. We're near St Andrews and I understand that you have a big community nearby. Could we join up with you? Safety in numbers and all that."

"We are located around Dundee, not too far from you," said Father Caspian. "As for dinosaurs, some of those on the outskirts of Dundee were killed by missiles. There don't seem to be many left around here now. You should be quite safe. But, I can send an escort to help bring everybody up here. You would be very welcome. We have plenty of room."

"How about the authorities, do you get much interference there?"

"We hardly ever see them. This is too remote from London for them. They laid down the law a while ago, then just left us to it. If we pay our taxes, they don't really care what we are doing up here."

"Sounds perfect. Let's make the arrangements."

By the end of the call, it was fixed that an escort party from the Dundee congregation would come in two days' time with transport for them. Apparently, there were quite a few ex-military with serious weaponry in the church and Father Caspian didn't seem to think there would be any problem.

"Okay, everyone, we need to pack up everything we will need in our new home," he said breezily to the others back in the rec. room. We're going to live in Dundee with a new community."

There was a buzz of excited chatter at the thought of moving to live alongside other people. Nobody had liked to admit it, but many of the community had been feeling that their life inside the bunker was drab and featureless. It was just too dangerous to venture outside. They missed the open air and the wild seascape of Gallanvaig.

They had also lost members of their little community whilst they had been there, including young Joanna, who was still much missed.

Nobody felt much of an attachment to the bunker and they would be glad to leave this phase of their lives behind.

Marta's anger was building. How dare these mutants hold them prisoner like this? They were the *Elite*. Not part of this awful, miserable place. She didn't know why their ancestors had decided to settle here, but it was becoming very tedious.

She tugged at the cords fastening her to the seat. Tight, but not unbreakable. Not if she changed form.

She glanced at Corinne, Fabbiana and Rosa and slightly inclined her head towards their bound hands and feet, whilst watching Inola and Nashoba closely. They were occupied in eating the snacks and drinking the champagne that the butler had brought.

Corinne mouthed a question, her eyebrows raised. "Gaj?"

Marta shook her head very slightly. Gaj could look after himself, she was sure.

She nodded firmly and started to quickly shapeshift into a huge, broad-jawed reptile, with snapping teeth and sharp claws. The others followed suit and they strained against their bonds until they broke like weak threads. The reptiles leapt up from their seats, as Inola and Nashoba realised what was happening. With a start, they dropped their food and grabbed for their guns.

"No, you don't," snarled Marta and with a sweep of her long, scaly tail, she swept them off their feet and grabbed one of their guns.

With an angry roar, Fabbiana grabbed the other and fired it straight at Inola's chest. Inola tried to throw a firebolt at Fabbiana, but in her agony from her chest wound, she missed.

Marta fired the other gun at Nashoba and hit him in the head. He dropped like a stone.

Hearing the commotion, Nicholas and Shappa rushed in to find out what was happening. Nicholas saw the injured guards and tried to teleport away from Marta, who was aiming her weapon at him. In his weak state from the GM sickness, which was at last overtaking the Jinn, he failed to move fast enough. Marta changed aim and fired. Shot in the back, Nicholas yelped in pain. The other Jinn rushed in and seeing the commotion started to create thunder and firebolts. The air in the galley crackled with electricity.

Gaj realised his opportunity to escape and shapeshifted, easily freeing himself from his bonds. Balthazar, who was still stuffing himself full of gourmet food, assumed that his followers would take care of the commotion in the galley.

But, as he realised that Gaj was free, he leapt up and tried to create a forcefield to hold Gaj captive where he was. But, he was also weakened by the sickness and Gaj swept him onto the floor, grabbing him by the throat with his strong jaws.

Balthazar was weakening. He knew that he had seconds to escape before this vile enemy succeeded in strangling the breath out of him. With a muted growl, he used every ounce of his energy force to throw Gaj backwards. As soon as he was free, he sent out a signal to his followers to retreat.

In a second, he had disappeared, just as Gaj lunged at him once more, jaws snapping.

Balthazar fidgeted angrily, whilst Cherie tried to clean the wound on his neck with antiseptic fluid.

"Ouch! That hurts," he whined.

"It has to be cleaned, Master, it might get infected," she said, trying not to anger him. He wasn't very nice when he was angry. Was he getting weaker or something? She had never seen him return to base so wounded. He would normally be able to fight anyone off, using his psychic powers.

She looked at him appraisingly as she cleaned the wound. "Okay, that's as clean as I can make it. I'll just bandage it."

"Oh, don't fuss," he snarled, but sat still whilst she bandaged his neck.

He still felt very unsettled by the recent battle with their enemies. Never had he failed to win against mere humans. Except, they *weren't* human, were they? He smiled grimly. Did that excuse his poor performance? Maybe it did, but it didn't make him feel much better. He was unused to defeat of any kind.

"How is Nicholas?" he asked Cherie. He had arrived back in pain from a wound in the back where a bullet had struck him.

"Tanaya managed to dig the bullet out. Eventually. He made such a fuss. But, we don't have access to anaesthetics here. I gave him a swig of whisky instead. You'd think he'd be grateful," she muttered, falling quiet as she saw Balthazar's thunderous expression.

"So, he will survive? He is my right-hand man. What about the others?"

"He will be okay, I think. As for Inola, Tanaya did his best with her chest wound. But, I think the bullet hit her lung. He took it out and stitched her up. I just don't know if she will recover. Her breathing is very ragged. And as you know, Nashoba didn't make it back. Inola said he took a bullet in the head. Everyone else is okay. Except nobody is feeling very well. I don't feel well myself."

"Oh, stop complaining, just be grateful we didn't make you go out and fight our enemies," snapped Balthazar.

Cherie fell silent and cleared away her equipment. He could bloody well look after himself now.

She went out, careful not to slam the door, in case she angered her Master even more.

Balthazar was thoughtful. In their weakened state, he knew that they couldn't take on those monstrous reptiles. But, his human enemies. They were different, vulnerable.

He had taken out the troublesome Jessie, who had shot him in Edinburgh and her friend too.

But, as for the one who had caused him several setbacks and defeats, the one named Calum.

He still had his punishment to come.

69. Pastures New

They were pleased with the result of what they hoped was their last battle with the hideous Jinn. The mutants hadn't seemed their usual arrogant, powerful selves.

"I'm sure they are sick," Marta told the others. "They were all so pale and they had the terrible rash that the humans got from the GM food."

"Their psychic powers were definitely diminished," said Fabbiana. "They couldn't hit their targets for toffee and their teleportation was pathetic."

"They still managed to become invisible and teleport out of here, though," said Corinne.

"Anyone else feel like they are done with this planet?" asked Marta tetchily. "It has become very tedious, so polluted, so many sick inhabitants. And the dinosaurs. We still haven't managed to rid the place of them. Look."

She pointed out of the window. They were flying over the African plains, where a herd of the horrible monsters charged after a group of smaller animals.

"Bloody Novagentech."

"Well, I think we have sucked most of the resources out of planet Earth anyway," said Fabbiana. "And our nice homes are all gone. The Alliance rebels aren't going to stop chasing after us, nipping our heels, any time soon. What are you suggesting?"

"We still have the ships. Why don't we pack our treasures and our bloodline families and move to a more inviting place?" said Marta. "There are many suitable planets with inhabitants that we can enslave."

"Let's get to Rio, then we will have a base to make our arrangements," said Fabbiana. "But I agree, this place is just getting too troublesome. So much violence and pollution. Let's leave it to the sick Jinn and the pathetic Alliance crew."

They all sniggered, knowing full well their role in the pollution and poisoning of the Earth's people and environment. Not to mention the Jinn and the dinosaurs, which their genetic meddling had caused to reappear on Earth, or the huge tracts of land made uninhabitable by nuclear missiles.

Yes, they were done here.

The chopper flew on towards South America. Which, coincidentally, would be very convenient for their escape plan, because of its proximity to a certain secret base.

Calum opened the door of the farmhouse above the bunker to admit the unit of military guards that Father Caspian had sent to escort them on their journey.

"Captain John Fraser, at your service," said their leader, saluting Calum and then shaking his hand. "Are you all ready to move?"

"Yes, but would you like some refreshment first?" asked Calum.

"We have had food and drink on the journey," said the Captain. "If it's all the same to you, we would like to get back to Dundee before nightfall. These dinosaurs are a big challenge to cope with anyway and in the dark, it's a nightmare."

"Okay, I'll muster everyone together then. We really appreciate your help in escorting us to Dundee. Thank you."

"No worries," said Fraser. "Now, we have lots of room in the personnel transporters for all of you. And luggage and animals can be placed in the trucks."

An exodus of assorted people with suitcases and animals straggled out of the bunker warily, looking around nervously for dinosaurs. But, all was quiet now.

"My unit will help you load your belongings," said Fraser. "Mr O'Connell, would you like to travel in the lead armoured carrier with myself?"

"Yes, if I can bring my team here," answered Calum, indicating the youngsters, David, Chloe and Rob. "And Buster of course," he added with a grin, pointing to his dog.

"And Shep," said David, whose dog was jumping up and down, tail wagging, thinking they were going for a walk.

"Of course," replied Fraser.

The loading was quickly completed with the help of the military unit and the convoy set off, eager to get back to their community and relative safety.

Calum hoped that this would be a good move.

They had lived through so many bad relocations. But, he didn't feel that he could keep people safe here.

Not with so many threats and being so few in numbers.

He was feeling the loss of Jessie and Joanna particularly badly.

And after sighting the huge dinosaurs in the area, he knew he couldn't defeat them and couldn't stand to lose anybody else.

"Okay, Calum?" said Rachel, noticing his withdrawal.

"Yes, sweetheart. Everything's going to be okay."

But, he sounded more optimistic than he felt.

The armoured trucks trundled along the road towards Dundee. There were few houses, just miles of green fields and hedges. After a while, Rob exclaimed.

"Would you look at that!"

Everyone looked in the direction he was pointing.

"Oh, my goodness," said Chloe. "Look at those things."

In the fields to the left of the road there was a herd of huge dinosaurs.

"Are they dangerous?" asked Rachel, staring at them nervously.

"Well, Eamon would know. But, he's in one of the trucks further back."

"Don't worry," said Fraser. "This type is common around here. Harmless. They eat grass and trees, that's all. I think our scientist said they are 'Camptosaurus.' or something."

The beasts were about fifteen feet long and stood upright on two stout back legs. They were using their short forearms to move foliage from the tops of the bushes into their huge mouths.

"So, have you seen any more dangerous ones where you are based?" asked Calum. He did hope that this wasn't a case of out of the frying pan and into the fire.

"Don't worry, there are very few that venture into the Dundee area. Too many humans. They seem to fear us and I can't say that I blame them, after the recent nukes destroyed a lot of their herds."

"Good point," said Rob. "I guess the ones we saw around our bunker just thought that the farmhouse was an empty building. Underground, we would have been invisible to them."

"Has Father Caspian found us accommodation do you know?" asked Calum. "We would like to stay together if possible. I know it's a big ask, with this lot. But, we've been through so much together."

"Oh, don't worry. You have been assigned a very good home and there will be room for all of you," said Fraser. "Good defences, too. And you will be quite near Dundee, where our community is, if you need anything."

"You're being very mysterious, but thank you," said Calum. "We appreciate your taking us all into your community."

Calum could see a town in the distance.

"Is that Dundee?" he asked.

"Fraser said, "Yes, that's your new home. We're about to cross the Tay Bridge."

Ahead was a long, straight road bridge across a wide river.

"Father Caspian will meet us at your new home. Here we go."

Reaching the other side of the bridge, they turned right and headed along a road parallel to the River Tay.

"Very picturesque, I'm sure," muttered Rob. "But, where are you taking us? This road seems to go out along the estuary, away from Dundee."

"Yes, that's right," said Fraser, smiling. "But, you will see why soon enough. Just be patient."

Rob grunted.

"Now, Rob," said Chloe. "These people have been very friendly, giving us transport and an escort to our new home. We should be *grateful*," she emphasised, giving him a nudge.

They couldn't afford to upset their new community. Not yet anyway. And then, only if it all turned out wrong. She really would have to stop thinking negatively like this, she thought. It was bad for the little one.

She smiled at Rob.

"Okay?"

He gave a grudging smile back.

"Now, can we get to our new home without any further bickering?" laughed Calum. "Wow look at that."

Everyone looked. Ahead, at the water's edge, was a five-storey, stone castle, topped by walled turrets and a flagpole, within a high-walled enclosure. Cannons could be seen on top of the wall.

"Wow," said James. "Are we going to be living here?"

"Cool," said Sean.

"Is it haunted?" said Rachel. "I hope it is."

"Welcome to your new home, Broughty Castle," said Fraser. "It was built in the late fourteen hundreds to protect Dundee from attack from the sea. It was an important fortress in warfare, being difficult to breach from the water because of the fortifications and the strong river currents. It was used as a museum for a while, but, more recently after the GM outbreak, it was used to accommodate people fleeing from the trouble in the bigger towns and cities. Those initial refugees have since moved into houses in town, so it is currently vacant."

"Luckily for us," said Chloe. "What a beautiful building."

The convoy stopped inside the castle gates and the troops helped them to unload everything into the entrance hallway.

A cheerful voice shouted.

"Hello, I'm Father Caspian. Welcome to your new home."

A tall, thin man appeared from a reception room. He wore a black robe and a white dog collar.

"Calum?" he queried.

Calum strode forward and shook his hand.

"Pleased to meet you. It's very good of you to invite us stay here in your community in this beautiful place."

"Not at all. New members of our congregation and community are always welcome."

"Well, I don't know that we're all convinced of your message yet," said Calum, glancing warily at Rob, trying to head off any cynical comments. "But, we are pleased to join you and we will be willing listeners."

"And that is all we ask," said Father Caspian. "Now, let's show you to your accommodation."

"I'm afraid that contact with the so-called living is difficult, once you're here," said Veronica. "I mean, your dad and I tried for ages, didn't we, Graham? We wanted to let you know that we were okay. You were so sad when you found us in our house."

"I never knew," said Jessie. "*How* did you try?"

"There are channels, conduits," said her mum. "Some on this side have the ability to be guides and give messages for others. On Earth, as you knew it, there are individuals who have a gift for communicating with spirits. But, the chances of linking up with the right person who can give a message to a specific person on Earth is very small. Especially in the time after the GM catastrophe first hit, when there had been a breakdown in civilisation and so many deaths. People were just trying to survive. And there were many who had passed over here who were desperate to get a message back."

"Something is still puzzling me," said Jessie.

"What is it, darling?" asked her mum.

"Well, you talked of Hell before and people who did wrong on Earth having to go there. Well, er, it seemed to us, that is, Calum and me, that you had taken pills when you died. Maybe because Dad had been killed by the Genies? Doesn't that count as suicide? And wouldn't that have been a bad sin?"

"I wondered about that too, once I realised where we were. But, I have talked about it with the elders. They say that is *was* a sin, but not evil enough to be banished forever. I was distressed, couldn't live without your father. Especially not in a world with evil Genies trying to kill us. I couldn't see any other way out. They say my mind was disturbed, I wasn't thinking straight. I didn't do what I did out of evil, just desperation. And, once I recognised my mistake, it was forgiven."

"That is amazing," said Jessie. "And I'm so glad that you were forgiven, otherwise we would have been parted forever."

She hugged her mother. Just then, there was a noise beyond the meadow where they were sitting. Jessie heard someone muttering, then sobbing. Who could it be, to be so upset in this wonderful place?

Her parents looked at each other, smiling. They knew what it was.

Jessie stood up and, with Hannah, started to move towards the sounds.

A shimmering appeared in the atmosphere, a darkness beyond. Then, someone moved into the bright, beautiful light.

Someone that they recognised straight away.

"Jessie!" cried the figure. "Hannah!" And then rushed towards them, arms outstretched.

"Joanna, sweetheart, you shouldn't be here. Not yet," said Jessie, tenderly. "It's far too soon. What happened?"

"We have been so worried about you two, since you disappeared in the storm in Gallanvaig. Where have you *been*?" The words came tumbling out. "Anyway, I have been trapped in a sort of dark tunnel. I could smell *earth*. And there were noises. Horrible noises. Where are we anyway?"

"Come and sit down over here," said Hannah, putting her arm around the girl. "Meet our parents," she added, realising that Joanna hadn't met any of them. "This is my mother, Norma and my father, George."

They both hugged Joanna.

"And meet my mum, Veronica and my dad, Graham," added Jessie. "This is our very dear friend, Joanna, who has been through so many adventures with us. I told you about her and her brother, James, sister Rachel and their friend, Shaun."

"Yes, we know," said Veronica, smiling. "We are very pleased to meet you, darling. And I think you might soon see a couple of other people who can't wait to see you again."

Joanna sat between Jessie and Hannah, looking very confused. "But, where *are* we?" she asked. "We were living in an old army bunker underneath a farmhouse in Scotland. It was Christmas and we had a tree, we decorated it, just like we used to. Then, I remember being ill, I was so *hot*. A wolf bit me. Doctor Nazeer thought I might have caught rabies. Then, I didn't feel good at all. The next thing I remember is being in the dark tunnel. Where *are* we?"

"Sweetheart, we have all moved on from life on Earth," said Jessie, gently. "When we were caught in the storm, Hannah and I passed on to this place. Our parents passed during the first wave of Genie violence, after the GM crisis."

"What are you saying? That I'm *dead*?" said Joanna in a panicky voice. "So why am I still here with you all? I don't understand?"

"We are in a far better place, darling. You might call this Heaven, where we will live forever, with no more disease, famine or war. We still don't understand everything ourselves. But, there's no doubt that this place, wherever it is, is very beautiful. Just look at the colours of the sky, the sea, the flowers and trees. Aren't they more intense than they ever looked back home?"

"But, where is Calum? And James and Rachel and Shaun? I miss them."

"Me too, sweetheart, me too. But, one day we will all be together again, I promise you."

Joanna looked around, finally, at her surroundings.

"It *is* very beautiful here. The mountains and the sea remind me of Gallanvaig a bit, when we were all so happy. But, with more colour, more *real* somehow."

Jessie laughed. "I know what you mean. Now, I'm starting to feel hungry."

"Is that real here?" said Joanna. "Do we still need to eat? Or are we just souls or something?"

"Of course, we eat here," said Graham, smiling. "It's one of life's pleasures, which would surely not be denied to us in Paradise."

"Yes, remember it says in the Bible that Jesus told his disciples at the Last Supper that they would 'eat and drink at my table in my kingdom,'" said Veronica. "The food here is more delicious than any you ever tasted on Earth, I can promise you. Let's go and find something to eat, then."

They wandered off to the orchards, Joanna still asking many questions. The trees were heavy with ripe fruit and they picked as much as they wanted. Bread and olives and jugs of wine had been set on long tables and everyone sat and ate their fill.

"This food is delicious," said Jessie. "Everything tastes so much better here."

"Mmm," said Joanna, her mouth full of bread and olives. "This is *so* good. I was *starving*."

People started to join them, as lunchtime approached. Their parents knew everyone by name and everyone greeted Jessie, Hannah and Joanna as if they had known them all their lives.

Then, two people approached the tables where Jessie and the others were sitting.

"Hello, darling," said a voice behind Joanna.

Joanna looked up and immediately burst into tears.

There stood her mum, Anita and her dad, Bill.

Joanna leapt up and hugged them both for some time.

They were all crying with joy.

Calum's room was on the top floor of the castle beneath the turrets. It was roomy with comfortable furniture, colourful décor and exposed beams crossing the ceiling. It was very peaceful; the only sounds were of the sea and the gulls wheeling around above the town.

Exhausted by recent events and the trauma of moving their base yet again, he had fallen into a deep sleep as soon as he put his head onto the pillow.

In the dead of night there was a small scratching sound in the room. Then, another. Calum slowly started to awake. He felt that somebody was watching him. Was he dreaming of Jessie again? He didn't really want to open his eyes to see that she wasn't there and he was alone with his grief.

Then, the noise got louder and there was a thump, thump sound. Calum's eyes shot open and he looked around.

There, outside the window was the scarred, leering face of Balthazar and he was banging on the window. *Hovering four floors above the ground.*

Calum jumped out of bed and rushed towards the door to raise the alarm. But, Balthazar was too fast. He materialised inside the room in a flash, together with three of his followers.

"Hello, my old friend," he sneered. "What leaving me already? Just like that girlfriend of yours. She went away too. Seen her lately?" he sneered.

"Don't you dare talk about Jessie, you monster," snarled Calum, grabbing the nearest weapon to hand, which turned out to be a heavy, brass table lamp with a coloured, glass shade. He threw it towards Balthazar, with a roar of anger and fear.

Balthazar raised his arm and deflected the lamp against the stone wall, where it smashed into pieces.

"That's not very nice," he said. "Not very friendly, are you? When I have come all this way to see you as well."

In a swirl of disturbed air, Balthazar was suddenly right in front of Calum and he grabbed him by the throat.

Calum gasped and clawed at Balthazar's hands, trying to loosen them enough so that he could breathe.

"This is what we do to our enemies," crooned Balthazar to his followers. "This man has been a thorn in my side for too long. But, it ends here."

The other three Genies sniggered.

They liked the fact that Balthazar had another enemy to focus on. Too many times, his anger had been turned towards his own followers, whenever they disappointed or denied him in some way. He had been constantly angry since the defeat by the lizard people. And he knew their thoughts, so they daren't risk ever thinking bad of him. But sometimes, they couldn't help it. It was like walking on eggshells.

Calum started to choke and lose consciousness. Would he die now, here in this castle, where he had just moved to keep his community safe?

Just as he started to slip to the floor, the door banged open and Father Caspian, Rob, David and Millie rushed in.

"Calum are you okay? We heard a crash," started Rob. Then, he saw who was in the room and he David rushed to pull Balthazar off Calum.

"Hello, David and Rob, long time, no see," said Balthazar. "And *Millie* isn't it?" He put his head on one side, searching. "Yes, Millie," he said, as she shook her head, trying to get him out. "And a Man of God too," he added, staring at Father Caspian.

Rob and David struggled to pull Balthazar's hands away from Calum's throat and finally they loosened a bit. Calum slumped to the floor.

"Right you lot, back off or get a bullet in the head," yelled Millie, pointing her weapon at Balthazar.

Balthazar swept his hand towards Millie and the gun flew from her hand and clattered against the wall.

Shocked, she looked around for another weapon. She saw a ceremonial sword on the wall and grabbed it.

"Oh, no you don't, my dear," said Balthazar. He moved in a flash to grab the sword from her and brandished it in front of her face. Millie gasped in fear.

"In the name of the Father and of the Son and of the Holy Ghost, leave this place, you *demons*," said a voice from the doorway. Almost forgotten in the melee, Father Caspian stood in the shadows. As he spoke, he held up his crucifix towards Balthazar and the others.

Balthazar recoiled from the priest and his followers shrank behind him.

"I banish you from this place, in the name of God!" thundered Father Caspian.

In an instant the room was clear of Genies. They had all disappeared.

Rob and David helped Calum to sit up.

"Are you okay, mate?" asked Rob.

"I am now. I'm a bit sore around the neck, but you all saved me. Thank you. And thanks to you Father, I'm sure your words were what made them leave." He coughed, rubbing his throat.

"I think we should have Nazeer up here to check you out," said David. "I'll go and fetch him."

"I'll be okay," protested Calum hoarsely.

But, David was already on his way to Nazeer's room.

"*Are* they devils do you think, Father?" asked Calum. "After all, they responded to your crucifix and your invoking of God."

"Well, I have been researching this topic after joining the Revelation Army. The Jinn, or Genies in English, were also known as demons, or evil spirits in Arabian theology and mythology. There is also some evidence that the name Jinn derives from the Aramaic language, where early Christians used it to describe pagan gods, or demons. So, yes, I believe that they *are* demons. Just look at all the evil they have done on Earth. The killings, kidnappings and destruction. And, you saw the effect that the crucifix had on them. That is an obvious sign of a demon."

"Well, I knew they were evil, but *demons*, in this day and age?" said Rob.

"You have seen for yourself that all the signs of Armageddon are around us, have been so for two or three years now," answered Father Caspian. "Once you acknowledge that fact, it is a small step to recognise angels and demons."

"Did anyone else think they looked more sick than usual?" asked Calum. "I saw them pretty close up and I mean, they never looked particularly healthy, but those awful red rashes and skin lesions."

"Maybe they're sick," said Rob. "After all, if they're still consuming GM material hoping for more psychic powers, that isn't going to be doing them much good."

They were interrupted by the return of David with Nazeer, followed by Rachel, James and Shaun, who had all heard the commotion.

"Calum," cried Rachel. "Are you okay? David said that Balthazar was here. Did he hurt you? Will he come back?"

"I'm fine, sweetheart. Yes, he was here, but Father Caspian stopped him in his tracks. And, I think we now have a weapon against him and his filthy followers, eh, Father?"

"Always trust in the Lord," said Father Caspian, nodding and holding up his crucifix.

"Do you have any more of those things, by any chance?" said Rob.

Everyone laughed.

"What, our biggest sceptic now wants to trust in God?" said David, laughing.

"Well, it seemed to work," he answered, running his hand through his hair. "That's all I'm saying."

"I'm sure we can provide you all with them," said Father. "I will see to it in the morning. Meanwhile, can I suggest that we all wait out this night here, with the protection of God, should we need it?"

Nobody was in any mood to argue. The invasion of their latest haven by the Jinn had shocked them all.

They settled down and talked and drank coffee until daylight. Nobody was very tired anymore.

At breakfast, which had been brought by the Revelation Army community, conversation was muted. Those who had slept through the disturbance were shocked to hear that the Genies had been here, inside the castle.

"Are we safe here?" said Douglas. "We never had visits from the Genies when we were in the bunker."

"I know," said Calum. "But, they may have been busy fighting their other sworn enemies, the Elite, or Annunaki. Maybe now that we have destroyed all the

Annunaki homes and they have gone to ground, the Genies see that battle as won. I don't know. But, we do have a proven weapon that we can use, should they turn up again."

Everyone looked up in interest, just as Father Caspian entered the large dining room.

"Morning, everyone. I think I have the answer to your Genie problem right here."

He lifted the box he was carrying.

"Help me hand these out will you, guys?" he asked Rachel, James and Shaun.

Everyone was handed a crucifix on a chain, or a string of rosary beads with a crucifix at the end.

"I raided our church shop," said Father Caspian, smiling. "We will have to order more, but this should be enough for now."

"Father Caspian used his crucifix to great effect against the Genies last night," said Calum. "The fact that I am here at all to tell the tale is due to him and his crucifix. So, keep these with you at all times."

"And if anyone would like to offer up prayers for the human race's battle against the Jinn and the Annunaki, you are very welcome to join us in Saint Anne's church, just down the road in Dundee. Ten o'clock today."

Some people obviously intended to take him up on that offer and they finished their breakfast and went off to get ready.

"That's a step too far for me," said Rob, as Father Caspian left with some of their community.

"Well, we're going," said Douglas and his wife Annie nodded. "I want to see what it's all about first-hand."

"Me too," said Rachel. "Can I come with you?"

"You can go with me," said Calum. "The least I can do is offer thanks to whichever great power saved me from Balthazar and his band. And, who knows, we might even learn something that might help us."

"James and Shaun, come on," said Rachel. A little reluctantly, they followed her out of the room. But, the priest had saved their beloved Calum, so they were prepared to give it a chance.

Quite a few left the castle to attend the Revelation Army service.

And those who stayed behind were sure to keep their crucifixes with them.

They were taking no chances.

72. Fury

Balthazar stamped around the room, yelling at his followers.

"You're all cowards! Why didn't you back me up? Now, they think that they have us beaten. And the damned lizards are just too slippery to bother with. Who cares what *they* do anyway? We're okay here, they can't touch us. Oh no, you *don't,*" he exclaimed, as he saw several of his followers trying to sneak out of the room.

"Get back in here!" he shouted. There was a flash of bright light, as Balthazar threw a thunderbolt in their direction. There were a few howls as the bolt stuck home. He swept through their minds, trawling for any opposition to him. His followers cringed at the aggressive attack inside their heads.

He must be careful, it wouldn't do to finish off his followers. He needed as many as he could get. Just scare them a bit, so they did his bidding without question. After all, he *was* the Master, they must obey him. He hardly noticed, as trickles of blood started to flow from his nose and mouth.

"What is *wrong* with you, Nicholas?" he snapped, as Nicholas' face screwed up in pain.

"I don't know, Master. I'm not feeling good."

Balthazar was dismayed as he saw the blood seeping down the faces of Nicholas and some of his other followers. Then, horrified, he felt the wetness on his own cheeks and blanched when he saw the red smear on his hand as he wiped it away.

What the hell was *wrong* with them all?

"There it is," said Rosa, delighted, as she spied her mother's summer estate below.

Lush palm trees waved in the slight breeze and the beach was white with fine sand. The sea was a deep, azure blue. The house itself was more like a luxury hotel, with many bedrooms, pools and annexes.

The chopper landed on the helipad and the butler unloaded their luggage, whilst the party went inside, followed by the waiters, bringing chilled champagne and gourmet food.

Later, they sat by the pool drinking champagne.

"So, tomorrow, we contact all from the bloodline and instruct them to travel here as soon as possible. We will leave as soon as the ships can be made ready. The technicians are already working on it. I am looking forward to being out in the cosmos again," said Marta. "We will get away from whining humans, who I am finding so tedious now. They don't like the big *corporations*, they don't like the *bankers*, they don't like what's happening to *animals*, or the *environment*. They don't like working for our *companies*, they don't like the *medicines* that we produce for them, or the *food*. They don't like *anything*. Ungrateful lot. I will be glad to be rid of them. Maybe we should nuke the whole planet on our way out," she added, with a wicked grin, showing sharp teeth.

"I don't suppose anyone would miss it," said Fabbiana. "Still, can you be bothered?"

"Well, if we have time, I might consider it. After all, what will they do without us to tell them what to do and what to think anyway? They will be lost, like little children. It would be a mercy."

She sniggered.

"Anyway, is there any sacrifice material around here for tonight, Rosa?"

"By which you mean little children who may be lost – or not?"

"Just a little mercy killing of our own."

"I'll get the staff to look into it," Rosa replied. "There is much poverty on the mainland and many unattended children, whilst parents are out trying to find work. They pretty much run riot in the slums."

"Well, that sounds perfect," said Fabbiana. "Set it up for tonight. Tell your staff that we are taking the children in for some free food. It won't be for *them*, though."

Everyone cackled.

The sacrifice was always good in these underprivileged places. There were few police resources around to stop them and people went missing all the time anyway. And the children were so worn down by the time they were old enough to understand their poverty and their hopeless situation.

They would enjoy themselves whilst they waited for their ships to be ready and the bloodline families to arrive.

The congregation started crowding into Saint Anne's church long before the service was due to start. Calum and the others had walked from the castle and now stood in line, waiting to enter.

"Popular little gig isn't it," quipped David.

"Ssh David," urged Chloe. "These people take their religion seriously. You shouldn't mock. Anyway, I want to hear what they have to say."

"Sorry, Chlo," said David. "But, it all seems a bit Sunday School to me. It's just not my thing."

"Well, give it a chance at least," said Chloe. "You never know, you might like their ideas."

He pulled a face.

"And, he did save our precious Calum, don't forget. And Father Caspian has given us all protection against the Jinn. So, I for one am very grateful."

It came to their turn to enter through the arched wooden doorway into the relative cool and darkness of the church. Candles flickered in front of a large, wooden altar covered by a white cloth. The benches were crammed with people of every age and description.

Calum found a bench near the back and they all squashed in together in anticipation.

A hush settled over the church, as Father Caspian strode to the podium at the side of the altar.

"Good morning and welcome to our Sunday service. Welcome especially to our visitors and new members of the congregation." He looked around for Calum and smiled when he saw the group at the back.

"Today, I want to talk about the Jinn. It is said in mythology that the Jinn were demons or fallen angels. Legends say that they could change shape, fly and become invisible. This indeed sounds very familiar to those of us who have encountered the Genies, a devolved form of humans that resulted from the effects of GM transgenes on human genes. This caused genes long left redundant to regenerate and become active. The Revelation of Saint John says that, at the Apocalypse, demons will be thrown into a pit for a thousand years. And these Jinn, who are modern day demons, will not be spared. So, I tell you that, until they are banished for good, we must be on our guard. Only yesterday, they visited our Castle and attacked one of us. But, the protection of God was called down against these demons and they were defeated, with God's grace and the sacred power of my crucifix here."

He pointed to the cross on a chain around his neck, as the congregation looked shocked at this incursion into their community.

"So, you must remain alert. Always keep your crucifixes with you, for your own protection. Now, let us pray for our deliverance from the menace of the Jinn."

"Our Father, who art in Heaven," he began.

The congregation joined in with one voice.

Later, at the castle, the friends discussed the service.

"Father Caspian seems very reasonable to me. I thought the early Revelationists were a bit manic, but he talks a lot of sense," said Calum. "And the idea of keeping the crucifixes with us seems like a good idea. You saw the effect that Father Caspian's cross had on Balthazar last night. And, if it's true that the Roman Catholic Church is involved with slaughtering their rivals, the Revelationists, then I know whose side I want to be on."

"I agree," said Chloe. "I feel very safe with the protection of this congregation around me. They have been nothing but friendly to us. And if they have come up with a protection against the Genies, then I admire them even more."

Rob grunted.

"I'll reserve judgement for now, if you don't mind."

"You don't trust anyone do you mate?" said Calum grinning. "I think we're safe here for the time being anyway. As safe as we can be anywhere, that is."

73. The Bloodlust

The bloodline families that had already arrived by plane and helicopter joined the Elite in the large basement beneath Rosa's family estate.

Those who had been next in line to be Masters, but reluctant to take on the responsibility, due to the violent deaths of their predecessors at the hands of the Genies, were eager to leave Earth.

"This place has become hostile towards us now," said Mark Vanderbilt, Edward's son. "And our secret is out anyway. The humans know what we are. I can't wait to be on the move."

"You have never known space travel, though. How can you know it will be so much better than life on Earth?" commented Marta. "I mean, our ancestors came here thousands of years ago. This is the only home you have known. Don't get me wrong, I am eager to leave too. But, we need to go with our eyes open. There may not be another susceptible planet out there to be exploited."

"Yes, but this isn't *our* home is it? It's the wretched human race's home. Those of little ambition, or intelligence. All we do is exploit and sacrifice them. It's got very boring."

"Yes, I agree," said Marta. "Now, we need a good number of sacrifices tonight to draw strength from for the long journey ahead. I think Rosa has come up trumps."

They donned the hooded robes and the music and drums started to play rhythmically.

They approached the stone altar in the centre of the room. Behind it was a huge statue of the horned, goat-headed being, Baphomet, whom the Elite had worshipped for years.

Upon the altar were at least a dozen struggling bodies, tightly wrapped in sheets.

The Masters were given pride of place and as the drums reached a crescendo, they took out the long daggers and with shrieks of ecstasy, plunged them into the struggling bundles.

The bodies soon stopped moving. The Annunaki had shape-changed into their preferred, actual form, as huge reptilians. No need to hide what they were any more. What could a few humans do against them anyway?

With growls of pleasure, the Annunaki loosened their robes and retired, chatting and laughing, to a first-floor hall. The butlers soon appeared with trays of glasses filled with red liquid., glancing nervously at the huge reptiles.

With sounds of appreciation, the contents of the glasses were drained and then re-filled, until all the precious liquid was gone.

This nourishment would stand them in good stead for tomorrow's journey.

The next day, members of the bloodlines started to turn up in earnest. Fleets of planes, luxury jets and yachts arrived at the island's airstrip and harbour. The human servants who flew the planes and piloted the yachts took the vehicles away to a neighbouring, uninhabited island to make room for new arrivals and await further instructions.

The new arrivals had needed to be fed, so fresh sacrifices were made. The butlers were kept busy, fetching food and champagne.

"Well, isn't this nice?" said Marta, grinning. "It's great to be all together for once, in our natural forms.

And there's no need to hide from the pathetic humans, who might be scared to see our real faces."

Marquees and covered sleeping quarters had been set out around the island. There was insufficient room for everyone to have a room on the estate, but the weather was warm and the food and drink plentiful. Everyone was quite happy with the arrangements.

"Hello, Miguel," said Rosa, shouting down the phone, above the multitude of voices, growls and shrieks of pleasure and laughter echoing around the estate. "Are the ships ready yet? We want to make a start, either later today, or tomorrow at the latest."

"Sim estamos quase prontos, Madame," came the reply. "We are nearly ready, Madame. Maybe later today. We will fly the ships over the island and use the scout ships to collect you."

"Okay, call me when you have an ETA."

Rosa put the phone down, looking pleased with herself.

"At last," she beamed to the other Masters. "We are going to be getting out of this dump later today."

The reptiles made sounds that passed for laughter in their own form.

But, to the few human servants around, it sounded more like a huge, growling, shrieking cacophony.

"Is everybody here?" asked Fabbiana. "We don't have much more time. We must be ready when the ships arrive."

"Everybody has been checked against the database on arrival," replied Rosa. "So, together with the number who were already here, we have twenty-nine thousand and fifty-five bloodlines present."

"There should be twenty-nine thousand, one hundred," snapped Fabbiana. "Forty-five still missing."

"If necessary, we will find out where they are and send scout ships for them. It will be quicker that way," said Marta.

But, by mid-afternoon, all the known bloodline family members had finally arrived and were ready for their journey.

"The time is approaching," said Veronica. "The elders have communicated this to us."

"When?" asked Jessie. "I didn't see anyone."

"You cannot quite see, yet," said her mum. "Wait." She whispered something to someone that Jessie couldn't see.

Suddenly, a veil was lifted from her eyes and those of Hannah and Joanna.

Their attention was drawn to the sky above, where they glimpsed a movement, fluttering.

"Oh, my *God*," whispered Jessie.

"What are they?" breathed Joanna. "They are so *beautiful*."

Above them hovered hundreds of beings, whose bodies were so delicate-looking that they seemed almost transparent. They floated on wings spread out like shining feathers. Their faces were incandescent with joy. Suddenly, Jessie could hear a chorus of voices, singing a most heavenly song.

"Oh, Mum, they are so beautiful. Are these the Elders?"

"Yes, my dear. These are the ones who have been explaining everything to us. They are saying that time for the Earth is running out, as predicted in the Bible and many other prophetic texts. The final days, the end times are here."

"But, what does that even mean?" asked Jessie. "Is it the end of the world? What about *this* world here?"

"This is the new home for the people of the light," said her mother. "The world as you knew it will end. There will be a massive filtering out of evil ones, who will be banished to the pits of Sheol. The good will be brought here, to the place of eternal light, for evermore."

"Mum, I'm scared. What if Calum isn't one of them? I miss him so much."

"You'll just have to wait, darling," said her mother smiling.

"But, what will happen to Calum, Rachel, James and Sean?" asked Joanna. "Will they be hurt?"

"No, I don't believe that the good will be hurt, darling. But, we just need to wait and pray. This is such a difficult time for everyone here. We all have such ties to people on Earth, people that we desperately want to join us in eternal life here. But, will they make the grade? We just don't know."

"I don't want to stay here without them," said Joanna firmly.

"Honey, that's not a choice you can make," said Norma, Hannah's mother. "We just need to pray and hope for the best."

"Come on, let's all say a prayer," said Veronica.

Jessie felt so helpless. This was a wonderful place, but would she ever see her beloved Calum again?

Balthazar growled his anger. He could see in his mind that the hated Calum was living freely in his castle in the land of mists and mountains. Why couldn't he destroy him, just like he had so easily destroyed so many before? But, he was sick. His followers were too. Nobody felt well, nobody had eaten for days. Doctor Tanaya had done his best, but, he too was sick now and couldn't help them.

Balthazar tried to send out a clone to attack Calum, far away in Scotland. It materialised over Dundee, but, broke up into wisps of smoke and he roared in anger, as he lost concentration in the agony of his sickness.

He was suffering from the failure of his internal organs, attacked over many years by genetically-modified food. So-called 'food' that poisoned people and polluted the environment. With the genetic make-up of the Jinn that they had regressed to, the Genies had some inbuilt immunity and avoided sickness for some time. They had used their GM diet to develop more and more psychic abilities, giving them an advantage over anyone who they decided was an enemy.

But now, suffering from final organ failure, all the Jinn could do was lie on their beds and moan for someone to come and help them. But, there was no-one.

Everybody was very sick.

The Gulf of Mexico was quiet, peaceful. The sun was strong in the sky, the heat was rising as the day reached its hottest part. Seabirds wheeled in the blue sky, searching for fish below the unbroken surface of the sea. A peace that was about to be shattered.

With a huge explosion of seawater, gigantic cigar-shaped motherships shot out from their underwater bases and broke the surface. Moving at enormous speed into the sky above Rio de Janeiro, they manoeuvred until they were hovering above the island. The ships were several miles long and had an ecosystem designed for the Annunaki's life support over long periods of time, a city in the sky.

As they hovered, to the delight of the spectators below, waiting for their delivery from this now inhospitable place, doors in the side of the mothership opened and smaller ships shot out into the air, flying towards the island below.

"At last, our ships," exclaimed Rosa.

The first scout ship landed on the airstrip at the island and the waiting passengers crowded forward, crooning and growling. Their snouts were wide with sharp teeth, their cries were deafening. Their anticipation of the treats that would be available to them once on board was overpowering.

"Back, back," shouted Fabbiana, shoving other reptiles aside. "Know your *place*. We, the Masters, will be first to board the ship."

The five remaining Masters and those who had refused to become new Masters out of fear, pushed their way to the front. Gaj, Corinne, Marta, Fabbiana and Rosa were first to board the scout ship. They were closely followed by the ones they considered cowards, Eleanor Goldman, Chao Chan, Mark Vanderbilt, Sora Mori, Johnny Kaufman.

But, there would be plenty of time to make sure they understood their shortcomings.

Meanwhile, they would concentrate on escape.

And destruction, of course.

The scout ship soared straight up, as soon as the Masters were on board. The rest could wait. A fleet of scout ships was landing to pick them up. The scout ship docked with the mothership and the very important passengers disembarked.

"Ah, that's better," breathed Rosa. "Earth air is so tiring, don't you think? This is so much better. I'm going to enjoy our journey."

They took seats in the luxury lounge, where the food and champagne has already been set out.

"Ah, champagne," said Marta smiling. "That is one thing about Earth that I will miss. I used to love our Russian variety. Do you think we could have some made?"

"How hard can it be?" said Fabbiana, sniggering. "I'm sure our on-board vineyards can sort something out."

"Now, Miguel, have you prepared the Wormwood missiles?"

"Sim, Senhora. All is ready. Just give me the word," said Captain Miguel.

The fleets of scout ships were thick in the air, as they ferried the reptiles to the motherships.

Marta waited for her final triumphant blow against the pathetic human race.

They would not forget the Annunaki in a hurry. Oh, no.

"They will soon wish that we were back there, taking care of them, telling them what to do," she said.

"You think so?" asked Fabbiana.

"I do. And we'll give them a leaving present to remember us by," she cackled.

They all laughed, a horrible growling, grating sound.

There was a serious discussion going on at Broughty Castle.

"Look, I still can't quite believe that the Apocalypse, End of Days, End of the World, or whatever you want to call it, is an actual thing," insisted Rob. "Put it down to my natural scepticism."

"But, you have heard what the Revelationists have to say about it. How they have linked current events to those described in the Bible. And you saw the impact that the crucifix had on the Jinn," said Calum. "You must admit, that it seemed like the reactions of a demon to a cross?"

"Maybe. But, does it make everything else *true*?" he asked.

Secretly, Rob hoped that there *was* a hole in their arguments. The alternative was too enormous to even contemplate.

405

"And you saw the database of everyone in the human race and those they call Annunaki," said Hogan. "You must admit that something strange has occurred in the history of the Earth. I mean, we all saw the footage of the shapeshifting reptile. These things aren't human. Their DNA showed that. So, where did they come from?"

"Well, our DNA is obviously inextricably linked to theirs," said Calum. "So, there has been some interbreeding, or at least some genetic meddling. Are you okay Chloe?"

He had noticed a pained expression on her face.

"Is the little one kicking again?" said David, concerned.

"Aah, no, it's worse than that," gasped Chloe, holding her stomach. "I think my waters have broken."

David gasped and jumped up to help Chloe.

"Can you walk to the car?" said Nazeer. "I think the baby has decided now is the time."

"Let us know as soon as there's news," said Calum, as they left.

David and Nazeer helped Chloe to the car and they set off for the delivery suite in the hospital up the road with Yvette, who was a former midwife.

"Will Chloe be okay?" asked Rachel. She had lost too many close friends and family already.

"Well, she's in very good hands," said Calum. "And it's a very natural process, you know, having a baby. I'm sure she'll be fine, sweetheart."

"What do you know about it?" asked Millie, sarcastically.

"All this talk of babies is making me feel queasy," said James, pulling a face.

"We can go and see Chloe this afternoon, if she is well enough," said Calum. "How about that?"

He was a bit worried about Chloe too. These were different times and he didn't know how good the local facilities, or expertise would be. Chloe and David had become very good friends over the years and he didn't want to see them lose the baby. Anyway, these little ones were the future of the human race. They were needed.

"Okay," said Rachel.

"Think I'll pass," said James and Shaun agreed.

In the delivery suite, Nazeer donned his surgical gown and gloves and Yvette did the same. He had already called the anaesthetist, who was administering gas to Chloe.

David sat by the bed looking very worried. He had never ever seen a baby being born and he was hoping that he wouldn't pass out or do anything embarrassing.

"Okay, darling?" he said, brushing damp hair off Chloe's forehead.

"Not really, no," she answered. "It bloody *hurts*."

"Sorry, sweetheart."

"Okay, Chloe, I think we're ready for you to push now," said Nazeer.

Chloe pushed hard and immediately screamed in pain.

"Good, that's it, keep going, you're doing fine," said Yvette.

Chloe motioned for more gas, with a pained expression.

Would this baby ever make an appearance?

The Motherships were fully loaded with passengers and supplies. Everyone had been served the finest food and champagne.

They would travel in luxury to their next destination.

"First of all, I want to do a little farewell lap of the world," said Marta, smiling. "Say goodbye *properly*."

Everyone laughed, as Miguel gave the orders and the ships wheeled off in an orbit of the Earth. The huge ships blotted out the sun wherever they flew.

The coast of Africa came into view and they were soon flying over the land mass.

"Okay," said Marta to Captain Miguel.

He spoke to the control room.

The command was given.

In Lagos, Nigeria, office workers were leaving their offices for their lunch break. Shoppers were browsing the clothing and food stalls in the local market. In the local water park, parents were swimming in the sunshine with their children.

A dark shadow crept over the sun and those who looked up saw the enormous ship blotting out the sky above the city. A huge bright flash lit up the sky and then the force from the missile flattened buildings within the immediate blast range. People out in the open were instantly killed.

The mothership flew with frightening speed over the skies of Africa and unleashed a firestorm across all the territories below. Little was left standing.

The second mothership had flown over India and then towards China, destroying several massive hotel buildings in Saudi Arabia on the way. Homes and parks, shopping malls and people, all were destroyed in an instant. The densely-populated Beijing was flattened, its skyscrapers collapsing in heaps of rubble. The blast waves hit the great Wall of China and huge sections collapsed into dust.

A third mothership was above Europe and deadly missiles rained down on Paris, London, Madrid, Berlin and Istanbul. The Eiffel Tower was hit and crumpled to the ground in tumbling metal and clouds of dust. The Houses of Parliament at Westminster disappeared in a mushroom cloud of toxic fallout, killing all within instantly. The Brandenburg Gate in Berlin was destroyed, its columns and the crowning figures of the horses and chariot, carrying Victoria, the goddess of Victory, were vaporised. The Leaning Tower of Pisa was struck and fell sideways, crushing sightseeing tourists. The Colosseum in Rome collapsed in a heap of rubble.

Marta was in the first mothership. She was laughing hysterically, every time a missile struck home. She really hated this place. These *people*.

The others were delighted at all the destruction and blood-letting, it was what they fed on. Each time there was a hit, they all raised their glasses.

In Copenhagen, those who had been relaxing at the quayside jumped into boats and tried to flee the city, only to be swamped by a huge radioactive blast, emanating from the missile's ground zero. The Summer Palace in St Petersburg disappeared in clouds of dust and nuclear fallout.

Sydney Opera House was one moment hosting a sell-out operatic concert, with an audience of over two thousand, the next its magnificent structure, along with everyone inside, had collapsed into Sydney Harbour.

The already-devastated United States of America was once more hit by nuclear missiles, flattening everything still standing in their path.

The ailing Genies in their bunker at Dulce lay sick, as the missiles dropped, one after another, from the huge mothership above America. Balthazar sensed the approach of the deathly missiles and in a huge release of energy, he and his followers roared in fury. They projected images of themselves across all the world, where they appeared in the skies. They howled their anger at another attack by their sworn enemies.

Those below that were still alive, saw the mighty signs in the sky and were afraid.

But, this time the Genies' underground base, weakened by previous attacks on America, succumbed to the massive blasts. The tunnels and the underground network of facilities collapsed onto the residents, engulfing them in fumes and radioactive dust.

The signs in the sky slowly faded, as life finally drained from the Genies.

In Broughty Castle, the friends had gathered for lunch. Calum glanced out of the window, was it clouding over? A minute ago, the sky had been blue, the wintry sun quite warm through the glass. But now, it was darkening.

"Are we expecting a storm?" he asked.

"Don't think so," said Rob. "You can never tell with Scottish weather though, fine one minute, the next pouring with rain."

Calum laughed. But, there was something about this darkness.

"What's going on?" he asked. "This looks odd. I'm going out to have a look."

He was followed to the foreshore outside the castle by the kids and Rob. He looked up.

"Oh, my God," he exclaimed.

Firstly, they saw the faint faces of the Genies in the sky, howling their anger, cursing the world and its inhabitants.

Then, in the sky above the castle, they saw a huge, dark shape. It had blocked out the sun and was flying at enormous speed.

"What the hell?" said Rob.

"Is that what I think it is?" said Calum. "So, Chloe was right all along about the spaceships she thought she saw at Nellis base. Rachel, you were right too, sweetheart about the aliens and the Annunaki. Are they on board do you think? Is this their final exit from Earth?"

They watched amazed, as the spaceship manoeuvred across the sky.

In the huge craft above, Marta and the others watched on a large screen on the observation deck, as the growing devastation unfolded below. Then, as she suddenly saw the castle and a familiar face in the crowd outside, she cackled.

"At last," she breathed. "*Calum O'Connell*. Well, we won't be troubled by *him* anymore. Fire, fire, *now*!"

The supernova-bright flashes of the falling Wormwood nuclear missiles dazzled all below, who were immediately killed by the resulting blast.

The three huge motherships had done their dirty work, taken their revenge on the people of Earth for rejecting them and their rule. Now, it was time to make a victorious exit. Onwards to a better place, where the rich pickings would be even better.

But, as the huge ships wheeled and rose towards space and the stars, there was a massive crack, like thunder. The sky split in two and turned black. A huge bolt, like lightning thundered from the crack in the sky and struck the first mothership. Marta's victorious celebrations were cut off in a stroke. A second thunderbolt struck the next mothership and yet another, the third.

"No, no, no, this cannot be happening!" yelled Marta, furious at being attacked and their escape thwarted. Then, she lost consciousness, as a hole was blown in the ship's fuselage and it plummeted, the interior compartment fast losing its atmosphere. The ships were all on fire and one by one, they tumbled to earth, setting the trees and grass below on fire, adding to the devastation.

Not for them an escape to pastures new. This was where they would stay.

The dark gods Moloch, the flying lizard, the huge figure of the goat-headed Baphomet and the snake god Lilith appeared from dark shadows all over the Earth. Roaring and howling, they fed on the pain and misery of the human race and also those who had worshipped them for millennia. They greedily sucked in the energy of the dying millions. This would be their last feast on Earth and they intended to make the most of it.

The energy would sustain them for months until they found another place to lurk.

The blasts caused earthquakes and huge areas of the world were devastated, sucking millions of people into the bowels of the Earth. The missiles that fell into the oceans caused huge tsunami waves, swamping the land and all upon it with huge torrents of seawater.

"And there were flashes of lightning, loud noises, peals of thunder and a great earthquake such as had never been since men were on the Earth, so great was that earthquake."

Finally, once the destruction was complete, the sky brightened, the sun shone brightly.

The dark gods disappeared, sated, searching for their next fix of life energy. But, as they left Earth's orbit, they were struck by an enormous force from the sky and tumbled down into a deep, dark pit.

Nothing and nobody was left alive.

75. Epilogue

Jessie wiped tears from her eyes. They had just been given the devastating news about the Earth and its people.

Hannah and Joanna were also weeping.

"Ssh," said Veronica. "We are about to have a visit from Him."

Music flooded the land and the brightest light they had ever seen approached. They could see a vague figure inside the light. Those who hadn't seen this before shrank back, afraid.

"What is it?" said Jessie.

"He is allowing us to see him," said Norma. "This is indeed a great privilege."

"It's the *One*, God if you like," whispered Graham.

A huge voice boomed from the light and the figure became fully visible.

The One was dressed in loose, white robes. He had long, dark hair and the most beautiful face that Jessie had ever seen. Love shone from his brown eyes and his smile was wide and kind.

"Behold, God is with you. I will dwell with you and you shall be my people. I will wipe away every tear from your eyes and death shall be no more, neither shall there be mourning, nor crying, nor pain anymore, for the former things have passed away. But, as for the cowardly, the faithless, the polluted, as for murderers, fornicators, sorcerers, idolaters and all liars; their lot shall be in the lake that burns with fire and brimstone, which is the second death."

Then, the brightness faded and the figure was gone.

"What does it mean?" whispered Joanna.

"All life on Earth has been eliminated," explained one of the elders, sitting near them, her wings folded. "There has been great calamity on Earth, evil ones have destroyed a large part of the land and all of the life. But, God has sent his retribution on them for what they have done. The people of the light shall travel here, where there will be no death or sickness and where they will live forever with God. The evil will be banished to Sheol, or Hell, where they will live forever in misery."

"It was all really *true*," breathed Jessie.

"Yes, sweetheart, everything you were told and didn't altogether understand, or dare to believe, was true," said Veronica. "It's just hard for us to understand yet. But, we don't need to worry anymore. All the evil has gone, banished. The Jinn, Annunaki, all of them."

"But, where are Calum and the others?" said Jessie. "Are they *dead*?"

"I think they must be, darling," said Graham. "But, that doesn't necessarily mean the end. As you have discovered for yourself."

Jessie looked around desperately, tears shining in her eyes.

"How can it be that all life on Earth is gone? What brought this about? And *where* is Calum? How will he find me?"

Her mother put her arm around her shoulders.

"Don't worry darling, the new arrivals have a way of turning up just in the place where their loved ones are. Listen, darling."

Jessie stopped crying and listened. Then, she heard the sounds.

A faint murmuring noise could be heard in the distance. Then, it increased in volume and resolved into many separate voices. Some were crying, some seemed to be asking questions that she couldn't hear. There were the tumultuous sounds of many people approaching.

Then, she saw them.

Through a bright opening that gradually increased in size, hundreds, maybe thousands or more people appeared, blinking in the bright sun.

"Where *are* we?" cried a young girl. "I'm scared."

A few of the elders went to welcome them and try to explain as much as they could.

"You're safe now. Everything is okay. You're protected and loved here," they repeated over and over, trying to calm frayed nerves and fears.

Impatiently, Jessie scanned the faces, searching for the one that she held so beloved. Was he here? Joanna was searching for Rachel, James and Shaun.

Soon, the place was thronged with people, all asking questions.

"Where *are* we? Who are you people? How did we get here? Is this Earth? Are we *dead*?"

A few people saw family members in the group and rushed to greet them.

Then, two familiar faces appeared in the crowd. Jessie ran towards them joyously. One was carrying a small bundle. The other led a dog.

"Chloe, David!" she cried and grabbed them both in a bear hug. "Shep!" she laughed, as the dog jumped up and tried to lick her face.

"Mind the little one," said Chloe laughing.

"Oh, my goodness, you had the baby," gasped Jessie, drawing back to look at the child, who was waving its arms around and whimpering a bit.

"It's a girl," said David, proudly. "And we're calling her Hope, because that's what we have for our future. What *is* this place anyway? We were in the

416

hospital and Chloe had just delivered Hope, when there was a huge explosion and we found ourselves in darkness with the baby. Then, we were here. Where *are* we?"

"Yes, and where have *you* been?" said Chloe. "We couldn't find you after the tsunami in Gallanvaig. So much has happened since then. What happened to you? Oh, Hannah, you are here too!" she added as Hannah rushed up and gave her a hug.

There was tinkling sound like a bell and one of the winged elders stood on a podium nearby.

"I know that you all have many questions," she said. "The main one I know you all have is; where are you? I am afraid that you have passed on from your life on Earth."

There was a gasp from the crowd, as their suspicions were confirmed.

"But, the good news is that you have reached Paradise; a place where there's no war, no sickness, no evil and no more worries. This is where you will live now. There is plentiful food and drink, the scenery is stunning, as you can see. There is no darkness. And we are all *loved*. I'm sure you'll have many more questions and we will try to answer them as best as we can. But, first, you must all be hungry after the recent stressful events and your journey through the darkness. Please join us for some food, there is plenty for everyone. I can assure you that it is the most delicious food you have ever tasted."

The crowd started to move towards long tables, that were set with wonderful-looking fresh fruits, salads, olives, bread and wine.

Hannah suddenly saw a familiar face and rushed eagerly to hug him.

"Hannah!" cried Rob, crushing her in a bear hug. "Where have you *been?* We thought you were gone forever."

"I was lost in the darkness, then I met Jessie in a tunnel and we arrived here," she replied after a while. "We're all safe now, don't worry."

"Do I look worried?" he said smiling, throwing an arm around her shoulder as they walked. "Not now that I'm with you again. But, I'm still not sure what's going on."

"Give it time. Neither are we really."

As the crowd moved along, Jessie heard someone call her name. She turned around. The face she loved and had longed to see again gazed back at her, a slow smile on his lips, looking more handsome, younger than she ever remembered him.

"Calum!" she cried.

They ran to each other and hugged for a very long time, determined that they would never again be parted.

"Darling, what *happened* to you?" he said, as they parted at last and the kids, who had arrived with him surrounded them, laughing and hugging Joanna. Buster ran around barking with joy at seeing Jessie.

"I didn't think I would ever see you again! We were so worried. We were forced to leave Gallanvaig without ever finding out what happened to you and Hannah. Was that an *angel* who just spoke to us? She had *wings!* Are we all *dead?*"

"Well, I haven't been here too long myself," said Jessie, laughing as his questions tumbled out. "But, as far as I can make out, yes, we are what we used to call 'dead.' But, I feel so *alive*, more than ever before. I think all death means is that we move on from our Earthly life, full of pain and problems, to a life here in Paradise. So, I for one welcome it."

The kids were happily chatting and teasing each other as they ate and drank. It was amazing how quickly they adapted to changing situations, thought Jessie.

Then, there was a stir as they were joined at the table by a couple more people.

"Hello James, Rachel," said Anita. "And Shaun too, how are you?"

"Mum!" yelled Rachel, flying into her open arms. "I've missed you *so* much. Calum said that those bastards murdered you, to stop the facts about GM from getting out. Was that true?"

"Hush, sweetheart, that's all over now."

James hugged his Mum, then stood there looking a bit bewildered. Their dad, Bill grinned at them all.

"You kids finally arrived here then?" he joked. "And Shaun, there's someone here to see you too."

He stood aside and there was Tony and Deborah, Shaun's parents, who had died from the GM sickness.

Shaun's face crumpled with emotion and he knocked over his chair as he ran to them.

"You're safe now, son," said Tony, his arms enveloping him.

As the newcomers sat and ate and drank with their families and friends, they could see that this really was Paradise. All of those who they had lost over the years were there, all looking young again, all healthy and happy. There were many squeals of reunion, as people found loved ones again.

And later that day, the One appeared and spoke to them all.

"This city has no need of sun or moon to shine upon it for the glory of God is its light and its lamp is the Lamb. There shall be no night here."

"On either side of the river, the tree of life with its twelve kinds of fruit, yielding its fruit each month and the leaves of the tree for the healing of the nations. There shall no more be anything accursed. You are loved unconditionally. Everything is love."

And they did indeed *feel* loved.

"We will never again live in darkness," said Jessie. "No pain or wars and food and drink in abundance. Everything we could ever need and all our loved ones are with us."

Later, the friends went for a long walk in the sunshine. They talked about the recent events, as Calum and the others explained what happened to the world, about the spaceships they had seen and the Jinn appearing in the sky. They swam in the clear blue sea. They admired the beautiful mountains and perfect beaches.

"I wish I had known about this life to come, when I was still on Earth," said Jessie.

"Why?" said her mother. "You wouldn't have been able to fully live your life in that place and time if you had known. Nobody would have enjoyed anything. Nobody would have struggled to survive, suffered in unrequited love, known the meaning of war, loss and death. It's because you lived that life, not knowing, that you can appreciate this now."

"Oh, Mum. You're so wise."

"Well, it all becomes clear, after a while here," said her mother smiling.

"This is perfect," smiled Calum, kissing Jessie.

"I know, darling. And we will never be separated again," she replied with her familiar wide grin.

"I love you so much."

"Yuck," said James laughing. "Enough already. Anyway, do you think they have any games for my tablet here?"

"Oh James, trust you," laughed Jessie.

Calum ruffled James' hair, laughing.

Then, in the distance he saw familiar figures, walking towards him, smiling. And some smaller figures, who were running headlong.

"Mum, Dad," he exclaimed, delighted. "And Michael, Niamh and the kids!"

His parents, brother, sister, nieces and nephews surrounded him, chattering excitedly about their journey here and what they were going to do.

Later, Jessie and Calum smiled as they sat companionably together, in the place they had been given to live. They raised their glasses in a toast.

There was no need for words. There was a true union of minds. Everything was now exactly as it should be. They were together and truly happy.

And families and friends were reunited in the light and there was no more sickness, or evil. This world that was just like their Earth, but not quite.

It was better, more perfect.

More perfect by far.

THE END

If you have enjoyed this book, please submit a review on Amazon.co.uk, Amazon.com or your local Amazon. It helps other readers to find books that they might like. Thank-you, I really appreciate it!
Catherine Greenall

author.to/CatherineGreenallAuth

Keep in touch with Catherine Greenall

Amazon Author Page

http://www.amazon.co.uk/-/e/B003WQCIE0

Facebook
https://www.facebook.com/pages/Catherine-Greenall-A-Quirk-of-Destiny/672514749502441?ref=hl

http://www.facebook.com/?ref=home#!/pages/Catherine-Greenall/286294433711

Twitter
http://twitter.com/CathyGreenall

Blog
https://catherinegreenall.wordpress.com/

■■

References and Further Reading

GM Food

1. Martin Teitel, PhD and Kimberly A.Wilson, *'Genetically-Engineered Food: Changing The Nature of Nature'*, Park Street Press, Rochester, Vermont, 1999

2. Gundula Azeez and Coilin Nunan, *'GM Crops – the health effects'*, The Soil Association, United Kingdom, 2008

3. The Soil Association, *'L-Tryptophan: what made this GM food supplement kill 37 people and disable 1500?'* United Kingdom, 2003

4. GM Freeze, *'Summary of 2010 Gfk/NOP Poll on Labels for GM-fed Products'*, United Kingdom, 2010

5. Institute for Responsible Technology, *'Dangers of Genetically Engineered Foods'*, Fairfield, Iowa, USA, 2005

6. Friends of the Earth, *'What's Feeding Our Food?'* United Kingdom, 2008

7. The Soil Association, *'Land of the GM-Free?'* United Kingdom, 2008

8. GM Freeze, *'GM Labelling and Traceability Enforcing Enforcement'*, United Kingdom, 2006

9. Tom Philpott, *'Amid Monsanto's antitrust troubles, another study questions effects of GMOs'*, http://www.grist.org Washington, USA, 2009

10. Don Lotter, *'The Genetic Engineering of Food and the Failure of Science – Part 1: The Development of a Flawed Enterprise'*, International Journal of Sociology of Agriculture and Food, Vol.16, No.1, pp.31-49, Cardiff University, UK and Florida Atlantic University, USA, 2008

11. Joël Spiroux de Vendômois, François Roullier, Dominique Cellier and Gilles-Eric Séralini, *'A Comparison of the Effects of Three GM Corn Varieties on Mammalian Health'*, International Journal of Biological Sciences, France, 2009
12. Dr Brian John, GM-Free Cymru, 'German Mon810 Feeding Trial Results are Worthless', Wales, UK,
13. GM Foods, Labelling and Safety Assessments, http://www.food.gov.uk/gmfoods/gm , Food Standards Agency, UK, 2011
14. Unintended Effects of Genetic Manipulation, A Project of The Nature Institute, Project Director: Craig Holdrege http://natureinstitute.org/nontarget/
15. GM Crops in the US Pew Trusts http://www.pewtrusts.org/uploadedFiles/wwwp ewtrustsorg/Fact_Sheets/Food_and_Biotechnolo gy/PIFB_Genetically_Modified_Crops_Factshe et0804.pdf
16. 'BT is a Toxin' GM-Free Scotland, September 2008 http://gmfreescotland.blogspot.co.uk/
17. 'Causes of Water Pollution - GMO Farming, Glyphosate, Big Contributors, Mike Barrett Natural Society, 28 June 2012 http://naturalsociety.com/glyphosate-causes-of-water-pollution/#ixzz22rw6wxez
18. 'Technical Fact Sheet on Glyphosate', US EPA
19. 'Glyphosate surface water contamination' Eigis European Glyphosate Environmental Information Source, 4th November 2002, http://www.egeis.org/home/glyph_info/papers.h tml?article_id=153

20. 'Glyphosate and AMPA in Drinking Water,' WHO Guidelines for Drinking Water Quality, 3rd Edition, 2004.

21. 'GM Corn Polluting Mid-West Streams' http://www.non-gmoreport.com/articles/november2010/gmcornpollutingmidweststreams.php

22. 'Insecticides Modified in GM Corn Polluting US Waters,'_____Elizabeth_____Renter Activist Post, 6 August 2012, http://www.activistpost.com/2012/08/insecticides-modified-in-gm-corn.html

23. 'GM Crop Production,' http://www.gmo-compass.org/eng/agri_biotechnology/gmo_planting/142.countries_growing_gmos.html

24. 'GM-Resistant Weeds Mean Harsher Chemicals,' Rachel Swick Mavity, Jul 11, 2012, http://capegazette.villagesoup.com/capelife/story/herbicide-resistant-weeds-mean-harsher-chemicals/854197

25. 'Health and environmental impacts of glyphosate,' Friends of the Earth, July 2001, http://www.foe.co.uk/resource/reports/impacts_glyphosate.pdf

26. 'Roundup Herbicide 'This Menace Killed 50% of Rats Tested - But It's Hiding in Your Water, Air and Food,'' Dr. Mercola, mercola.com, January 10 2012 http://articles.mercola.com/sites/articles/archive/2012/01/10/herbicide-poison-groundwater-supply.aspx

GM and Animal Feed

27. Alliance for Natural Health https://www.anhinternational.org/2010/04/21/e

uropeans-consuming-gm-animal-feed-unknowingly/

GM Genes transferring to other crops

28. Paul Brown, *'Scientists shocked at GM gene transfer'*, The Guardian, UK, Thursday 15 August 2002

Genes and Aggression

29. Wikipedia Article 'Aggression' http://en.wikipedia.org/wiki/Aggression#Genetics

30. Wikipedia Article 'Genetics of Aggression' http://en.wikipedia.org/wiki/Genetics_influencing_aggression

31. BBC News, *'Missing Gene Link to Aggression'*, United Kingdom, 26 January, 2003

32. Thomas J.H. Chen, Kenneth Blum, Daniel Mathews, Larry Fisher, Nancy Schnautz, Eric R. Braverman, John Schoolfield, Bernard W. Downs, David E. Comings, 'Are dopaminergic genes involved in a predisposition to pathological aggression?: Hypothesizing the importance of "super normal controls" in psychiatricgenetic research of complex behavioral disorders', Elsevier Ltd, USA, 2005

Genes and Allergies

33. *Dr. Barry Starr,* **'Are peanut allergies genetic?',** Stanford University *School of Medicine, The Tech Museum, Understanding Genetics,* http://www.thetech.org/genetics/ask.php?id=224

34. Martin Teitel, PhD and Kimberly A.Wilson, *'Genetically-Engineered Food: Changing The*

Nature of Nature', Park Street Press, Rochester, Vermont, 1999

Genes and Psychic Abilities

35. Global Psychics Inc, *'Family Genetics and Being Psychic'*, 2007, http://www.globalpsychics.com/weblog/2007/1 2/18/family-genetics-and-being-psychic/
36. Mary Desaulniers, *'Psychic Powers and DNA Activation'*, 2010 http://ascensionenergyprogram.blogspot.com/2 010/01/psychic-powers-and-dna-activation.html

Discrediting of Scientists Raising Concerns about GM

37. Spin Profiles, *Arpad Pustzai*, 2009
38. 'Controversial Seralini Study Linking GM to Cancer in Rats Is Republished' The Guardian, 24th June 2014 http://www.theguardian.com/environment/2014 /jun/24/controversial-seralini-study-gm-cancer-rats-republished

Organic Food

39. Natalie Geen, Chris Firth, *'The Committed Organic Consumer'*, Henry Doubleday Research Organisation (HDRA), Garden Organic, Coventry, UK, 2006
40. European Commission, 'Research on organic consumers in Europe; Condor Project, Consumer Decision Making on Organic Products', 2005

World Population and Earth Resources

41. The Soil Association, '*Telling Porkies – The Big Fat Lie About Doubling Food Production*' United Kingdom, 2010
42. Martin Desvaux, Optimum Population Trust, '*Towards Sustainable and Optimum Populations*', United Kingdom, 2008
43. Johan van der Heyden, '*Current World Population*', http://www.geohive.com/, Netherlands, 2009
44. The Vegan Society, '*Global Food Security*', Birmingham, UK, 2009

Military Information
45. Royal Air Force
    http://www.raf.mod.uk

Area 51 and Nellis Air Force Range, USA
46. Rahni, Anomalies Unlimited, '*Underground Bases*', Skokie, USA, http://www.anomalies-unlimited.com/Bases.html
47. Wikipedia, '*UFO and other conspiracy theories concerning Area 51*'; '*Area 51*'

Apocalypse
48. Wikipedia
    http://en.wikipedia.org/wiki/Four_Horsemen_of_the_Apocalypse
49. The Holy Bible, Revised Standard Version, Catholic Truth Society, 1966

Illuminati and Freemasons
50. 'The Biggest Secret', David Icke, 1999, David Icke Books
51. 'Human Race Get Off Your Knees; The Lion Sleeps No More' David Icke, 2010, David Icke Books Ltd.

52. 'Top Ten Illuminati Symbols,' Tom Hidell, Illuminati Rex,
http://www.illuminatirex.com/illuminati-symbols/

Places

53. Carlsbad Caverns National Park New Mexico, US National Park service
http://www.nps.gov/cave/naturescience/index.htm

54. Cimarron Canyon State Park, New Mexico,

http://www.americansouthwest.net/new_mexico/cimarron-canyon/state-park.html

55. Matagorda Island Lighthouse
http://www.lighthousefriends.com/light.asp?ID=156

Native Americans

56. Legends of America
http://www.legendsofamerica.com/index.html

Fluoride

57. Fluoridation: Mind Control of the Masses,' Ian E. Stephens, Alex Jones Infowars, July 9, 2010
http://www.infowars.com/fluoridation-mind-control-of-the-masses/

58. 'Fluoridation of Drinking Water' Drinking Water Inspectorate, September 2011

Underground Government Bases

59. 'The Kelvedon Hatch Secret Nuclear Bunker,'
http://www.secretnuclearbunker.com/

The Vatican

60. 'Cardinals, Conclaves and a New Pope,' Father William Saunders, http://catholiceducation.org/articles/religion/re0787.html

Native American Names

61. **SnowOwl**

http://www.snowwowl.com/swolfNAnamesandmeanings.html

Jinn

62. Jinn, Wikipedia, https://en.wikipedia.org/wiki/Jinn

Rabies

63. NHS UK, https://www.nhs.uk/conditions/rabies/

David Icke Books

64. Biggest Secret
65. Human Race Get Off Your Knees
66. The Perception Deception
67. Everything You Need to Know but Have Never Been Told
68. The David Icke Guide to the Global Conspiracy

Other Books & Journals

69. Proof of Heaven, Eben Alexander
70. Return to Life, Jim Tucker MD
71. Memories of Heaven, Dr Wayne W.Dyer, Dee Garnes
72. Flying Saucer Review
73. The Holy Bible, Catholic Edition, Catholic Truth Society, 1966

Annunaki

74. Gaia
https://www.gaia.com/article/annunaki-saviors-or-tyrants-human-race
75. Annunaki, Wikipedia
https://en.wikipedia.org/wiki/Anunnaki

Zecharia Sitchin

76. Official Website Zecharia Sitchin
http://www.sitchin.com/
77. Wikipedia
https://en.wikipedia.org/wiki/Zecharia_Sitchin

Barcodes, Financial Systems and the Mark of the Beast
78. Alamongordo
http://www.alamongordo.com/tag/six-hundred-sixty-six/

Dinosaurs
79. Can Scientists Turn Birds Back Into Dinosaur Ancestors? Carl Zimmer, *National Geographic*

http://phenomena.nationalgeographic.com/2015/0
5/12/reversing-bird-evolution/

80. Dinosaurs found in UK, Natural History
Museum
http://www.nhm.ac.uk/discover/dino-
directory/country/united-kingdom/gallery.html

81. How T-Rex Evolved into Modern Bird,
Telegraph
http://www.telegraph.co.uk/news/science/dinosaurs/
11122181/Graphic-How-Tyrannosaurus-rex-evolved-
into-modern-bird.html

82. Evolution of Cows, Dogs & Cats, Wikipedia
various

Useful Websites

GM Freeze
http://www.gmfreeze.org
GM Free Cymru
http://www.gmfreecymru.org
GM Free Scotland
http://www.gmfreescotland.net
GM Free Ireland
http://www.gmfreeireland.org
Friends of the Earth UK
http://www.foe.co.uk
Greenpeace UK
http://www.greenpeace.org.uk
The Soil Association
http://www.soilassociation.org
Institute for Responsible Technology
http://www.responsibletechnology.org
Ban GM Food
http://www.bangmfood.org
Wikipedia
http://www.wikipedia.org
Center for Food Safety
http://www.centerforfoodsafety.org
GeneWatch
http://www.genewatch.org
Google Maps
http://maps.google.co.uk
Food Standards Agency UK
http://www.food.gov.uk
The Vegan Society
http://www.vegansociety.com
GMO Seralini
http://www.gmoseralini.org/en/

Printed in Poland
by Amazon Fulfillment
Poland Sp. z o.o., Wrocław

49025741R00255